Books of Merit

The Sky Is Falling

ALSO BY CAROLINE ADDERSON

Pleased to Meet You
Sitting Practice
A History of Forgetting
Bad Imaginings

CAROLINE ADDERSON

The Sky Is Falling

A NOVEL

THOMAS ALLEN PUBLISHERS

TORONTO

Copyright © 2010 Caroline Adderson

All rights reserved. No part of this work may be reproduced or
transmitted in any form or by any means – graphic, electronic, or
mechanical, including photocopying, recording, taping, or information
storage and retrieval systems – without the prior written permission
of the publisher, or in the case of photocopying or other reprographic
copying, a licence from the Canadian Copyright Licensing Agency.

Library and Archives Canada Cataloguing in Publication

Adderson, Caroline, 1963–
The sky is falling / Caroline Adderson.

ISBN 978-0-88762-613-5

I. Title.

PS8551.D3267S59 2010   C813'.54   C2010-903596-8

Editor: Patrick Crean
Cover design: Black Eye Design
Cover image: Oliver Barmbold / Source: PHOTOCASE

Published by Thomas Allen Publishers,
a division of Thomas Allen & Son Limited,
145 Front Street East, Suite 209,
Toronto, Ontario M5A 1E3 Canada

www.thomas-allen.com

ONTARIO ARTS COUNCIL
CONSEIL DES ARTS DE L'ONTARIO

Canada Council
for the Arts

The publisher gratefully acknowledges the support of
The Ontario Arts Council for its publishing program.

We acknowledge the support of the Canada Council for the Arts, which
last year invested $20.1 million in writing and publishing throughout Canada.

We acknowledge the Government of Ontario through the
Ontario Media Development Corporation's Ontario Book Initiative.

We acknowledge the financial support of the Government of Canada through the
Book Publishing Industry Development Program (BPIDP) for our publishing activities.

BRITISH COLUMBIA
ARTS COUNCIL
An agency of the Province of British Columbia

We also acknowledge the support of the British Columbia Arts Council.

10 11 12 13 14   5 4 3 2 1

Printed and bound in Canada

In memory of my mother

2 0 0 4

Last night I had one of those dreams again. Nothing happened, nothing ever does—no central dramatic event. Usually I'm so busy puzzling over some vague inconsistency, some hint that I'm actually asleep, that I hardly notice the drifts of dread settling all around me. This time I found myself downtown at midday, or so it seemed from the quality of the light, the eye-smacking noonishness, though the empty streets contradicted it. I came to Eaton's, which is Sears now. (This was what I was puzzling over, not the eerie lack of traffic, the bizarre absence of pedestrians, but *Was Eaton's back in business? Since when?*) I pushed open the glass door and wandered around for a bit. Cosmetics. Women's Shoes. Soon I began to feel uneasy. Sick. Something wasn't right. Where was everyone? Well, in the shelters obviously, I realized just as the shrill whine of the approaching missile became audible.

The slap of the newspaper landing on the front porch woke me. These early-rising immigrants who fling the news on our city streets, they're unsung heroes in a way. How many innocent sleepers have they saved from annihilation? I should leave ours a card. I thought of this after my perfectly timed rescue, when I couldn't get back to sleep because of Joe making glottal sounds. Eventually I must have slept because the alarm went

off, reset by Joe, who has to be at the hospital early. This time I
got up well before the apocalypse.

Our front door mat reads "Go Away." Lying on the joke,
helplessly bound by elastics, was the very paper that had saved
me. I carried it to the kitchen, poured the coffee, sat at the table.
It had snowed in the night. No. Spring had come. Spring was
right outside the window. Filling the frame, our snow-white
magnolia, peaking. I thought of *The Cherry Orchard*, all of us
reading it on the front porch while we swilled plonk. The truth
is every spring when the trees bloom I think about Chekhov and
everything that happened, how Pascal betrayed my friend Sonia
and she him in turn. We wanted to get rid of all the bombs, but
look what happened. It was partly my fault, that bad, bad decision that we took. Only this year it all came together because,
when I peeled the rubber bands off the *Vancouver Sun* and laid it
flat on the table, Sonia was staring up at me. Not a recent picture, but Sonia when I knew her all those years ago.

The shock of seeing her again, the dis-ease of the dream.
The inevitable self-loathing. Pete's picture was below hers. It
took me a moment to notice him. As soon as I did, I turned the
paper over. It was a funny thing to do, a token of respect, like
covering the face of the dead. Except both of them are still alive.

But what about the boy? Whatever happened to him?

1 9 8 3

I'm not from Vancouver. I came in 1982 to attend the University of British Columbia and, until I met Joe, I didn't know anyone who had been born here. Everyone in the group was from elsewhere, Sonia from up north, 100 Mile House, Pete from Toronto, Belinda—Isis!—from somewhere in Nova Scotia. I don't remember where Carla or Timo were from. Pascal had escaped the same small town in Saskatchewan that Dieter had grown up in, Esterhazy, which turned out not to be a coincidence after all. I'd fled too—a strip-malled neighbourhood of Edmonton where I'd been miserable for no good reason other than there always has to be someone to pick on and it's usually the smart, socially awkward person with the funny last name, skulking the hallways, binder raised up like a shield. Me.

During my first year at university I stayed with my father's sister, my aunt Eva, who manned her stove in a suburb to the east of Vancouver, cooking through cases of dented cans and frostbitten cuts of meat, by the vat, as though against some desperate contingency. Every day I had to travel all the way across town to the city's western point, the UBC campus, a three-bus journey. The commute took an hour and a half or more each way, I explained the following summer to my father, who had wanted me to go to university at home in the first place and now didn't want to pay for me to live in residence. "Read on the bus," he said. "I get sick," I lied. In fact, I'd grown so accustomed to the trip I never looked out the window any more, not even to check if my stop was coming up, somehow always feeling for the cord and ringing the bell at just the right moment even while absorbed in the evolution of Doric-order proportions or the impact of the Crimean War on modern warfare. I just wanted to be closer to campus and to get away from my aunt, who seemed more and more an embodiment of all I was destined to become, lonely and eccentric and obsessively cheap. By the end of the summer, I succeeded. I convinced my father that my grade point average was in jeopardy despite the fact that, hitherto, everything I handed in came back scarletted with the letter A.

When I returned to Vancouver in the fall to begin my second year, I stayed with my aunt again while I looked for somewhere closer, the very next day taking the long, familiar bus ride and spending the morning at the Student Housing Office making calls. I had come too late. The inexpensive basement rooms with a hot plate and a bathroom sink to serve all washing functions had been snapped up. The idea of a shared house unnerved me, but I made a few calls anyway only to discover that the cheaper of these had been taken as well. Although I had a full scholarship, it covered only tuition. An apartment was out of the question.

My preferred place to study the previous year had been in the stacks under the old stone Main Library. I went there again after my disappointing morning, descending to the remotest and deepest parts of the bunker-like levels where the obscurest, bookiest-smelling tomes were stored. The carrels were tucked away singly wherever there was a bit of space. Under the glare of the fluorescents, the books emitted their wise scent. (I imagined print powdering off the pages, that I was breathing knowledge.) I found the Russian books and selected one at random.

Cyrillic seemed vaguely runic. Latin letters were sprinkled in but the cases were mixed. R was backward. I should have been looking in the classified ads for a room but for the moment I felt so perfectly alone and happy.

Afterward I went to the Student Union Building to buy a cookie, a detour that entirely changed my fate. I actually went for a newspaper, then, overcome by temptation, got in line at the cookie kiosk, hiding behind the paper the way I used to hide behind my binder, like some cartoon Cold War spy. A new study had just come out of MIT predicting that more than 50 percent of Canadians would be immediately killed in the event of a nuclear war. The pretrial hearing of the Squamish Five, a local terrorist group, had begun. The Great Lakes were an acidic broth. All of it reminded me why I never paid attention to the news. The line moved forward, bringing me closer to a bulletin board next to where the coffee was accoutred. *Rides. Used textbooks. Accommodations.* I stepped away, losing my place, drawn by a notice with a fringe of phone numbers on the bottom.

A man answered immediately, like he'd been poised by the phone. "Did you hang up on me a second ago?"

"No," I said.

"Sure?"

"Yes."

"Fuck."

"I'm phoning about the room," I said. "Is there a good time to come and see it?"

I could almost hear him shrug. "Come right now." Then he hung up, forcing me to dig in my change purse for another dime. "*What!*"

"I need the address," I whimpered.

It took fifteen minutes to get to the house, which was in Kits, one lot in from the corner, on a street otherwise lined with genteel homes. Next door was a knee-high garden statue of a black man in livery holding up a lamp, as though to illuminate the adjacent eyesore. I walked past the Reliant patchworked with political bumper stickers parked in front—*Extinction is Forever. One nuclear bomb can ruin your whole day. Impeach Reagan*—and up the path that cut through a steppe of unmown grass, climbed to the wide, crowded porch—bicycle, wearily flowered chesterfield, cardboard placards with their messages turned to the wall—and knocked on the rainbow on the door, knocked several times until at last a young man appeared, shirtless, but wearing a kerchief on his head. The year before, fishing for a major, I had cast my net wide over many subjects, among them Art History. Only now did I understand what the professor had been saying about beauty and its relationship to proportion.

He looked right at me, unblinking, in a way I was unused to. "I phoned," I said and he smiled. To show me he was capable of it, I thought, or to show off the investment (which was patently wrong, I would find out). In their perfect even rows, his teeth glowed. "Go ahead," he said. "Look." I stepped into the vestibule and, since he was barefoot, stooped to remove my shoes. By the time I straightened, he was gone.

To the right was a set of French doors, each pane painted with a dove or a rainbow or some other optimistic symbol. I kept thinking about the fifteen minutes. How my life would open up if I were living just fifteen minutes from campus. I poked my head in the living room. Shag carpet, beanbag chair, posters. A fireplace extruding paper garbage. On its hearth stood a statue identical to the one in the next-door garden except for the sign taped to the lamp: *It's payback time!!!* Instead of curtains, a poncho was nailed to the window frame. Then I started because someone was sleeping on the chesterfield, lying on his back with a beret over his face. I ducked right out.

Bathroom: chipped, claw-foot tub, tinkling toilet. The cover of the tank was broken, half of it missing, the workings exposed.

It embarrassed me to see someone else's plumbing. Above it hung a poster buckled with damp. *Is Your Bathroom Breeding Bolsheviks?*

I peeked in the bedroom at the end of the hall and, seeing it looked well lived in—there were stuffed animals on the bed—returned to the vestibule with its battered mahogany wainscotting and went up the stairs. None of the three bedrooms on the upper floor was empty either. All had bare fir floors and plank and plastic milk crate shelves. The front-facing room, the largest, had a view of the mountains and the ubiquitous Rorschach Che painted on one wall. The middle room was an ascetic's cell with a pitted green foamie for a bed, the end room a postered shrine to Georgia O'Keeffe and Frida Kahlo, reeking of incense. I went back downstairs to the kitchen, which also smelled but of a more complex synthesis—ripe compost, burnt garlic, beans on the soak—so different from the cabbage and mothball overtones at my aunt's. It was untidy too. Dirty, in fact. I glanced at my socks with their dust and crumb adherents. The fifteen minutes more than made up for it.

The shirtless one was outside on the deck smoking, leaning against the railing, his back to me. I could make out each distinct vertebra. They seemed decorative. When I tapped on the window, he waved me out through a door beside which a rubber Ronald Reagan mask hung on a nail. Out there in the overgrown yard the decorous history of the house still showed in the unpruned roses in their unmade beds and the old pear tree scabbed with lichen. The garage though, slouching and moss-covered, was practically in ruins.

"Which room is available?" I asked.

He exhaled his acrid smoke and pointed up to the window of the O'Keeffe/Kahlo room.

"I'd like to take it."

"You have to come for an interview. There's a sign-up sheet." He threw the cigarette over the deck railing and led me back inside where a loose-leaf page lay on the kitchen table, three names and phone numbers already written on it. I felt sick and made my writing neater than the others', only realizing after the fact that it would probably work against me.

"Jane," he read off the paper before flashing his teeth again. "How do you say your last name?"

Most of the rooms that were advertised in the newspaper and still available were almost as far away as my aunt's, near Fraser Street or Knight. I went to look at a few only to leave undecided and anxious that someone else would get the place if I took too long to make up my mind. Then someone called "from the Trutch house," she said, though the house I'd seen was actually on one of the numbered east-west streets. Trutch was the cross street. She told me to come at six-thirty.

I got there too early and waited on the steps. In the house across the street, the living room curtains were open and I could see through to the dining room, where a family was sitting down to supper. A child lobbed an oven mitt across the table. Someone and his dog walked past the stickered Reliant. The dog smiled but the man's straight-ahead gaze seemed to emanate hostility.

At exactly six-thirty, I rang the doorbell. A thin girl answered, her hair long and dark and not particularly clean. Despite this, despite dressing like a scarecrow and the deep shadows under her eyes, she was quite pretty, which made me leery and more nervous than before.

"Are you Jane?" She introduced herself as Sonia and led me in.

Pete from two days before was sitting at the kitchen table. Today he wore a shirt, almost a blouse, with full sleeves and a ruffled front and cuffs. He'd dispensed with the kerchief and I saw now that his hair was dirty blond and shoulder-length; he'd seemed Greco-Roman when we'd met previously, but my second impression was Renaissance for sure.

Two other men were at the table, one of them wearing glasses with big plastic frames and a T-shirt entreating the U.S. to vacate Central America. His hair was dark and wiry, nose very narrow, like it had been squeezed in a book. This was Dieter. The third man seemed cleaner than the rest. It took me a moment to notice the girl leaning against the counter, but as soon as I did she became the most obvious person there because of the deep coppery mane hanging halfway down her back and how her freckles contrasted with her creamy skin. Belinda, Sonia, Pete, Dieter, this other person—five complete strangers who didn't know anything about me, not my tormented high school years, not how I had blown it last year. Last year had been my chance to start over, to make friends, but I had forfeited it, blaming the bus ride. I couldn't imagine it had anything to do with me.

Seeing me hovering in the doorway, the cleaner man stood and shook hands smilingly all around. My heart sank when he picked a violin case off the floor and walked past without acknowledging me. He was my competitor. I felt like turning and running because no one would ever choose sweaty, bookish me over someone who could play the violin.

I sat and Sonia introduced everyone. Pete uncrossed one arm to wiggle his fingers at me. "This is Jane," Sonia said.

"Jane Zed," said Pete.

"That's easier," I admitted.

Except for Pete, they looked everywhere but at me so I felt cut out of the picture, as I usually did. Then I was flooded with embarrassment, for I knew it was childish to want two contradictory things: to be left alone and to be included.

"I'm Belinda," said the girl at the counter, who had not been introduced.

"Belinda's the one moving out," Sonia explained.

Pete: "She needs her space."

With two exaggerated tosses of her head, Belinda threw her hair over each shoulder. Years later, on nights I couldn't sleep (frequently, in other words), I would sometimes scroll the muted channels in search of a soporific. Belinda would flash past, executing this same ribbon dance, in the service of selling hair conditioner. But now she was indignant, telling Pete, "I do!"

"I know you do," he said and it was impossible to decipher his tone, whether he was sarcastic or earnest. He could be acidly sarcastic, but I didn't know that yet.

Belinda humphed and leaned back with crossed arms. The other two, Sonia and Dieter, seemed anxious to keep the interview going. Dieter took over the talking, stapling his eyes to the place I always thought of as my upper right-hand corner. Theirs was a communal rather than a shared accommodation. They each participated equally in the running and upkeep of the house. "We have a chore sheet." He got up to unmagnet it from the freezer door for me. I saw their different writing styles, Dieter's tight and precise, Pete's backward leaning, Belinda's too large for the space. Sonia had printed her name in a round, elementary-school hand.

"We rotate chores monthly. You do your assigned chore once a week. Every Sunday we put twenty dollars in the kitty. From that you buy the groceries when it's your turn to cook. We eat supper together. House meeting once a month. *Eso es todo.*" He pushed up his glasses with his middle finger.

I was not a serious candidate. His perfunctory delivery and the fuck-off adjusting of his glasses made this obvious. Sonia had been sucking on the little gold cross around her neck, but now she let it go to add, "We're vegetarian."

"So am I," I said. It just came out. I was surprised too, because I had just decided I didn't want to live there anyway so

I didn't care about being rejected by them. But now everyone straightened and Sonia smiled, acknowledging this specious point of commonality.

They asked what I was studying. "Arts," I said.

"Me too!" Belinda bubbled from her corner. "I'm in Theatre!"

"I'm in Education," Sonia said. "Dieter's in Poli Sci and Spanish. Pete's in Engineering."

Pete: "I'm an anarchist."

Belinda: "I'm a feminist."

"Me too," Dieter seconded.

"Actually," Pete said, "I'm an anarcho-feminist."

"I'm a pacifist," Sonia sighed, and Dieter tugged a lock of her hair twice, tooting, "Pacifist! Pacifist!"

Pete: "More precisely, I'm an anarcho-feminist-pacifist."

Declarations winging by me, fast and furious. I nearly ducked. I was relieved they didn't ask because I, I was nothing.

I moved into the Trutch house officially the Sunday before classes started, after transporting my belongings in my suitcase over several trips throughout the week. My aunt didn't have a car and, anyway, I didn't want to involve her. Belinda was still occupying the room the first time I came; Pete was there, too, lolling gorgeously on the bed. He smiled right at me while, blushing violently, I stacked my things in the corner Belinda had indicated with a careless, freckled wave. Each time I came back there was a little less of her in the room and none of Pete.

On Sunday the bed was still there, the mattress stripped. I crept downstairs for a broom. Dieter was in the kitchen with another man, older, well into his twenties and dark-complected, who was reading but stood politely when I came in. He wore granny glasses, the gold rims of which matched one of his front teeth. "Ector." He put out his hand.

Dieter was boiling coffee in a saucepan, watching it so intently I got the impression he was deliberately ignoring me. I asked about the broom, but then Pete came in and told everyone to freeze. "You and you and you. Come."

Ector and I obeyed. We didn't think twice. We followed him out and waited in the vestibule while Pete took the stairs up two at a time. A moment later he and Belinda started down with the mattress between them. Ector snapped to when he saw Belinda, pulling a beret from his back pocket, donning it, then opening the door for them to hurl their burden out. He insisted on taking her place, then up he went with Pete. There was banging. From the swearing, not the fucks but the words I couldn't understand, I realized that the chivalrous Ector spoke Spanish, also, when Pete screamed out his name, that it was actually *Hector*.

"Hector! Hold it!"

They manoeuvred the heavy frame down the stairs, further distressing the walls, out the front door and down the steps with Belinda directing them like an air traffic controller. "Jane and I will take the mattress," she said when they dropped it in the long grass. "You guys take the bed."

Pete turned to me. "What do you think of that, Zed?" I didn't know what he meant. He was the one who had recruited me. "A real fair-weather feminist," he said, pointing his chin at Belinda. "All for equality until there's something heavy to carry."

Hector squatted, ready. "Come on, Peeete."

"Oh no. We'll *all* carry it."

"God," said Belinda, rolling her eyes.

Single-handedly Pete threw the mattress on the frame, then we each took a corner of the bed. It was heavy. We shuffled down the walk and straight into the middle of the street. When a car came up behind us, we moved to the side to let it pass.

"How far?" Hector asked.

"Blenheim Street," Belinda said.

Hector looked across the bed at me. "I'm forgetting your name."

"Jane."

"I'm Ector."

"Yes," I said.

At the corner we set our burden down and breathed collectively for a moment before struggling on another block. By then my hands were screaming. I wanted to stop, but didn't. Hector voiced my feelings. He said carrying the bed was killing him. Belinda said that if we died, it would not be in vain, she would erect a plaque.

"To the Glorious Committee of the Bed-Carrying International!" Hector cried.

Another car came up behind us. "Keep going," Pete told us.

"Move to the side," Belinda said. "God."

The car honked. We were panting now.

"Why?" asked Pete. "Why should cars have the right of way and not beds? If beds had the right of way—do not let go, people!—this world wouldn't be so fucked up!"

The driver craned out the window. "Excuse me?"

"Get a bed!" Pete yelled. "Make love instead of polluting the world!"

I dropped my corner. Everyone stumbled forward, and Pete, using the momentum, tackled Belinda on the bed. It seemed he couldn't let her go after all. She shrieked, then succumbed, letting him twine his body around hers, squid tight, as they necked, demonstrating for her, or us, their interconnection. He flipped onto his back so she was on top, her astonishing hair falling around them, a privacy curtain. Hector burst into applause. When the driver got out of the car, I turned and ran.

My main occupation that first day was putting together the futon I'd bought as a kit and alternately dragged and carried on my back like a peddler all the way from Fourth Avenue without any help from anyone. I found the broom and swept, opened the window to uncloy the air of sandalwood, piled my books against the wall in alphabetical order. Now I lay on the futon trying to read *Anna Karenina*, but mostly fretting as suppertime approached. I didn't know why they had picked me. Were there so few vegetarians around? When I went downstairs, would I be accused of letting them down when I let go of the bed? I truly couldn't have held on a moment longer. Then why did I run away, they would want to know. Because I was scandalized. Was that how people really acted?

"Supper!" one of the men called.

I was first to arrive except for Dieter, who was at the sink dumping the contents of a pot into a colander, the lenses of his glasses opaque with fog. Maybe he really didn't see me this time. "Supper!" he screamed.

Sonia appeared next, pretty and unbrushed, fingering her cross, then Pete, who skated across the floor in socks. As soon as Dieter thumped the pot of spaghetti down in the middle of the table, Pete lunged for it while Dieter waited, poised to get the tongs next. It surprised me, the carnivorous way vegetarians ate; Sonia and I had yet to serve ourselves. She gestured for me to go first. I took half of what remained, she a few tangled strands. The moment the tongs were returned to the pot, Pete snatched them and claimed the rest.

No one spoke—because of me, I presumed. Because I'd dropped the bed. I fixed my self-conscious gaze on the flayed face of Ronald Reagan on the opposite wall, the nail jutting from his empty eye socket. The men seemed intent on their food, Sonia too, but while they ate with gusto, she was a baby bird grappling open-throated with a very long worm. I suspected, though, that if I got up and left the room they would probably start twittering like birds at the precise crack of dawn. Twittering: *She dropped the bed! She dropped the bed!*

Dieter inflicted a goofy smile on Sonia, who grimaced and turned her tired eyes to me. "Are you all moved in?"

I gulped some water so I could speak. "Yes. There wasn't much to move."

Pete had already cleaned his plate! He went to the fridge for a loaf of bread and a tub of margarine, slapped a nubbled slice down, painted it with the spread. There was a jar on the table full of yellow powder, which he dumped on his bread. Only now did he and Dieter begin to talk, heatedly, as though they were picking up an argument they'd called a truce on before supper. When Dieter called, I'd been reading that scene in *Anna Karenina* where two prominent Moscow intellectuals come to Oblonsky's for dinner. *They respected each other, but upon almost every subject were in complete and hopeless disagreement, not because they belonged to opposite schools of thought but for the reason they belonged to the same camp.* Dieter was defensive, emphatic, offended, Pete aloof. "You agree?" Dieter asked. "Don't you?" He would glance over at Sonia every time he made a point, to see the effect it had on her.

When Sonia pushed away her plate, Pete used the excuse of scooping the remaining noodles off it to end his conversation with Dieter and go out on the deck, the strands hanging from his mouth, like hay. Dieter began stacking the dirty dishes. He paused to tug Sonia's hair and say, "Ding dong, Avon calling!" which drove her immediately from the room. That left just me sitting at the table. It was over, the agony of my first supper, with no one mentioning the bed. I'd hardly been required to speak at all. "Thank you," I said to Dieter before slinking out, relieved. He looked blankly at me through his big plastic frames.

Back upstairs, in my near-empty room with *Anna Karenina*, I thought that if it was going to be like that every night I would probably survive, which was, anyway, all I ever expected.

The year before, I'd come to Vancouver with only a general idea of what I wanted to study. I'd made a shopping list of possible courses, but when I showed up to register I discovered it really was like shopping, my least favourite thing, the gym a marketplace crowded with hundreds of students. For every course you had to stand in line to receive a computer card, first-come, first-served. It was a hot day and I was perspiring madly in the crush. At the Slavonic Studies table the line was negligible. I'd always wanted to read *War and Peace*.

Later in the year Professor Kopanyev told me he'd assumed I'd enrolled in his survey course because of my Polish background, but this was not the case. My father had come to Canada when he was my age, eighteen, so had lived most of his life here. He never talked about his childhood. When I came to stay with my aunt, she told me cabbage rolls were his favourite dish, but we always ate Canadian—pork chops with Minute Rice, Sloppy Joes, McCain frozen pizza. Other than an unpronounceable last name, nothing remotely Polish could be said about me.

In the first semester of Slavonic Studies we covered the history, geography, and economy of the Soviet Union. I wrote a paper on the emancipation of the serfs. We turned to literature in the second semester with Kopanyev presenting a biographical lecture on the greatest writer who ever lived—Turgenev, Dostoyevsky, Tolstoy, Chekhov, Solzhenitsyn—depending on the week. We read a sample work by these authors, discussed them in tutorials, then selected one as a subject for a paper. At the end of the year someone put up his hand and asked, "How can they all be the greatest?" It seemed obvious to me by then.

Kopanyev was tall and bearded, always tweedily dressed in shades of brown. One day he asked me to stay after class, which was when he commented on my surname. He said that my paper on Chekhov was both entertaining and insightful and he hoped I would continue in the department the following year. Ours was a small class, not even a dozen students, so I knew not to take his praise too much to heart. But I did. All year I had slunk from lecture to lecture praying that no one would notice me but now I was both thrilled and grateful that someone had.

My paper was titled "Boredom and Sadness in the Short Stories of Anton Chekhov." I'd chosen a collection of eleven of his stories in a popular translation and counted how many times he used words associated with these emotions. *Bored* appeared sixteen times, *bore* three times, *boringly* once. *Not interesting, uninteresting*, and *uninterestingly* once each. People, society, life— these were described four times as *dull*, and a further seven as *monotonous. Monotony* was used three times, *dissatisfaction* twice, *dissatisfied* once. One character gazed *apathetically* at her empty yard. I didn't count the condition of the yard, but I did include her later feeling of *emptiness*. Also the fact that on first impression Dmitry Dmitrich Gurov thinks there is something *pathetic* about Anna Sergeyevna, "The Lady with a Lapdog," soon to be the great love of his life. I interpreted *pathetic* as *sad*, an emotion referred to ten other times in the collection. *Sadly* (3). *Sadness* (2). *Unhappy* (2). *Sorrow* (1). "Were these *depressed* (3) characters full of *melancholy* (3) and *despair* (3) because life was *boring* (5), or does perpetual *boredom* (3) lead to a *mournfully* (1) *depressing* (1) and *despondent* (1) life?"

Kopanyev flipped through my handwritten pages. "I read some out to my wife. We had good laugh."

"Really?" I said.

"This word *skuchno*. It implies boredom, of course. But also sadness, desolation, gloom, yearning. Russians are always sad and it's boring. Aren't you?"

I stared at him.

"No?" He rolled my paper into a tube and poked me with it. "Come back next year. Take Russian."

And so I did.

Kopanyev assured us learning Russian would be easy because, he claimed, it was a phonetic language. But right from hello, from *zdrastvuytye*, I realized this wasn't always the case. There was the matter of stress, too, how an unstressed *O* will convert to an *A*, for example. If you stressed the wrong syllable, the meaning of the word would change. "Like with *pismo*. *PisMO*. Letter. *PISma*. Letters."

He seemed even more ursine this year as he handed out the alphabet. Cyrillic, he explained, was named for the Byzantine monk who gave the Slavs a written language. He'd had to draw on Greek, Hebrew, and old Latin. Three full alphabets plundered to represent all the Russian sounds. My eye went straight to the familiar letters, but only five of these actually corresponded to their English equivalents. An *M* might have sounded like an *M*, but *B* was *V*, *P* was *R* with a roll, *X* a truncated gargle. A gargle! *A* and *O* were ostensibly the same, but then Kopanyev was shouting at us, "They are long! Long! Open your mouths! Open them!"

There were two special symbols, sort of lower-case *b*s, that were not letters per se, but signs meaning *soft* or *hard*. "You must soften preceding consonant. Like so." And he showed us what was happening in his mouth, his tongue cozying up against his palate. He drew a picture on the board.

"Okay. First letter: A. Repeat: A like fAther. Like I am doctor looking down your throat."

We recited the alphabet. That was all we did until, walking out of the room at the end of the fifty minutes, I felt like I was drowning in unutterable sounds.

Now everything had a different name. *Dom.* (House.) *Spalnya.* (Bedroom.) *Kniga.* (Book.) I took over Belinda's chore, vacuuming upstairs and down, practising my Russian as I worked. In the living room, the *gastinaya*, Hector was playing the guitar. He didn't live there, but he often stayed over, and when I came in with the vacuum he perched on the chesterfield, like a crow on a power line, so his feet wouldn't be in my way.

I was still wrangling the machine, the *pylesos* (I'd stopped vacuuming to look it up), when Sonia burst in the front door. The way she looked at me, I thought of Anna Sergeyevna without her Pomeranian. Anna Sergeyevna, uncombed. But how could Sonia be pathetic? If I'd been her, of course, I would have been the happiest girl in the world.

"Did you hear?" she asked me. "The Russians shot down an airliner."

Strum! went Hector's guitar. Sonia made a sound, too, like the last of her wind was being forced out in one invisible squeeze, a little huff of terror, as she bolted past me to her room.

A few hours later, Pete and Dieter came home and consulted the rabbit-eared black and white TV. I hovered in the French doors to find out more. A Soviet jet fighter had shot down a South Korean civilian airliner, sending two hundred and sixty-nine souls plunging into the Sea of Japan. A U.S. congressman, five Canadians, and twenty-two children were among those aboard.

Hector left after the news and Sonia wouldn't come out of her room, so it was just the three of us at supper that night. "This is it," Pete announced. "This is the shot that rang out in Sarajevo. Get ready, people."

Dieter: "It had to be a spy plane, don't you think?"

"I don't think anything yet."

"They just happened to be flying over Soviet territory? Right over where the Soviets just happen to have bases? Flight 007. Get it? Double O seven? Isn't that just a bit of a coincidence?"

"I don't believe anything the media says."

Dieter squeezed his nose in his fist. Then the telephone rang and they both turned to stare at it on the cluttered counter, tethered to its twenty-foot cord. *Telefon*. It rang a second time, yet neither of them moved. They suffered some collective neuroses regarding its functioning, I'd noticed. They would come running only to stare like this, as though it had summoned them and they were sore afraid in its mighty presence. An ordinary yellow phone, their golden idol. It wasn't for me, that was for sure. Finally Pete took a chance and answered, then covered the receiver. "Sonia! Mommy's calling!"

Sonia stomped in, swollen from crying, and snatched the whole phone up, carried it off in her arms, the cord unwinding with her departure, loop after loop. I finished the dishes and went up to my room, which was directly above Sonia's. There was a decorative metal grate in the floor for passive heat exchange. I could see right down onto her dresser. At night, when I woke, the light coming from below would cast a filigree pattern on the ceiling, like a leaded glass window. Sonia's insomnia gave me a night light. Her sleeplessness gave her those dark dramatic circles around her eyes. Maybe she was a sleepwalker, a *lunatik*. Someone who walks on the moon.

She was still on the phone, murmuring below me. I heard her sigh and say, "Ma? I'm so scared."

Then Pete came up. I could differentiate their footsteps now, Pete's stomping, Dieter's soundless sneaking, the creak of the wood giving him away. Pete was the door-slammer. *Slam!* He put his music on (Hendrix). When Dieter banged in protest on the adjoining wall, Pete, out of principle, cranked it up. By the time he relented, Sonia had hung up and I still didn't understand what she was so afraid of.

On the weekend, I took the long bus trip back to Burnaby to have supper with my aunt, fulfilling the promise I had made about Sundays, which assuaged both her hurt feelings and my guilt. This actually worked out well because every Sunday there was a potluck at the Trutch house, followed by a meeting, neither of which I was invited to.

My aunt answered the door, throwing open her arms, pulling me to her size Z bosom. I smelled her perfume, Eau de Thrift Store Sweater. "I made your favourite," she said, and I knew she intended to lure me back.

I piled on the sour cream, the fried onions, the bacon. Lots and lots of bacon that probably straddled the Best Before date, but I didn't care. My aunt took note. When I moved out, she had inflicted on me doleful glances and squashy, overlong embraces, their implication being I would not thrive. Beyond her protection there awaited only loneliness and constipation. Now her cheeks, squiggled with capillaries, glowed in triumph.

"Have you been eating?"

"Of course," I said, but the truth, we both knew, was not enough. I hadn't really felt full since I'd moved to the Trutch house. I wasn't getting the protein I required. Also, competition for food was fierce.

"You look thinner."

"I'm not thinner."

Though I was always conscious of her accent, strangely, I never heard my father's any more. She was older, in her late fifties, the one who'd sponsored him to come to Canada all those years ago. Briefly they'd lived together, then my father went to Alberta where there were more jobs. He didn't like

Vancouver. People were unfriendly, he said, and the red two-dollar bills looked phoney and it rained all the time.

"How are you sleeping?"

"Fine."

"And?" She meant my bowels.

"Yes, yes."

"Your studies are coming along?"

"Yes."

"Tell me about the girls you're living with. Are they nice?"

I hadn't mentioned that two of them were boys. And while I didn't think of my new housemates as nice, neither did I consider them unkind. Unkind was names scrawled on my locker, papier mâché projectiles fired through an empty Bic. In high school these torments had come erratically, and I was by no means the only one who suffered them. In fact, on the scale of universal adolescent suffering I might not even have attained a rank. It was the haphazardness that caused the most damage. For weeks some other victim would suffer, then it would start up again, usually under some friendly guise—"Jane, do you want to eat lunch with us?"—so I learned always to be on my guard, like some armoured wallflower with its tin petals tightly closed.

As for my housemates, I never expected to make friends with them. I had my books and the people in them were more than enough. Except for supper, I ate toast in my room. Toast was quick to prepare and I could get out of the kitchen fast. But I definitely wasn't getting enough protein.

What to tell her? Belinda was around a lot, having sex with Pete. She stayed overnight several times a week because, I'd overheard, the house on Blenheim Street was "Women Only." I talked about her as though she were still living there—leaving out the sex. "She's very dramatic." I said she walked like she was doing an interpretive dance and got up to imitate her gliding step. As for Pete and Dieter, apart from the phone idolatry and the fact that they argued all the time, I had a slight impression of them, hardly more than Pete was an anarchist as conceived by Botticelli and the owner of the patched Reliant. Dieter was a zealot for composting (I'd learned by mistakenly throwing a banana peel in the garbage), and possibly a Marxist. Both more or less ignored me, but I still didn't want my aunt to know about the anarchism, or the possible Marxism, or that the house wasn't "Women Only" but a locus of premarital sex. She'd surely write my father.

I said Sonia was pretty and very nice. My aunt retorted that I had "beautiful eyes."

Sonia *was* pretty, yet she neglected her appearance and, since the airliner incident on Thursday, she seemed in distress. Anti-Soviet demonstrations were taking place across the country. In Toronto, performances by the Moscow Circus were cancelled. The circus business seemed especially to wound Sonia, causing her to stare uncomprehendingly at her plate all through Friday's supper. In "Lady with a Lapdog," Chekhov wrote that Anna Sergeyevna's *long hair hung mournfully on either side of her face*. He wrote, *It was obvious she was unhappy*.

"I'm glad it's working out," my aunt said. "You're young. You should be having fun." She dabbed at her eyes with her napkin.

After dinner we cleaned up. There were a number of dented cans by the side of the sink, which I rinsed and stripped of their labels. Then my aunt removed the tops and bottoms with the opener and took them out on the back porch where she savagely stamped them flat in readiness for her basement repository. This was how we'd spent Sunday evenings last year: she in front of the TV unravelling the old sweaters she would later reknit into odorific Christmas and birthday presents, me studying in the kitchen. Tonight I joined her for the start of *The Wonderful World of Disney* until I could politely escape.

When I got back to the Trutch house, the porch was more crowded than usual due to additional bicycles. "*Oni velosipyedy,*" I said out loud, to no one. *They are bicycles.* (I was starting to form sentences.) I hoped to stash the care package of perogies in the freezer and slip up to my room unnoticed, but there was no need to tiptoe around. The double glass doors to the living room with their floraed and faunaed panes were still closed. I knew what their meetings were about because of the leaflets and petitions foisted upon apathetic students like me almost weekly. Voices overlapped, several conversations going on at once, while, in the kitchen, the dirty dishes from the potluck stood around on the table daring me not to do them. Then someone began singing. It was a woman's voice, quavering and strange. "We shall live in peace, we shall live in peace . . ." Others joined in. "We shall live in peace some da-a-ay!"

I shivered and hurried up the stairs.

The bus stop was two blocks away, on Fourth Avenue. In the morning buses came at convenient intervals, though some-times, if one was too crowded, it would speed indifferently past. Every time this happened, I took it personally, which was what I was doing when Sonia came around the corner nicely dressed for once in a skirt. Not until she was almost at the stop did she realize it was me. "Oh! Hi," she said.

I wanted to say something consoling about the airliner, but had no idea of the etiquette in that particular circumstance so, as usual, I defaulted to saying nothing and feeling awkward. The bus arrived and we got on and Sonia followed me to the back. All the seats were taken there too. She could barely reach the strap, so I wordlessly gave up the pole and we do-si-doed, exchanging places. "What time is your first class?" she asked.

I told her. She said she had to go out to a school and observe a grade two class that day. "That's why I'm dressed up like this."

Meanwhile the bus lurched along, accumulating more passengers before making a run for the hill. When it reached the top, a view opened over the plated ocean. I lived mere blocks from it now, but had yet to go and see it. Sonia glanced at me from time to time, as though deciding whether or not to speak. At the campus loop, we were disgorged, and with everyone pushing to get off, she got ahead. I didn't expect to see her again until supper, but she was waiting when I stepped down.

"Did they shoot it down on purpose?" I asked.

She knew immediately what I was talking about. "They thought it was a spy plane. Now who knows what the Americans will do? Probably start firing." She pressed her fists into her temples. "Which way are you going?" I pointed and she walked with me toward the Buchanan building. "I don't know what to do about Dieter," she said.

"What do you mean?"

"He always sits next to me at supper. Haven't you noticed? He knocks on my door for no reason. Now he's started pulling my hair. It's driving me crazy. I don't like him. I mean, I like him. I like everybody. He's in my group! But I don't like him *that* way."

So what I'd always suspected was true: other people's problems were shockingly trite.

"His father died last summer."

"Really?" I said. "That's terrible."

"It makes it hard, though, to say I'm not interested. Last night he came in and lay on my bed and said he'd protect me." She turned to me, exasperated. "How does he think he's going to do *that*?"

Outside the library she plucked entreatingly at my sleeve. "Jane? Sit beside me tonight?"

I thought of that little tug as I took a seat in my seminar. The fabric pulling against my arm, her plea for my presence. The other students meandered in with their backpacks and throwaway coffee cups, chatting, but not to me. No one talked to me. I always sat in the same chair, at Kopanyev's right hand, and always the seat on the other side of me was empty. No one wanted to sit next to the overeager girl. Keith, the punk, clomped in. They were completely freaked out by him. Then Kopanyev arrived, folders bursting under his arm. He was not the most organized lecturer. Frequently his tangents tangled us up and, in this, a second-year course, Nineteenth-Century Russian Literature in Translation, he seemed to recognize that he was an unreliable driver and so threw the reins to us. We were given a reading list and assigned a date, not to make a presentation per se, but to offer a passage, a character, or simply an observation, as a topic for discussion.

He ticked our names off with a massive fountain pen. "Now, my conversationalists." Looking around the table, rescrewing the cap. "Michael? Ha! Did you see him jump? What have you brought for us to talk about today, Michael? What have you been reading? Speak! Speak! We are waiting."

A wing of blond hair hung over Michael's eyes. He performed the affectation, sweeping it aside. "Chekhov."

"Ah. The greatest writer who ever lived. And?"

"I notice, well, a couple of things. First, the stories are unbelievably gloomy. Second, the characters always, or often, seem to be in love with people who don't love them back."

"Unrequited love," Kopanyev sighed.

"They're even married to people who don't love them back."

Kopanyev: "Example?"

"'Three Years,'" I said.

"Remind everyone, please, Jane. Summarize story."

"Go ahead," I said to Michael but he only made a face.

"Laptev is in love with Julia, a friend of his sister Nina," I said. "Nina's dying of breast cancer. Actually, Nina's also a victim of unrequited love because her husband lives in another part of town with his mistress."

"Men!" expleted the ponytailed girl at the end of the table and everyone laughed, except Mohawked Keith who generally limited himself to expressions of contempt.

"Laptev proposes. At first Julia refuses because she doesn't love him. Then she agrees. Because Laptev's rich and she doesn't see any other opportunities for herself. The story basically relates the first three years of their marriage."

Michael swept his bang away again. "Their *unhappy* marriage. It's completely *depressing*."

"Chekhov is funny too."

"What's funny about that story? Find me one funny thing."

"I don't have the book with me."

"Cancer? Ha ha ha."

"Doesn't their baby die?" someone asked. "That's the same story, right?"

"That story is more sad than funny," I agreed, "but others are really funny. The people are funny."

"And we have two cases of unrequited love," said Kopanyev. "Can anyone think of other stories with this element?"

"'Lady with a Lapdog.'"

"That's not *unrequited*. That's *doomed*."

Turgenev's Bazarov and Odintsova were proposed, but Kopanyev asked that we restrict our discussion to Chekhov. The heavy girl who kept poking at her cuticles said, "There's that story. I don't remember titles. Where the creepy husband pisses off the wife who's trying to help the famine victims."

"'My Wife.'"

Another professorial nod for me.

"'His Wife,'" I added.

Blank looks all around.

"Where he finds the telegram from his wife's lover saying he kisses her sweet little foot a thousand times?"

"Ha ha ha!" roared Kopanyev. "So wife can be villain? I thought women could only be victims."

The three other girls in the class rolled their eyes but wouldn't take the bait, not even Ponytail. "The wife's the villain in 'The Grasshopper,'" a male pointed out.

"'The Grasshopper'!" Michael moaned. "I read that last night. Another riot."

At Kopanyev's request, Michael summarized it: wife runs off with arty friends while doctor husband pays for everything, catches diphtheria, and dies.

"That's actually quite a funny story," I said.

"But in that story," the heavy girl said, "the wife didn't hate the husband. She just thought he was boring."

"She was having an affair."

"But she still *liked* her husband, so I don't think you can call that"—four fingers with ragged cuticles, two from each hand, went up and scratched the air—"unrequited, per se."

"'The Kiss'!" Keith blatted.

"Most definitely." Kopanyev asked for a summary.

"This army captain? He goes to a ball. Hangs around feeling like a loser. Later he goes into a dark room where this lady's waiting for her boyfriend. She kisses the loser by mistake. This pathetically transforms the guy's life. He spends months fantasizing about the mystery lady, hoping for a chance to go back to the house. Finally the opportunity comes up and he goes and realizes what a complete and utter loser he really, truly is."

Kopanyev stroked his beard for a full minute. Sometimes he treated his facial hair like a living thing, a cat clinging to his face. It seemed to help him think. "You don't sound very sympathetic, Keith."

"He's a loser."

For some time we talked about "The Kiss," whether being in love with a hypothetical person could even be considered unrequited love, whether Staff-Captain Ryabovitch was indeed worthy of sympathy or merely deluded, and when the majority expressed scorn, Kopanyev declared that we were either preternaturally hard-hearted or had been remarkably successful in love despite our youth. He went on to confess one of his own early trials—he had adored a classmate and was rebuffed—regaling us with humiliating details until he noticed his watch. "You're not serious!" He clapped his hands. "My dear little children. My pupils. My timepiece has been unkind to us, as usual. Thanks to Michael for excellent topic, which we have barely scratched."

And, sighing, he rose just like a bear being prodded to stand upright.

Chekhov began his career as a writer of comic stories in order to support his family. I was baffled that my classmates couldn't see the humour in his work. That evening, searching for something funny in "Three Years," I underlined the passage where Julia is travelling back home from Moscow by train with her philandering brother-in-law, Panaurov. "*Pardon the pub simile,*" he says to her, "*but you put me in mind of a freshly salted gherkin.*"

And later, when Laptev's friends, Yartsev and Kostya, walk drunkenly back to the station, unable to see a thing in the dark: "*Hey, you holiday-makers!*" Kostya suddenly shouts out. "*We've caught a socialist!*"

Sad (5), *sadly* (4), *unhappy* (4), *miserable* (1), *lonely* (1), *depressed* (2), *depression* (2), *disgruntled* (1), *boring* (9), *bored* (5), *dull* (1), *monotonous* (2), *apathetic* (1).

Sonia tapped and looked in. "Supper."

Downstairs, a pot of soup and a tray of airy, row-provoking biscuits waited on the table. "Sit," she said, before taking the chair beside me and shouting to the other two. They thundered down. Supper was the only time they ever responded promptly to a call.

Dieter: "I usually sit there."

Sonia said nothing, while Pete, who was loading biscuits on his plate, exhaled a single word. "Fascist." Dieter took the chair across from Sonia and knuckled up his glasses. "I'm a creature of habit I guess."

"You're a creature," Pete said.

"What's that supposed to mean?"

"You are. I'm a creature, you're a creature. Zed's a creature."

Sonia: "Her name is Jane."

"She'll let me know if she doesn't like what I call her."

"Whoa!" said Dieter, taking two biscuits off Pete's plate and returning them to the tray. "We'll divide these up evenly. What do you say?"

While Dieter was busy divvying up the biscuits, Pete ate his entire ration. Then he double-checked the empty pot. "Sonia?"

"What?"

"You'll never eat three. Give me one."

Dieter: "No."

"I'm not asking you."

"Three each."

"I'm asking Sonia."

Sonia kept her head low to her bowl, blowing ripples across her spoon.

"Sonia?"

She was by far the best cook. The biscuits were buttery, cloud-light. Dieter wasn't touching his; I assumed he was saving them for last so he could eat them in front of us when ours were gone.

Pete said, "Sonia, why do you always make so little food? It's not the end of the world yet."

She dropped her spoon. I realized before Pete and Dieter did that she was crying. I was sitting next to her and, dumbfounded, saw the tears rain in her soup.

"I'm still hungry," Pete bleated, clasping his hands. "Feed me. Feed me."

She leapt up. "How can you joke about the end of the world? How?" Before he could answer, she snatched a biscuit off the tray and hurled it. It struck Pete square on the forehead, then bounced off, leaving a floury mark. He sat, momentarily stunned, before letting go a long, crazy, primeval whoop, a pterodactyl call. "It's not funny!" she shrieked. "Not at all!" and she stumbled from the table and out of the room with Dieter hurrying after her. "Asshole," he hissed at Pete.

Pete took advantage of the moment to jam a fourth biscuit in, the one that had ricocheted off him. "Do I go too far, Zed?" he asked when he had finally choked it down. I didn't reply. I didn't think he cared what I thought. When he left, he took another biscuit with him.

I cleared the table and put the dishes in the sink, though cleanup was the cook's job. I could hear Pete talking in a funny voice and Sonia begging him to stop. When he wouldn't let up, I went down the hall to see if she was all right. Her door was open and she was sitting on the bed hugging a stuffed toy, Dieter kneeling on the floor at her feet, Pete on the bed behind her, massaging her tiny shoulders. "Leave me alone," she was moaning, "go away," while Pete kept telling her in a duck's voice that everything would be okay.

That night I woke to the leaded glass window on the ceiling. I stared up at it, wondering what time it was. Maybe Sonia was afraid of the dark. Maybe that was why her light was on so often at night.

It was true she never made enough food. I was hungry again.

I felt my way into the dark hall and down the stairs. Moonlight penetrated the living room, rebounding off the white surfaces—the note taped to the lamp, *It's payback time!!!*, and the statue's painted grin—relegating the rest of the room to obscurity. I carried on past the French doors, to the kitchen where I saw the glow and stopped.

A bright orange spiral.

The stove was on. My first thought was that this was why I'd woken. Sometimes it was the front door slamming, or Belinda and Pete's noisy exertions. But Belinda wasn't there tonight so I must have instinctively sensed danger. I'd just taken a step to shut the burner off when I realized someone else was there—Sonia, moving toward the stove at the same time, her face and upper body washed in the thin orange light. Palm down, fingers outstretched, she was reaching for the element, lowering her hand over it. When she got close enough to the coil to make me wince, she drew her hand back and shook it out. She tried again, getting closer the second time.

I crept back upstairs and lay on my futon staring at the pattern on the ceiling, wondering what to do. When Sonia's light finally snapped off, I turned my own on, tore a sheet from my notebook, tore that in half, wrote. I folded the note until it was compact enough to wriggle through the grate. Then I listened for it, the small sound of it landing on the dresser below, the soft tap of my message reaching her.

She seemed so tormented, but if I lost any sleep over Sonia's problems, it was only because her light woke me up. Those first months in the Trutch house I mostly tried to avoid my housemates, staying in my room and getting up earlier than everyone else. But I couldn't escape our communal supper or the awkward dashing to and from the upstairs bathroom that I shared

with the men. And in the afternoon, when I came home, someone was inevitably there. Pete would be there, or Hector with
his gold tooth and his beret, watching *Looney Tunes* with Pete.
Sometimes if Dieter was there, he and Pete would exchange a
look when I came in, their unsecret signal to close the subject,
which was always politics. But maybe it wasn't. Maybe it was
them wondering about me and just what my problem was.

What was my problem? I wondered it myself.

Then one afternoon I came home and found my bedroom
door open. I always kept it closed, but it was open now and Pete
was there, in my room, his back to me, hair in a ponytail, T-shirt
inside out. I saw a tag and seams.

"What are you doing?" The words came out in a quiet rasp.

"Looking for a pen."

He wasn't looking for a pen. He was lying on his side on the
floor, one hand propping himself up as he studied the spines of
my books. My private, treasured books. My room received the
sun's afternoon attention and he was basking in it, in a bright
cloud of dust motes. "There are pens downstairs by the phone,"
I said.

"Can you get me one?"

"No."

"See?" he said. "It's too far to go. You read a lot of novels."

"Some of them are short stories."

"It's a waste of time."

Now I mustered a tone nearly appropriate to what I felt.
"Can you get out of my room, please?"

The books were arranged in three pillars. He pulled one out
from the middle, causing the whole stack to collapse, opened
it and began flipping, pausing to read the underlined bits. "*Art
is just a means of making money, as sure as haemorrhoids exist.*"
He looked over his shoulder at me. Utter delight. Complete

self-satisfaction. My expression seemed not to register with him. "I rest my case. It's written right here. What *is* this?" He glanced at the cover.

I wanted to snatch it from him, whack him with it. Riffle the pages in his face—*literature farts at you!* Instead I dropped my backpack to the floor and began digging. Pete read on to himself but, finding nothing else of interest on the page, tossed the book back on the pile. "You need a bookshelf, Zed."

I pulled out my pencil case, unzipped it. "Here."

"Oh, good." Before he left, he took the pen and scribbled on his arm to make sure it worked.

I don't know if he could hear me, crying, over his music. When I had calmed down, I took a decision. I couldn't live there any more. These people were horrible. I hated them. Pete was a drug addict. (What he smoked out on the deck was marijuana.) Dieter was a control freak. Sonia hadn't even mentioned my note. I'd go back to my aunt's and live there until I found another place. I didn't care about the bus ride, or that she was crazy. *They* were crazy. I knew I was overreacting, but at that time I felt I had nothing, nothing except my privacy.

I heard Sonia's call to supper and Pete and Dieter bolting, racehorses out of the starting gate. Sonia called again. A few minutes later a tap sounded on the door, though I hadn't heard any steps. Sonia was weightless.

She put her head in. "Aren't you eating?"

I didn't look up from my book. "No."

"Are you sick?"

"Yes." I was sick with anger.

"Do you want me to make you some toast or something?"

"No," I said. "Thank you."

"I hope you feel better."

"Thank you."

I put the book down as soon as she closed the door.

Pete came up directly after supper. When I didn't answer his knock, he thudded to his room. A moment later my pen shot through the gap under the door. "I'm returning your private property!" he called.

I heard him go away, then come right back. "I need to borrow that again." I was afraid he'd barge in so I got up and kicked the pen back under the door. It came skating through a second time, followed by a piece of paper I could read from where I had retreated to my nest. *Property is theft.*

I threw the covers off and stomped to Pete's room, where he was apparently anticipating our clash, standing with arms crossed, half smiling. "I don't go into your room!" I shrieked.

"You're welcome to," he said. "Any time."

"I don't want to! And I don't want you going into mine!"

"Anything I have is yours."

He wasn't mocking me. He mocked Dieter mercilessly all the time and that was not the tone he was using now. I hurled the pen but, other than dodging it, he didn't react, just stood there, a beautiful statue that had briefly come to life. "Hold it," he called after me.

I slammed my door. Pete opened it—without knocking!— and set down two yellow milk crates. "I don't want those," I said.

He returned with two more, blue and red, then the boards. Kicking my books over a second time, out of the way, he began assembling the shelf. Two crates, a board, two more crates, another board. I sank down on my futon, face in my hands, and sobbed.

"There. You want me to put the books back or do you want to do that yourself?"

I looked up, streaming. "What do you *want*?"

He was still on his knees but, to my horror, he changed position, got comfortable interlacing his fingers behind his head and falling onto his back—all to ponder his reply. It didn't take long. "I want a fairer world," he said. "What do you want, Zed?"

"I want you to ask permission before you come into my room."

"I don't ask permission."

"You should!"

"Why?"

"Because it's polite! It's respectful!"

"Polite is bullshit. It's bourgeois. I don't recognize private property and I don't respect it."

"I'm not talking about respecting property! As if I care about a stupid pen!"

"Oh," he said. "But I respect you, Zed. You're intelligent. You don't play games. You're funny."

"Funny?"

"Dry. Anyway, I didn't want to go all the way downstairs to get a pen. I was curious about what kind of books you read."

He spoke so reasonably to my hysteria. At least that was how it seemed now. I scrambled for a tissue. "You might say sorry."

"That's another thing I don't do."

"Fine." I blew my nose with an embarrassing quack. "Can you get out now?"

"I can." But he stayed exactly as he was, on his back, naked foot tapping the air. When I threw up my hands, he laughed. "You asked me if I *could*."

I felt dizzy after he left. I couldn't believe he thought those things about me. I looked over at my scree of books and, though it actually pained me to see them in disarray, I resisted putting them away. Then a voice quavered through the grate. "Is everything all right up there?" I went over and peered down. "Toast?" Sonia asked.

A few minutes later she came up with a tray. "Thank you," I said.

"There wasn't any supper left."

"No doubt."

She sat on the floor and hugged her knees, watching me eat. "I heard you and Pete," she said with a glance at the grate. "Don't mind him. He acts like that because he's smarter than everybody else."

I huffed.

Sonia: "It's true. He doesn't even go to class. He studies on his own in the library. Engineering's unbelievably hard. I admire him so much. He has discipline. He lives by his code."

"His anarcho-feminist-pacifist code?"

Sonia nodded. She didn't seem to get sarcasm. "His family's rich. He won't have anything to do with them. He has a trust fund, but he gives most of it away. He gives Hector money all the time." And though Pete paid the kitty, she told me that he wouldn't take any money out because he didn't believe in it. In money. He shopped on the five-finger discount, which explained the bizarre miscellany of groceries he always unloaded from his pack. Tomato sauce, popcorn, frozen peas. I'd seen him come home from university with a roll of toilet paper under each arm.

"Remember that time he said, 'Jane will tell me if she doesn't like what I call her'?"

I finished the toast and, licking my finger, gathered up the crumbs. "Zed. He calls me Zed."

"If you tell him not to, he won't."

"I don't care."

"Ask for his shirt, he'll give it to you. But you have to ask."

"Ask and I shall receive?"

I meant, *Does he think he's Jesus?* but Sonia brightened. "Are you a Christian?"

"No."

She felt for the little cross around her neck, as though to reassure herself she was. "The other thing. Pete separates out his feelings. Unlike me." Tears appeared then and were blinked back fiercely. "We are *this* close to a nuclear war," she said, pronouncing it "nucular." There was precious little space between the finger and thumb she held out. "Ever since they shot down that airliner, I've been waiting. Waiting. It's killing me. I can't talk about it now. I'll be a wreck. I have a project due tomorrow. As if it matters." She let go of her knees and lurched over to hug me while my own arms hovered in the air, not knowing what to do. "Actually," she said, letting go, "would you like to help me? Are you busy?"

My whole body tingled, like a limb gone to sleep, or waking up.

We went downstairs to her room. Sonia collected Japanese things. There was a teapot and two tiny handleless cups on the dresser, strings of origami cranes, a calligraphic banner. The stuffed toys looked Canadian. I went over to the dresser and peered up into my room, but all I could see was the blank of the ceiling. "Do you know Japanese?" I asked.

"No."

"Drink—more—tea," I pretended to read off the teapot. Then I saw my note behind one of the cups, still folded budtight.

"Let's have tea," she said, so I passed her the pot and cups. The moment she left the room, I tossed the note into her open closet where it fell among her shoes.

She returned shortly with the tea and sat down on the floor. I sat the same way, cross-legged, facing her while she poured with demure, faux-Japanese gestures, the little white cup balanced on the tips of her fingers as she bowed to me. I accepted it, bowing in return.

"It tastes better in these cups," she said.

I sipped. "It actually does."

We were going to make origami cranes for her practicum. Sonia spread out the coloured paper. I chose a yellow square,

Sonia a pink one. She flipped aside the braided rug to start. "Okay. Like this."

I reoriented the square as a diamond, like she did. I repeated each step, each fold and turn, fascinated, even distracted by her deft little fingers. It was like watching the manipulations of a baby or a raccoon, except her nails were chewed down and raw-looking. I wondered if they hurt. We made a tighter diamond, transformed it into a kite, pleated and repleated what we'd done. Then, somehow, out of this intricately wrapped present of air, we coaxed two birds. "That's good, Jane. Your very first crane." Which was how she talked to her seven-year-olds, I presumed. "Keep it if you want," she said.

We paused to sip our tea then bowed again over new squares, the crowns of our heads almost touching. "A hundred and fifty thousand people died when they dropped the bomb on Hiroshima." Sonia looked up, gauging my reaction.

"Really? That's awful."

And it was. Awful.

"Not a day goes by that I don't think about it," she said.

I helped her fold twenty-four cranes, for which she hugged me again. Afterward, I went back upstairs where I set the yellow one on the grate so she would see it roosting there if she happened to look up. Then I moved my books into their new home. *Art Through the Ages. The Science of Life.* Chekhov. Turgenev. Dostoyevsky. Tolstoy. When I was done and I slid back for a better look, a line from *The Cherry Orchard* popped into my head: *My dear venerable bookcase, I salute you.*

Mid-terms came and I wondered how I had allowed myself to be flattered into taking Russian. It was nothing like French, the only other foreign language I'd attempted. French was a mouthful of feathers. Russian was spitting out stones. But if only I *could* spit them! I was able to read simple sentences now and even understand the absurdist dialogues in the language lab, but I choked on the stones. In addition to Russian and Russian Lit, I'd enrolled in the stupefying Canadian Poetics, and Biology 100, the obligatory science credit I'd sidestepped the year before. After exams were over, when I could with great relief recap my highlighter pen and file away my index cards of notes, a house meeting was called. The main item on the agenda: what to do about Halloween.

Pete: "If we're not going to use it as a consciousness-raising opportunity, then I'll boycott it as a bourgeois ruse."

"How is Halloween a bourgeois ruse?" It was the first time I'd spoken during a meeting.

"Zed," Pete said, shaking his gilded head. "What happens at Halloween?"

"Children dress up. They go door to door."

"Yes. Essentially begging. A friendly adult disperses candy—for free! How fun! But what does it teach them? That the society they live in is generous and benign? Zed? Imagine a genuinely needy person begging door to door. And is that candy really free? Is it even sweet? Under what conditions did the workers in the factory labour to produce it? And what about the virtual slaves toiling in the sugar cane fields?"

"Oh dear," Sonia said.

I wondered what he would have to say about Christmas.

Dieter: "I see your point about candy. Maybe we can hand out something else."

"We could hand out cranes," I said.

Sonia literally lifted off the seat of her chair, making excited flapping motions with her hands. "Yes!"

"How does that raise consciousness?" Pete asked.

"The crane is a symbol," Sonia said. "It's a symbol of peace."

"They don't know that."

"We could write a message explaining it," I said.

Pete smiled, showing all his perfect teeth. "Okay. Let's write messages on the cranes. I'm fine with that."

"Do we have consensus then?" Dieter asked.

We did and I felt pleased because it was my idea. Sonia went to get the origami papers from her room, then we set to writing. *The crane is a symbol of peace*, I wrote. I didn't know what else to say. When I got bored writing that, I just wrote *Peace*, but that, too, became tedious. The others were writing more than I was. Pete appeared to be composing a manifesto. Dieter kept leaning over to read Sonia's messages, leaning close so she almost had to fold her little self sideways to avoid touching him. *Think about what peace means*, I wrote, though I had never given it any thought myself. I glanced at what Sonia was writing.

No more Hiroshimas!

We worked for half an hour then all of us but Pete were done. "I need a smoke," he said. "I'll finish later." When Dieter tried to read one of his messages, Pete pounced, slapping his hand over it. "Do you *mind?*"

Dieter stalked away, offended. I stayed and offered to help Sonia fold the cranes. "Did you write this?" she asked, reading one of my banal messages.

"Yes."

"That's good, Jane," she said.

"What did you write?" I asked.

She showed me.

Give peace a chance.

Later that night as I lay reading in my room, something made me look up from my book: a green square sliding under the door, fed slowly through from the other side. Then an orange square, then a red.

UNCLE PETER ANSWERS YOUR QUESTIONS ABOUT ANARCHISM!

1. What is Anarchism, Uncle Peter?
   Why, that's a good question! Let Uncle Peter tell you. Anarchism is the name of a political philosophy based on the rejection of any form of compulsory government.

2. What a funny word, Uncle Peter!
   Yes, Sonny. It's derived from a Greek word meaning "without rulers."

3. How can I tell if someone is an Anarchist?
   Judge people by their actions, not their appearance. Above all, beware of men in suits.

4. But Uncle Peter! My daddy wears a suit!
   See #3.

UNCLE PETER ANSWERS YOUR QUESTIONS ABOUT ANARCHISM! (PART TWO)

1. Uncle Peter! I'm only eight years old How can I be an Anarchist?
   It's never too early to start living by the principles of Anarchism, Sonny! The first thing you must do is identify the authority figures in your life.

2. What are authority figures, Uncle Peter?
   The people bossing you around. Mommy. Daddy. Big brother or big sister. Teacher. Principal. These are the most likely culprits. At this stage of your life, they stand in for "compulsory government."

3. Then what, Uncle Peter?
   Question everything they say. If they say, "Eat your peas," you say, "Why?"

4. Uncle Peter, what if they answer, "Because I said so"?
   You say, "That's not a good enough answer."

5. Uncle Peter, do Anarchists often get spankings?
   Yes.

UNCLE PETER ANSWERS YOUR QUESTIONS ABOUT
ANARCHISM! (PART THREE)

1. Uncle Peter, how can I be a good Anarchist at school?
   The same way you are a good Anarchist at home: question authority.

2. Dear Uncle Peter, can you give me an example?
   Certainly, Sonny. Never turn in your homework.

3. Why not, Uncle Peter?
   Because homework is simply a tool for authority to extend its control of children outside of school.

4. But I'll fail, Uncle Peter!
   You won't. You'll take the test and ace it.

5. What else can I do, Uncle Peter?
   Take this crane to school and show it to your classmates.

In the morning I woke to find a whole paper mat of squares at my door. I read them while I was eating my toast in my room. By the time I'd finished folding them into cranes, Pete's music had come on (The Doors) and, with the men jockeying for the bathroom, the day's fresh disputes began.

"Zed!" Pete called to me later as I was coming down the stairs. "Did you see what I put under your door?"

"Yes."

He stepped out of the kitchen, peanut butter jar in hand, and, taking the spoon out of his mouth, asked, "What did you do with them?"

"I turned them into birds."

He threw his head back and let loose a peanutty peal that filled the hall. "Did you read them?"

I'd barely recovered from mid-terms and now I sensed another test. He'd stopped Dieter from reading what he'd written, but I settled on the truth. "Yes."

"And?"

I zipped my jacket, hefted my texts onto my back. "You really want my opinion?"

"Yes."

"I laughed."

I thought he might be offended, but he looked pleased.

Pete had a suit! At supper, it induced a fit of giggling in Sonia every time she looked at him. "What?" he asked, deadpan. "It's Halloween."

"What are you supposed to be?" I was innocent enough to ask.

"A capitalist," Sonia told me.

Pete smirked as he margarined his bread. "You can say that again."

We were still eating when the first chorus sounded. "Trick or treat!" Pete got up, plucked Reagan's face off the wall, snugged it over his own, and tucked his hair in.

Dieter: "You should have said you were dressing up. I would have been Margaret Thatcher."

"You'll scare them," Sonia said.

Reagan: "That's the whole idea." The mask distorted his voice. He didn't even sound like Pete, and I recoiled though I had only ever thought of Ronald Reagan, if I thought of him at all, as affable and doddering. Pete threw open the front door, booming: "Who have we here?"

"Trick or treat!" UNICEF boxes jingled furiously.

"Here's a little something for each of you."

"What is it?"

"A peace crane. And there's a special message inside it. When you get home, ask your mommy and daddy to read it to you."

"Thank you, Mr. Reagan."

"You're welcome. Now be careful tonight. You never know when I'm going to drop the Big One."

He shut the door and came back to the kitchen, still the president. Dieter had gone for the belt of his bathrobe and was tying a tea towel over his wiry hair. "Who are you?" Reagan asked.

"Arafat, you Yankee scum."

Sonia and I went to the living room where, kneeling on the chesterfield, we watched the procession out the window. Voices rang out all along the street, screeches too, then a firecracker discharged, and Sonia cringed. "Oh God. It's like a war." As soon as she said it, I saw it too, a tattered exodus, pillowcases stuffed with belongings, dragged along. They carried on right past our house, though our porch light illuminated a welcome. When a pirate broke free and started for us, an adult called him back. Finally a few older, unchaperoned kids took a chance. Reagan and Arafat answered.

"What's this?"

"It's a peace crane. Inside there's a special—"

"Don't you have any candy?"

"No, you ingrate. You're fat enough already."

"Fuck you!" said the child.

Sonia leapt off the chesterfield. "What do you guys think you're doing?"

The kids fled down the walk. Two of them were playing with the cranes, using them as bombers, flying loop-the-loops, colliding mid-air. Sonia dismissed Pete and Dieter. "Go. Leave. Jane and I will hand them out."

We put on coats and shoes and took the bowl of cranes with us. From our new post at the end of the walk, we intercepted the next group that came along, Sonia crouching before a child in a hooded coat with rouge-appled cheeks. "Hello, sweetheart. Are you having fun?"

"I'm cold," the girl said, and Sonia cupped both her hands and breathed on them until a smile appeared.

"Do you want a birdie?"

I had relieved Sonia of the bowl so she could conjure the smile. Now I thrust it at the child. Her mother asked, "What's that you're giving out?"

"Origami cranes."

"What for?"

"They're pretty," I said.

She frowned. "Okay," she said to the little girl, "just take one and say thank you. Jeremy! Wait for us! Say thank you."

"Thank you," the girl told Sonia.

"You're very welcome," Sonia told her, standing again. "Stay warm."

As soon as the woman turned her back, Sonia stuck out her tongue. "She doesn't want her kid to have a paper crane. It's okay, though, to rot her teeth with candy. People are so stupid. They hate us on this street. Have you noticed? They never talk to us. The woman next door gives me a dirty look every time I walk by. They think we're Communists. If you want peace you must be a Communist. It's stupid."

"Are you Communists?" I asked.

"No!"

More children came. Sonia stepped in front of them too and, scooping a crane from the bowl, flew it, twittering it into a sack. The children watched her, rapt. I watched their father, saw him take note of the house, its psoriatic paint and overgrown yard, then Sonia—her *mournful* hair, the button on her anorak: *Think Peace*. She was speaking to his children in birdsong, exuding harmlessness, but his lip curled anyway and he bustled them along.

And so it went, all Sonia's overtures rejected. Then a loud *WEEEE!!* sounded, followed by a *BANG!*, and she grabbed the nearest child and clutched too hard. She only wanted to protect him, but he started wailing; his outraged mother snatched him back. The bowl was empty anyway so we went back inside where I put the kettle on. Sonia gnawed her nails, looking miserable.

Don't, I wanted to say, just as a single voice called out from our darkened porch, "Trick or treat!"

We both went to the door. "Oh, God! What are you *doing*?" Sonia cried.

The fruity weight of the breast, nipple projecting into the cold air. The left one. The other side was draped in filmy white fabric that hung off one shoulder and fell in folds around her Birkenstocks. "Come on," Belinda said. "You have them too."

"Not like that!"

The freckles petered out on her chest, making her look snowed on. She raised her arms. White feathers were attached and, in her armpits, aigrettes of auburn. "I am the Goddess," she intoned, flapping.

"Inside," Sonia hissed. "The neighbours."

Belinda followed us in and through to the kitchen. "How did it go with the cranes?"

"Okay, I guess. Jane helped hand them out."

"Did she?" The Goddess glanced at me through judgemental slits.

"Please," Sonia begged. "Put it away."

And the general mood was autumnal, Chekhov wrote. My umbrella was on the porch with the old placards, drying out. A beaded curtain of rain poured off the ruined eaves. Things had changed. I thought it was that fall had officially come and with it the infinite rains, the dirty batting of cloud, the sadness. I looked forward to the sadness. It made me feel like I shared something with other people, even though it was just a mood. I went down the front steps, past Pete's car. The next-door neighbour was standing in her front window in her flowered housecoat, hugging herself, face resigned. I felt like calling out, "Me too!"

At the bus stop I joined the ranks of the damp, our small shivering group physically separate but united by this resigned melancholia. Soon the bus came, but as it neared we saw that it was full. No one was surprised, not even when, in passing, it sent up a tidal wave of dirty water. By the time I got to campus, my hair would be stringy, my runners saturated. My feet were already cold and would be for the rest of the day. I could switch the hand that held the umbrella and warm the other in my pocket, but my feet were defenceless. If I'd been a character in a Chekhov story, I would have put on galoshes. (It was the same word in Russian: *galoshe*.) *Ga-losh-es*. *Losh* like *slosh*. Sloshing through puddles. Through *luzhi*. Galosh, galosh. A comical word, yet how sad they actually looked on a person's feet!

And so, standing in line for public transit, I found a subject for my first Russian Lit paper of the year. Chekhov and shoes. The stories are filled with them—galoshes, felt boots, slippers. Dr. von Koren in "The Duel" challenges the dissipated Ivan Layevsky partly because he wears slippers in the street. Podorin in "With Friends" (I'd read the story the night before) feels at home with the Losevs only when he borrows a pair of slippers. Later, weary of the visit, the slippers define his estrangement. *Then he sat silently in one corner, legs tucked under him, wearing slippers belonging to someone else.*

The following Sunday, when I came home from my aunt's, I stood staring at the jumble of shoes in the vestibule, wondering what I could discern about the group behind the closed French doors based on what they wore on their feet. Sonia's clogs were set neatly against the wall. I already knew she was from 100 Mile House, that both her parents were high school teachers. Her mother taught Home Ec and her father Math. She had a younger brother, Jared, and a Sheltie named Skipper. They lived on an acreage where they raised sheep. But the clogs allowed me to imagine her slipping them on in spring and running out to the barn to greet the lambs that had been born in the night. Kicked in the corner were Pete's Birkenstocks, the cork soles crumbling, plastic bread bags stuffed inside them, his trust fund untouched. Dieter's Adidases were there too, a Marxist-leaning red. As for the other shoes, including a giant's rubber boots, I couldn't begin to guess who owned them because what had really changed with the season, with the arrival of autumn, was that my housemates were starting to become fleshed-out characters.

I decided to study in the kitchen. With the addition of the bookshelf, my furniture situation had greatly improved, had, in fact, doubled, but I still didn't have a desk. In the kitchen I would have the luxury of a table. They always broke with that song and, as soon as I heard it, I could flee upstairs. I brought down my translation homework and cleared a space among the potluck dishes.

1. *Comrade Popov says that he received a letter every day from his wife in London.*

2. *This author will spend a long time writing and in the end he'll write a good novel.*

3. *Where was Masha going yesterday when we saw her?*

I could hear their voices in the other room, the different pitches—when a woman was speaking and when a man was— the melody of assent, the appassionato of disputation, but I couldn't make out the words. Outside, rain drummed impatient fingers against the window. I struggled, brain attempting to convert the English word into its Russian equivalent, hand to write the symbol that corresponded to the Russian sound, all the while feeling that maybe it was English I couldn't understand. When I had got through about half the exercises, the French doors clattered open unexpectedly and Dieter said, "Let's take five." A man I didn't know, tall and heavy with a head full of sloppy yellow curls, passed by the kitchen without looking in. One of his pant legs was rolled to his knee.

Then Belinda appeared, the only person I'd ever met who made freckles seem glamorous. Without acknowledging me, she headed to the sink where she filled a glass with water and drank from it, her back turned, forcing me to be her audience. She was so dramatic I could see why Pete enjoyed being cast as her leading man, but I didn't want to be in the play about her. Despite how enthusiastic she'd sounded when I was chosen for the house, in all our subsequent encounters her disdain for me was plain. I was finally starting to feel comfortable and knew she could easily ruin things for me by just a few calculated comments. The popular and beautiful have such powers.

Belinda drank a glass of water three feet away from me and, when she finished, she set it on the counter with an attention-getting rap, turned, and swept over, saying, "Hmm. I wonder what Jane studies? Accounting, I bet."

Instinctively, I covered the page—too late. She hovered above me, hair grazing the table. "Is that Russian?" she asked, dropping the stage voice.

"Yes."

"You're studying *Russian?*"

"Yes."

"Say something."

Of course I couldn't. The stones stuck. I tried to read what I'd written, but I hadn't worked out the pronunciation yet. Then out of my mouth came one of the sentences I'd translated. "*Tovarishch Popov govorit, chto on poluchil pismo.*"

Dieter bellowed for everyone to gather, and Belinda, first hesitating, blinking at me with new respect, swished out again. "Jane knows Russian," she said to the blond man I'd seen a moment ago with the rolled pant leg who was coming back down the hall.

"Who-who-who's Jane?"

"The other housemate."

He looked in at me. His cheeks were round and pink, like a baby's. I heard Belinda in the other room: "Pete! Guess what? Jane knows Russian."

I'd already closed my book and was just waiting for the opportunity to bolt upstairs when Pete strode in. "Do you speak Russian, Zed?"

"A little. I read and write it better."

"Say something."

"I don't want to."

He came over. "Show me the writing then."

Now Sonia appeared and, behind her, Belinda again, followed by a pale girl I'd never seen with shorn beige hair. Pete held the page in the air. Belinda snatched it and passed it along. "Jane!" Sonia cried. "What does it say?"

I repeated the Masha question. "Where was Masha going when we saw her yesterday?"

Dieter was there now. "Say something."

Pete: "She doesn't want to."

Belinda piped up, "She said something to me. It sounded delicious."

Dieter: "I prefer the Romance languages."

"You would."

"What's that supposed to mean?"

"It means you prefer the Romance languages," Pete said. "Why are you offended? You said it yourself."

"It's your tone."

"Are you the Tone Police?"

"Excuse me," I said, making a break for the door.

"Let's finish the meeting," Sonia pleaded and they all followed me out, though I turned right at the stairs and went up where they turned left at the living room. They didn't bother closing the French doors this time and a few minutes later, the song started up.

"Why didn't you tell us?" Sonia asked the next day.

"I said I was in Arts."

"Arts is anything. Dieter's in Arts." She added quickly, "Not that there's anything the matter with Dieter."

"He has a lot of rules," I said and Sonia cringed. A few days ago he'd tied a grease pencil to a piece of twine and taped it on the fridge door. It was for writing our names on our bread and yogurt and milk. Only supper was communal. But Pete, of course, was drinking from any milk carton he liked. He'd drunk from mine right in front of me.

"Anyway. Can you help me?" she asked.

There was a demonstration at the art gallery. The Americans were trying to deploy more missiles in Europe. At first, the West Germans wouldn't take them, but now that the Soviets had shot down the Korean airliner, it looked like it was going ahead. Sonia wanted her banner to be in Russian.

"What do you want it to say?" I asked.

"End the arms race."

I suspected this couldn't be directly translated. I could write "weapons" for "arms," but maybe you couldn't refer to it as a "race" in Russian. *Finish the weapons' athletic competition!* No one would be able to read it anyway. "I need my dictionary," I said, then did my best up in my room, working out the phrase and bringing it back down to her on a clean sheet of paper. *Ostanovi-tye gonku vooryezheniy!* She was in her room, cutting a bedsheet in half lengthwise. Then she laid it, a white runner, in the hall. Pete was on the phone in the kitchen. We could hear him saying, "Why can't I go in through the window?"

"I'm going to write the letters first, then paint them," Sonia said.

"Do you want help?" I asked.

"Would you? It's chicken scratch to me."

Pete: "I'll climb."

Pete: "Well, that's just fucked."

Then he roared. Hammering—the receiver against the counter, again, again. Sonia and I rushed to the kitchen where Pete was redialling. We heard Belinda's faraway hello. "Did you hang up? You didn't? Are you sure? They cut us off then, the *fuckers!*" He hurled the receiver and charged past us, knocking aside Sonia. She went over, picked the phone out of the sink, and, with the greying dish cloth, wiped some tomatoey stuff off the earpiece. "Belinda?" she said.

Upstairs, a door slammed. Crosby, Stills, Nash and Young. *O-hi-o.*

"He's mad," Sonia said in the phone. "He went upstairs. Were you really cut off? Jane and I are making the banner. Maybe she will. Anyway, I'm going to ask her to the movie. Are you going? Nobody's going? So? I've seen it before too. I've seen it four times. All right. I'll ask Jane."

"That was Belinda," Sonia said, on the way back to the hall. "She asked if you were coming to the demonstration."

I said no, I had to study. "Is there something the matter with the phone?" I asked.

"It's probably tapped," she said.

Which was why, apparently, it provoked such awe. I didn't believe it, though I didn't say so. I just nodded and tried not to show how silly I thought that was. Meanwhile, Sonia settled cross-legged to watch me sketch out the Cyrillic letters.

"That's amazing."

"What?"

"That you can write Russian."

I shrugged, though I was pleased. I stored the compliment the way my aunt socked everything away in bread bags—the shoes in her closet, her bits of costume jewellery, little pastel shards of soap. My aunt would pick an expired bus transfer off the ground and put it in her pocket, as though it were legal tender. I'd saved the things Pete had said to me, too—that I was funny and intelligent—and a comment Kopanyev once scrawled on the bottom of my paper: *Jane, you are a very sensitive reader.*

After a minute, Sonia asked, "Why are people afraid of the Russians?"

"I don't know."

"I think it's because they haven't met any. If they knew a few, they wouldn't be so afraid."

"That makes sense," I said.

"Personally, I'm more afraid of the Americans. They have more bombs. Do you know a lot of Russians?"

"Not that many," I admitted.

When I was nearly done, she went to her room, walking on the edge of the banner, one tiny foot placed in front of the other, close to the wall. She returned with brushes and a plastic yogurt container half-filled with paint, which she set in the middle of the banner. We each started at an end and worked our way toward the centre, filling in the letters.

"There's a movie playing at the SUB. *If You Love This Planet* with Dr. Helen Caldicott. Have you seen it?"

"No," I said.

"Do you want to go? You don't have to study on Friday night, do you?"

She extended the invitation to Hector and Dieter too. I thought for sure Dieter would come, but he only pushed up his glasses and sneered. "It's a fundraiser for SPND, isn't it? I wouldn't give them a cent. They're useless."

"What's SPND?" I asked Sonia as we were putting on our coats.

"Students for Peace and Nuclear Disarmament. I used to be in SPND when I lived in residence. Dieter and Pete were in it too, but we broke away. All they ever do is have bake sales and march in the Walk for Peace."

Hector was in the living room watching a sitcom. "*Adios,* Hector," Sonia called. "Are you sure you don't want to come?"

Hector pointed to the TV. "I'm watching this."

Once we were out the door I asked, "Is Hector living with us now?"

"Oh dear," said Sonia. "I think we'd better have a meeting about Hector."

The night was clear and cold, the only clouds formed by our breath. I could even see stars, puncture holes in the night, rare for November. Sonia had put on a funny knitted toque with earflaps and a couple of sweaters, both of which looked like they came from my aunt's stash. Over them she wore an anorak and scarf, yet she still seemed too thin. Her clogs resounded on the wooden steps as we went down them.

"They bring speakers in too."

"Who?"

"SPND. That's what they're into. Education. And that's why I joined. But education isn't enough if you don't do anything with it."

It occurred to me then that nothing I studied had any practical application whatsoever.

Sonia: "We've got to do something. Right now."

The bus was nearly empty and, when we arrived, the campus seemed deserted too. The forested Endowment Lands cut the university off from the city, though in the residences and the frat houses, in the Pit Pub under the Student Union Building, life was undoubtedly going on. We saw scant evidence of it, however, as we walked past the glass wall of the Aquatic Centre; only a few swimmers were clocking laps. The SUB itself felt evacuated, the cafeteria closed, the cookie kiosk too, the couches mostly empty with barely a handful of people milling around before the movie started.

The lobby was down a set of stairs. More people were there, maybe twenty, all of whom Sonia seemed to know well enough to embrace. We bought our tickets from a girl she introduced as Ruth. "This is Jane, my housemate."

Ruth wore a fringed paisley scarf like a sloppy bandage around her neck. Her long blond hair was divided evenly by the part and her eyes were a very pale blue. Sonia took her ticket and wandered off to talk to someone else. Ruth held on to mine. "You live in Trutch house?" she asked.

"Yes."

The way she looked at me, so intently, I felt washed in blue light. "But I've never seen you at anything."

"Here I am."

"I tried to get in there."

"In the house?"

"Yeah," she said.

"Move in, you mean?"

She nodded. I only remembered the man with the violin, not the other names on the interview sheet. Yet Belinda had told me I was the only woman to apply. She'd said they needed "gender balance" and that was what I thought she meant. "Are you vegetarian?" I asked Ruth.

"Yes!" She sighed. "It must be great living with Pete and Dieter. They're so committed. Dieter's probably going to Nicaragua next summer. Are you in NAG!?"

"In what?" I said.

"Non-violent Action Group! I thought everyone who lived there was."

An older couple approached the counter and Ruth finally handed over my ticket. Sonia was standing with her back to me, an arm around a much taller person's waist. I bought popcorn and a Coke and waited in the corner until the theatre doors opened and people started filing in. Sonia looked around then, smiling when she saw me.

We sat at the very back, near the door. "That girl Ruth?" I said, holding out the popcorn.

Sonia refused, wrinkling her nose. "Ruth's in SPND," she said. "She's really nice."

"She wanted my room."

"I know. I felt bad when she didn't get in. It's horrible rejecting people."

"Why didn't she?"

"A couple of reasons. Well, one. No, I can tell you. Two. We thought she was using it as a way to get into the group. She really wants to be a Nagger. Afterward, I phoned her and told her she should get some people together. And make a new group. Like we did." She pulled off her toque and tossed it on the empty seat in front of her. Staticky feelers of hair reached toward the light. "She cried. I felt terrible."

"What was the other reason?"

Sonia glanced around before answering. "Belinda was worried about Pete. He sleeps around."

"Really?" I said. Wasn't he doing it enough with Belinda? It seemed I was always trying to shut out their groans and laughter. If I was studying or writing a letter to my parents, I'd screw toilet tissue into my ears. If I was trying to sleep, I'd muffle them with my pillow. Yet in the morning, crossing paths with Belinda in the hall or on the stairs, I'd be the one to blush. "Then why did she move out?" I asked.

"It was getting too intense," Sonia said, disappearing inside the anorak then shucking it like a cocoon.

"How many people applied?"

"To move in? Lots." She smiled. "I'm glad we picked you."

Belinda had picked me. She'd picked me to keep her boy-friend safe. I was offended. Hurt. I was sensitive. Overly sensi-tive, my mother told me all the time. "It's not always about you," she would say. Last year Kopanyev had written it on the bottom of my paper. And then the lights dimmed and the movie started and I didn't think about the humiliation of being Belinda's foil again, not for years and years.

The funny bits were first, clips from old black and white Ronald Reagan movies and hokey newsreels from the war. I leaned back with my popcorn and my drink. Then Dr. Caldicott, lecturing in a pink blouse and pearls, began to describe what happened the morning the bomb fell on Hiroshima, her Aus-tralian accent counterpointing the chorus of angels on the soundtrack. I had seen footage of an atomic bomb exploding. It was not unfamiliar to me: a white ball of light gradually detach-ing from a flat plain of smoke, rising slowly, levitating, while underneath it a boiling pillar formed. Then the head, the ball, changed too, expanding, growing petals of ash. The glow inside was horrible, yet beautiful too, the way it folded in on itself and bloomed. And the angels sang higher and higher until they were keening, and the flattened city stretched before us, a treeless ruin. There were mountains behind it, just like Vancouver. That bomb was small, Dr. Caldicott said. Today's hydrogen bombs were twenty megatonnes, equivalent to twenty million tonnes of TNT, and today the United States had 35,000 of these bombs, enough to kill every Russian forty times, while the Soviet Union had 20,000 bombs, enough to kill every American twenty times. The probability of a nuclear war occurring by 1985, a little over a year away, was fifty-fifty. Many famous and brilliant scientists believed this to be true.

I set my drink on the floor. It tipped over and some detached part of me could hear the can rolling all the way down to the front of the theatre. The other part listened as Dr. Caldicott

explained in exact clinical detail what would happen in the event
of a nuclear war. In the remaining eternal half-hour she presented to us our certain fate. How every person within six
miles of the epicentre would be vaporized, then up to a radius
of twenty miles killed or lethally injured, thousands severely
burned. The film showed what these burns were like on Japanese survivors. I saw a skinless child lying on a cot, a man face
down, his back a map, the countries burned on him, rivers of
scars. Living people melted, like wax. We saw footage of houses
imploding in nuclear test blasts, dummies being sucked out windows, dummies lying dismembered in the rubble. She warned us
about the flying glass, the steel thrown around like toothpicks.
What was left of the buildings would be lying in what was left of
the streets. And if you looked at the blast even from forty miles
away, if you happened just to glance at it, you would be blinded.
As she said this, the hideous burned face of a living person
turned its poached eyes toward us. Everything that was flam-
mable within an area of three thousand square miles would start
to burn, creating an unstoppable conflagration so that everyone idealistic enough to have taken refuge in the bomb shelters
would be pressure-cooked or asphyxiated. Afterward, the mil-
lions of decaying corpses would cause uncontrollable outbreaks
of disease—polio, typhoid, dysentery, plague—uncontrollable
because no medical infrastructure would remain. Unlike in
Hiroshima and Nagasaki, there wouldn't be an outside world
to come and help. Civilization, the doctor said, would be laid
waste. Almost more sickening to me was her explanation of what
this meant: no architecture, no painting, no music, no literature.

Dr. Caldicott: "And the survivors would die of a synergetic
combination of starvation, radiation sickness, epidemics of infec-
tion, sunburn, blindness, and grief."

At these words Sonia, who had been quaking next to me,
lurched from her seat and bolted for the door. It opened with a

yawn into the silence on the other side before thudding closed again. I was still sitting in the theatre, stunned, but I knew I would follow her through that door and that on the other side everything would be different now.

We huddled together on the rocks. More than cold, we were frightened. I was nearly numb. This is what people feel like when the doctor tells them they have cancer, I thought. I thought: I'm going to die. I have until 1985. I have thirteen months to live. We'd gotten off the bus at our usual stop, but instead of going home, Sonia had taken my hand and led me the two blocks to the beach. We staggered together, helping each other along an unlit path between two houses, down a set of slippery concrete steps. I'd hardly been to the beach, never at night or by this secret route, so when I looked around I really was seeing it for the first time. Across the strait, the mountains wore tiaras— lights from the ski hills. West Vancouver twinkled at their feet. I saw the void of Stanley Park and the Emerald City brilliance of the West End. In thirteen months it would all be gone.

Sonia put her head on my shoulder and began to cry. After a few minutes she stopped. It was physically impossible to keep shedding tears at the rate she had. "I'll never get married," she said, using her sleeve to dry her face. "I'll never have children. I'll never have grandchildren."

I started crying too when, the moment before, I'd been in shock. I never expected to get married and have children either, but the fact that Sonia wouldn't seemed unspeakably sad. But what Dr. Caldicott had said about the end of civilization, the end of literature, that was what broke my heart.

No Turgenev. No Tolstoy. No Chekhov.

Sonia: "For me it's the children. The children who'll never be born and who'll die so horribly."

I asked her what we could do.

"We've got to talk to people, Jane. Tell them the truth. All over the world it's happening. People are saying no. They're saying these weapons aren't making us safer. The opposite!"

The house was dark when we got back. Hector was asleep in the living room and Pete and Dieter were out. Sonia brought me to the kitchen. I felt for the light switch but when I turned it on, she immediately snapped it off and, letting go of my hand, shuffled away in the dark. I heard a click. Gradually my eyes readjusted and I saw the shape of her waiting at the stove, hands clasped like she was praying to it. The coil blushed and, as the colour deepened, I could make out her face in the glow. She was grimacing.

"This is what I do," she told me, letting her hand hover above the burner. "This is how I'm getting ready for the burns."

Many times that weekend I started a letter to my parents, both to warn them and assure them that, contrary to the impression I might have given over the last few years, I loved them very much. Unable to find the words that truly expressed our predicament, I tore the letters up. I thought of my father at the bus depot in Edmonton telling me that if anything bad ever happened to me he'd buy a horse, a dog, and a gun and ride away and no one would ever hear from him again.

"What will you call the horse?" I'd asked, like I used to when I was little.

"Casimir."

"And the dog?"

"Patches."

"The gun?"

"Black Beauty."

There wouldn't be a horse. There wouldn't be a dog or a gun.

I decided to tell them when I went home for Christmas. If it hadn't already happened.

I'd handed in my shoe paper the week before. Now I was supposed to come up with a discussion topic, but when I looked to my venerable bookcase, I could think only of the incinerated libraries and the books that would disappear forever. I mourned them all, but mostly the Russian ones.

Finally, I opened the first page of "The Duel."

The stout, red-faced, flabby Samoylenko, with his large, close-cropped head, big nose, black, bushy eyebrows, grey side-whiskers, and no neck to speak of, with a hoarse soldier's voice as well, struck all newcomers as an unpleasant army upstart. But about two or three days after the first meeting his face began to strike them as exceptionally kind, amiable, handsome even. Although a rude-mannered, clumsy person, he was docile, infinitely kind, good-humoured and obliging. He called everybody by their Christian names, lent money to everyone, gave medical treatment to all, patched up quarrels and organized picnics, where he grilled kebabs and made a very tasty grey mullet soup.

I couldn't imagine a world without Dr. Samoylenko! These characters were realer than most real people, more important to me than the students in my seminar where we discussed them. That was why I was learning Russian. So I could know them better. Kitty and Levin, the Nihilist Bazarov, old man Kirsanov with his cello and his tears—after my parents, they were the people I cared about most, as well as, and especially, Chekhov's characters. That slippered fool Ivan Layevsky, Alexei Laptev, the Hamlet of Moscow, even poor, bewhiskered Staff-Captain Ryabovitch in "The Kiss"—they had all endeared themselves to me with their foibles and struggles and depressions. Heroically, or unheroically, they endured the boredom of provincial life, the disappointments of love. *I* loved them. I loved their galoshes and felt boots and smoky icon lamps, their black bread and tea with jam, the old men in slippers sleeping on the stove. I loved the mud and the vodka, the wasted days, the gambling, the flies. I loved that dog named Syntax. It was easy to imagine them perishing, not just the books they lived in. The people in the film were Japanese, but who could tell, they were so badly burned. They were human beings. Only human beings, like Anna Sergeyevna and Alexei Laptev and Dr. Samoylenko, burned and blinded and dying of grief.

I stayed in my room the whole of Saturday, and when I came down for supper Sonia jumped up from the table and hugged me. At that moment I passionately did not want to die. I thought I would cry again, but didn't, because of the men. Our embrace aroused enough curiosity that they paused with their forks in mid-air. After a few minutes Hector remarked, "The ladies are very quiet tonight."

Dieter said something in Spanish.

"Excuse me. I had just been told there are no ladies present here. Only two very quiet women."

"Jane is upset," Sonia explained. She sounded oddly triumphant.

Concern flashed across the little round lenses of Hector's glasses. It glinted off his tooth. "You are sad, Jane? Why?"

"Have you seen *If You Love This Planet*, Hector?" Sonia asked him.

"This is the movie you invited me to last night? Then I'm glad I didn't go. The world is full of cruelness and injustice, but Friday night is not for suffering."

"Has your life changed, Zed?" Pete asked.

Sonia: "Don't tease her."

"I'm not teasing her. I'm asking her a question."

They all looked at me. "I feel horrible," I said.

"As you should," said Dieter. "The bombs could start raining down at any moment. Quick! Go to the window! Check! Are they falling yet?" He grinned when, predictably, Sonia wailed and had to be comforted. Stiffening against his chest, she struggled free.

Pete had finished eating but instead of going for his second course of bread and margarine, he folded his arms on the table and addressed me. "This is what's going to happen, Zed. First you'll feel frightened. Then you'll feel depressed. This is normal given the circumstances. You've just learned that you might die at any moment."

Hector: "Anybody might die at any moment. It is a fact of life."

Dieter: "This is more than death, Hector. This is annihilation. The entire planet."

Sonia resumed picking at her dismantled burrito. "Is there meat in this, Hector?"

"After the fear, after the depression," Uncle Peter went on, "you'll begin to get angry. This is good because when you're angry enough, when you're sufficiently pissed off, then change can happen. You'll say, 'This is not right. This is unacceptable to me.' At that point you'll commit to action."

"First mourn, then work for change," Sonia said and Dieter nodded.

"What am I supposed to do?" I asked.

Sonia: "We could let her in NAG!"

"No, we couldn't," said Dieter. "We would need consensus. Have you heard of SPND? It's a group on campus. Students for Peace and Nuclear Disarmament."

"Nu-clee-ar," I said.

"What?"

"It's pronounced 'nuclee-ar' not 'nucular.'"

"No, it's not."

"It is."

Pete: "Whoa. This is premature. Let's wait till Zed gets mad. I've seen her mad. She showed promise."

On Sunday morning I brought the sacred yellow telephone to my room and called my aunt. "What's wrong?" she asked. "You are upset about something. I can hear it in your voice."

"I can't talk about it." The dread was rising in my throat, acidic, like reflux. "I'll come next week. Not tonight." I hung up before the tears started. How could I confide in a person for whom the worst thing in the world was constipation?

Sirens kept going off. The fire hall was a few blocks away on Balaclava Street. I'd always tuned out the shriek of the trucks, but I heard them now and every time thought of the newsreel schoolchildren in *If You Love This Planet* donning gas masks and crouching futilely under their wooden desks. Finally I opened my Chekhov again and got to work. Just before the duel between Layevsky and von Koren, I underlined two sentences. *Layevsky experienced the weariness and awkwardness of a man who perhaps was soon to die.* And this: *It was the first time in his life he had seen the sunrise.*

The meeting was still going on downstairs when I finished preparing for the next day's discussion. I wrote another note to Sonia, the same thing as before, *Are you all right?* but this time I snuck down and put it in her clog. And I wrote it in Russian, so she would know it was from me.

The next day she brought it to me so I could read it to her. "It says *Vsyo normalno?*"

"Jane," she said, staring at me, twisting her little cross in agitation. "I'm not normal."

"What do you mean?"

"Everybody goes around like—like everything is fine. But it's not. I know you understand. I know you feel like I do. Don't you?"

I told her, "Yes."

2 0 0 4

Their faces in the newspaper. It all came back, everything that happened that spring. The spring those pictures were taken. I decided to skip my first day of work. I wouldn't be able to concentrate anyway. I'd go out somewhere. Where? And if the paper was still on the table when I got home, if Maria hadn't put it in the recycling, then. Then I would read what it said.

Was it Maria's day? She comes every second week to clean for us and vex us. For example, our most needed utensils? She deliberately hides them, I'm sure of it, yet when I ask her politely and respectfully and without a hint of criticism to put things back where she finds them, she merely informs me that I put them in the wrong places. "Jane, do it the way I do. Because it's better." She's Slovakian, short and muscular with a yellow bob and chapped hands. Joe Jr. claims she pays inordinate attention to his underwear drawer, that his briefs are always meticulously folded and stacked and, occasionally, on some Slovakian whim, transferred to a different drawer. "It freaks me out," he says.

"Yet this same woman," Joe Sr. says with a finger in the air, "this same woman will not dust."

Maria would make the newspaper vanish. She would say that we had our chance to read it and we lost that chance. She's done it before. But it was Monday, I remembered then. Tuesday is Maria's day.

I went to wake Joe Jr. for school. He's fifteen so this can be a challenge, though, surprisingly, he was already awake. I heard sounds before I knocked. "Come in," he said.

He was sitting on the edge of the bed in his boxers with the cello between his bare splayed legs. Instead of the bow, a bamboo backscratcher. "What are you doing?" I asked.

"I didn't want to wake you," he said.

"I don't mind being woken by the cello."

"I'm not that good yet. Listen." And he played a little silence for me.

I was supposed to begin copyediting a manuscript, the first job I'd accepted all year, but even before I could feel guilty about playing truant (I hadn't checked my e-mail to see if it had arrived yet), even before I had decided where to pass my truancy, the phone rang and I left Joe Jr.'s room to answer it. It was the editor phoning from Toronto to say there had been a delay. I cleared the gladness from my throat. "Oh well."

"I apologize," she said.

I like this woman, Morna Crane, whom I've worked for before though never met in person. She does things like this— phone instead of e-mail, then take the trouble to prolong the conversation to a friendly length, which she did by asking, "What's the weather like out there?"

Though I've never been to Toronto in the early spring, I had a snowbound childhood and remember the season's fetid start— the dirty snow receding, the sordid revelations: candy wrappers, plastic bags, dog shit. "Do you really want to know?" I asked as Joe Jr. finally emerged from the bathroom, handsome despite all the holes he's punched in himself, hair gelled into glistening tufts (an operation so time-consuming breakfast must be taken on the run). He stood in the open door of the fridge swigging milk from the bottle. I'd set out the day's provisions—bun wrapped in wax paper (breakfast), five-dollar bill (lunch). He took them, kissed me on the phone still held to my ear, and left for school, dragging the cello down the hall.

"Tell me everything, Jane," Morna said. "Don't spare me."

"Our magnolia is blooming. The cherries too."

She sighed. "I saw on the news that it's snowing in Calgary. That comforts me a little."

And I got an idea. I'll go look at the beautiful trees, I thought.

On the crest of the hill, at the four-way stop just before the descent to Arbutus Street, there's a bit of a view northward toward the mountains, over other cotton-candied streets. Two varieties of flowering trees were in bloom, one a darker and one a lighter shade of pink. I drove through the frothy tunnel of 33rd Avenue, past the bright armies of daffodils amassing in the mansion gardens of Shaughnessy. All these carnival colours. All this spring cheer. It's a bit much, I thought.

The radio brought the story up again while I was driving. I could have switched it off but was better prepared now after an hour of consciously avoiding thinking about it. It was over in a few sentences anyway. Sonia Parker, one of the "masterminds" of a 1984 bomb plot gone awry, had been released yesterday. Peter English would be released in 2009. The next item, in keeping with the terrorist theme, was about the Guantanamo Bay detention camp.

When I reached the parking lot, I sat in the car for a few minutes until I was breathing normally again.

Queen Elizabeth Park is the highest point in the city proper. I hadn't been up there for years. On the plaza in front of the geodesic dome, a contingent of senior citizens was Catching the Monkey's Tail as they Tai Chi-ed in perfect unison. I made my way past them, feeling clumsy, and headed for the lookout where three life-sized bronze people stand waiting for their picture to be taken. According to the nearby plaque, they've been posing there since 1984. The view behind them is entirely obscured by trees now, which seems fitting since the present skyline would have been unrecognizable in 1984. We couldn't have imagined how the city would grow and change, upward and outward, its concrete leavened. Because we didn't believe it would still be here. Only the mountains would be left standing. Or so we thought.

I headed through the Quarry Garden, over the Japanese bridge, down to where I'd seen the largest group of trees as I drove in. Walking under their collective canopy was like entering a cloud. I remembered bringing Joe Jr. here when he was about five, him in his baseball cap standing under a tree like the one I was standing under now, letting his head fall back as he gazed up through the ruffled branches. The cap tumbled off his head. "Mom," he said, sounding like he hated to be the one to disabuse me. "They're not really real, you know."

I sat on the damp grass under the tree. Then I lay down. How wonderful and sublime, the scent of the blossoms. I only noticed when I closed my eyes. Naturally, I thought of Chekhov, Chekhov on his deathbed and how the doctor gave him champagne. Chekhov sat up, smiled, and said to his wife: "It's been a long time since I drank champagne!" He drank it, then he lay back down and died.

I don't know how long I'd been lying there when my purse rang under my head and startled me upright. It was Joe calling from work. Of course I expected the worst. What else? "Nothing's wrong," he said. "Did the book arrive?"

"No. There was some kind of delay. Tomorrow maybe. Shouldn't you be working? Isn't somebody dying over there?"

"Not at the moment. Ma for dinner? That all right?"

"Fine."

"Maybe we'll play a few songs for her. You remember Simon's coming?"

"I didn't, but it's okay."

"It's not too much?"

"It's fine." I wondered if Joe had seen the paper, if that was what the call was really about. There was a pause full of hospital sounds—nurses being bossy, carts rattling by.

Joe: "I wanted to ask your opinion. The Streptococci?"

"The what? Oh. I like The Joes better."

"Won't Simon feel left out?"

"You're kind. And literal. Were The Ramones all named Ramone?"

"Yes," he said.

"Really?" I was stunned. "The Ramones were *brothers*?"

"Well, not from birth."

I walked around the park. I had lunch in the café next to the organic grocery store, then stopped in to buy more food, grocery shopping being sort of a second job these days, part-time and volunteer. I was stalling, though I wouldn't have if I'd known Joe's mother was already sitting patiently on our porch with a casserole dish in her lap. When I pulled up later that afternoon, Rachel called out, "I'm early!"

I came up the steps and hugged her, thinking, as usual, that every time I do she's smaller while every time Joe Jr. is bigger. The hug went on a little too long. One of us wasn't letting go. Who? The one with the heavy dish in her hand, or me? Finally, we separated and I turned to unlock the door.

"I still find this mat rude," she said. "*Go Away.*"

"It's not meant for you."

"Are you sure?"

Then I remembered the newspaper lying on the mat that morning, the reason I'd stayed out most of the day. It was on the kitchen table now. I didn't want Rachel to see it so, while she dealt with her shoes and coat, I hurried ahead to get rid of it. When I got to the kitchen, though, the paper was gone.

Rachel set the casserole dish on the counter. "That's apple crumble."

"I'll get the groceries," I said, slinking off, perplexed. I brought in the first set of bags from the car and Rachel asked if she should put them away. "I'll do it," I said. "There's more."

"I'll put the kettle on," she said.

Two more trips to the car so the metabolic furnace inside the resident fifteen-year-old might be stoked. Rachel, meanwhile, was already making her rounds of the houseplants, pushing a finger into the soil to check for moisture, plucking off dead bits. No judgement was implied by this. She's one of those super-seniors. Active Native Daughter of British Columbia, editor of the Heritage Society newsletter. Every autumn she hikes into the mountains to collect, catalogue, and consume wild mush-rooms. She's also handy with a needle. Among Joe's most prized possessions is a petit point Sex Pistols album cover Rachel made for him in the eighties, *God Save the Queen*, no less. She's doing one for Joe Jr. now, The Clash's *London Calling*, but in crewel because petit point, she says, is murder on the eyes. Anyway, I am so far from threatened by her solicitude and competence that I never even look at the plants.

"I haven't seen paper grocery bags in years," she said, com-ing in from the living room with dried leaves cupped in one hand.

"That's why I shop there."

When she opened the cupboard under the sink to get at the compost, I took advantage of the moment to stash a box of dish detergent. "Hold still," she said, pulling something out of my hair. She showed me what it was. "What have you been doing?"

"Buying groceries with sticks and grass in my hair," I said.

"Flower petals, too, by the looks of it."

I jammed the blocks of ice cream in the freezer then went to the bathroom to check how bad I looked. A paper didn't just disappear. I'd left it there that morning face down on the table. We have a key hidden in a spot so obvious no thief would bother looking. Rachel knows about it, so why didn't she use it? Then I remembered, belatedly, that she receives the newspaper herself every morning and listens to the CBC all day long, and I sank down on the edge of the bathtub and cried into a towel. I was crying out of gratitude. For her tact. For everything she's ever done for me.

Every year around this time, I have to grapple with these memories and feelings. Spring is difficult. Spring is a challenge.

Joe Jr.'s door was closed. I don't usually go in without his permission, but now I tapped on the door and opened it with the intention of looking for the lost paper. Surprise! Joe Jr. curled up in bed with the iPod clutched in his fist. Sometimes when I look at him I see every stage of his life in superimposition, the culmination of a whole person, not just the disinterested grunter he is so often now. It's almost overwhelming. I closed the door again.

In the kitchen Rachel asked, "What's wrong, Jane?"

"Joe Jr.'s home."

She frowned. "I rang the doorbell."

"He's plugged in."

She nodded. "Is he sick?"

"Oh, God. I hope not."

"Well, don't fret. Joe will have a look at him."

This is the kind of brave talk you get out of people who eat wild mushrooms. Every time he gets sick, I think he's going to die. Of course, I didn't know if Joe Jr. was sick. *I* felt sick thinking there might have been something about me in the paper. Since I hadn't actually read the article myself yet, I couldn't be sure, but

I doubted it. Then I remembered the recycling (belatedly again) and stepped out onto the back deck. Opened the blue bag, and yes! There it was, the prodigal *Vancouver Sun*, at the very top, all the sections intact. I was losing my mind. I glanced at the headline again—*Opposition Mounts to Iraq War*—but when I flipped the paper over to see their long-ago faces, to read what was being said about Sonia and Pete now, the article was gone.

Strips of newsprint border hanging down like the empty arms of cut-out dolls.

"Tea," Rachel called.

I stuffed the paper back in the bag and staggered in, trying not to show my shock. Joe Jr. must have cut it out. But why? He's never expressed an interest in current events.

Rachel was at the table, watching me through the steam of her raised mug, waiting for me to sit. "Jane? Are you all right?"

"Yes." I sat and stared out the window until the magnolia gradually came into focus, giving me something to say. "You asked what I did today. I went to Queen Elizabeth Park to look at the trees."

"How nice. The cherries are blooming."

Apparently there are hundreds of different varieties in Vancouver. She named about a hundred of them, also several kinds of plum, but I was barely listening. I was hoping, desperately, that it wasn't Joe Jr. who had cut the article out, but who else could it have been?

"What were you looking at?" Rachel asked.

"What? Oh. They were very—cloud-like."

"Pink?"

"Yes."

"Fragrant?"

"Mildly. I didn't notice at first."

"I wonder if they were the whatsits. Akebono." She turned her head and spring suddenly arrived on her face, full bloom.

"Ho ho! Here's the guy who wouldn't answer his grannie's feeble knocks!"

Joe Jr. stood in the doorway, scratching, gelled spikes relaxed, flattened by the nap. I was at his side in a second, feeling his forehead, checking his piercings—the rings in his eyebrow, the stud under his lip—for telltale redness. "What are you doing home?" I asked.

"I skipped," he said, yawning.

"You're not sick?"

"I was bored." He shrugged me off and made for his grand-mother, who was waiting with arms wide, ready to fling around his waist. She tolerated the noogie then smoothed her hair back in place. "I rang the doorbell," she teased. "You left me sitting in the cold."

Joe Jr. pulled away and began to pogo violently and strum the air. "Da, da, da! I rang the doorbell! You left me sitting in the cold! I rang the doorbell! You left me sitting in the cold! Sitting in the cold! Sitting in the cold!" His muse tried not to look horrified. Then, abruptly, he turned back into a boy. "I have to write that down, Gran."

"Are you serious, you skipped?" I asked because, now that he didn't have meningitis, I was annoyed.

He'd already transferred his transient attention from Rachel to the fridge and, finding the fresh package of smoked meat in the drawer, began pushing it breadlessly into his mouth. "It was boring."

"So?"

He turned to his grandmother. "Are you going to stay and hear us practise?"

"I could."

"Is Simon coming over?" I asked, suddenly worried about the paper again. "Because there's something I'd like to talk to you about before he comes."

Joe Jr. shot me a glance, which seemed both significant and calculated not to be. I would have to tell him, I knew it then. More meat went in his mouth and when there wasn't enough left in the package to make a decent sandwich, he tossed it back in the drawer. Instead of answering me, he said, "Gran, did Mom tell you I started the cello?"

"What?" Rachel turned to me for confirmation.

"It's true," I said.

"I'll show it to you." He beckoned to her and Rachel got up and followed Joe Jr. out of the room.

"After that," I called to Joe Jr., "I need to talk to you."

We've never told him about the trouble I got into when I was young. I didn't want him to know his mother has a criminal record, despite the fact that the actual conviction is not very impressive. I didn't want him to be ashamed of me, or someone at school to find out. I would never, ever want him to be ostracized.

While Rachel was in the bedroom with Joe Jr. and the cello, I made burritos. Joe Jr. was using the bow now, hitting about 50 percent of the notes (enough accuracy to plunge me into melancholy). And I remembered our terrible cooking, Dieter alternating between spaghetti and payloaded chili. Nutritional yeast dumped over everything like yellow snow. Sonia, preparing for a time when food would be scarce, always served an approximation of bread and water. Pete was the most creative, a liberal spicer. Once I came into the kitchen when he was cooking and saw a half-dozen garlic cloves stripped and lined up on the cutting board. "Smash, smash, smash the state!" He brought down the knife, scraped the chunks into the pot. One lone survivor, having leapt to safety, quivered on the counter. Pete popped it in his mouth.

The doorbell rang. I went to answer it and found Simon slouching on our mat, a six-foot-tall reminder of how like the newborn stage these teen years are—parents blind to the repulsiveness of the age except in other people's offspring. *Go Away* indeed! Simon had an Adam's apple now; it looked like he was gagging on a Russian word. There were the inevitable wires too, pumping in the jangle, and his teeth serving a three-year sentence in a metal cage. Compared with Joe Jr., Simon has taken self-skewering to a whole new level with actual grommets in his lobes I could see the light of day through. Yet when I opened the door, *he* took a step back, right off the mat, when, rightly, it should have been me recoiling from him. Under all the acne, I definitely perceived a flush.

"Hello, Simon."

He did that darty thing with his eyes, sniffed, made an utterance. Hi, I presumed.

"Joey's in his room," I said, standing back to let the guitar case through.

He's not so bad. He actually reminds me of Joe years ago. And he took his boots off, which, considering the laces, was a major concession, though I wasn't prepared to wait. "Go on in when you're finished," I told him, assuming he could read lips.

I went back to the kitchen. A few minutes later I glanced up from grating cheese and saw him in the doorway, staring. "He's in his room!" I added hand gestures.

Right after Joe got home and washed his hands, literally and metaphorically, of the day's suffering, we sat down to dinner. I never got the chance to ask Joe or Joe Jr. about the article.

"Joey! Simon!"

They looked up—startled, innocent, already helping themselves—and seeing Joe's signal, jerked the earbuds out by the wires.

"So how was everybody's day?" He turned to me and kissed my cheek. "How was your day, my darling? What happened at school, boys?"

"Nothing," they chorused.

I tattled. "Joe Jr. says he skipped a class. He came home and slept instead."

"It was boring," Joe Jr. said.

Joe turned to me. "I think that's reasonable."

"Joey played the cello for me," said Rachel. "I never thought I'd live to hear someone in this family playing Bach."

"Was that Bach?" Joe Jr. asked, looking pleased with himself.

I noticed how Simon kept glancing at me from across the table. I could see right in his mouth as he chewed, beans stuck on his braces, mud on a wire fence. When I met his eye: dart, dart. Normally Joe Jr.'s friends ignore me. When I come into the room they immediately mute themselves, except for the yelps when they punch each other, or the snickers. They hardly look at me, not the way Simon kept looking at me now. How to describe it? With *interest*.

And a horrible thought came to me. Joe Jr. *did* have the article. He had it and he'd shown it to Simon.

Joe: "Boys? What do you think of this? The Streptococci?"

Thumbs down from Joe Jr. "Nobody'll get it."

"What is it?" Simon asked.

"Then how about The Cankers?"

"I thought we were going to be The Cretins," Simon said. "Like? One, two, three, four, Cretins wanna hop some more?"

"Jane has a problem with The Cretins. She doesn't think it's very nice."

"I like The Joes," I said.

The boys groaned.

"Think of it as a tribute. Joey Shithead. Joe Strummer. Joey Ramone. Joey Normal and the Fuck Ups."

Rachel frowned. "What's all this nasty talk about?"

"We need a name. We're, like, a punk band, Gran."

"You're like one or you are one?"

"Dad's getting us a real gig."

"I'm working on it," Joe said. "I still have connections, Ma."

"Though half of them are lawyers now," I pointed out. "You remember Molly? She's a lawyer."

Rachel: "How about The Tone Deaf? Are you playing the cello in this band, Joey?"

"No, that's for school. No one else was playing it. Mom told me that story so I thought I'd try it."

"What story?" I asked.

"You were reading that book. About the guy who brings his crazy friend home and is embarrassed because his dad plays the cello."

"You mean *Fathers and Sons*?"

I'm the odd reader out in this family. The Joes have no use for books; they live for the music I mostly tune out. I was so touched that my son had actually paid attention to something I cared about that tears came to my eyes. Quickly, I wiped them with my napkin because crying is a hundred times worse than playing the cello, even old Kirsanov knew that. Joe rose from the table and went into the kitchen to get dessert, trading a concerned glance with his mother on the way. Then I really felt foolish, because I knew for certain that they all knew what had happened to that article. They all knew and I didn't. I was the cretin.

The apple crumble hit the trivet; the boys attacked. Joe set the ice cream down beside it and I remembered that Russian word, the one I'd imagined bulging in Simon's throat. *Morozhenoye*. I got up to put the tea on. When I got back to the table Simon was saying, "There's, like, a demonstration." He glanced at me, ears reddening around the peepholes. "You should come." He seemed to be saying this to me specifically. Inviting *me*.

"*I* should?" I asked.

The colour spread from his perforated lobes. "You all should," he said. "It's totally illegal, their being in Iraq."

"Where's the demonstration?" I asked.

"At the Art Gallery. It would be awesome if you came."

Awesome? What the hell? I wondered. What was that kid thinking about me?

After dinner they went downstairs to practise. Joe Sr.'s lair is down there, a TV, a stationary bicycle, an unambitious set of weights. It's also where he stores and listens to his vast punk record collection. Maria is not allowed, not even to get at the black hole of the bathroom.

When Joe Jr. was around twelve, he began spending time in The Lair. While it hurt to be replaced as the preferred parent, I knew it was only fair. I'd been tightly and intricately attached to Joe Jr. I never sent him to daycare or preschool. When he started kindergarten, I used to lie on the living room floor for the entire two and a half hours, imagining all the calamities that could transpire while he was out of my sight. Earthquake. Fire. Gunman walking in spraying bullets. Pedophile lurking in a bathroom stall. Out-of-control car careering through the playground. Somewhere, some rogue state firing off something nuclear. I believed that if I worked through each of these scenarios, they would be less likely to happen because, statistically, the chance of thinking of a bad thing happening before the bad thing actually happens is much smaller than a bad thing happening. More people are killed in car accidents than people who think they might be killed in car accidents. Needless to say, it was a trying year.

Downstairs, the racket started as Rachel and I loaded the dishwasher in tandem. "I could hardly look at that poor boy," she said.

"Simon?"

"It nauseates me."

"His acne or his ears?"

She grimaced. "Acne is natural. Self-mutilation isn't."

I nodded. "Ugly is the new beautiful."

"Again," she sighed. "They never learn. Look at Joe. His ears are in tatters from all those pins. Is he a physician or an embattled tomcat? I'm sure his patients laugh at him behind his back."

"I don't think so. They're probably just happy to see him after the six-hour wait."

She nudged me. Simon had come up the stairs. He gawked at us briefly—well, me—then disappeared down the hall, returning a moment later with an enormous boot in each hand. Before closing the basement door again, he cast me a backward glance.

I felt annoyed by his attention now. The grey-haired Shaughnessy matron mimed a finger down her throat. "At least they didn't tattoo themselves back then," she went on. "You remember Silly Putty?"

"Sure. It's still around."

"Joe used to push it onto the Saturday comics, then stretch it out of shape. That's what those tattoos are going to look like in fifty years. These kids don't realize they're going to be old one day."

And I thought: maybe they're not.

A new song started up downstairs. Soundproofing spared us the lyrics, but we could hear that one of the three chords was different from the three chords in the last song.

"Does Joey have a tattoo?" Rachel asked.

I hated to tell her. It was a sore point for me too. "A very small one. Tiny. Joe went with him to get it. To make sure about the needle. Anyway, all this is wonderful for Joe. It's the dream of every punk rocker who ever sold out. His offspring is picking up the torch."

"I guess."

Then they called us, so we dried our hands and started down the stairs to where the walls are painted black and the light bulbs red. "Rachel?" I said, before I lost the chance. "Did you see the article?"

She turned around on the stairs and, under the light, looked drenched in blood. "That's why I came so early. I thought you might want to talk. But you seemed distracted. I've been waiting for you to say something."

"I'm sorry, Rachel."

"Are you all right?"

"Yes, but I didn't get the chance to read it. It didn't mention me, did it?"

"No."

"I feel better now. Thanks."

"All that was a long time ago, Jane."

"I know," I said.

It's a gallery of album covers down there: D.O.A., Pointed Sticks, The Clash, The Ramones, The Subhumans, the petit point Sex Pistols, framed, in a place of honour. Strings of interlocked safety pins hang in the doorway like a beaded curtain. Drawing it aside for Rachel, I wondered how many safety-pin factories had closed since the demise of punk. Joe had probably single-handedly kept one in operation. As well as the curtain, he once made himself an entire suit of safety-pin chain mail. This was during med school, which, according to Joe, was one long, jittery Wake Up–pill high. The problem with the suit was it wasn't safe to sit in.

I sat on the weight press bench while Joe led his mother to the only chair, an armchair rescued from the Dumpster, his threadbare throne. He'd changed into his Sex Pistols T, a decade unwashed at least. (He claims it's too fragile to get wet.) Joe Jr. wore something affectedly torn. Simon wasn't wearing a shirt at all, treating us to the full spectacle of his bubonic back and chest. They had their boots on and the dog collars bristling with studs. While Joe fiddled with the amp, the younger Joes bounced up and down like tennis players warming up.

"Ready?" Joe asked.

Joe Sr. armed himself with the bass, the boys their guitars. They one-two-threed and exploded into a raucous "Now I Want to Sniff Some Glue," segued into "Fucked Up Ronnie," leaping dervishly, crashing into each other, Joe's forty-three-year-old pectorals bouncing along with him. The exertion of punk is all the cardio he gets and, already, he shone with sweat.

At the end of the medley, Rachel burst into applause. "How stirring!"

Rachel went home after the concert. The boys retreated to Joe Jr.'s room, Joe Jr. having successfully avoided talking to me all evening. Joe Sr. was in the shower. I had the feeling he was doing it too, avoiding me, so I went to bed where I lay in wait for him. I took *Fathers and Sons* because I thought maybe I could get Joe Jr. to read it, since he'd already expressed an *interest*. The first thing I did was look for that Bazarov quote.

The shower shut off in the next room and a minute later, Joe came in with a towel tucked around his waist. He smiled and, turning his back, dropped the skirt, effectively mooning me. "Ha!" I said as he fell naked between the sheets. "That's perfect. Listen. *Art is just a means of making money, as sure as haemorrhoids exist.*"

He laughed. "Someone came in with a bleeding case a few weeks ago. Really gory. The guy wept for joy when I told him what it was. He thought he had cancer. Everyone thinks they have cancer."

I closed *Fathers and Sons*. "What was wrong with Simon tonight?"

"What?"

"Didn't he seem to be acting strangely?"

"He's fifteen. I know! How about The Piles?"

"Is something going on?" I asked.

He immediately reached for *The Journal of Emergency Medicine* lying on the lid of the laundry hamper for a pretence of reading before sleep. "Masturbation probably."

"Tonight?"

"Continuously."

"Did you see the paper?"

He pushed his face a little deeper into the shielding pages. "I glanced at it."

"You saw the article?"

"Yes."

"Yes! So where is it now?"

He tossed his magazine on the floor and turned to me, pouchy under the eyes, I noticed now. The poor man was tired. "I called Joe Jr. at school and asked him to get rid of it. I thought you hadn't seen it, Jane. I didn't want you to be upset."

And I was filled with shame because it's easy to forget that my moods affect them too. In our early years, Joe was convinced I had an off-season sort of SAD. Every spring he would bring me pills the way other husbands bring cheering flowers. Really, there's nothing clinically wrong with me. I just feel guilty whenever the trees flower.

"Rachel said I wasn't mentioned."

"It was the same old thing. Those two. The bomb. You know it all by now."

"Did Joey ask why you wanted him to do this?"

"No."

"Did he say anything about it tonight?"

"No."

"That's funny," I said, though really, why would he be curious about his mother? Except that Simon seemed to be. "So where is the article now?" I asked.

"He's got it, I guess. You want me to get it?"

"Tomorrow," I said and, satisfied he was just trying to help, I kissed the good, long-suffering doctor, heroic lancer of haemorrhoids, and let him get some sleep.

Chekhov was a doctor. His stories are full of medical men and women, the occasional scoundrel, but most of them sympathetic and hardworking. Dr. Samoylenko with his kebabs and mullet soup. Dr. Ragin in "Ward Number Six," who ends up committed to the same asylum as the patients he neglects. The frustrated, overworked Dr. Ovchinnikov in "An Unpleasant Business." Joe is, I think, most like Dr. Osip Stepanych Dymov from "The Grasshopper," in the background making everything run, taking no credit. No one remembered Dymov until exactly half past eleven every night when he threw open the dining room doors and announced, "Ladies and gentlemen, supper is served." Throughout dinner his wife would call him her darling *maître d'hôtel* and extol his charms to her arty guests. *"Gentlemen, look at his forehead! Dymov, turn your profile to us. Gentlemen, look! The face of a Bengal tiger, but an expression as kind and charming as a deer's. Oh, you sweet darling!"* Yet she started an affair with her painting teacher, and when the doctor found out, he began inviting a friend to dine with them so Olga would not have to lie. And after dinner, when his friend played the piano, Dymov would say, *"Why, hang it all, my dear fellow, let's have something really sad!"*

Joe has a raptor's face, but a deer's expression too. He would, of course, ask for something really angry.

When Joe Jr. was younger I was fearless. Nightly I would brave the obstacle course of Transformers, the carpet land-mined with Lego, slippery with hockey cards. Willingly I risked these childish hazards because I needed to be sure he was actually still there in his captain's bed, tucked in and breathing and safe. Safe from the harm I'd imagined throughout the day. But as he got older and slept less soundly, he'd sense my intrusion and wake. I had to stop checking on him despite my urge to protect him, which persists even now that he's a foot taller than I am and perfectly capable of looking after himself. It should be easier, but it's not. It's worse than ever. The older he gets, the more imperilled, or so I feel anyway. Because of Pascal. Because, what if the same thing happened to Joe Jr.?

I tossed and turned. I curled my toes up tightly, then relaxed them, did the same with my feet, then my calves, and so on, like you're supposed to, but gave up. Gave up and gave in to the compulsion and went to Joe Jr.'s room to make sure he was okay.

Standing in his bedroom doorway, I faced different hazards now. His scorn, for one. I couldn't even see him, but I heard him. He breathes like his dad. All that was visible were the fluorescent constellations stuck to the ceiling, still glowing after all these years like the heavenly bodies they represent. When I noticed them, I was amazed, just as I am nightly amazed by the reappearance of the stars and how they prove that, against all odds, the world has endured another twenty-four hours. They gave me courage and so I shuffled in, feeling my way with my feet until my shins collided with the bed. I froze while Joe Jr. slept on, oblivious to my bumbling—until I sat down.

"Ow!"

I sprang up. "Oh, God. I'm sorry. I woke you."

Groggy. "Mom? You sat on my leg."

"Sorry!"

"What time is it?"

"Shh. Go back to sleep. I'm leaving," I said.

"What are you doing in my room?"

"Nothing. I'm leaving."

I turned and walked straight into the edge of the door. It felt like a punch. More stars, brighter now, and a waterfall in my eyes. My nose sang with pain and when I cupped it, I felt something warm running out. Joe Jr. switched on the lamp.

"Are you okay?"

As soon as I could see, as soon as I ascertained that blood had not been shed, I turned to Joe Jr. sitting up in the bed. These days I rarely see him undefended by attitude like this and, in that moment, he looked exactly like his baby self. The clock on the bedside table, its face round and reproving, jabbed its hands past two-thirty.

"You want the article, I guess," he said.

What I actually wanted was that he would always and forever be safe.

Joe and I have tried to raise Joe Jr. in such a way that lying would be unnecessary. It seemed we were successful, for his confession spilled right out. "Dad asked me to take it. That was why I came home early. *And* because I was bored." But the next thing he said just floored me.

"Were you a terrorist, Mom?"

1 9 8 4

A grey quilt thrown across December. I glanced up and, remembering the missiles, quickly hoisted my umbrella. As though a bit of nylon stretched over some flimsy metal ribs could save me! Then the Reliant, so motley, so cheerful, pulled into the bus stop and honked. Dieter unrolled the passenger window so Pete could call out from the driver's side. "Get in, Zed!" To Dieter, Pete said, "Let Zed sit in front."

Dieter: "What?"

"You heard me. Don't be such a creature. Mix it up."

Dieter, lips rosebudded, got out of the car and slammed the door before getting in the back. "Oh, thanks," I said.

"I'm not going to hold it open for you, Jane. That's sexist."

I got in. The sticker on the glove compartment read *Military Intelligence is an Oxymoron*. Dangling from the rear-view mirror, a plastic Virgin Mary with a man's bearded face cut from a book and pasted over hers. Pete saw me staring at it. "That's Kropotkin." A jab started the figure pirouetting on its string.

"She doesn't know who Kropotkin is," Dieter said from the back.

"Did you before I told you?"

I felt for the seat belt but the buckle had been cut off. Only one windshield wiper worked, luckily the one on Pete's side. It was raining seriously now and my side was all smears. He turned in the direction of Fourth Avenue, then immediately into the alley. "Where are you going?" Dieter said. "I have an exam."

Pete: "I forgot something."

We drove down our own alley, past the pristine back yards, then the moss farm that was ours, around the corner and onto our street, circuit complete when Pete pulled into his original parking spot. "Unroll your window, Zed." I did and he looked out at the house next door where the drapes were fully open now. The neighbour, usually in melancholy vigil in the morning, was gone. Pete stepped out of the car into the rain and, keys jangling, went around to unlock the trunk.

"What's he doing?" Dieter asked me.

Strolling toward the house. Then he veered off the path and cut through our long grass, which lay down for him. When he reached the neighbour's emerald turf, he suddenly bolted for the garden statue, the black man in livery, twin to the one on our living room hearth. "Fuck," Dieter said, which summed up what I felt, though in different words. After a brief struggle, Pete wrested the statue free. It had been wired to something; I saw metal feelers protruding from the base as he ran with it CFL-style back to the car. A thud, then the trunk slammed and Pete slid into the driver's seat with a single bead of rain hanging off his nose, just above the smile. I shrank down in the seat.

"Great," Dieter said. "I'm officially late."

Pete turned to me and placed a hand carefully on my forehead. I pulled away from his touch. "Stick out your tongue," he said.

"Are you nuts?"

He caught my wrist in a tight clasp and took my pulse. "Still depressed" was his diagnosis when he finally let me go. "I'll check on you later, Zed."

My parents wrote me every week I was away at university. To save postage, my father always included his letter with my mother's, versions of *My dear Jane, I am glad to hear your studies are going so well.* He would cut off the unused portion of the page for his next letter until all that was left was a strip like you'd pluck out of a hat for charades.

That Christmas they waited for me to come home before putting up the tree. My father did the man's work, bringing the box up from the basement, grappling with the assembly, swearing, while my mother and I unpacked the ornaments. Last year I'd been so happy to come home to the only people in the world I could be myself with, but this year I was different, wiser I thought, older than my years.

"How did exams go?"

"All right, I guess." In my hand was the innocent toilet paper angel I had made a thousand years ago, before I knew I'd be dead at nineteen.

My father paused in his cursing to say, "All A's, I bet."

"Not necessarily. I won't find out for sure until I get back. I'm going back earlier than I said." They both looked at me. "I've got things to do," I told them.

"What things?" my father asked.

"I have to buy a desk."

They were hurt. I shouldn't have mentioned leaving so soon, but it was all I wanted to do. During the bus trip home I'd been amazed at how quickly we entered winter. Just past Hope, the season had been lying in wait. It made Vancouver seem all the more vulnerable, ever draped in the fragility of spring, never donning winter's frozen armour. I felt an urgency to get back and somehow guard it.

A few days before, Sonia had invited me to go downtown. I'd finished my exams and felt like being with other people before the world came to an end. I felt like being with Sonia. At the bus stop, we met up with Belinda and Carla from the "Women Only" house, Carla who seemed colourless next to Belinda in her padded Mao jacket and bright pink harem pants. Sonia hugged Carla and Carla hugged Sonia and, to my dismay, Carla, whom I didn't even know and had only seen once, the night they found out I was studying Russian, hugged me too. Belinda was swinging on the pole; we had to stand back to avoid the red lash of her hair. She twirled over to Sonia and hugged her. Then she saw me and cried, "Ho ho, Jane! Congratulations! Sonia finally got you!"

I turned to Sonia, who was beaming. "It's how we'll save the world, Jane. One person at a time."

Then Belinda, of course, hugged me, breathing in my ear, "I hear Sonia gets little Russian notes in her shoes." She pulled back and looked at me. "I want a note."

Carla husked, "Me too."

We were going to The Bay to put stickers on war toys. They'd already been to Eaton's and Woodward's, Sonia told me on the bus, smiling and leaning over the seat ahead of where I sat with Carla. "We got kicked out of Woodward's," Carla boasted. My shock must have shown because she hastened to add, "Don't worry. They can't arrest us."

Never in my life had I intentionally done wrong. I hadn't even handed in an assignment late. I had, of course, given my parents the usual teenage grief, but I didn't count that. "I don't want to get in trouble," I said.

Belinda and Carla exchanged glances. Carla said, "You can be support. Are you okay with that?"

"What does that mean?"

"You'll be the lookout and if anything happens to us—"

"Nothing will happen," Sonia assured me.

"You let the others know."

"Who?"

Belinda: "Call Pete."

"All right," I said.

The plan when we got off the bus was to fan out and enter separately, then meet up again in the third-floor bathroom. "The handicapped stall," Carla said.

"What if someone has to use it?" I asked and Belinda spread her arms and pulled me to her again. She smelled of patchouli and B.O. "Jane," she cooed. "Everything will be fine."

"It's her first time," said Sonia. "It's normal to be nervous."

I felt her little hand pet me.

Inside, the store was shiny with Christmas, tinkly with piped-in carols. A harried clerk looked up from her register as I passed. There would be security guards, too, posing as Christmas shoppers on the watch for shoplifters. I insinuated myself into the crowd on the escalator and was the first to reach the bathroom. *Please Do Not Throw Sanitary Products in the Toilet* read a notice on the back of the stall door. A tap. I unlocked the door for Carla, who immediately crouched to unzip her backpack and hand me a sheet of stickers.

> *Warning: This is a war toy.*
> *Studies show violent games*
> *make violent children.*
> *This Christmas, think peace.*

She took a black marker from her backpack and wrote under the sanitary products notice: *Ronald Reagan is a criminal! Throw HIM in the toilet!* Then the door handle rattled and Belinda bellowed on the other side, "Hey! What's going on in there?"

"Are you okay, Jane?" Sonia asked when we were all crowded in the stall together. "You can bail if you want."

I shook my head.

Carla distributed the sheets of stickers to the others. "Toys are at the top. Pretend you're shopping. If a clerk gets suspicious, employ distraction. We'll meet up afterward."

"Where?"

"The cafeteria."

"No. It's on the same floor."

Belinda suggested Santa's Workshop. Then she dropped her harem pants and peed in front of us. After they left, I stayed behind for a minute dashing cold water on my face and wiping it with paper towels.

The escalator delivered me up in Furniture and Appliances. I had to stagger around looking for Toys. When I found it, Carla was working independently, Sonia and Belinda together. I passed behind them, nonchalantly I hoped, and heard Belinda ask in her stage voice, "God. What do you think? Will he like *this*?"

"Nope," said Sonia, slapping a sticker on the box.

"This?"

"Nope." Slap.

"*This* then?"

"Nope." Slap. Giggle.

I looked around for a clerk but there wasn't anyone except an elderly woman in a knitted beanie hobbling toward me. She seemed exhausted. "Where are the Cabbage Patch Kids?"

"Sorry. I don't work here."

"They have squashy faces."

"Are these them?" I asked, pointing to some nearby dolls.

"That's not squashy."

I suggested she talk to a clerk and, as she limped off, I hissed to the others to clear out. Belinda and Sonia separated at once, heading in different directions. I had to go over to Carla with a second warning before she took off. It would look suspicious if I left then too, so I picked up a box and pretended to be interested in model building. The picture on the lid showed a green army airplane raining down bombs.

The old woman came back. "No luck," she told me. "They're sold out." Then she thanked me for helping her.

"I didn't do anything."

As soon as I said it I knew I didn't want those to be my last words.

Living on the West Coast had softened me. I couldn't tolerate the Prairie cold any more. When my mother insisted on taking me to the West Edmonton Mall for clothes I didn't want, I dashed from car to store and, even in that short time, sprang a nosebleed. My mother yearned for me to feel pretty. She urged me to try on frilly tops and skirts, even though she didn't dress that way herself. (She was the slacks and sweaters type.) When I was in high school she seemed to think that if I dressed differently my problems would be solved, I would make friends, when what I'd really needed was to be inconspicuous, not to make enemies. Anyway, all of that was in the past. It was trite. There were enough missiles pointed in my direction to kill me twenty times. It didn't matter what I wore. Sonia didn't care about clothes either.

Faced with my mounting sullenness, my mother finally gave up and we ran the frigid gauntlet back to the car with a new pair of runners. I vowed not to step outside the house again for the rest of the visit.

She turned on the heater and, while we waited for the engine to warm up, she studied me. "Don't," I said, bringing my mittens to my face.

"What's the matter?"

"Nothing."

"Did you have a fight with your aunt?"

"No."

"Then why aren't you going to see her any more?"

"I was busy with exams," I said.

"She was kind to you last year," my mother said. "I'll just remind you of that." Then, tentatively, she asked, "What about those girls you're living with?"

Worried, fretful little Sonia with her sudden bursts of joy. I had one too, at the thought of her. "Remember I wrote you about Sonia? We've started doing things together."

My mother pounced on this. "You've made a friend?"

What a freak she'd given birth to! She never said that, of course, but I intuited it every time she tried to help me. The heater pumped out its chinook, but I answered coldly, "She's really nice. That's all I'm saying."

"So what's wrong then, sweetheart? What's bothering you?"

I winced and drew a circle on the window.

"What?" she asked.

"Do you ever think about dying?"

"Not if I can help it. What are you nursing morbid thoughts for? It's Christmas."

A line to bisect the circle, then two drooping arms. Peace. "Mom? We're on the very brink of a nuclear war."

I wasn't expecting her to be relieved, especially not to laugh. "My goodness! Is that it?"

"Yes!" I told her.

"Why waste your time worrying about problems you can't fix?"

"Maybe we can fix it!"

"Jane. That's silly." She put the car in reverse and began to inch out of the parking spot. "And don't mention this to your father. You know how he feels about Communists."

"Not wanting the world to blow up has nothing to do with Communism! That's just so ridiculous! The nuclear clock? It's at three minutes to midnight. There's a fifty-fifty chance of a nuclear war occurring by 1985. That's not me talking. That's the generals. The scientists. Nobel Prize winners."

We were halfway out of the parking stall. My mother had braked for my outburst and now she sighed. "They're always talking about it on the news. But, please. We haven't seen you in four months. It will ruin the holiday, Jane. Just ruin it."

Barely three weeks before I'd felt exactly the same way. I knew the threat was there but somehow it lacked imperative. It was hard to understand now how I could have been so blasé about my own annihilation. If someone had held a gun to my head, I would have run screaming, but twenty thousand guns had had no effect. Were we all hypnotized? Was there something in the water? Yet if not for Sonia and Dr. Caldicott, I would still be carrying on like my mother was. "Don't you get it?" I said. "Holidays don't matter any more! There might never *be* another Christmas!"

The way she looked at me I wondered if I'd actually gotten through to her.

On Christmas Eve we played Scrabble. My father joined us in a game and, according to tradition, stormed off in a huff when we laughed at his spelling. Later he always crept back asking, "Who's the smartest girl on Earth?" Being smart wasn't enough now. I would need to be brave. I thought of Sonia practising bravery at the stove; so would I, in my own way. Mummied in outerwear, I went out to run a hurried loop around our cul-de-sac. The street lights cast their sequins on the shovelled driveways and the fresh snow crackled under my boots. In Russian the vocabulary for winter is immense. There are three words for *blizzard*, two for *a hole in the ice*. Single words that mean *a thin layer of slippery ice*, or *newly fallen snow*, or *a frozen snow crust*. It was minus thirty-one degrees and every painful breath I took asked me if I seriously wished to live. *Yes*, I exhaled. *Yes!*

Two days later, at the bus depot, my father gave his spiel. The horse, the dog, the gun. My mother cried and so did I.

I was sure I'd never see them again.

I thought I would have the house to myself when I returned, but as it happened Dieter had come back early from Saskatchewan to fill the sink with unwashed dishes and the compost bowl with rotting matter. Reagan hung flaccidly from his eye socket, face to the wall, disgusted by the sight. I knew Dieter was responsible because when I went upstairs I heard him laughing with a girl behind his closed bedroom door. Given his tireless pursuit of Sonia, I decided he was more of a Marxist-pacifist-hypocrite than anything else he claimed to be.

I hadn't slept a minute of the overnight bus trip so, as soon as I got in, I went to bed for the rest of the day. When I woke, it was to darkness and voices and music downstairs. I would have preferred to avoid Dieter and his paramour, but hunger made our meeting inevitable.

Only the girl was there when I went down, looking through the cupboards, a patterned scarf turbaned around her head. The music was Pete's, CCR. It was his boom box, too, on the counter. The girl gasped when she saw me. "Where did you come from?"

"Upstairs," I said.

"Have you been here all along?"

I nodded, pulling a bag of perogies from the freezer. She opened another cupboard and spoke hollowly into it. "I'm making a stir-fry. Do you want to eat with us?"

"No thanks."

"Don't you remember me? We met at the film." I turned and the pale blue guilt in her eyes washed over me. "Ruth," she said.

At that moment Pete walked in from the deck. After not seeing him for a week, I was freshly struck by the oxymoron. He was a commanding anarchist. "Zed! You're back!"

"She's been here all along," Ruth said.

"Where's Dieter?" I asked, though it was obvious now that he was still in Saskatchewan.

"How should I know?" Pete turned to Ruth. "Bye-bye."

"I'm making a stir-fry," Ruth said.

"No, no. Time to go. Zed's here now."

"Don't mind me," I said.

"I bought all the stuff," Ruth said, moistening.

"Take it with you."

Pete opened the fridge and started shoving bags at her. It took some cajoling to get her out of the house; she was sobbing by the time she left. Meanwhile, I cooked my perogies and sat down to eat them in the kitchen, unable to get to my room because of the drama playing out in the hall. Before Pete closed the front door, I heard Ruth ask, "Are you doing it with her too?" I couldn't believe it. As if I would fall in love with someone like Pete. I'd never fall in love, period.

"What's for supper?" he asked, coming into the kitchen.

"Stir-fry, I hear."

"Zed, is this really you? You didn't talk like this before." He checked the fridge—"Oh look. She left something"—and sat down across from me, tossing his long hair back. I wasn't going to say a word about him betraying Belinda, but I felt sorry for Ruth. I told him he was mean.

He bit into the forgotten pepper, shook the seeds into his palm, and pressed them with his tongue. "Why?"

"You hurt her feelings."

"I did not. I'm not in charge of how she feels. I didn't make her come here. She came of her own free will."

"Does Dieter know you used his room?"

"You're not going to get started on that, are you?"

"You said you were going home."

"No, I didn't."

"I asked you if you were going home for Christmas and you said yes."

"You asked where I was *spending* Christmas. I live here, Zed. This is my home. Here. With you." He waited for me to redden before adding, "And the others." Then he tossed the stem of the pepper across the room, basketting the compost perfectly.

I continued eating, watched by Pete, until I couldn't stand his canine gaze another minute. "Get a plate then," I said. "If you can find a clean one."

After supper I went out to buy more food. I checked the kitty while Pete was at the sink singing along to his boom box, well into the dishes, for which I was unreasonably grateful. Pennies. I didn't want to ask him to contribute. I didn't want to give him the impression that I was prepared to eat with him every night.

Later, when I returned from the store, not only had he finished the dishes, he'd emptied the compost. I went up to my room and, as I was passing the bathroom, Pete called to me. "Zed?" I stopped in the doorway. He was lying in the tub, reclining in its clawfoot embrace, a veil of steam hanging around him, concealing nothing. "What?" I quavered.

"Bring my boom box up from the kitchen?"

I did that for him. I went downstairs, unplugged it, and brought it up.

"Great. Can you plug it in?" A long, dripping arm pointed to the outlet. I sidled in, keeping my back to him.

"Do you want me to turn it on?"

"Can you get another tape? In my room. There's a box."

I crossed the hall. His books were still homeless, walls bare, sleeping bag balled up on his foamie, the cassettes in yet another milk crate. "Which one?" I called.

"I don't know. Read them to me."

They were all dubs with handwritten labels, mostly music from the sixties and early seventies. He was always lamenting he'd been born too late, that his prime was wasted on the eighties. The surprise was that he had Mozart. He settled on Hendrix.

"Jimi lived here, did you know that?"

"No." I fed the cassette to the machine, snapped closed its plastic mouth.

"His father was born here. Imagine. A black person in Vancouver."

"There are Chinese," I said in defence of my adopted city.

"Fuck the Chinese. I'm moving to Seattle when I graduate."

Crouched over the box, my back turned, I awaited further instructions. "Should I turn it on?"

"What do you know about Kropotkin?"

I glanced over my shoulder.

"I take that to mean nothing. You're studying Russian and they don't teach you about Peter Kropotkin? What about Bakunin? He was Russian too. *What?* No Bakunin either?" Pete slid down the sloped back of the tub and disappeared from view. While he was underwater releasing his intermittent glubs, I could have escaped, but I felt compelled to stay and see what he would do next, which was burst through the surface, gasping, the smooth planes of his face streaming. He tossed his head, splattering droplets across the wall. "UBC sucks. Sit down."

If I stayed low on the floor, he'd be higher and all I would see of him would be his head and arms and shoulders above the tub's rim. I could pretend he wasn't naked. What did I even know about anarchism, he asked. I'd read what he'd written on the origami cranes. I knew, though roughly (Slavonic Studies 105 had been a survey course), that anarchists were scurrying around nineteenth-century Russia with all those nihilists and revolutionaries. It was a time of social upheaval, of government repression, revolutionary cells, and political assassinations.

Pete said, "That bomb stuff is such a stereotype. Genuine anarchism is peaceful. It's about community."

"But there aren't any rules, right?"

"In the sense that I'm not going to tell you how to act, that's correct."

"But if everybody just acts however he wants?"

"What business is it of anybody else's how I act? I'm accountable to my personal conscience, that's all."

It struck me that he might be talking about Ruth, and I blushed. "What if a person doesn't have a conscience?" I asked.

He ran a disdainful hand down his face, as though he expected a more sophisticated argument from me. "Obviously that's not going to work. You have to constantly balance your own desires with the good of the community. That's just common sense. More than common sense. It's survival. Kropotkin had a theory. Social animals engaging in mutual protection, not competition, maintain the species. What are humans? Social animals. What does this say about us? That we are doomed unless we organize ourselves into harmonious, decentralized, voluntary associations. In other words, anarchism is our natural state and we are fallen creatures, Zed."

"Were you named after him?"

"Who?"

"Kropotkin. You said his name was Peter."

He looked truly shocked. "Oh, sure. My father thought, 'After whom shall I name my first-born son? I know. An anarchist.'"

He spoke so venomously I had to ask what his father did. "He rapes the earth," Pete said. Then he just sat there in the water staring straight ahead for a full minute before he thought to ask what mine did.

"He fixes appliances."

"That's noble."

Pete lay back. A pink foot rose out of the water and started snuffling blindly for the faucet. I made a move to leave but he held up a hand until he had shut the water off. I couldn't help thinking of a chimpanzee or a raccoon—other social animals that perform tasks with their feet.

"You're nice to talk to, Zed."

"Thanks."

"That's a compliment. Most people are full of shit."

I went to the university to study the next day. We'd received a surprise visitation by the sun that week and, though I was tempted to stay above ground and enjoy it, I descended to the stacks where I felt safe. If the bomb fell and I survived (unlikely, but anyway), at least I'd have something to read. At lunch I resurfaced to eat my sandwich in the pruned-back rose garden and, as happened when I occasionally lifted my face out from behind a book, I was startled to find myself in so beautiful a place—Bowen Island, West Vancouver, the North Shore Mountains laid out before me in so breathtaking a panorama I imagined some deity arranging landforms over breakfast, the way you might toy with the salt and pepper shakers and the sugar bowl. Along came Kopanyev, probably on his way from his office in Buchanan Tower to the Faculty Club for lunch, wearing a trench coat and a hat, maybe even a fedora. I wasn't sure. I just liked the word. I hoped he wouldn't see me, but as I was the only one around, he did. He came right over and, standing hugely before me, asked, "What do you think? Do I look like KGB agent?"

I was hideously shy in his presence though when I wrote a paper I actually pictured him reading it. I wrote it *to* him, like a letter, a *pismo*, hoping for his approval. Now he threw himself down on the bench beside me. "Look!" The view sat in the palm of his outstretched hand. "That makes it all worthwhile, ya? Rain. Grey. Depression. Poof! I read your paper."

I blushed.

"Were you implying he had fetish?"

"No!"

"I didn't think so. I actually never noticed these feet references, but you are quite right. In 'Duel' it's practically reason they fight."

I quoted von Koren's scathing summary of Layevsky's "moral framework." ". . . *slippers, bathing and coffee early in the morning, then slippers, exercise and conversation; at two, slippers, lunch and booze . . .*"

Kopanyev laughed and laughed.

"And von Koren wears *yellow* shoes!" I said. "I think that's worse."

"I do too! I am completely in accord! I would shoot any man first for wearing yellow shoes, second for wearing slippers in street. Then in 'Three Years,' like you said, it is heartbreaking, devastating, that he imagines Julia limping on foot he's kissed. But sometimes it's just detail. I'm not convinced galoshes have special significance. Half year Russia's covered in snow, other half in mud."

"In 'Man in a Case' Belikov's 'great claim to fame' was going around in galoshes."

"Yes." He stroked his beard. "Anyway, I enjoyed reading it very much." He bowed forward to peer at my new runners, then lifted his own foot clad in an expensive-looking dress shoe. I didn't know what he wanted me to say about it so I said nothing.

"How's Russian coming along?"

"It's hard."

"Stick out your tongue."

"What?"

"Stick out your tongue. Just little. Come on."

I poked the tip out and retracted it.

"As I thought. It's much easier if it's forked."

When I returned home later in the afternoon, I saw that the next-door neighbour had replaced the stolen statue of the black servant with a vaguely malevolent gnome. When it had actually appeared, I couldn't say, but this was the first time I'd noticed his red-hatted presence, his pursed, painted lips, and—unbelievable!—*yellow* shoes. Pete's car was gone. He didn't come home that night. Sonia wasn't coming back until New Year's Day. While I certainly didn't miss Dieter, it was depressing to be alone in the house with a menacing plaster figure lurking on the lawn next door.

The Chekhov story I read that night seemed strangely coincidental. "My Life—A Provincial's Story" is about a young man in conflict with his father over his way of life. The son of a prominent, corrupt architect in a corrupt provincial town, Misail refuses to take the path dictated by his rank. He explains: "*The strong should not enslave the weak, the minority must not be parasites on the majority, or leeches forever sucking their blood.*" His father despises him for working as a common labourer. Eventually Misail marries the rich daughter of a former employer, and together they move to the country, joining the back-to-the-land-type movement going on in Russia at the time. They set up as farmers but soon the farm and marriage fail. When Misail's sister, a consumptive whose whole life has been devoted to their tyrannical father, has an affair and becomes pregnant, she too is disowned. Yet Misail goes to see his father and, despite everything, tells him, "*I love you and can't say how sorry I am that we're so far apart.*" The story ends with Misail steadfast in his convictions, raising his orphaned niece alone.

Sad (10), *sadly* (1), *sadness* (1); *dissatisfied* (1); *unhappy* (1); *morose* (1), *morosely* (1); *depressed* (3), *depression* (1); *despondent* (1); *miserable* (1); *gloom* (1), *gloomy* (3); *sorrow* (2); *suffer* (1), *suffering* (2); *woe* (4); *lonely* (4), *loneliness* (1); *bore* (1), *boring* (5), *boredom* (1), *bored* (6); *monotony* (1).

Pete showed up the next night and, without explaining his absence, offered to cook me supper. Though I declined (I'd already eaten), I made an effort to sound friendly. I felt I understood him a little better. (Like Misail, he'd gagged on his silver spoon.) I felt I knew something about him. (He secretly loved his father.) It occurred to me, too, that perhaps he didn't even know this secret thing about himself. From my desk, new that day—a foldable card table—I could hear his noisy preparations. He even cooked like an anarchist. Banging, chopping, crashing, then smoke from the inevitable bomb of burning garlic.

Half an hour later he stomped up the stairs. "Come out with me, Zed," he called through the door.

I got up and opened it. "Where?"

"I've got to do something. Right now. I promise it'll be fun. Can you drive?"

"Yes."

"Really? You're full of surprises, Zed. Here." He tossed the keys.

I had learned the previous summer, but hadn't been behind a wheel since. Pete got in the passenger side and helped me move the bench seat forward. I wiped my sweaty palms on my thighs. "Where are we going?"

"We'll stick close to home tonight."

"Why can't you drive?"

"It'll be easier if you do. I'm going to keep hopping out." He began unloading things from his backpack onto the dashboard— Ronald Reagan mask, snaggled towel, a piece of manilla tag with letters cut out.

"You should drive," I said.

Pete pointed to Kropotkin in his dress dangling from the rear-view mirror, as though that might bolster me. We both laughed and, strangely, I did feel braver. I started the car, turned on the wipers to clear the windshield. I shoulder-checked. Each of these steps I named and ticked off in my mind. Behind us, the wet street shone under the street lights, all our neighbours home, their curtains open, the light from their televisions blue-ing their living rooms. No sooner had I pulled from the curb when I braked, startled by the feel of the vehicle obeying me. We were tossed forward, and Pete, tucking his hair up under the rubber mask, struck the dashboard.

Then I was driving straight down the middle of the street, slower than a jog. From the corner of my eye I saw him remove an aerosol can from his pack. The little ball rattled as he shook it. "Are you going to deface something?"

His voice came out rubbery. "Zed. What a nasty mind you have."

"That's spray paint, isn't it?"

"I'm going to modify some signage."

It seemed to take a week to reach the corner. When Pete, or Ronald, called for me to stop, I hit the brake harder than I meant to, sending both of us lurching forward again. He plunged out of the car, towel in one hand, paint and cardboard in the other, leaving the door ajar. In fluid, practised move-ments, he swabbed the stop sign, slapped the cardboard on it, blasted it with paint.

STOP
the arms race!

By the time the cloud had settled, he was back in the car telling me to drive.

"I start to get this itchy feeling, Zed. It's unbearable. I have to act. Can you possibly go any faster?"

"No," I said.

He rocked side to side in the same rhythm as the windshield wipers. "Stop then," he said the second before he jumped out, arms and legs pumping below the grotesque cartoon head, all the way to the next stop sign. When I pulled up beside him, the job was done. He opened the door, said, "Bayswater," and took off running again.

Bayswater Street was busier. I had to pull over to let a car pass, which was when I finally noticed the wipers shrieking against the dry glass and shut them off. Two blocks ahead, under the street light on the corner, Pete was lingering at the scene of the crime. He waved, then darted across, forcing me, if I wished to follow, to turn onto Point Grey Road where there was even more traffic. For the whole long block until the fork onto First Avenue, I held my breath. By then I'd lost him. One moment he was streaking ahead of me, then he wasn't. I drove all the way to Trafalgar Street, but the sign there was intact.

The neighbourhood looked unfamiliar through a windshield. I was lost just blocks from the house. I considered abandoning the car and walking back, but didn't know how I would face Pete later, so I carried on, trawling the treed streets, avoiding the main arteries, alert in my peripheral vision. Other nocturnal creatures popped up green-eyed in the headlights—a cat, a raccoon. A man with a dog crossed the road and, while I waited, I read the street sign. Balaclava. Not the face mask. The Crimean War. There was a Blenheim, too, a Trafalgar, even a Waterloo. The streets were all named after famous battles. It was the first time that I noticed.

I came to more stop signs that had been changed and, confident I was on his trail, kept driving, a full five minutes before something else occurred to me. He was intentionally evading me. He'd promised fun. Was this what he meant? A game of tag? I pulled over and shut the engine off. Kropotkin revolved slowly in his dervish's robe while I huddled, thinking of Ruth, how Pete had humiliated her, how he was humiliating me now.

A loud smash, like something had dropped out of a tree and landed on the trunk. I swung around. Nothing. When I faced forward again, I screamed. Ronald Reagan was pressed up against the windshield, doubly grotesque.

Pete got in the passenger side, laughing and breathing hard.

"You scared me!" I said. "Take that off!"

He tossed the mask onto the dash, shook his hair out. He looked elated.

"Where did you go?" I asked.

"I was right behind you. Here. Slide over. I'll drive."

It was awkward switching places. For a moment, when I was almost in his lap, he seemed to hug me. I could feel the bellows-like movement of his chest. He turned in the seat. "What's wrong? You seem angry. Are you angry, Zed?"

"Let's go."

"Are you angry?"

"Stop it!"

"Are you?"

"Yes!" I said.

When I wouldn't meet his eye, Pete took my face in both his hands. I was too rattled to pull away. I thought he was going to kiss me. He seemed about to, but then he didn't. "Sonia wants you in the group," he said. "She brought it up at the last meeting. Do you want to help save the world, Zed?"

It turned out that the liveried garden statues were more than booty. They were functional too, propping the flip-chart agenda against the fireplace, *Warm Up: Sonia* the first item of business. Last week, when Sonia returned from Christmas holidays, I'd been shocked by her advancing thinness; now, as she got to her feet, she actually had to hoist her pants. She looked around at our expectant faces—Pete and Dieter, Belinda and Carla, Timo (the facilitator that night), me (spurting sweat)—and began to sing. "If you're happy and you know it, clap your hands . . ."

Sonia wasn't the singer I'd heard so often closing their meetings, the one with the shivery voice, but soon the others drowned out her off-key warbling. They clapped and stomped and danced around the living room, taking wild swings at each other with their hips, giving up a rousing *Yeehaw!* when the song dictated. They were at ease with each other. They knew each other. I knew no one, barely myself. Yet I wanted to be there. I'd been dragging my loneliness around for too long. Also, I didn't want to die. When it was over, after Belinda had, to my mortification, implicated me in a polka, and everyone had collapsed on the floor, a silence fell, or rather everyone stopped laughing so the only sound was our common struggle, at that particular moment the struggle for oxygen. I lay panting, inhaling everyone's commingled exhalation, and vice versa, feeling close to these people, at least closer than I had to anyone in years.

We resumed our places, me on the chesterfield buffering Sonia from Dieter, Timo perched on the hearth, a giant baby in overalls, cheeks flushed from the warm-up. He was the only one in NAG!, the only Nagger, I hadn't been introduced to, the one with the big rubber boots and blond, dessert-like lashings of hair, and that curious affectation—the right pant leg rolled. As he read over the rest of the agenda, some of the words stalled in his mouth. It seemed arbitrary which ones would trip him up. "Does anyone have anything to aaaaadd?"

Hands went up and, while Timo wrote new names on the agenda, Belinda, who was leaning against the beanbag chair Pete sprawled in, gathered her hair from behind her and tossed the scarf of it over her shoulder, striking Pete full in the face.

I saw him flinch, then lift the hair that had fallen across his chest. He examined the ends, sniffed them. Then he put them in his mouth and, suddenly, he seemed so vulnerable, like a kitten weaned too young.

My acceptance in the group had been contentious, I was pretty sure of that. Nevertheless, when my name came up on the agenda, *Welcome Jane!*, they came over and one by one initiated me with a hug. I really hated this part. I didn't want to die but neither did I want to be hugged all the time. There would be no escaping the hugs. Timo was the softest. Pete crawled across the dirty shag and laid his golden head, heavy with ideology, in my lap. Carla presented me with a Guatemalan peace bracelet she'd woven herself. And here was proof that Sonia had diminished over the holidays; while still in her skeletal embrace, I decided I would be the one to fatten her up.

The main task of the evening was to revise and approve the rough copy of a leaflet we were going to distribute at a technology conference that was taking place in a few weeks at the Hyatt Regency. Some of the participants were involved in arms manufacturing; one in particular made components for the cruise missile. What struck me especially was that the cruise missile was being tested in Alberta, my home province, because the northern terrain there resembled the Russian steppe. The missile flew low, below enemy radar, following the contours of the land and, because it couldn't be detected, it was considered one of the new "first strike" weapons in the American arsenal, evidence that they had moved away from the old policy of deterrence.

A long discussion followed about whether or not to have contact information on the leaflet. "As if we don't have phone trouble already. Now we'll have assholes calling up," Dieter said.

Sonia put a hand on her heart. "If a hundred assholes call and we reach one of them, it will be worth it."

Dieter sniffed. "Okay. Fine."

Sonia volunteered to deal with the assholes, Timo to photo-copy the leaflet. Belinda would get the suits. "Help, anyone?" she asked. Sonia and Carla put up their hands, then I did.

"*Liaison SPND*," Timo read off the agenda. He was the li-aison. "They're having a rummage and bake sale on campus to raise money for the Walk for Peace. Do we want to get involved?"

Dieter pulled a sock off and threw it into the middle of the room. "They can have that." Everyone laughed.

Next, Pete gave a report on his stop sign work. Over the Christmas holidays he'd changed thirty-one signs. "Half of those I did with Zed." Everyone turned congratulatory eyes on me and Sonia squeezed my hand and kept it. Until we finally took a break, it grew clammier and clammier and the only thing I could think about was when she planned on letting me go.

I used the downstairs bathroom, the one with the broken toilet tank lid and the poster about Bolsheviks. I thought of it as Sonia's bathroom as she was the only one with a bedroom on the main floor. The bottles on the side of the tub were hers, among them, unsurprisingly, No More Tears shampoo.

In the kitchen, Carla and Belinda were picking at what was left in the dirty potluck dishes, their heads together, like con-joined twins. Belinda looked up and said, "Oh, Jane. We were just talking about you," as Carla edged past me and out of the room. I couldn't have been more surprised by what Belinda said next. "You didn't sleep with Pete, did you?"

"What?"

"You were here with him over the holidays, right?"

"For a few days."

"You seem so friendly now. He didn't try anything?"

"No!"

"Okay. I'm not accusing."

She didn't sound accusing. She was smiling, but I remem-bered another time her expression hadn't quite matched her words. After we'd finished putting the stickers on the war toys, we met up again at Santa's Workshop. It had been Belinda's idea to get our picture taken. We lined up and, when our turn came, crowded onto Santa's lap. Santa got quite jolly, his droll little mouth drawn up like in the poem, until Belinda said in a girlie voice that what she most wanted for Christmas was for men to stop staring at her breasts. In a twinkling, he spilled us off. Everyone seemed to agree that she'd really put old Saint Nick in his place.

"You'd be the first to say no," she told me now.

"Sonia's slept with Pete?" I asked.

"God, no. Not Saint Sonia. She's saving herself."

Carla popped her head in and we both looked at her. Belinda said, "God! He wouldn't *dare*! But everyone else has, believe me. SPND is at his feet."

She was warning me. I stepped away and got my drink of water, drank it down in relieved gulps while Belinda waited. Then, with her freckled arm draped over my shoulder, we went back to the meeting. "My feminism's in conflict with Pete's anarchism," she confided in a low voice.

"He says he's a feminist."

"Words aren't important. Actions are."

We resettled in the living room to deal with the new business. Pete's name came up on the agenda again and he repeated what I'd told him about the street signs. "Which ones are battles, Zed?"

"Trafalgar. Balaclava. Blenheim. Waterloo. Dunkirk—"

All around the room heads shook in outraged disbelief.

"—Alma and Dunbar."

"Dunbar! The food co-op's on Dunbar!"

"Warmongering in hippy Kitsilano. Shocking, isn't it?"

"God!"

"We've ggggot to rename them."

A committee was struck.

Sonia got the last word. She rose to her feet. "This has been such a good meeting. I missed you guys at Christmas. I love you all so much." Then she started to cry. "It's 1984—"

"Shades of Orwell," someone whispered.

"I feel like we have one year left. Just one year. If we can't stop this madness in the next twelve months, we're doomed. All of us. I know in the past I've always been a support person."

Dieter became defensive. "Support is just as important. We're all equal."

"Yes, but I was a support person because I was worried about having a criminal record and not being able to teach when I graduate. Over Christmas it finally sank in. There won't be any kids to teach if I don't act. I want you all to know that this year I'm going to do everything I can."

Everyone formed a silent scrum around Sonia, embracing her in layers of arms and bodies, a swaying mass of love, while Sonia sobbed. Someone began to hum, then they all joined in. Strangely, it was Carla with the husky man's voice, the beige hair and beige eyelashes and, more often than not, beige clothes, who had all her colours in her throat. "We shall live in peace," she fluted, "we shall live in peace . . ."

They formed a chorus. "We shall live in peace some da-a-ay!"

Then I, too, overcame my shyness and began to sing. "Deep in my heart, I do believe . . ."

It didn't matter how I sounded. It mattered that I meant it.

I ran into Dieter in the upstairs hall. During the meeting, during one of the many diversions, people had talked about the holidays. Belinda said she'd fought non-stop with her mother, mostly because she'd wanted to spend Christmas with her dad. "He's a film director," she said, tossing her hair. He made cable TV commercials for local businesses. Carla had been as miserable. She was adopted and didn't fit in. There was a big scene when she wouldn't eat any turkey. For Dieter, it had been his first Christmas without his father.

"I'm sorry about your dad," I told him now.

He blinked rapidly behind his glasses, "Me too," and for a moment we stood in embarrassed silence, in the no-man's land between each other's room. In Pete's land, actually, his music leaking out around our feet. *Riders on the storm.* When I turned to go, Dieter asked, "Can I talk to you?"

We went to his room where the monochrome Che loomed on the wall. I didn't know anything about Che. I knew a bit about Trotsky, how he'd been stabbed with an ice pick in Mexico. Che was just a black and white stain to me, but he reminded me of Hector, probably because of the beret. Hector hadn't slept on our chesterfield since before Christmas when he'd got an under-the-table job in Victoria delivering pastries.

Dieter sat on his desk chair, leaving me the bed that Pete had been in with Ruth. I hadn't told Belinda. It never crossed my mind to tell Dieter. "You're a good friend of Sonia," he began.

I smiled. So I was. It was as though I needed someone objective, not my mother, to point it out. When I got back after Christmas, I'd written Sonia a note of welcome, tied it to a piece of yarn, and left it hanging from the grate. Every night and every morning since her return I'd checked the grate, hoping more for her reply than an actual letter from my parents in the mailbox. Now I felt like flying to my room and calling down to her.

Dieter kneaded the back of his neck. "And you get along with Pete."

I seemed to. I liked him now. I knew he was as vulnerable as anyone, maybe more so, because it was hard to live by your principles. Hardly anyone understood that. They either idolized him or thought he was an asshole, or both. Why? No one thought Misail was an asshole. They thought he was a fool.

Ostensibly Pete and Dieter's conflict was ideological. Dieter, because of his interest in Central America, leaned toward Marxism and rules and procedure, which naturally irritated the resident anarchist. But theirs was also a conflict of personalities. Dieter was insecure. He wanted Pete's approval. He didn't seem to understand as I had early on that Pete respected people who stood up to him. You could call him on anything and he would consider your point of view.

"Sometimes I think he hates me," Dieter said. "Everything I say, he questions."

"That's his anarchism."

"You make it sound like a disease." He dropped his head to his chest then slung it over his shoulder and around the back until it cracked audibly. "You're like me," he said, not noticing how I recoiled. Dieter was an incurable corrector. He had a single eyebrow like a headband, concealed by the frames of his glasses. "You study hard. School's important to you. I care about my marks, too, right? And then there's my family. And what Reagan's doing in Central America. Not to mention this whole nu-clee-ar situation. Then I come home and Pete's arguing with me constantly. I'm so fucking tense all the time." He looked pleadingly at me. I didn't know what to say, what to do, until he told me.

"I was wondering if you'd put in a word to Sonia for me."

Finally, in the morning, a reply to my *Welcome back!* I threaded the yarn up through the fretwork and plucked the twist of paper out.

I have to talk to you.

Fulfilling the promise I'd made to myself at the meeting, I stopped at the store on my way home from university and bought a tiny tub of the most expensive brand of ice cream, the one with the faux German name, happy to squander my meagre allowance on an umlaut. Except that Sonia refused it. She sat on her bed with her head hanging, face curtained by her mournful hair.

"Why not?"

The curtain opened, revealing the earnestness behind it. "I'm trying not to eat so much. There won't be any food left after a nuclear war."

"Sonia," I said.

She sighed and, looking wretched, squeezed shut her eyes. I popped the lid off, dug into the pink with the teaspoon, tapped on her pursed lips; reluctantly, they parted. As the ice cream melted inside her, I read the predicament on her face. She was an ascetic. Pleasure actually hurt her.

"How is it?"

"Delicious," her anguished answer.

"What did you want to talk to me about?"

"The meeting," she said, and I took advantage of her reply to spoon more ice cream in. "What did you think?" she asked, coughing.

I doubted the plan they had—we had—for leafleting the Hyatt would bring us any closer to world peace, yet for those two and a half hours that we talked about it I felt less helpless, as though our death sentence had been temporarily stayed. I admitted to her now, though, that I didn't want to get arrested. "My parents would kill me," I said.

"You can be support with Dieter. It's just as important."

"How many of you have been arrested?"

"None so far, but it's going to happen. It might happen at the Hyatt. I'm ready. You've heard of the Berrigan brothers? They're brothers and priests. They broke into a silo and hammered on the nose cone. They poured their own blood on the missiles."

"We're just putting the leaflets under the doors, right?"

"Yes." Then, despite what she'd said at the meeting, she confided that she felt estranged from the group. "How can Dieter make these plans to go to Nicaragua next summer? We don't even know if we'll be alive. They have all these other causes. When Belinda and Carla start talking about equality, I want to scream that it'll happen soon enough. Soon we'll all be equally dead. We have to focus on peace. Because, without peace, there won't be anything left."

She met my eye. "You're right," I said.

"Really?"

"Logically, yes." I held the spoon out again.

"No more."

"You have to eat or you'll lose strength."

Dutifully she opened her mouth. "I'm jealous of you, Jane," she said and I almost dropped the spoon. "You've just found out how things really are. You're going to get more and more empowered. I'm afraid of burning out."

"You won't," I told her, for which she rewarded me with her most wistful Anna Sergeyevna smile.

A few nights later we went together to the Blenheim house to help work on the radiation suits. From the outside it looked less like student digs than ours, except for the portly papier mâché Venus of Willendorf blown up to four feet standing guard on the porch. Belinda opened the door, brandishing a smile and a slip of paper checkered with creases. "What does it say?"

She'd asked me for a note, so I'd written a word in Cyrillic and slipped it in her shoe. Now that she wanted me to translate it for her, I didn't know which to say, *actor* or *actress*. She'd claimed that words weren't important, but that was simply untrue. Not just at the Trutch house, but in my classes too, there was often a feminist cabal enforcing correct usage. Kopanyev had a terrible time in Nineteenth-Century Russian Literature in Translation—not that he didn't deserve or enjoy the frequent ideological lashings he received. He got all twinkly when voices turned shrill. There was a small, seething faction in our already small seminar that loathed him. In Russian, though, everyone adored him, which seemed odd to me. Was literature inherently more controversial than language? But wasn't it language itself that feminism sought to reform? Perhaps there wasn't any point in even trying to remake a gendered language like Russian. In any case, I was as far from mastering—mistressing?—the politically correct English lexicon as I was from speaking Russian, though I was learning fast.

Belinda waited. "Actor?" I hazarded.

Delight! Incensey hugs all around! She waved us inside and in a single glance I understood why she wanted to move from Trutch to Blenheim Street despite its militaristic connotations. A brown tartan behemoth filled half our living room. The shag had alopecia, the walls were a four-sided bulletin board. Here everything was homey and neat. We followed Belinda to the kitchen, where I almost had to shield my eyes from the rare, bright sight of dishes gleaming in the rack. There were curtains, too, and four matching chairs around the table, the radiation suits heaped over the back of one. Then Carla appeared from some other immaculate room for another round of hugs.

At the Trutch house we wouldn't have been able to work on the kitchen floor. The chore sheet notwithstanding, it simply never got washed. Now we set up an assembly line, Carla using a homemade stencil to draw the radiation symbol on the backs of the suits, the rest of us colouring it in with markers.

"Tell them what Dieter said," Carla told Belinda.

"God! He asked me to talk to Pete for him. I asked why. 'You're his *girlfriend*,' he said. I said, 'What do you mean by that?' 'What do you mean "what do you mean"?' So I actually had to tell him. 'I'm nineteen. I'm not a girl. I menstruate. Are you a boy or a man?'"

She flipped her hair, indignant all over again.

Sonia was surprised. "But he's good about saying 'woman.' He corrects me all the time."

"So he says"—Belinda thrust out chest and voice—"'I'm not going to be manipulated by semantics!'"

Sonia: "The poor guy."

"Why? Someone's got to tell him he's sexist. I don't mind."

I said, "There are two words in Russian, *dyevushka* for young woman and *dyevochka* for girl." I worried I sounded pretentious until I saw they were in awe.

Belinda said, "This one's done. Put it on, Jane. Let's see how it looks."

I went to the bathroom. As I was climbing into the suit, I noticed pillows of calico fabric hanging on the towel rack. I had no idea what they were for but because in size and shape they resembled menstrual pads, I felt embarrassed, the way I used to last year when my aunt would carry her wooden clothes rack into the back yard and drape it shamelessly with her nylons and underpants and gallon-cup brassieres, the way I had a minute ago when Belinda said *menstruate*. In the mirror, I adjusted the particle mask over my mouth and nose and drew up the hood. When I opened the door, a girl—a *woman!*—with cropped hair and a silver charm dangling from one ear was passing by. The charm was an axe, which made me think she must be in Forestry. Without even glancing at the suit she introduced herself as Nellie, Carla and Belinda's housemate.

I pulled the particle mask under my chin. "Jane."

"Oh, you're the Russian! I've heard about you."

I blinked at her. Then I remembered something. My aunt calling the house before Christmas and Sonia whispering, "She's

Russian," when she passed the phone to me. Pete and Dieter glancing at each other. Even Dieter looked impressed as I toted the phone away. Now I smiled a lie at Nellie and went back to the kitchen where they oohed over me in the suit. I certainly didn't put them straight about my dull Canadian mother and my cranky, Polish-born, anti-Communist father, and the Sloppy Joes and frozen pizza.

Afterward, as Sonia and I walked the dark streets home, I mentioned how clean the Blenheim house seemed compared to ours. "Our house is gross," I said.

"Yes but—" Sonia squirmed. "Some things are gross there too."

It turned out that the calico pillows in the bathroom that I thought could not possibly be menstrual pads were. They laundered and reused them. "And did you see the chart on the fridge?" she asked.

"The chore sheet?"

"It's not a chore sheet."

"What is it then?"

"They record their periods."

"No!"

"I'm still a feminist," Sonia avowed.

We reached our street, the exact spot where I had let go of the bed last fall. In the corner house a child was practising the piano, the same plunked notes over and over. Televisions strobed in living rooms. "Carla's a lesbian," Sonia said.

Confusion. Sonia clogged blithely ahead, hands in pockets, chin high, the flaps of her funny toque like blinders. A few paces on, she stopped to wait and, when I caught up, she acknowledged my distress. "I didn't know either until Belinda told me. Apparently I'm naive." Then she changed the subject. "I hope Belinda and Pete don't break up."

"Are they fighting?" I asked.

"They're always fighting. But if two people really love each other? They can work it out. What hope is there for the world otherwise? How can we expect strangers and enemies to get along when people who are actually in love can't? Also, it would be bad for the group."

We went up the front steps. On the porch, Sonia turned to me. "Have you ever been in love, Jane?"

"No," I said.

"Me neither."

A strange thing happened that week. I opened my book and, as was often the case with Chekhov, I fell right in, tonight into the first story, "The Kiss."

Off the top Chekhov sets up Staff-Captain Ryabovitch as a poor foil to his superior, Lieutenant Lobytko, a *tall, strongly built officer* whose *ability to sniff a woman out from miles away* earns him the nickname *the setter*. By contrast, Ryabovitch is a *short, stooping officer, with spectacles and lynx-like side whiskers*. The ladies call him *vague*. *Timid and unsociable* Ryabovitch, the *most modest and most insignificant* officer in the brigade.

The officers are invited to the local manor house. After tea, everyone moves to the ballroom where *the grand piano suddenly thundered out. The sounds of a sad waltz drifted through the wide open windows and everyone remembered that outside it was spring, an evening in May, and they smelt the fragrance of the young leaves of the poplars, of roses and lilac.* While the other officers flirt and dance, Ryabovitch, *filled with sadness*, wanders off, soon managing in his bumbling way to get lost in the big house. He enters a darkened room and it is here that an anonymous woman rustles forward and, encircling his neck with her fragrant arms, delivers the eponymous kiss. But when she feels his lynx-like whiskers (Chekhov implies), she shrinks *backward in disgust*.

Ryabovitch flees, but as the shame lifts he begins to give himself up to a *totally new kind of sensation. Something strange was happening to him* as a result of the misplaced kiss. Feeling almost drunk, he now boldly enters the party. The tingling *peppermint drop* sensation on his left cheek, just by his moustache, persists so that by the time he arrives back at the barracks that night, he has abandoned himself to an *inexplicable, overwhelming feeling of joy.*

Sonia called that supper was ready.

I brought the giddy feeling in the story down with me, the high point I had left off at when I tossed the book aside, though I knew for Staff-Captain Ryabovitch disappointment would prevail. "The Kiss" was one of Chekhov's most banal tragedies.

Pete was just coming in off the deck, pink-eyed, wearing a sarong. "What are you smiling about?" he asked.

"Nothing."

"Is it my dress?" He started jigging around the kitchen and Sonia and I laughed, Sonia hefting a heavy pot of soup onto the table before going back for cornbread. Pete peered in the pot. "Stuff's floating in the soup."

She rushed over. "What?"

"Solids. Potatoes. Carrots. Don't tell me. The Americans finally ratified SALT II."

She dropped the two large pans of cornbread on the table so she could assault him with the oven mitts. "Jane says I have to keep my strength up."

"Zed. Let me kiss your hand."

"How sexist," I said and Dieter, taking his place at the table, laughed.

Dieter wasn't so bad. We had too much in common, were on the same pole, I decided that night as we talked over supper. That was why we repelled each other. Last year Dieter had come to UBC from Saskatchewan and, like me, had been overwhelmed by the beauty of the place. Then the skies had lowered and covered it all like dust sheets over the furniture. He couldn't get out of bed. He had SAD. His girlfriend at the time ("so-called") dumped him. One of his dorm mates was in SPND and dragged him out. The scales fell off his eyes, just like mine had, but also plunged him deeper into depression. His involvement in Peace and Justice for Central America was what snapped him out of it. "Latin Americans have passion," he told us. "Not a common trait in Saskatchewan."

Each of us could trace the provenance of our commitment like this. For Sonia it was seeing a lamb euthanized when she was a child, for Pete his years at a private boys' school watching the lone black kid get hazed year after year. In the woods behind the stone walls, they warmed their hash over a lighter. Pete said, "My dad made this." He meant the little foil bowl, but when he looked into the pink, sorrowful eyes of his black-skinned friend it all came together—aluminium, South Africa, and nasty, brutish prep school boys in faggy blazers.

Pete dredged his bowl with the cornbread and bowed to jam the soggy mess in his mouth. Dieter, too, had entered the race for seconds but when they both reached for the ladle at the same time, the strange thing happened: each insisted the other go ahead. I looked at Sonia and she at me. Could it be true? I gave Chekhov partial credit for my mood. Also, tomorrow I would take part in my first real action. Pete had smoked a joint. Sonia was indulging Dieter with guilty smiles because she felt bad Belinda had been so hard on him. So, yes! Provided there was enough food to go around, we could be the harmonious, decentralized, voluntary association Pete dreamed of.

He said, "We should play Monopoly tonight."

This, I learned as I helped Sonia clear the table, had been a favourite pastime during the last academic year. Dieter went to get the board.

"The object of the game—" he began pedantically.

"I've played before," I said.

"Not like this."

Sonia was shuffling the title deeds and divvying them out.

"You divest yourself of everything. Give it all away. So if you land on Park Place, for example, the owner will pay you what it's worth and give you the first hotel. If she's out of hotels on that property, you get a house. No houses, you get the deed."

"What about Chance and Community Chest?"

"They stay the same. Whoever's the biggest capitalist in the end loses."

Out of the handful of die-cast tokens of militarism and greed, Sonia chose the thimble, Pete the iron, Dieter the wheelbarrow. Naturally, I took the shoe.

The year before, even the month before, nothing short of a catastrophe would have kept me from the lecture hall. But now that I understood an unimaginable catastrophe, while not yet upon us, was alarmingly imminent, that the time to act to prevent it was now, I did. On an abruptly sunny morning, the elements aiding and abetting our plan, I skipped class for the first time in my life and, with my housemates, piled into Pete's car.

At the Blenheim house I watched Carla swagger down the walk. She always dressed in cords or jeans and today wore a plaid shirt like my father favoured, buttoned high. As she neared the car, the urge to stare was so great I realized I wouldn't be able to look at her at all, which was, of course, the same problem I had. People sensed my awkwardness and averted their eyes. But Sonia and Pete, Belinda and Carla—they didn't. Not even Dieter did any more. I was a Nagger now.

Belinda handed the bundle of suits off to me before getting in the back with Carla and Sonia. Timo was biking down.

Pete said, "Why don't you sit in the front?"

Belinda closed the car door. "I'm already back here."

"I see."

She bristled. "What do you see?"

"I see you're in the back." When he started the car, it was the engine that sounded angry. Belinda gathered up her hair, hurled it behind her. "God."

Carla tapped my shoulder to say hello. My smile felt exaggerated, stretched, but as soon as I faced forward again and started stuffing the radiation suits in my pack, all I felt was nervous. Off we drove, off to save the world in that crazy quilt of a car, a confirmed lesbian in the back.

We parked a few blocks from the hotel and pooled our change to feed the meter. Our group hug blocked the sidewalk. (Let the capitalists walk around us!) Then we split up, Dieter and I, support, going ahead. We had decided to pretend to be a married couple staying in the hotel. "In you go, my darling wifey," Dieter said, ushering me inside the revolving door. Centrifugal force propelled us into the atrium, where we stood blinking and disoriented, as though we had passed through to another dimension, one shiny with marble, bulwarked by velvet couches, inhabited by suited men with name tags. In that chandeliered world, almost everyone carried a briefcase. There were other guests, obvious tourists, not conference goers, but despite our efforts at dressing up we were out of place among the suits and uniforms.

I was much more nervous than I'd been at The Bay. Surprisingly, though, now that I was actually in the hotel, I discovered getting arrested wasn't what I really dreaded. Hanging around the lobby, wondering what the others were doing, wondering if they'd been caught yet, seemed worse now that every minute of every day was spent waiting—waiting for the world to end. There was a fifth suit, a spare, in my pack. If they tried to arrest me, I would run.

I pushed on the door to the ladies' room, slippery with my sweat, and said to Dieter on his way to the men's, "I'm going up."

"What?"

"I changed my mind."

A quick glance up and down the corridor and he came over to where I was still holding open the bathroom door, my pretend husband, so chivalrous a minute ago. "This is the first rule in any action: do not stray from the plan. Maybe nobody explained that, Jane." All at once I pictured him losing at Monopoly the night before, rubbing his hands together, cackling over the play money. He hadn't seemed that disappointed. "You're jeopardizing the whole action," he told me.

I stepped inside where he couldn't follow me and, in a stall, put on the extra suit. Carla came in a minute later and I handed hers to her. "I'm going up too."

"Oh, good. You remember about going limp?"

"Yes."

Now that these words had passed between us, I could be myself again with her.

Sonia hugged me when I told her. "Dieter's mad," I said.

"Never mind. This is more important."

We were going in two trips, the women then the men, starting at the top and working our way down. Timo and Pete would leaflet the odd-numbered floors, the rest of us the even. As well as distributing the suits, it was supposed to have been my job to stand at the end of the corridor and make sure the coast was clear, but Dieter did this on his own now, shooting me a disgusted look when I stepped out with the others. At his signal, we sauntered into the lobby and over to the elevators.

"Act normal," Belinda had primed us, adding with a snort, "if that's possible." It seemed to be working. We waited with downcast eyes and, somehow, in that logic peculiar to toddlers and ostriches, no one paid any attention to us. Even as the elevator door slid away and we stepped aside to let the descending passengers exit, we received no more than a few curious glances.

An elderly couple got in with us. "Thirty-two," said Carla and I pressed the button. The man, stooped and sporting bulbous hearing aids, asked for the sixteenth floor. We ascended in silence, my gaze flitting nervously from Sonia to the numbers illuminating in excruciatingly slow sequence above the door. I could hear the elderly couple breathing behind us, no doubt staring at the radiation symbols stencilled on our backs, putting two and two together. The elevator stopped—on the fifth floor, not the sixteenth—and in that eternal pause before the door retracted, we exchanged a look of panic. To be caught so soon, with the pockets of our radiation suits bulging with undistributed leaflets.

It was Pete. Pete alone, staring off to the side, the mask under his chin like a huge white goitre. Until then I wasn't aware his charm was something he could control, that it was more than the sum of his good looks and orthodontic work, but now he saw us in the elevator and turned on all his lights. (*Radioactive* sprang to mind.) When he beckoned, Belinda took a tranced step toward him. We all did. We shuffled obediently out. Behind us, the old woman said to her husband, "There's another one! Is there something going on in this hotel?"

"They have conferences!"

"Oh!"

The door closed on them, leaving us standing in the hall with Pete. "What are you doing?" Belinda asked. "Where's Timo?"

"I want to talk to you." He made a sweeping motion to dismiss the rest of us and Sonia pressed the elevator button.

"Are you crazy?" Belinda said. "We're in the middle of an action!"

When the elevator came, Sonia held the door for Carla. "Go," Pete told her but Carla crossed her arms and wouldn't budge. Sonia and I got in and travelled up alone, floor numbers lighting up all over the panel as though we were already being pursued. We got out on the thirty-second floor, according to the plan, and worked the long hall without incident, sliding a leaflet under each door, meeting no one, the only sound the friction of our suits. In the thrill of the work, we forgot about Pete being such a hot-head, finished, and went down two more floors, also as planned, stooping before each door again, sliding our warning through. I was taking action. As long as I was taking action, we were safe. Here and there a room-service tray bore the congealed remains of a midnight snack, pop stagnant in the bottom of a glass, wadded napkins—a still life of waste. I stepped right over it. I'd fallen into a rhythm: stoop, drop the leaflet. One sharp tap to send it under the door. Three paces to the next room: repeat. Tap. The leaflet shot through.

"What's this? Pizza?"

I was still bent over, staring now at a pair of long bunioned feet with frosted nails. Slowly, I straightened, the way you would if you chanced upon a bear. Against the bright white of her robe her paper-bag cleavage seemed years older than her face, her raised eyebrows two thin lines in a child's drawing. I turned to see where Sonia was. Way down at the end of the hall, staring back at me. Condensation formed inside my mask.

The woman leaned out the door. "Oh. There's two of you." She beckoned to Sonia, kept moving her hand, winding her in. I searched Sonia's eyes above the mask as she drew closer. We could easily bolt but Sonia showed no sign of wanting to. The woman, meanwhile, tried reading the leaflet from several distances before giving up and asking us in. She hummed a few bars of "London Bridge" as we shuffled under her arm. "You are girls?"

Sonia pulled her mask down. "We're women."

All the gold in her mouth showed when she laughed. "Fine. Little women. I'll call you—can I see you?" We both took off our hoods and she scrutinized me. "I'll call you Jo. And you," she told Sonia, "you are surely Beth."

She walked over to the beds with their unmade floral spreads. Her glasses were on the side table next to some prescription bottles. She put them on and looked around for the leaflet, turning a complete circle before Sonia picked it off the floor and handed it to her.

"Thank you. Sit down. There's—there they are." By the window, two armchairs no one made a move to sit in. Sonia and I watched her read. "Oh. You're protesters." She looked at us over the top of the glasses. "Sit down."

Sonia sat on one of the beds, so I did.

"Can I offer you girls—excuse me. Jo. Beth. Can I offer you a drink?"

"No, thank you," Sonia said. "We're working."

"I'll have one if you don't mind. Jo?"

I shook my head.

She crouched before the miniature fridge so her legs jutted through the robe's opening, all the way to the tops of her veined thighs. I averted my eyes. When I looked next, her backside was swaying before us, huge and white. She had dropped onto one knee and was gripping the shelf of the mini bar, trying to get back on her feet. As soon as she was steady again, she disappeared into the bathroom. Though there were clean glasses right there on the bar, she came back with one that had a toothbrush in it, adding a few shards of nearly melted ice from the bucket, then the clear contents of the bottle she uncapped with her teeth. She crossed the room and sank into one of the armchairs. "Now," she said, stirring with the toothbrush, tossing it aside. "Tell me all about this awful missile."

Sonia told her. She opened one of the leaflets and referred to the grainy pictures and graphs as she talked. "It's a first-strike weapon. They think—"

"Who?"

"The Americans. They think that nuclear war is inevitable and that they can win by launching a pre-emptive strike. But they're insane if they think you can win a nuclear war. It's suicide. Back in September? After the Soviets shot down that Korean airliner? Do you remember? We were this close. And Trudeau is allowing the Americans to test the cruise missile in Alberta. So we're implicated as much as they are."

She talked about how many weapons the Americans and the Soviets had amassed, how many times over we would all be killed. She mentioned the Doomsday clock. "That's awful," the woman said. "Just awful. They really are a bunch of bastards," and she drained the glass and slammed it on the table. "I see you have more of those flyers."

"Yes," we said.

"Because, Jo, Beth, I'll tell you what I'm going to do. I'm going to go early to dinner tonight and I'm going to put them under everybody's plate." She thrust her chin in the air the way I'd seen Belinda do. "*Everybody's*. What do you think of that?"

Sonia stared. "Are you with the conference?"

"Not really. I get dragged around." She sniffed and waved a hand toward the window behind her. "I do like this Robson Street." Then, as though reminded of the world outside, she turned, showing us the sleep-matted back of her head.

Sonia and I got up and went over to the window and the three of us looked down. The West End high-rises looked so tiny. We saw Stanley Park, a miniature Lion's Gate Bridge, water water everywhere giving off a silvery sheen. Sonia tapped the pane. "We live over there. In Kitsilano."

With my eye I followed the beaches—Jericho, Locarno, Spanish Banks. Around the end of Point Grey was Wreck Beach, the nudist beach at UBC. I couldn't see it from here, but the Buchanan Towers, where Kopanyev had his office, were perfectly visible. He was probably sitting there right now, puzzling over my absence.

"What's that big island?" the woman asked.

"Vancouver Island."

"I thought we were on Vancouver Island."

Sonia leaned against the glass, prepared, it seemed, to fall right into the city. Her mouth left a foggy circle, like the translucent shadow of the radiation mask.

"It's very beautiful here," the woman said, yawning.

"Yes. Can you imagine it destroyed?"

"Unfortunately, I can. I'm from Detroit."

Sonia turned to her with clasped hands. "Would you really put leaflets under the plates?"

"Oh, Beth. It would give me tremendous pleasure. You have no idea."

Sonia went over to the bed and counted out twenty leaflets and placed them on the table. "Will that be enough?"

"Whatever."

"Thank you so much. Now we have to finish handing these out."

The woman was still gazing out the window, her eyes half shut, glasses cocked, but she came to enough to wave to us. "Farewell, little women!"

In the hall outside, Sonia bounced on her toes. "Jane, I'm so happy. See how easy it is? No one wants to die. We just have to explain the situation like we did with her."

I wasn't so sure the woman would even remember the leaflets by dinner though I didn't say this. I let Sonia bounce.

I let her be a rabbit. After all, who knew what effect our words would have? Maybe we would be her provenance. We continued leafleting and soon came to a door propped open with a cleaning trolley. The maid was standing in the middle of the room, a rag in her hand, hypnotized by something on the television. Sonia had her in her sights, but I wanted to try now. I tapped on the door. The maid snapped the TV off and swung around to face us. "Sorry to bother you," I began. "We're wondering if we might talk to you about something that's going on in this hotel."

She gestured vigorously. "No Ingleesh!"

In the elevator I still felt charged. It was what kept the Mormons and the Jehovah's Witnesses going despite how many doors are slammed in their faces. If one soul could be saved, even one. Sonia said, "Now I don't know what to do. I feel like we should keep talking to people. But *someone* has to get arrested."

"Pete will, I bet."

"I hope so," she said as the elevator opened and we stepped right out into the waiting arms of a crimson-faced security guard. "Stop," he said. It was a plea, rather than a command. I was momentarily horrified, but Sonia could not believe our luck. She smiled and put her hands up like in a Western.

"Thank you," he told us, breathlessly. "I've just been chasing your friend around."

"Who?" Sonia asked.

The guard took a handkerchief from his breast pocket, the one appliquéd with the Hyatt crest, and wiped his face. Now that he had us, he switched to sarcasm. "Sorry. I didn't catch his name." A staticky ejaculation sounded from deep inside the jacket and he whipped a walkie-talkie out, clearly deriving a childish pleasure from handling it. We got a brief glimpse then of the other thing in the jacket—the belly straining against the belt. "Interception on twenty-eight. Two more coming down." He reholstered his toy. "You have to come with me. Not that way. We gotta take the stairs. Here." He seized Sonia's arm, then mine. This was when we were supposed to go limp. I waited for Sonia to go first. She pulled her mask off. "We won't run away."

"Sure you won't."

"What did he look like?"

"The big guy?"

"Timo," Sonia said to me. "If he was alone, that's not good. Where's Pete?"

When we got to the stairwell door, the guard nodded for Sonia to open it since both his hands were full. It shut heavily behind us and we found ourselves in a concrete shaft much like a bomb shelter. A vertical bomb shelter with thirty-some floors of Escher handrails. Our steps echoed as we started down, the suits swished, and the guard's breath came in nasal spurts. "Are you going to call the police?" Sonia asked him.

"That depends on how much trouble you are."

"Oh, we won't be any trouble."

"Then you should be fine."

"It's the people at this conference who are making trouble," I said, with a glance at Sonia. She nodded, adding, "But you can call the police if you want. We'll go peacefully."

We reached the next landing. She pulled her hood down and shook out her hair, which I took as a signal. "You probably wonder why we're here," I began.

"Nope."

"There's a conference in this hotel. One of the companies involved is making the guidance system for the cruise missile. Do you know anything about the cruise missile?"

"Sure. I read your leaflet."

"Then you understand," I said.

"No, I don't. I don't understand at all. You look pretty young. You should be in school, shouldn't you?"

"That's true. We should be, right, Sonia? If we felt safe, we would be in school, but we don't. We feel—imperilled."

Sonia liked this word. She smiled. By this point the guard's hold on us was procedural rather than restraining. The more laboured his breathing, the more symbolic his touch, which alarmed me for we were only going down. He wasn't old. After-shave emanated from him, stronger as he heated up.

"Are you married?" Sonia asked.

"I don't have to answer your questions."

She raised the arm he was holding and looked at his wedding band.

On every second landing, we passed a heavy metal door like the one we'd entered through, with the number of the floor painted on it. The guard was perspiring copiously now and, worried for him, I asked to take a break. He looked relieved as he shepherded us into the corner of the stairwell, spreading his legs wide to block us in, yanking out his handkerchief. "Sorry about the trouble," Sonia said.

"Sure you are."

"We are. We really are."

He swabbed the back of his neck and face, then meticulously refolded and restored the soggy cloth. I sensed he was stalling. His chest heaved. Sonia asked, "Do you have kids?" just as the walkie-talkie woke up with what might have been "Jack?"

"Yeah. We're on our way down," he answered. We heard the word *situation* in the reply. "So I should just leave these ones here?" he asked.

"*Ah?*"

"I'll be there when I get there. Over." And he sighed.

"Is your name Jack?" Sonia asked.

"He called me Jock."

"It's Jock?"

He looked at her sidelong. "It's a joke. No more chit-chat. Let's get going."

"I'm Sonia. This is Jane."

He smirked as we started down again. I could hear that his breath sounded more normal now for a too-fat man. I kept glancing at Sonia, who was making tartar of her bottom lip. She was, I guessed, thinking of another plan. Sure enough, as we neared the next landing, her eyes slid sideways, slyly, to meet mine the second before she slipped. Her bum hit the concrete stair and, with the guard still holding us, she almost brought me and him down on top of her. "Ow! Ow! Ow!" Her howls reverberated in the shaft. "My ankle!" she cried, rubbing her tailbone.

"I'll get some ice," I said.

"Wait!" Jock shouted as I bounded back up the stairs and burst into the hotel proper. I was gone less than three minutes, jogging the halls in search of an ice machine, but when I returned, Jock was sitting on the stairs with Sonia, showing her a photograph, apparently to distract her from her pain. She beamed over her shoulder at me. "See? I told you she'd come back. Look, Jane! Aren't they cute?"

I exchanged the ice I'd carried in the bowl of my mask for the photograph. Two little girls posing on a fur rug. One was missing a tooth. "How old are they?" I asked.

"Seven now. They were five when that was taken."

Sonia rolled her sock down and delicately painted her ankle-bone with an ice cube. When the walkie-talkie sounded off again, she told him, "Just don't answer it. Is it fun, having twins?"

"It's fun now, but in the beginning—oh, my God. I wouldn't wish that on anybody."

"*Jock? Jock?*"

"Can you put any weight on it?"

"I'll try. Ow! Ow! Just a sec." She sank back on the stair and filled the sock with ice. It actually looked sore then. Using the railing, she hoisted herself to her feet. The grimace was real. "This should be interesting," she said, hopping down a step.

"I think we can use the elevator."

"No," said Sonia. "I don't want to get you in trouble. I can do it." She hopped down another step. I tried to look as blank as possible. There was a kind of bird that did this very thing, I remembered. It would feign a broken wing to save its offspring.

"That's the way," said Jock. "You're doing great."

When we had made it down to the twelfth floor, Sonia said, "I can't believe you don't worry about them."

"Who?"

"Sara and Michelle."

She knew their names!

"Who says I don't?" Jock said.

"I mean that you wouldn't do absolutely everything in your power to keep them safe. You seem so nice." He pulled his head back, insulted, and a few extra chins appeared. Sonia said, "I'd do anything for my child. Except that I don't have one and I never will."

"Why not, if you're so keen on them?"

"I couldn't. I couldn't bring a baby into the world knowing what's going to happen." She gripped the railing. Hop.

He stopped. "It's just a job, okay? A person has to have a job."

I jumped in again. "That's what everyone says. The people at the conference who make the weapons. Reagan. Andropov. They're just doing their jobs."

"We live in a free country," said Jock. "I'd like to keep it that way."

"Me too," Sonia said. "I hate politics. But this isn't about politics. It's about life."

"I get your point. I even agree with you—somewhat. But I still can't let you run around in here dressed up like that. I'll get fired. Then how am I going to feed my girls?"

"Would you call the police?" Sonia asked.

"Why? I'm here so the police don't have to be. I'm going to escort you out. Peacefully, right?"

"Of course," Sonia said.

I thought of something then. "We still have leaflets. You could put them with the tourist brochures later. No one would ever know it was you."

To see a person change his mind. It seemed more beautiful and moving than any sunset or spring flower. Here was a man who had believed one thing twenty minutes ago, who, before our very eyes, became convinced of something else. I gave Sonia all the credit. How had she done it? Not so much with words, though pleading was part of her success. It was mostly that you took one look at her and saw she embodied the fears of every child. You wanted to save *her* from any harm.

She took her remaining leaflets and turned to me for mine. The guard accepted them, slipping them into some secret pocket of his wonder jacket without a word. We went down the last three flights in silence, holding our breath in case he changed his mind. "Thank you," Sonia told him when we reached the bottom. Her eyes shone. "Thank you. You did a good thing today for Sara and Michelle. For the world. You should be proud of yourself."

He blushed, more so when she kissed him. Then she turned to me and did the same. She wrapped her thin arms around my neck and pulled me close. It was the first time anyone not related to me had kissed me and a tingling sensation started up where her lips touched my cheek. Jock opened the door and, cued by Sonia's nudge, took our arms again. We stepped out into a short corridor. Until we reached the lobby, the commotion didn't register. I was still dazed from the kiss.

"Fuck you! Fuck you all!"

A pair of guards in the same navy jackets was dragging Pete toward the revolving doors. All around the marbled atrium people stood and stared—the clerks at the front desk, the bellhops and the doormen, the men in suits, some scandalized by, some laughing at, Pete's tormented flailing.

"Fucking warmongers! I hope you all die!"

They shoved him—"Die, warmongers, die!"—into the glass cell of the door where we couldn't hear him any more. But we saw him—pounding on the glass, face twisted and unbeautiful.

Meeting afterward at the car was about the only thing that went according to the plan. No one got arrested. Except for Dieter, who had slipped unobtrusively out, we'd all been dragged or shoved out, depending on our state of limpness. Sonia and I didn't even try to go limp. We were too horrified by what Pete had yelled.

"What the fuck was that about?" Dieter asked him as we drove away. But Pete was disinclined to explain himself, why he had ignored the plan and, worse, discredited us.

"Something happened to me and Jane," Sonia piped up tearfully from the back. "We met this woman from the conference? She took a bunch of leaflets. She's going to give them out."

Pete snorted.

"She said she would! Didn't she, Jane?"

"He's always so negative," Belinda said.

"I'm always so negative? Why is that, I wonder? Maybe it's because the world is run by homicidal despots. Maybe the death sentence we're living under makes me feel just a little bit down."

He honked the horn. We were passing Timo on his ten-speed, crossing the bridge to meet up with us in Kits, one pant leg rolled to the knee so it wouldn't catch in the chain. He lifted his giant mushroom helmet and, when he saw us, glumly waved.

"And we made friends with our security guard. He was going to hand out leaflets too," Sonia said.

Pete: "Really? Maybe he'd like to join the group."

"Ha ha. He wouldn't anyway. He wouldn't because you yelled horrible things at everybody."

"Pete," said Pete, "was only trying to get arrested. Pete thought that was the point."

It had been. All over the world it was happening, all over Canada too. There was a group in Ontario, CMCP, the Cruise Missile Conversion Project, whose members were arrested regularly. There was ANVA, Alliance for Non-Violent Action, and ACT, Against Cruise Testing. All the way home I kept thinking that if we got pulled over, we would probably be arrested because Pete had cut the seat belts out of his car. And I wished we had a better acronym. Mostly, though, I thought about Sonia's kiss.

"Drop us off," Belinda ordered.

"I thought we were going to debrief," Pete told her, keeping his eyes fixed on her in the rear-view mirror—until I got nervous and tapped him on the arm. "Fuck," he muttered, accelerating.

After we let Belinda and Carla out on Blenheim Street, we drove home. Dieter stalked straight into the house while I lingered by the car. Neither Pete nor Sonia showed any signs of getting out. Pete was still behind the wheel in some furious kind of trance. Though Sonia had opened her door, she seemed to lack the strength to stand. "Is your ankle all right?" I asked.

"It's my bum that hurts," she said.

When Timo rode up on his bike, Pete finally got out and slammed the door. "Will you look at that?" he said, pointing. He must have noticed the gnome before, when it first sprang up with the snowdrops. It was merely the first available object on which to vent. "Is that or is that not," he said, rounding the car and heading for it, "the *second*-most-offensive lawn ornament you've ever seen?"

"Pete," Sonia bleated. "Don't."

"Sizism!" Pete bellowed. "I call that sizism! And here we've got a short person living next door! We've got Sonia! How's she going to feel looking at that every time she leaves the house?" Sonia grabbed his arm to hold him back but he jerked free and cupped his hands around his mouth. "SIZISTS!"

We all went in then, Pete upstairs to his boom box; Sonia and I debriefed with Timo in her room. I was glad Timo was there. Because of the kiss. I felt embarrassed now. Embarrassed by the kiss and embarrassed that I was still thinking about it and feeling its peppermint tingle, like Staff-Captain Ryabovitch with his lynx-like sidewhiskers. As soon as I thought of Ryabovitch, a different feeling overtook me, a nervous, trapped-bird fluttering.

Now that I knew it wasn't an affectation, I loved how Timo kept his pant leg rolled. It was the kind of detail Chekhov would put in a story. Panaurov lighting cigarettes off icon lamps; Timo Brandt, yellow curls damp and flattened by the helmet, going around with one pant leg calf-height. It summed up his character, his practicality, his enviable indifference to how he looked. Timo was soft. He was lazy. His feet were size sixteen. When he lay on the bed, the mattress roiled under his weight and the stuffed toys toppled. Sonia nestled beside him, her head on his chest. He looked right at me and patted his stomach so I crawled over too. We were like two children curled up with a damp, docile St. Bernard.

Sonia: "Do you think he put the leaflets in the rack?"

"What are you ttttalking about?" Timo asked.

"The security guard who caught us. He was going to put the leaflets out for us. What are the chances, Jane, of running into the two nicest people in the whole hotel?"

"You were the nicest person in the hotel," I said.

"Then Pete—" She sighed. "Now Jock probably hates us. He probably thinks we're the Squamish Five."

The trial of the Squamish Five was well under way now. Pete and Dieter were following it, talking about it every night at supper. Pete disagreed with their use of violence, but as he didn't believe in the court system or punitive justice, he was against the trial too. Dieter supported the group's goals but not their means, though he understood what had driven them to use force. By coincidence, the Squamish Five's most notorious bombing had taken place in Ontario, at the headquarters of the very company whose presence we had been protesting that day.

Timo stroked Sonia's hair. "You don't know what he was thinking."

"Look." She pulled up her sleeve to show us an arm mottled with what seemed like dirty fingerprints. Jock had changed back into his old self in the end—worse than his old self. He'd handled us quite roughly and I felt a delayed outrage now. How could Jock, or anyone, hurt Sonia? The marks were so blue against her skin.

"He seemed so nice," Sonia moaned.

"I know what you need," said Timo. "You need Chchchipits."

"No Chipits."

"Yes Chipits. They're in my pack, Jane."

I was beginning to feel sick anyway, my head rising and falling on the swell of Timo's belly. I got up and found the Chipits in his bag. Timo propped himself against the headboard and opened the package with his teeth. When he poured some into Sonia's hand, she gave me a look that said she would eat them, but only because of me.

I knew Timo was studying psychology so I asked his advice. "I'm worried about Sonia. She takes everything so hard."

"She's displaying a genuinely appppropriate response. We're sitting on six hundred thousand Hiroshimas."

"I'm burning out," she said. "I'm a falling star."

"She doesn't sleep," I said.

"Of course not," Timo said. "Listen. I've got an idea about renaming the streets. Can I tell you? The leaders of famous non-violent campaigns. So, Rosa Ppparks Street. Mahatma Gandhi Street. Nelson Mandela Street."

"We should name a street after Sonia," I said.

"Sonia Parker Street!" Timo cried. "Flowers everywhere! Free rides for children!"

Me: "Ice cream!"

"Isn't Timo wonderful?" Sonia asked me.

"Yes," I said. Except now, when she praised him, I felt a little rush of jealousy.

Not until Sunday's meeting did we learn the whole story of what went wrong. Instead of leafleting with Timo according to the plan, Pete had joined up with Belinda and Carla, following behind them, getting between them. This had enraged the women. They felt harassed. Finally, Pete gave up and went down to the lobby, where he started handing out leaflets to everyone in "fascist dress."

Meetings. Meetings to debrief the fiasco. Meetings to debrief the debriefing. Meetings to reaffirm our commitment to peace and non-violence. Accusations (aimed at Pete—I was relieved Dieter never brought up how I, too, had abandoned the plan), weeping (Belinda, Sonia), then reconciling hugs (everyone) and (finally, finally) we moved on without ever extracting an apology from Pete, though that was what everyone seemed secretly to want.

"People? What I meant was 'go ahead and die *if you want.*' That's what it amounts to. That's the choice they're making.

I didn't mean I personally wanted them dead. That's ludicrous. I'm an anarcho-*pacifist*."

As soon as we began planning the next action, it became obvious that a coolness had developed between everyone and Pete. Physically it manifested in the way, during these meetings, he drifted off alone on the ice floe of the beanbag chair while the rest of us stuck to the shore on the other side of the room. I felt differently toward him too, warier, though I believed his explanation. Certainly relations froze over between him and Belinda because, after that, she was never at the Trutch house except for meetings.

All this internal strife affected Sonia. If the group was fighting, we weren't working for peace. If we weren't working for peace, we were slipping perilously closer to the apocalypse. The downing of Korean Airlines Flight 007. The stationing of cruise missiles in West Germany. Now Andropov was dead. She resumed her visits to the stove, something she hadn't done since the night she brought me to *If You Love This Planet.* But I found a way to stop her. I began reading through the grate.

"*The appearance on the front of a new arrival—a lady with a lap dog—became the topic of general conversation.*"

"Stop!" she called up.

I changed books and began again. "*On 20 May, at eight o'clock in the evening, all six batteries of a reserve artillery brigade, on their way back to headquarters, stopped for the night in the village of Mestechki.*"

"Not that either!"

They were too sad. Instead of "Lady with a Lapdog" or "The Kiss," she preferred "A Case History" and "The Fiancée" with their idealistic heroines, Liza and Nadya, both of them insomniacs, like Sonia. I read to her until she fell asleep and, afterward, I read on silently, now and then pausing to underscore something else that seemed written expressly to me.

Whether the sky is covered with clouds or the moon and stars shine in it, on returning home I always look up and think that I shall soon be dead.

What we learned from the Hyatt action was that we needed more than a plan. We needed to rehearse, so for the next action, renaming the streets, we conducted practice runs and for part of every meeting acted out scenarios that Belinda devised and directed. Since we couldn't realistically change all the signs in the city, we settled on a single neighbourhood, our own, Kitsilano. In a single night we would turn it back into the peaceful haven it had been in the sixties when hippies instead of yuppies lived there. Getting arrested wasn't part of the plan. This time we aimed for something nobler: that the morning after, everyone living on those streets previously named for slaughter would wake and find themselves at peace. So Trafalgar Street became Caldicott Street and Balaclava, M. L. King Jr. Street. Blenheim changed to Gandhi Street and Waterloo to Mandela Street. People on Dunbar now resided on Chomsky Street. Alma became *Kropotkinskaya Ulitsa*.

During the preparatory weeks I found myself wondering if words alone could really make a difference. I knew from studying Russian that they sometimes did. *Morozhenoye* is so difficult to pronounce that Russian children aren't allowed to eat it until they can say it. It was not ice cream as I knew it in a plastic tub from the store, but a hand-churned nineteenth-century confection jewelled with wild strawberries. The strawberries were mandatory. *Chay* was drunk in a glass with a saucer of jam on the side. And I wondered, if we lived a few blocks east, where the streets were named after trees instead of battles—Larch, Balsam, Yew—would we quarrel so much?

We had to wait for a clear night. They weren't that common in late February, but finally one arrived and we set off after midnight on bicycles. Pete and I were the vanguard. "Imagine if we lived here in the sixties, Zed? In the sixties *student* was synonymous with *radical*. Now it's synonymous with *polo shirt*." As the vanguard, we blacked out the original names while the others followed with the stencils.

It was the first time I'd been out all night. It was also the first time I'd drunk beer, which I didn't like even when Sonia diluted it with lemonade, the way she preferred it. Yet the little I drank had an exhilarating effect, as did the lot everyone else drank. Pete brought down his boom box and we pushed aside the furniture and danced in a circle to Janis Joplin and The Doors. With Timo jogging on the spot, curls bouncing, and Belinda whipping the floor with her hair, "*Come on, come on, come on, come on!*" no one knew, or noticed, or probably cared, that I'd never danced before.

When it started to get light, we stepped out of the house holding hands. *It was the first time in his life he had seen the sunrise.* Rechristened, the streets were indeed peaceful at that hour. People were only starting to leave for work. As we broke the flesh and blood chain of our clasp to let each car through, everyone waved. "Excuse me?" Belinda called to a paperboy flinging lies onto porches. "Do you know the way to Gandhi Street?" He grinned and returned the peace sign that we flashed. I don't think I imagined the perfumed air. The only disappointment this time was how quickly the status quo was restored. Two days later, all the signs had been changed back.

Because of this action, as well as the more ambitious one we started planning for next, my studies began to suffer. I felt distracted in tutorials and barely scored 70 percent on my Russian quiz on irregular past tenses. I couldn't blame this entirely on my desire to save the world. Filling Sonia's shoes with Russian words, drinking tea with her (Japanese style if we went to her

room, Russian style in mine), rearranging my room so that my
futon was next to the grate, reading to her through it—for me,
these were the real actions. After she dozed off, it would take me
an hour or more to calm myself because, near her, even if there
was a floor between us, I felt jittery with happiness. I couldn't forget the kiss any more than I could forget its literary antecedent.

   Still, I wouldn't name the feeling, couldn't admit to love,
not even to *lyubov*.

For the subject of my final term paper in Nineteenth-Century
Russian Literature in Translation I chose *Anna Karenina*.
I wanted to write something about Levin's second proposal to
Kitty, whom he asks to marry early in the book, only to be
refused because Kitty expects an offer from the dashing Count
Vronsky. It takes Levin another three hundred and sixty pages
to get over his wounded pride and ask for her hand again, which
he finally does while Kitty is sitting at a card table doodling with
a piece of chalk. Fear of a second rejection renders him mute.
Levin takes the chalk and writes the letters w-y-t-m-*i-c-n-b*-d-y-
m-n-o-t? He means, *When you told me* it could not be—*did that
mean never or then?* He hands her the chalk and she writes: T-I-c-
n-a-d. *Then I could not answer differently.* They continue like this,
writing on the felt top of the table, declaring their love in code.

   I was intrigued by the scene. In one way their reserve seemed
anti-romantic, a contrast to Anna and Vronsky, who have no dif-
ficulty communicating their passion. Yet as the novel progresses,
Anna and Vronsky's ideal romance flags while Kitty and Levin's
marriage, portrayed with all its flaws, grows more delightful.
I hadn't begun to formulate my thesis. All I knew was that it
had to do with language and that I wanted to write a paper that
would please Professor Kopanyev and make up for my stuporous
performance of late.

In the chapter where Kitty first meets Anna, I read this sentence: *It was obvious that Anna admired her beauty and youth, and before Kitty knew where she was she felt herself not only under Anna's sway but in love with her, as young girls do fall in love with married women older than themselves.*

Do they?

I got up for a drink of water and, realizing then how stiff I was from lying on my futon all morning, decided to go out for a walk. I left the house and for several blocks walked with my head down, agitated but pretending not to be, trying to think about my paper without thinking about the implications of that line, so by the time I reached Kropotkin Street and looked up, what I saw stopped me in mid-stride: the avenue ahead in full frothy bloom, as though a pink mist was streaming down it on both sides. I crossed quickly over. A cumulus of blossoms. Overnight these few blocks of Third Avenue had been transformed. Nature had performed this action which, indisputably, trumped ours. All at once I felt like sobbing, the way I had at the end of *If You Love This Planet* when Dr. Caldicott declares how deeply in love she is with the world and how seeing it in spring especially makes you realize you have to change the priorities of your life. Maybe it was the tears in my eyes, but everything seemed magnified, more intensely coloured, *pinker*. I desperately loved the world! That was what I was feeling, I decided. The pure embrace of life.

I broke off a cluster of blossoms that, back home, I placed in a glass of water on my card table. Over the next few hours I kept glancing up at it, reassuring myself I hadn't dreamed what I'd seen and felt.

Mid-afternoon Sonia called up and asked what I was doing. "Reading," I said.

Ya chitayu.

I got an idea. I plucked all the petals off the branch, waited a minute, then called her name. When she appeared under the grate, I released them, pink, liberated moths, watching as they fluttered down on her smiling, upturned face.

One hundred and forty-nine pages later, Kitty, having been made physically ill when Vronsky abruptly transfers his attentions to Anna, is taken by her mother to a German spa. There she meets a Russian girl of her own age, Varenka, and *Kitty, as often happens, felt an inexplicable attraction to this Mademoiselle Varenka.*

The similarities disturbed me: *as young girls do, as often happens.* Did it? I knew it happened now, because of Carla, but I had assumed that lesbianism was a modern phenomenon, that it had to do with feminism, with taking a stand against men, not with love. But now I read in a book more than a hundred years old that Kitty *was aware, when their eyes met, that Mademoiselle Varenka liked her too.*

Five chapters are dedicated to Kitty's obsession with Varenka, chapters that had apparently not seemed very important the first time I read the novel since I barely remembered them. Varenka, Kitty decides from a distance, while pretty, is *not likely to be attractive to men.* The two women see each other daily in passing but, not having been formally introduced, are obliged to communicate with their eyes. Kitty's eyes say, *Are you the delightful being I imagine you to be?* and Varenka's answer, *I like you too, and you are very very sweet.*

Kitty begs her mother for an introduction until the Princess Shcherbatsky, weary of these entreaties, approaches the Russian girl at last. *"My daughter has lost her heart to you."*

Varenka: *"It is more than reciprocal, Princess."*

And so they finally meet. *Kitty blushed with happiness, long and silently pressing her new friend's hand, which did not return her pressure but lay passively in hers. The hand did not respond to her pressure but Mademoiselle Varenka's face glowed with a soft, pleased, though rather sad smile. . . .*

Exactly the way Sonia's looked when I showered her with petals! I remembered, too, how she had held my hand during that first NAG! meeting, and my confusion about what to do. I, too, had gone limp. Like Kitty, I blushed now.

Kitty becomes *more and more fascinated by her friend, enraptured* by her. Soon she learns that Varenka has also been wounded in love. "*Why, if I were a man, I could never care for anyone else after knowing you,*" Kitty tells Varenka.

"*How good you are, how good!*" *exclaimed Kitty and, stopping her, she kissed her.*

She kissed her.

I touched my face, feeling that tingle again. No, I couldn't write about it. As I reshelved *Anna Karenina* in the milk crate, the word *palpitations* came to mind, though it felt more like my heart was hurling itself against the bars of its cage. Eventually these protestations subsided. I had other, more pressing things to distract me: our date with the end of the world, my long mental slog toward another essay topic.

At our next house meeting we decided to have a party. After the requisite bickering, we reached consensus on a date—the following Friday—who, and how many people we would invite, and what each of us would do to get ready. Then, on Friday, I came home to an unusual domestic scene, Sonia on her knees angrily scrubbing the kitchen floor while Pete sat cross-legged on the table, well out of her way, shelling peanuts into his lap.

"Let me," I begged her. "I'll do it."

"That's not the point," she said.

The point was that we, the women, were yet again cleaning while they, the men, were not. Sonia glared at Pete. I hurried out with the teeming compost, knocking another rotting stave off the fence in my eagerness to stay in the we that included her.

When I came back with the empty bowl, Pete waved me over and dumped his shells in it.

Since hinting wasn't working, Sonia sat up on her haunches and asked him outright: "Pete! Why aren't you helping us?"

"I got the snacks." He waved the bag of peanuts.

"When we said we'd get the house ready, we meant put the food out and decorate. We didn't mean do everybody's chores."

"So put the food out and decorate."

Her little nostrils quivered. The effect was charming. "You go around saying you're a feminist! If you really were, you'd help!"

"Wrong. I really am a feminist, therefore I refuse to treat you differently than I'd treat a man." He cheerfully cracked another shell with his perfect teeth. "Ask Dieter. He'd be happy to patronize you."

This was why anarchism would never work, I thought. No one would ever want to wash the kitchen floor. When I made the mistake of voicing this, Pete replied, "Wrong, Zed. This is actually an example of how perfectly anarchism works. Someone always wants the kitchen floor to be clean. In this case, Sonia wants it to be clean, so she's washing it. She's washing it of her own free will. If I relinquished my principles and went ahead and washed it, even though I'm perfectly satisfied with the condition of the floor, I wouldn't be an anarchist. Because an anarchist will not be limited in the exercise of his will by fear of punishment or by obedience to any person or metaphysical entity. He—or she—is guided in his—or her—own actions by his—or her—own personal understanding and ethical conceptions."

Dieter walked in then and Sonia got up off the floor and threw the sopping rag at him. It slapped his chest with a horse-dungy plop that made me laugh out loud. Sonia shrieked that she was on strike and ran out.

"Asshole," Dieter told Pete.

"I didn't do anything."

Dieter dropped his books on the table and, tugging his pant legs at the thigh, got down on all fours. I knew then that he still liked Sonia, though he hardly bothered her any more. His glasses hung off his face as he worked, clinging to his temples by the arms. Pete kept on cracking peanuts.

I went after Sonia and, finding her lying on the meadow of her bedspread, sat down to watch the fortunate air filling her up, the unfortunate air leaving. I felt so awkward around her now, a different kind of awkwardness than when I had first moved in. Then I had felt invisible, but now I felt far too obvious, like the sleeve I wore my heart on was fluorescent or Hawaiian.

"I'm exhausted," she said after a minute.

"You should have waited for me to get home. I would have helped."

"It's not just that. Jane? After exams? After my practicum?"

"Yes?"

She was staring up at nothing. "Do you want to move out? We can get an apartment."

"Together?" I said.

"Yes."

It was hours before it really sunk in and the euphoria hit. What she said and her proviso: "If we're still alive, I mean."

We had said eight o'clock but no one came until almost ten, after which the house was full of noise. Some of Dieter's *amigos* turned up, including Hector, back from Victoria in the hope that his refugee application would finally be processed. For this Latin American contingent we played music happy with maracas, buoyant with unintelligible choruses, until midnight, when Pete brought down his milk crate of tapes and put on *Purple Haze*. People from SPND and EAR were there, too, and everyone from NAG! Belinda and Carla had set up in the kitchen, Belinda straddling a backward chair while Carla wove tiny braids into her hair. Several times during the evening Pete came in and asked, "Are you done yet?" to which Belinda replied, "God," without looking up.

I tagged along while Sonia hugged everyone and made sure they had drinks. Everything she did—replenishing the chip bowl, stashing a six-pack in the fridge—she did with grace. I was *fascinated, enraptured.* Then Ruth came over. "Can I talk to you, Jane?"

"I'm helping Sonia," I said and blushed. The adoration in my voice. So obvious! I followed Ruth out in case she'd noticed.

No one was in the living room despite all the effort Sonia and I had put into festooning it with cranes. Ruth closed the French doors after us then slumped on the chesterfield and, face in her hands, began to cry. I was supposed to hug her, I knew, but I didn't. I waited until she had blotted her tears on her paisley scarf. Taking a few pulls from the bottle jammed between her thighs, she said, "I'd do anything, Jane."

"For whom?"

She burped into her fist. "To get into NAG! I know you're in now. Sonia told me. How did you do it?"

I felt sorry for her and told the truth: "I live here."

"I knew it! I tried so hard. You have no idea how hard I tried to get in. I even sucked up to Dieter." Ruth started to sob in earnest now and, embarrassed, I looked out the ponchoed window. Someone was coming up the walk in moon boots. More than out of season, the glowing white boots were out of climate, but I was accustomed to strange garb by then, to T-shirts that screamed slogans, to tie-dye in the full spectrum of purple, to work socks worn with long Indian cotton skirts, to Birkenstocks, buffalo sandals, huaraches, clogs. He set down the duffle bag he was carrying and removed something from it—a book.

"I'm so depressed," Ruth said.

How strange that our roles should be reversed, that Ruth with her barely blue eyes and blond hair and her pretty peach-fuzzed face should be miserable while I was so exultant. Strange, too, that I had the power to save the night for her. All I had to do was tell her why I was so happy. Ruth was drinking with intent now. I said, "Sonia and I are moving out."

She looked at me. "When?"

"After finals."

"Thank you," she gasped.

"Together," I added, in case she hadn't understood that I loved Sonia. There. I'd finally admitted it.

"So *two* rooms will be free?" she said, incredulous.

The doorbell rang and, tingling all over from my confession, I went to answer it. The book was under his arm now, the duffle on the porch, a dark grey parka with a fake fur–trimmed hood draped over it. I only noticed because it was the same coat that got so many boys through Alberta winters, that boys all over Canada wore, presumably, but that I'd never seen in Vancouver because parkas were unnecessary. His hair, brown and wavy, flopped in his eyes.

"Does Dieter Koenig live here?" he asked in a voice thick with hope.

I nodded and stepped aside; he whisked the duffle in with him. There was something so comical about how he did it, bowing and bobbing and brushing away the hair, that the people who were hanging around in the vestibule smiled. Or maybe it was the boots. "Go ahead," I said. "I think he's on the deck." Just then Ruth came out of the living room, blotted and beaming, and I hurried after the newcomer before she had the chance to thank me physically.

"Through that door." I pointed.

Sonia, tidying the counters, collecting empties, smiled at me. *How good you are, how good!* I thought, as Dieter's friend in the boots came clomping back inside, the book clutched to his chest like a flat black breastplate. "I don't see him," he told me.

We went out together where about a dozen people braved the chill. Dieter was in the corner with Hector, the two of them talking with their hands. When Dieter spoke English, even when Hector did, their arms hung limply at their sides. English seemed to bring on a semi-paralysis, while Spanish animated everyone who spoke it. I wondered what Russian did. Made you drink vodka probably. "Dieter!" I called over the voices, the boom-box maracas, and pointed to Moon Boots, who raised a tentative hand and smiled. Dieter waved back blankly. A joint that was circulating reached us just then and Moon Boots took it with wide eyes, looking from the person who'd passed it, to me, as though he'd won a prize.

I went back inside where Sonia was telling a man in a Question Authority T-shirt about the renaming of the streets. "Far out," he kept saying. "Far out." Ruth was bubbling away to Pete, who unwound the scarf from her neck and draped it over her head like a dust cloth over a lamp. She carried on giggling and saying flirty things, even after Pete walked off. Then Moon Boots came in for a second time and, noticing Ronald Reagan hanging on the nail, stopped to put the mask on. The notebook slid out from under his arm and he stooped to retrieve it, almost tripping someone else coming in from the deck. He tugged the mask off, bobbed an apology, was just attempting an exit, seemingly before something else could go wrong, when Sonia nabbed him. "You don't have a drink."

His eyes darted. "Milk?"

Sonia poured him a glass out of her carton, handing it to him with a suppressed smile. We watched him glug it, saw the pump in his throat and the residue above his lip, the only moustache he looked capable of growing. His jawline was spackled with zits.

Sonia: "I like your boots."

He looked down at them. We all cracked up.

A siren woke me. I thought it was a scream until the fire truck rumbled past. It would be hours before anyone else got up, I assumed. But Sonia was at the kitchen table when I went down, in her pyjamas, cradling her headache in her hands. First I surveyed the devastation, then I put the kettle on. "Go back to bed," I told her. "I'll clean it up."

"Why should you?"

Because I wanted to. Because I loved her. Because I wanted to make her happy.

"It was fun last night," she said. "I feel so guilty whenever I have fun. That's when it's going to happen. When we least expect it. Reagan's just waiting for me to look the other way so he can press the button."

"Did you sleep?" I asked.

"No. Tell me the truth, Jane. Is my insomnia honourable or am I just torturing myself?"

This was a reference to Dr. Korolyov in "A Case History." "*So you're not sleeping,*" he tells Liza, the young, conscience-stricken textile factory heiress. "*It's lovely outside, spring has come. The nightingales are singing and here you are sitting in the dark, brooding.*" Outside, the watchman bangs two o'clock, and Korolyov sees Liza tremble and notices that *her eyes were sad and clever, and clearly she longed to tell him something.*

Korolyov: "*Your insomnia is something honourable: whatever you may think, it's a good sign.*"

"I want to be a Liza," Sonia said. "I want it so badly."

"You already are one."

"I'm not. I'm not. I won't be able to save anybody. The bomb will fall. We'll all die."

She'd saved me. I wanted to tell her that but just then she turned away, toward the window. I brought the teapot and jar of jam over, clearing a space in the mess to set them down. Then I saw what she was looking at. Someone was coming up the stairs to the deck wearing a bizarre sort of robe, long and padded with a fur-trimmed hood. He walked like he was dragging one leg behind him. My first reaction was shock, that some crazy person had wandered into our yard. Then the robe detached from the hood and became the sleeping bag he slung over the deck railing. I saw the moon boots. "That's Dieter's friend," I said.

Sonia tapped on the window. He swung around and looked at us and, in that moment, hair flopping in his eyes, he seemed very, very young. It was hard to tell how old anyone really was. Sonia looked young too, because she was small, while Pete, so forceful, seemed older. Belinda always struck me as being at the height of maturity—maybe as much as twenty-five. Hector probably was that old, but all of us in NAG! were eighteen or nineteen at most. We may have called ourselves *women* and *men* but we were barely adults.

Sonia opened the door to the deck for him. "Tea?" she asked, flitting to the cupboard for another mug. Sand rained on the floor as he shed the coat. He took the white boots off, then his socks, which were wet and, like the bottom of his pants, encrusted with sand. "Sorry." He tiptoed to the sink and wrung them out.

"Is it raining?" Sonia asked.

"No." He set the ball of socks on the table next to his mug.

"We've been drinking our tea with jam," she said. "That's how they drink it in Russia. It's delicious." She nudged the jar toward him and he added several spoonfuls, dipping each one again and again until the spoon came out clean and the tea looked like diluted blood. Sonia and I traded smiles the way we had the night before when he chose milk over beer.

"I slept on the beach," he said.

"Wasn't it cold?"

"No. It's like spring."

"It is spring," I pointed out.

"Really?" he said, which Sonia seemed to find funny. "Then, in the middle of the night? I woke up? There was water right up to my knees!"

"The tide came in," she said.

"I didn't know it did that."

"What's your name?"

"Pascal."

2 0 0 4

The residue of a dream was still on me when I woke, not surprisingly, given my conversation with Joe Jr. the night before. As for the dream's content, I remembered nothing; it was flying below the radar, low against the contours of my dread. My head ached at the temples and I lay there hoping the pain would pass. Eventually I gave in, put my slippers on, and went and took a pill. By then both Joes had already left the house. Joe Jr. must have had track practice. When I saw his empty bed, I felt even guiltier for having sat on him.

I looked at Tuesday's paper. (Tuesday—Maria was coming.) There was no mention of Sonia and Pete. It was old news now and I left it on the table for Maria to do with as she pleased. A second cup of coffee in hand, I went to my office and found lying on my computer keyboard the article that had caused so much agony the day before, retrieved by Joe, I guess. So I finally read it and, like he said, there was nothing new in it other than Sonia had completed her sentence and Pete had five more years to serve. It hardly warranted the fuss I'd made over it. It certainly didn't tell me what I wanted to know.

When I checked my e-mail, the promised manuscript was there to distract me, a novel, 528 pages long, partly historical, starting with the discovery of some letters in a Toronto basement.

The headache intensified as soon as I started reading, not so much because the device of found letters always rings false, though it does. Why? I know my own mother has kept every letter I've ever written her and probably stores them in a proverbial trunk. There was nothing wrong with the writing other than it strained to be poetic and wasn't by Turgenev or Tolstoy.

"Hello, Jane! I am here!" Maria called as she came in. I shouted back a greeting, then tried to forget about her even though I could hear her maniacal humming as she got to work bashing around in the cleaning cupboard. I glanced in the stained bottom of my mug, took down the first volume of the Shorter Oxford, checked the word *annealed*. What could she be doing to make so much noise? Finally she stopped but then a *clank, clank, clank* started up. Somewhere someone was banging on something. Nice for the headache. Very soothing.

I read more of the manuscript, but it was tough going by then and I felt like a member of a search party, whacking my way through excess description, desperate to find the missing story.

Several years ago I copied a quote out on an index card and tacked it to the wall above my desk. I had no idea where it had gone. Probably it fell behind the desk and, since it was obviously important, Maria vacuumed it up. The book I originally took it from was on the undusted shelf. (She sucks up cards but she doesn't dust.) I flipped through it until I found the familiar passage.

> *Here is more advice: when you read proofs, take out adjectives and adverbs wherever you can. You use so many of them that the reader finds it hard to concentrate and he gets tired. You understand what I mean when I say, "The man sat on the grass." You understand because the sentence is clear and there is nothing to distract your attention. Conversely the brain has*

trouble understanding me if I say, "A tall, narrow-chested
man of medium height with a red beard sat on the green grass
trampled by passersby, sat mutely, looking about timidly and
fearfully." This doesn't get its meaning through to the brain
immediately, which is what good writing must do, and fast.

It's from a letter Chekhov wrote to Maxim Gorky. The comment box on the screen expanded as I transcribed it, stretching
halfway down the margin of the page. When I finished typing,
I reread it, then, remembering my lowly station as a copy editor,
I backspaced it all away.

Until that moment I'd assumed the clanking was coming
from outside, but all at once I recognized the sound. The *clank,*
clank, clank of the watchman beating out the hour. The past
catching up. So this was it? The past was here? Now? I felt a
wave of nausea and put my head down on the desk.

Actually, it was Maria. Two more clanks passed in dishpan
annoyance, then I got up and followed the sound down the hall.
When I peeked in the kitchen, I saw her broad back, lumpy
around the bra straps, turned toward me, the cutlery basket
from the dishwasher tucked under her thick arm. With a furious
robotic regularity, she was tossing them, knife, fork, spoon, into
the drawer.

I sighed and went in. It's my kitchen, after all. "How are you,
Maria?"

"Wonderful," she said, lifting a red hand to wipe her forehead.

"Spring is here."

"Ya."

Maria is one of those short, broad women who compensate
for lack of stature with radiant health and intimidating energy,
a sort of Slovakian Mrs. Claus. Joe and I have reinvented her
life story many times during the three years she's cleaned for us.

We know for a fact she's a mail-order bride. Her aged Canadian husband, her cleaning pimp, drops her off and picks her up in one of those big American guzzlers that have got us into this latest mess. He looks about eighty so we know she must have escaped something awful to be so cheerful about her new life. Sometimes it's a sausage factory, sometimes a remote pig farm in the Tatra Mountains.

I started making a fresh pot of coffee. "I do it," she said.

"You're busy with other things."

"I do both. Sit." She pointed to a chair and, before she could take me by the shoulders and force me down in it, I obeyed. I hate how I go limp in her presence. I know I should be ordering her around, but she orders me. I watched her scoop the grounds into the filter basket with one hand and with the other remove the burner rings off the stove and immerse them in the sink full of soapy water with zeal enough to drown a bag of kittens. It made me so tired that I picked up the newspaper again.

The main story was about the ongoing commission of inquiry into the treatment of a Canadian man who had been arrested in transit in New York, flown in shackles to Syria, his country of birth, then kept in a grave-like cell for over ten months until a false confession was tortured out of him. Maria paused in her scrubbing to look over. "Ah," she tsked, seeing the innocent man's photograph. "Those terrorists."

Last night my son asked me if that was what I had been. When he said the word, I sank onto the bed, clutching my heart. "Is that what the article said?" I asked.

"No. It said those other two were."

"Pete and Sonia? It's not true."

"We Googled you."

"Who?"

"Me and Simon."

I should have guessed. This explained Simon's peculiar behaviour, the aberration of the normal optical pattern, the slowing of the dart, the *interest*. I was embarrassed on another count as well. I'm thirty-nine years old, I earn my living on a computer, yet I've never even thought of Googling myself.

Joe Jr.: "You got, like, three hundred and twenty-six hits, Mom. Simon's mom? She's a zilch." He puffed up a bit when he told me this. "Want to see?" The laptop was there on the floor, asking to be stepped on.

"It's all right," I said.

He was too excited to keep what he'd learned to himself, or to notice that I didn't want to hear it. "A couple of sites said you went by an alias."

"I did?"

"Zed."

"Oh my God."

"They said you were anarchists, or anti-nuclear activists, or terrorists. Did you help make the bomb?"

"Are you serious? I didn't know anything about it."

He canted forward, finger raised, and tossed the covers aside. "Hold on a sec. I have to pee."

I would never get back to sleep now, so I asked, "Do you want hot milk?"

"Sure."

I went to the kitchen and put the pot on the stove. My hands were shaking as I poured the milk, but I also felt a sort of wonderment to be talking to my son like this. I couldn't remember the last time I wasn't in competition with the soundtrack, the last time we'd had a real conversation. I talk all the time, of course, but without any confidence that what he hears bears any relation to what I'm saying, if he hears anything beyond an incessant flow of blahs. When I came back with the mugs,

I couldn't help but smile; he'd fixed his hair for me. "Thanks," he said as I passed him his drink.

"Joey, Dad told me he called you at school. I'm annoyed at him for going behind my back."

"Oh, he does it all the time," said the son we raised to be honest. "Just little things! So who made the bomb?"

I sat on the end of the bed, leaning against the wall, cringing. "We were *peace* activists. We dressed up in radiation suits and handed out leaflets."

I thought this would sound pathetic enough to douse his interest, but instead he asked, "For real? Where?"

"The Hyatt Regency."

"No way. Where did you get the suits?"

"They were paper coveralls like painters use. With radiation symbols drawn on the back." I guess he pictured me in this get-up with my trusted slippers on because he smiled. "Pretty hokey," I conceded. "Anyway, like I said, it was harmless."

"But you just mope around all day and read! You hardly even leave the house!"

"I do too!" I said. "How do you think all that food gets in the fridge?"

He filtered more hot milk through the smirk. "That's just so cool, Mom. It's so cool I'm having trouble believing you."

"I can see that. And I do work, by the way. I have a contract right now."

"Why didn't you ever tell me about this stuff? I wish you had!"

He didn't understand. How to explain the terror? "Remember 9/11? Remember how scared you were? That's what we felt like all the time. There were so many missiles pointed at us. The last thing we wanted was that somebody would get hurt. But people did."

"Just that one guy."

I didn't correct him. I didn't tell him about Pascal. I said, "One is too many."

"So where did the bomb come from?"

We could be up all night. He had school tomorrow if it wasn't too tedious, so, mustering some parental sternness, I relieved him of his empty mug. "It's almost three. Can we talk about it tomorrow?"

"You won't," he said. "You'll change the subject."

"I promise." My stomach churned as I said it, but Joe Jr. lay down. As a joke, I tucked him in and kissed him above his piercings. And he actually let me do these things.

That was last night. Now I found out my cleaning lady was caught up in the current "terrorist" frenzy. ("Communist" used to be the catch-all label.) "They should shoot them," Maria said, gesturing at the paper. "They are animals."

I bristled. "Maria, this man was falsely accused. No one denies it any more. He suffered terrible treatment. He was tortured."

The coffee maker made a loud, intestinal sound. I might have taken that as a warning, but I didn't. I decided to make a case for due process with my cleaning lady. I explained that even though al-Qaeda disdains due process, Western democracies have to take the high road. "They can't start playing dirty and kidnapping and torturing people, or holding them without charges for years. Then we're no better." And while she polished the stove and put it back together like a puzzle, I said, "I'm not condoning what real terrorists do, or saying that people who have been properly tried and convicted shouldn't be punished. But dissent is what strengthens democracy, not suppression. And while we're at it, we might listen to some of their complaints. They honestly believe that Western society is evil. I mean, *I* honestly believe some aspects of Western society are evil. I believe, for example, that excess materialism is evil. That plastic bags are evil. I heard on the radio the other day that samples taken from remote beaches in the Orkneys and Outer Hebrides—do you know where they are? These tiny islands in northern Scotland where there are practically no people?"

She set my coffee down on the newspaper.

"The samples were heavily, *very* heavily, contaminated with plastic molecules."

Standing there with her hands on her hips—yet another overbearing Slav in my life. How? I wondered. How had she got herself hired? And how had I got on to plastic bags? And what about the missiles, for that matter? The Berlin Wall came down, the Soviet Union collapsed, and almost overnight the arms race ended, making the entire anti-nuclear movement obsolete. A succession of causes rushed in to fill the void. Land mines. Globalization. War in the Middle East. Climate change. The sky keeps falling. But what happened to the missiles? No one mentions them.

No. What has really been bothering me, what has been eating me for twenty years, is that Sonia was no terrorist.

"Do you realize, Maria," I said, deciding to drop both the bags and the missiles and focus on the real point, that the innocent, sadly, are expendable, "like this man"—I moved the coffee cup to point at his photograph. It left a damp ring behind like we were seeing him through a marksman's sights—"many, if not most, of those people they're holding without charge over there in Cuba? They've done nothing wrong."

As I waited for her reply, I remembered how tragically she lost her first husband, in one version to crazed pigs, in the other when he fell into the meat-grinding machine. Yet she could still smile! Such fortitude! What an example she was! Her rosy face fairly crinkled with mirth as she told me, "Chop their heads off. That would be better. That's what they do to us. I get you sugar."

1 9 8 4

At first I didn't realize he was still with us. The morning after the party he helped us clean up, literally running the vacuum up and down the hall. He asked to use the shower, then hung around the rest of the morning waiting for his sleeping bag to dry out. I saw him roll and stuff it into the duffle bag and assumed, when he walked away, it was for good.

Most of the following week there was no sign of him when I got home, only Pete strung along the chesterfield, cheering on the Road Runner with the peanut butter jar balanced on his chest. But on Thursday I came home early because something upsetting had happened in Kopanyev's class. Pascal's book was lying on the kitchen table with a felt-tipped marker tucked in its pages. I opened it, saw our address and phone number on the inside cover. The rest of it was drawings.

In the beginning they were all of the same two people, a man and woman, each captured in an ordinary act—shovelling snow, cooking, reading the newspaper. There was a sketch of a ranch-style house I assumed the sketch couple lived in, then a self-portrait in a bathroom mirror. A Greyhound bus. The driver. Dozing passengers. Scenes out a window. I turned the page. Sonia! In a few lines he'd managed to capture her worried, soulful essence. There was a drawing of Carla braiding Belinda's hair. Of Dieter gesticulating. I hadn't noticed Pascal creeping around the party, executing us in ink.

Next (assuming he filled the book chronologically), he'd drawn scenes down at the beach: the view across to the mountains, an empty lifeguard chair, a huddle of old Vietnamese men fishing off the dock. The rest of the book was blank. He must have left it behind the morning after the party. Someone had found it and set it out. Or so I thought.

But that night it poured. When Sonia got up to practise with the stove, I woke too and hurried downstairs to stop her. I found her in the living room, cross-legged on the floor with something white cradled in her lap. I had to look twice.

A boot.

"Shhh," she said.

He was asleep on the chesterfield, palms together, cheek resting on the back of his hand. "He looks so peaceful," she said.

"There's a chore sheet on the fridge." Dieter pointed to it. "Sign up for something."

"Okay. Now?"

"Sure."

Pascal abandoned his toast, all the pieces making a crooked tower on the plate.

"Another thing. We take turns cooking. Sonia told you about the kitty, right?"

"There's a kitty?" He looked from the chore sheet to the floor around his feet.

"Here." Dieter flipped open the cupboard where our scant treasure dwindled in the bottom of the lidless Mason jar. "Every Sunday we each put in twenty dollars. What else?"

Upstairs, the music shut off and I instinctively braced for the seismic event of Pete stomping down. "Tell him about the compost," I said.

"There's a compost."

"What's a compost?"

Dieter was gobsmacked. "*What's a compost?*" Then Pete blew into the room and over to the fridge. "Another thing," Dieter went on. "On Sunday night? Our affinity group meets here. Are you going to be here on Sunday night?"

"I'm not sure. Can I stay till Sunday?"

"If you want, but you should make yourself scarce around five."

Pete fed himself a handful of granola, chasing it with milk from my carton. "Why?" he asked. "Maybe he'd like to join the group."

Dieter looked at his watch. "We should get going."

"If you weren't so busy keeping people *out* of the movement."

Pascal: "Can I use the phone to make a long distance call? I'll pay for it."

Pete said, "I wouldn't. The phone is tapped," and Pascal goggled.

When I'd first heard about it last fall, I'd dismissed the phone tap as just another conspiracy theory (there were plenty of those; rumours of RCMP spies abounded). Now that the trial of the Squamish Five was in the news, I learned that the RCMP *had* been tapping that group's phone. That was how they knew who had bombed the pornographic video stores, how they found out about the cache of stolen dynamite in the mountains. Except, Pete's outburst at the Hyatt notwithstanding, we were non-violent. On the other hand, we'd already started planning for a much more daring action, one that might, conceivably, give us trouble with our phone.

"Who needs a ride? Zed?" Pete asked.

I declined. I was skipping Russian.

After Pete got a street named after Kropotkin, I wanted a Chekhov Street, too, but by the time I'd formulated my case for his inclusion, we'd run out of streets. Rather than waste my thoughts, I used them for my second term paper in Russian Lit. Chekhov was a writer of his time. He wrote about a particular place (Russia) at a particular point in history (the end of the nineteenth century and a handful of years into the twentieth). So many of his stories feature sympathetic characters whose ideas would seem radical even today, like Misail in "My Life— A Provincial's Story," or Liza in "A Case History," or Nadya in "The Fiancée" who flees her bourgeois family and her cliché of a fiancé and escapes to St. Petersburg because her eyes have been opened and she wants to live. The miracle of literature is that the more particular the story, the more universal. I felt that those stories, set in that intensely political time, spoke for our time too, and I wrote more passionately about them than I had on any other topic, not so much because I had anything at stake in seeing Chekhov as a radical, but because after giving up on *Anna Karenina* I was eager to argue. I sensed only vaguely that this was so I wouldn't have to have a different, more painful argument with myself: should I, or should I not, tell Sonia how I felt?

Papers were due the last day of the semester, but I finished ahead of the deadline and read mine to Sonia through the grate. She thought it was wonderful and insisted I let Pete and Dieter read it too. Dieter praised my writing. He said I had a way with words. Pete said, "Fuck, Zed. We should have named a street after him."

When I slid the paper across the table to Professor Kopanyev after class, he scooped it up and pressed it to his tweeded chest.

"I wrote about Chekhov again. I hope that's all right."

"Of course, of course! He's greatest writer who ever lived." He made a show of flourishing the loose-leaf pages and reading the title from arm's length, "Chekhov the Radical." Oddly, his face seemed to collapse. He stood abruptly and started stacking his folders, placing my paper on top. Men are always occupying themselves with their facial hair in Russian novels—gathering it in their hands and sniffing it. Kopanyev looked like he was trying to rip his off his face.

The following week he turned up tardy as ever, twinkling as usual, books and folders in his arms. He leaned forward and dropped it all in a heap on the table. The books were part of a set, both with unillustrated manilla covers, and those of us who were also taking Russian leaned forward to read the Cyrillic titles—two volumes of Chekhov's letters. When Kopanyev finished tidying the mess, he announced that he himself had brought in a subject for discussion. "With apologies to Keith, who I'm sure was amply prepared and very much looking forward to guiding us through our conversation today."

Halfway through the year, to everyone's surprise, Keith, the punk, had blurted that his name was actually *Teeth*. Too late. Kopanyev never remembered. Now Teeth's tactic was not even to reply to Keith.

Kopanyev took up one of the twin volumes, torn bits of paper stuck in its pages. "Excuse me," he said, opening it. "I'm translating off top of my head. It's from letter to poet Pleshcheyev from Anton Chekhov written in—" He set the book down and frisked himself until he came up with a glasses case. "*1888*," he read, once the glasses were installed. "*Those I am afraid of*, he writes, *are ones who look for tendencies between lines and want to put me down definitely as liberal or conservative. I am not liberal or conservative, not evolutionist, nor monk, nor careless about*—Excuse me. *Indifferent to. Indifferent to world. I would like to be free artist— and that is all*. Those are Chekhov's own words. What do you say?"

No one said anything.

Kopanyev flipped through more pages. Scraps of paper fluttered out like dandruff. "Here. Here we have a letter to editor

Suvorin. Quote: *Now what about us? Yes, us! We paint life such as it is—that's all, there isn't any more. . . .* Should I go on? Here. Here. Same letter to Pleshcheyev. *I consider trademarks or labels to be prejudices.*"

The others didn't understand what he was so riled about. Eyes rolled here and there. I was in shock. I was his favourite. Everyone knew I was his favourite, but now I had disappointed him. My throat felt so parched that I coughed. He swung around. "Jane! Yes! Please! Speak!"

"I feel," I began before coughing again, "he presents the viewpoints of his characters so sympathetically that he must share them."

"I am completely in accord!" he roared. "It seems as though he shares them. Because he is artist, not disseminator of propaganda. What about Turgenev? Who here thinks Turgenev is nihilist? Who? Hands up. No one. Yet how we feel for Bazarov! I for one weep every time he dies in my hands. Yet Turgenev himself lived like dandy in Paris and Baden-Baden. That, my conversationalists, is mark of artist."

One of the women I'd overheard complaining about Kopanyev's paternalistic attitude sighed now. "So what are you saying? Chekhov wasn't a socialist?"

"He certainly wasn't! He says so himself, though critics in Soviet Union would very much like you to believe he was!"

How grey Kopanyev's teeth were. Normally you couldn't see them behind the beard and moustache. He laughed a lot—he was jovial—but he never smiled. Now as he bared them in the triumph of his argument, I saw they were dingy and stripped of enamel, as though he and my father and aunt had all got them from the same store, deep in the discount bin. Communist teeth, my mother called them.

"One thing I'm trying to teach you, my dear pupils, is to read what is really on page, to respond to it with all your hearts, as human beings. Literature will make you better person. It will teach you sympathy and compassion for all manner of peoples, but not if you read it with closed mind. Not if you read to prove your closed mind is right."

At Kopanyev's suggestion we turned to "The Fiancée," which most of us had read and because, he told us, it was Chekhov's last story and the one those despised Soviet critics always cited as an example of his revolutionary tendencies. Everyone agreed that it was the portrait of a young woman's political awakening, but not only that, Kopanyev insisted. "What is Chekhov really saying? Who stirs Nadya up in first place?"

"Her cousin?" Michael offered.

"Sasha you mean? Yes. And what happens to Sasha?"

"He dies of consumption of course. Ha ha ha!"

"Before that. Nadya goes to visit him, but she has different impression of him after her year away at university. Suddenly he seems dull and provincial. *Outmoded*. She has, in fact, outgrown him. And when she goes home, she sees her mother and her grandmother differently too, and town, even ceiling over her head, which keeps getting lower and lower. A year at university and she has outgrown them all. We see her at end of story longing for same elusive bright future so many of his characters yearn for. But where does it say that this is longing for revolution? Who has copy of story? Who? Nobody? I thought by now you would all be carrying Chekhov in your breast pockets, next to your hearts. Excuse me. Don't move. I'll return momentarily."

He left. We sat in silence. A full minute passed before I realized this was my chance to bolt. "I thought this was his most feminist story," the heavy woman commented as I gathered up my things.

"Yes," said another. "She broke free from patriarchal expectations. She didn't want to be that dope's wife."

Kopanyev returned as I was slinging my backpack onto my shoulder. He remained on his feet in the doorway. Blocking me in? Only when I had sat back down did he begin reading: "—*it would be forgotten, erased from memory.* This is Nadya thinking. She means past. *The only distraction for Nadya was the small boys next door. Whenever she strolled into the garden they would bang on the fence, laugh and taunt her with the words, 'And she thought she was going to get married, she did.'*" He lowered the book. "They banged on the fence! There is that motif again!"

The night watchmen, security guards of the nineteenth century, beating out the hours. Time is passing. The future is approaching. *Clang, clang, clang.*

"How many times in the story does she lie sleepless listening to watchman banging out time?" Kopanyev asked. "What does it mean?"

I sat there, head down, shamed, angry.

"And here is last line of story: *In a lively, cheerful mood she left that town—forever, or so she thought.* What does it mean? Why does he add this *or so she thought*? Why? Why?"

He was yelling at us.

Finally someone spoke. Teeth. He burst out: "So tell us! Why the fuck?"

"I don't care about politics," Sonia told me that night as I lay convalescing on her bed. "In my opinion, that's why we're in this mess. And I know how you feel, Jane. I failed my practicum last year."

"What? No! How?"

"I read them *Sadako and the Thousand Paper Cranes.* Do you know about her? The little Japanese girl who died of atom bomb disease? That's what they call leukemia in Japan."

"She died of leukemia? How old were the kids in your practicum?"

"Grade Two. I had to tell them, Jane. Through the children we'll reach the parents. Even cereal companies understand that. My supervisor said I was irresponsible."

"Ha! She's the one who's irresponsible!"

Sonia grabbed my hand. "That's exactly what I told her!"

We helped each other like this. That was why I loved her. She supported me and I supported her. Half the time I felt exultant (we were going to move out together, we could only grow closer), the other half acutely anxious (we'd probably be obliterated before that). The love reacted with the dread, and its product was a particular mood. Sadness and tedium and yearning. The lilac scent of unrequited love. A Russian mood. What if I did tell her? What if I said, *Ya tebya lyublyu?* I knew what she'd say. She'd say, so sweetly, "Oh, Jane. I love you too."

I shouldn't have written that paper. The force with which Kopanyev rejected it shattered my self-confidence. I'd write my exams but I wouldn't go back to class for the rest of the term. I couldn't face his tweeds, his mocking beard.

No doubt he would have loved my paper on *Anna Karenina.*

That spring the trees bloomed in succession, so many different kinds, each paler or pinker specimen bursting into flower just as its predecessor dropped her frilled skirt to the ground. Classes were ending and exams about to start, these spread over the month of April. We were trying to choose between a die-in outside the army recruitment office or chaining ourselves to the fence at the Boeing plant in Seattle. Belinda preferred the recruitment office action, which would involve bodies on the sidewalk outlined in chalk and fake blood splashed around. It satisfied her dramatic tendencies and was supported, of course, by Carla. But Pete argued that a recruitment centre was too general a target.

"People? Yes, we oppose all manifestations of militarism. But we can't ignore that time is running out."

Sonia seconded his opinion. "The watchman is clanging."

"It's time to stop beating around the bush. Code Blue here, right? We need to act specifically against nuclear weapons. Boeing manufactures the cruise."

Belinda, who had a head half-filled with Medusa braids, put on a pouty face until Sonia told her, "We can still have blood. We could do burns too."

Belinda perked up. "Burns would be neat."

Some of us still had misgivings—about getting arrested in a foreign country, about having to rehearse an action that would take place a three-hour drive away. Some of us were Dieter, but also me, though I was much less vocal. I waffled rather than opposed. The group talked it out. We talked and talked and in the end Pete, Dieter, and Timo formed a committee that would drive down to scout the plant before we made a final decision.

"We'll have to rent a car," Timo said. No one imagined they would make it over the border in Pete's Reliant.

There was one last item on the agenda that night which Carla, the facilitator, introduced by saying, "I think Isis has something to tell you." Before we could even ask whom she meant, Belinda rose and announced she was changing her name.

"To Isis?" Sonia asked.

"To Isis."

Everyone knew what was coming. Pete's "Fuck" cued Belinda's explosion. "Fuck *you!*" she roared. "You don't own me!"

"Why didn't I hear about this before?"

"Like I said, you don't own me! God!"

Timo: "Whoah-oah. Whoah. Pete. Belinda."

"Isis!"

"Isis."

Pete ignored Timo. "What is going on?"

"Can you stop threatening her?" Carla said.

"I'm asking a question!"

"I just said! I'm changing my name!"

"Okay." Pete got off his ice floe. "I have an announcement too."

Dieter: "You're not on the agenda."

He stood on the coffee table. "I'm changing my name to Spot."

Carla: "Pete! You are such an asshole!"

He stabbed a finger at her. "Spot! I demand you call me Spot!"

Timo could hardly get the words out. "I ddddon't think this is the aaaappropriate time—"

Isis: "I want a mediator. I'm not talking to him without one."

"Can we have a volunteer to mmmediate? Can you guys agree on someone?"

"I want Zed," said Pete.

Isis said, "Fine. I'm fine with Jane."

In the Chekhov story "The Duel," Layevsky and von Koren had two seconds each, as well as the deacon hiding in the shrubbery. Five witnesses to their folly. We were three—me, huddled on the hearth, flanked by the pair of mocking garden statues.

Belinda arrived early, dressed in fatigues, more of her hair braided now. Then Pete made us wait, so long that by the time he came down and flopped in the beanbag chair the atmosphere was tense. They kept their eyes fixed on me, a proxy for their anger. I felt their glares cut through me.

Sonia and Timo had offered a compressed lesson in active listening. They said I should remain as neutral as possible and repeat back to Pete and Belinda what they said to each other, rephrasing if necessary, especially when their meaning became obscured by emotion. "So," I said now and immediately pictured myself drowning in deep water and crying out this very thing—"So! So!" "Who wants to go first?" I asked.

Belinda signalled that she would. "I can't be with Pete any more."

I was taken aback. How to rephrase *that*? And it struck me what a terrible actress Belinda really was because none of her speeches had ever sounded as raw and pained as this. She was destined for commercials and summer stock. Tonight, though, she wasn't performing and Pete was obviously as shocked, in shock even, all his powers extinguished. I doubt anyone had ever broken up with him before.

Belinda began to cry. After a few horrible minutes, she wiped her face on her sleeve and gestured for me to translate. "Pete?" I said. "Belinda says she can't be with you any more."

"Isis," she corrected.

"Isis," I said.

"Why?" he asked.

"Pete wonders why," I said, feeling really stupid.

"You eat people," she said.

He looked confused. "Tell her I thought she liked that."

I opened my mouth but nothing came out.

"I mean you absorb them," she said. "You suck them dry." She squeezed her forehead, kneading out thoughts. "I've just been so in awe of you, Pete," she said to the shag carpet. "Of your commitment and your brilliance. Everything became about you. I forgot about myself."

"Really?" He sounded genuinely surprised. "I thought it was the other way around."

"I haven't grown. And I'm tired. I'm sorry to say this to you. I'm exhausted. You're exhausting to be with." She turned to me again and I stammered something about her feeling tired. "And tell him I hope we can still work together in the group," she said. "I wouldn't want to jeopardize that."

"No," Pete said.

"The work is too important."

"I agree."

Silence. My armpits were sopping but my throat was so dry I'd begun working my mouth to gather enough saliva to swallow. I dreaded that they would start screaming. Then the phone rang in the kitchen and we all straightened, alert as animals. It broke some of the tension.

"So," Pete said. "I guess that's it."

"Don't you have anything you want to say to me?" Belinda asked.

Sonia, I noticed, was trying to peep in through the doves and peace signs on the door panes. "Ask him," Belinda said in an urgent voice. "Ask if he doesn't want to tell me something."

"No," Pete said.

"Nothing?"

Sonia poked her head in. "Sorry. Pete, the phone's for you."

"Who is it?" he asked.

"I don't know. A woman."

Belinda, who had been leaning forward on the chesterfield, anxious for Pete to speak, fell back when Sonia said this. "Take a message," Pete said.

"It's long distance."

"Take a message."

Sonia gave me a stricken glance as she closed the door again, probably in response to the SOS I was transmitting with my eyes. As soon as she was gone, Belinda asked in a completely different tone, "Who was that, I wonder?"

Pete lifted his head and looked at her. I could see by his expression he was devastated, and now this too: confused. "Is this about sex?" he asked, like it was the last thing he would have blamed their troubles on.

"You slept with Ruth!"

"Who told you that?"

"Ruth did," Belinda said.

"In what context?"

"I asked her."

"You could have asked me." He turned to me. "I don't lie." To Belinda: "Is that what you're waiting for me to tell you?"

She rolled her eyes. "No. I already know that."

"Should I go?" I asked and they replied, "Stay!" in adamant unison.

Pete: "I said you could sleep with other men."

"Why, thank you."

"I'm not giving you permission! You have the right to do what you want. Now and then I feel like sleeping with someone else. And if she feels like it too, it sometimes happens. It has nothing to do with you. I'm completely committed to you."

Belinda tossed her snakes.

"I thought you were okay with it! You said you were!" He threw up his hands. "Christ, if this was the sixties this wouldn't even be an issue!"

"I don't want to sleep with other men," Belinda said.

"Then don't!" he shouted.

She yanked on her braids in frustration, as though she wore them as a prop. "Don't you get it? I don't even want to sleep with you!"

Pete sat, apparently absorbing this. After a long, blank moment, he sprang out of the beanbag. Belinda scrambled to her feet too, reaching for him, and they hugged for a long time, fused and swaying. When Pete started running his hands all over her back, Belinda abruptly pulled away and Pete lurched off through the French doors without looking back.

"God," she said to me, lifting her arm and sniffing. "I stink, I'm sweating so hard. Can you walk me home? I need to debrief."

Sonia came out of the kitchen as we were leaving. Belinda held up a hand to stop her from asking. No, Isis did. All that was over now. Sonia nodded; she would get the whole story from me later.

"That was the hardest thing I ever had to do in my life," Isis said as we descended the wooden front steps into dusk. "Correction. My stepfather once tried to get in my pants."

"Oh, my God," I said.

"This was the second hardest. Thank you." She hugged me.

"I didn't do anything."

"You did. You were there. I felt supported having another woman in the room."

"Pete wouldn't hurt you," I said.

We stopped at the bottom and Isis said, "All men are latent rapists as far as I'm concerned. But what a relief! What a relief it's finally over!" She threw her head back and inhaled. "God, the air smells wonderful. I love spring. Have you read *The Cherry Orchard*? Of course. You've probably read it in Russian. We should read it together. The group, I mean."

Then the street lights suddenly winked on and we looked at one another in surprise. Isis laughed and took my arm. Together we walked on, linked like schoolgirls crossing the street. "Was I too hard on him, do you think?" she asked. "See, I'm trying to be assertive. I'm trying to find my power." Before I could answer, Belinda—this time it was Belinda—pulled her arm out of mine and staggered over and sank down on someone's lawn. People were obviously home. Lights were on in the house. She toppled onto her side, howling, "He would never say he loved me! He would never use those words!"

I hurried over. "He won't say sorry either."

"You keep defending him! Are you sure you didn't sleep with him?"

"No!"

"But if he did, Jane? If he had once told me he loved me? If he had said it tonight? That's what I wanted. I need to hear those words. I'm so insecure."

This surprised me very much.

"My mother used to say the awfullest things to me," she went on. "Like my breasts are two different sizes. Who cares! She made me so self-conscious. I hate her."

She curled in a ball, sobbing, with me bent helplessly over her. "He kept screwing around. I said it was okay but it wasn't. I was jealous. I wanted to slit their throats." She looked up at me, grass and snot blending with her freckles, and her whole body spasmed. "*Hic!* Sorry. That's not non-violent. God! Now I've got the hiccoughs.

"He's jealous too," she went on. "He won't admit it, but he is. Remember what he did at the Hyatt? He's jealous of—*Hic!*— Carla." She rolled onto her back, used her sleeve on the tears, sighed. "Look. Stars."

I looked up and saw them, the first faint emanations that night. "Make a wish," she said and I did. "I'm always torn," she said, lying at my feet, "between disarmament and gender equality."

When she got up, fresh-cut grass was stuck all over her army pants. She brushed herself off and we continued down Gandhi Street. Every time she hiccoughed, I pretended to too, so by the time we reached the Blenheim house, we were laughing again. "Are you going to be okay?" I asked.

"Yes. Carla's home. Thanks." She foisted the mandatory goodbye hug on me, then started up the walk. Halfway she turned, wearing a different face altogether—pleased and smug. She said, "Carla worships me."

We didn't see Pete for three days. Except to cross the hall to the bathroom, he never left his room. Nor did he respond to Sonia's pleas, delivered through his door, to come down to supper. His heart was broken, Sonia said, but I thought it was more complicated than that. Getting Belinda back would have been easy. All he had to do was utter the formula she had doubtlessly given him many times, the three magic little words we all long for. He could probably have got her back without them, but he knew it wasn't fair. His looks, his manifold charms—they were inherited, not earned. If he turned his magnetism on, like he had done that time at the Hyatt, what message would it give to people like me who had none of his physical advantages? So he stayed in his room, pitting his heart against his principles. I knew he would come out when his principles had won.

Without the Reliant, both Dieter and I had to take the bus the last few days of term and, in the morning, we walked together to the stop. "I really don't want to do that action in Seattle," he told me. "It's a way bigger deal to get arrested down there."

"You can be support. That's what I'm doing."

"They'll arrest everybody. They're a bunch of Fascists. I'm going to Nicaragua in June. We're driving down. I'll have to get across that border again. But we need consensus, right? Are you with me?"

I thought he was asking if I understood. "Yes," I said.

"Good." After a pause he said, "What are you doing this summer?"

"I don't know yet." I was in a quandary. I was supposed to go home. My mother had asked in her last letter when they should expect me. But Sonia and I were moving out together. If I left for the summer, I'd have to sublet my room. I'd have to be apart from her for four months when I could scarcely endure the day's separation and often trudged halfway across campus just to eat my lunch near Scarfe, the Education building, pathetically hoping to catch a glimpse of her. Who knew what would happen during those four months? It was always there, the enormous matter of a nuclear war, the monster in the room, the ominous shadow falling over all our plans and dreams. And where did I want to be at the end of the world? Wherever Sonia was, I knew.

"Did you talk to Sonia about me?" Dieter asked when we reached the bus stop.

"No."

"No! Why not?"

"I didn't know what you wanted me to say," and by his crumpled look I saw he didn't know himself any more.

"Well, could you do this for me then? Could you find out if there's any other guy she likes at the moment?"

"There isn't," I said with complete confidence.

Pascal mostly kept to the living room, out of everyone's way. Or he hung around with Dieter when Dieter wasn't studying. I think he hoped being unobtrusive would earn him an extended stay. The night it was his turn to cook, I came into the kitchen and saw no evidence of food being prepared. When I went to remind him, he leapt off the chesterfield, killing the cartoons. The doorbell rang. "Supper!" he called.

Pizza was a treat, though a guilty one. "Cheese is made with rennet," Dieter explained—nicely. He seemed relaxed, almost jocular, now that he had a friend in the house he didn't feel the need to impress. Now that Pete was in seclusion. "See, rennet comes from the hooves of calves. We usually buy rennetless cheese at the co-op. Anyway, it won't kill us this one time, right?" he asked Sonia.

"It killed the calf," she said, stripping the stringy topping off her slice.

Pascal looked at her, rueful, his eyes big, like the calf's, so she couldn't help but excuse him. "You didn't know," she said. "Take some up to Pete later."

"I'm surprised the smell didn't lure him down." Dieter yelled at the ceiling, "Pete! We've got pizza down here! Yummy! Yummy!"

Sonia: "Leave him alone."

"Is he sick?" Pascal asked.

"He's heartsick," Sonia said.

"It's his pride," said Dieter, pushing up his glasses. "The worst possible thing that could happen to a guy just happened to him. His girlfriend became a dyke."

I'd already figured it out walking Isis home a few days before. She as much as told me. Still, I felt sick when Dieter brayed the word out so coarsely. Sonia seemed as shocked. "Who told you that?" she asked.

"It's obvious. They're a bunch of man-haters. You'd better watch it when you go over there. They'll convert you too."

"That sounds pretty sexist to me, mister."

"Sexist? Me?" Dieter tossed his crust into the box. "They can say whatever they like. They can make jokes like, 'What do you call a man at the bottom of the ocean?'"

"What?" Pascal asked.

"A good start."

Sonia and I laughed. "See?" said Dieter. "But if I said, 'What do you call a *girl* at the bottom of the ocean?' it wouldn't be funny. No. I'd get the lash for saying that."

Now Pascal laughed. He'd only just got the joke. Sonia leaned over and hugged him, because he was so sweet and naive, because he made us feel less so.

After supper, Pascal and Dieter went out to the back yard to kick a soccer ball around while Sonia and I lingered at the table. "I thought Belinda and Carla were best friends," she confessed.

Maybe if we weren't sitting on six hundred thousand Hiroshimas. Maybe if the hands of the nuclear clock weren't stuck at two minutes to midnight. Maybe without all that pressure, instead of feeling racked over what it was I felt for her— whether it was physical or not—I would have been thrilled to be designated a best friend. It might have ended my torment. But it was March 31, 1984. "We have to give a month's notice if we're going to move out," I told her.

When Isis and I had made our star-bent wishes, I'd put moving in with Sonia ahead of world peace.

"We can't have a meeting if Pete won't come down," Sonia said.

Outside the window the soccer ball soared past like a moon in an accelerated orbit. We could hear Dieter and Pascal laughing and the robins belting out their songs in the vaudeville of spring. I wanted to say, but didn't, that we could give our notice in writing.

"Let's try talking to Pete one more time," she said.

We crept up the stairs together, bearing the pizza box with the two pieces we'd saved at supper by slapping away greedy hands. "He'll come down if we call a meeting," I said.

Sonia stopped on the landing. "Jane. He's in so much pain."

"Do you still want to move out?"

She saw then, and heard in my voice, that I was in pain too, and squeezed my arm to reassure me. Her pupils were dark pools of compassion I wanted to dive into. "Yes, Jane. But we might have to put it off a month. Okay?"

She tapped on Pete's door and, placing her little shell ear against it, listened. "Pete?" She opened the door. Immediately a sickroom smell hit us—fetid and sour. Three days weren't enough to starve, but maybe he did other drugs besides pot. Maybe he'd overdosed. Two towels on the curtain rod shut out most of the light so it took a moment for our eyes to adjust. Sonia went over to the foamie and knelt. "Pete? We're so worried about you." She lay beside him and motioned to me to come too. I set the pizza box on the floor and went and knelt on the other side of him.

Sonia: "Pete? We miss you. We love you. You have to talk about it. You have to let your feelings out. Belinda hurt you, didn't she? You love her."

He turned onto his back. I saw grease-darkened hair, dry lips bleeding in the cracks. He smelled, not just of B.O., of something rotten. Now he was ordinary, like us. I didn't want to see him ungilded like that.

Sonia brushed his face with the ends of her hair. She painted his eyelids and cheeks. He stopped her hand and blindly guided the hair into his mouth. "We love you, we love you," she whispered and I hated him and wanted to be him at the same time. I wanted her to whisper those words to me.

Turgenev's Bazarov had reached this same stalemate, I remembered—love or principle? It killed him, but it didn't kill Pete. He sat up and spat Sonia's hair out. "What day is it?"

"Friday," she told him, staring at the miracle of his rising.

"Fuck. My sister's coming."

The next morning when he came down, he seemed himself again, though somewhat gaunt. He'd showered and it was hard to believe that terrible smell could ever have come from him. "You're back," Dieter said with a tinge of something in his voice. "When are we going to Seattle?"

Pete was obviously starving. He took a mixing bowl from the cupboard and filled it with all the granola in the jar. After jiggling each milk carton in the fridge to ascertain which was the fullest, he doused his cereal.

"Pete?"

"I don't know. My sister's coming for a few days. After that." He didn't join Dieter and Pascal at the table, but bowed over the bowl on the counter, feeding himself with a wooden spoon.

Dieter: "I didn't know you had a sister."

"Do you have a sister?"

"Yes."

"Wow. My life is completely altered."

Dieter coloured. My toast popped and I raced to scrape margarine across it and get out. Pascal, I noticed, was drawing Pete
in his book.

"Guess what?" Dieter said as I moved off with my plate.
"This is weird. Pascal and I are from the same town."

Pascal: "Esterhazy."

"He didn't know what a dyke was," Dieter added. "I had to
tell him."

Pascal put a hand over his embarrassed face. Dieter was
watching Pete, waiting for a reaction. Pete straightened and,
from where he stood at the counter several paces away, threw
the bowl he had been eating from into the sink. It crashed onto
all the undone dishes and, from the sound of it, more than one
thing shattered.

We didn't meet the sister immediately. Pete kept her away in
whatever hotel she was staying at. All along we'd thought he'd
severed his family ties, but now we realized he just didn't talk
about that part of his life. He was ashamed. He switched cooking nights with me and begged off both the potluck and the
meeting.

"You won't be at the meeting?" I asked.

If he'd told me he was joining the army, I would have been
less shocked.

It was a spiritless affair without him, first because the planned
scouting trip to Seattle that hadn't happened left an unfillable
hole in the agenda and, second, because now it was obvious how
much Pete's dynamism motivated us, even during his silences,

even when he lay back in the beanbag and furiously pumped his ankle, beating out the dwindling minutes of our lives while we argued over petty details and bruised feelings. We always felt judged, but now we realized we deserved it. Our efforts were half-hearted. We were weak.

In "My Life—A Provincial's Story," Misail's sister is saddled with the ludicrous name of Cleopatra by their egomaniacal father. A sickly, lachrymose sender of notes at the beginning of the story, she strives to reconcile father and son, visiting Misail secretly so as not to provoke their father's wrath, begging him to change his ways for the sake of their dead mother.

"Zed, this is my sister Dede," Pete said when I came into the kitchen. I'd noticed her shoes when I came in, loafers with two bright American pennies glinting in their leather slots. Now she was perched on a chair with her argyled feet twined around a rung, afraid of coming into contact with the floor, I could tell. She stared right at me. I encountered Dedes all the time on campus, a type that possessed not only dewy prettiness, but unnerving psychic powers; instantly they knew I was irrelevant.

"Hi," I said.

She turned her tight smile over to Pete, who was at the counter opening cans. He was the more striking of the two, but that didn't mean she was in any way flawed. Maybe her jaw was a little too large. It didn't seem as though she'd shed a tear her entire life.

"When did you learn to cook, Peter?" she asked.

"It's easy. Why don't you help?"

"What should I do?"

"You can chop the garlic."

"My fingers will smell. Zed's a funny name."

I looked up from where I was making myself a snack. "It's Jane actually. Only Pete calls me that."

She smiled. "He calls me Pea."

"Are you visiting for long?"

"Just a few days. I'm checking out UBC."

Pete set the can opener down too loudly then up-ended the beans into the colander in the sink. They made a sucking sound as gravity pulled them from the can. "Where are you studying now?" I asked her.

"We have Grade Thirteen in Ontario. Do I have to?" Pete passed her the garlic and, putting the heel of his hand to the side of her head, he gave her a little shove, which she seemed to like.

At supper Dede told us, "Oh, I'll live in residence for sure." Her eyes made a rapid blue sweep of the kitchen before coming to rest on the contents of her plate and, apparently finding them as disgusting, her lips pursed, as though on a drawstring. Dieter, who was sitting across from her at the table, chewed and smiled with an expression of delighted horror. "I'm thinking of majoring in English," Dede said. "Or maybe French."

"I hated residence," said Sonia. "I couldn't connect."

Dede blinked at her.

"It was so lonely," she said.

"Oh. I thought you meant the electricity didn't work."

Dieter laughed, then Pascal laughed.

"You did not," Pete said.

"I did!"

It was the only thing he'd said since introducing her. He seemed so subdued with her here. I imagined the sobering heart-to-heart the night before, Dede begging him to talk to their father, Pete refusing, saying, "He rapes the earth." We all ate in silence for a minute except for Dede, who poked. Then she asked us what we did for fun.

"Fun?" I said.

"I play soccer," Pascal offered when no one else answered. "I like to draw."

"Are you in Fine Arts?"

Eyes darting, he suddenly bent over his food, heavy brown waves flopping over his plate.

"What about you?" she asked me.

"I was going to major in Slavonic Studies. I'm not so sure now."

"I'm back to fun now."

"Oh. I'm studying for exams."

"That's right. I forgot."

Dieter was still staring at her. I wasn't sure she'd noticed, but now she met his gaze and smiled as though he were an interesting insect. "What about you, Dede?" he asked. "What do you do for fun?"

Pete stood and took both their plates to the counter.

"I sail. I play field hockey. I party quite a bit."

"Really?" said Dieter.

Pete squeezed her shoulder. "Smoke?"

"So you do have some!" She got up at once. On the way out to the deck, she pointed to the Ronald Reagan mask. "Cute."

As soon as they were gone, Dieter said, "Do you believe that?"

"I think she's nice," said Sonia. She looked at Pascal, who bobbed in agreement.

"Talk about bourgeois. *I sail. I play field hockey. I drink tea in the afternoon.*"

We could see them through the window, their backs to us as they leaned over the railing, passing the joint back and forth. Dede was talking, administering little jabs to her brother's shoulder. Pete kept shaking his head.

"I'm going out there," said Dieter gleefully.

"Are you a spy?" I asked.

He pretended to be affronted. "We're going to kick the ball around." He looked at Pascal.

"Let's go to the beach," Pascal said. "There's more room."

"I don't have that much time. My first exam's on Wednesday. Oh, never mind." Dieter put his plate in the sink and went upstairs.

"I'll go," Sonia told Pascal just as Pete and Dede came back in, looking much happier than when they went out.

"I'm definitely coming to school here," Dede told us, beaming. "Mom would be happy about that, wouldn't she?"

Pete collected the remaining plates and carried them to the sink without answering. I'd thought their mother was dead. I already knew Dede was no weepy Cleopatra; I'd been wrong about that too. I wanted to stay and listen, to find out if there was anything I'd been right about, but that would make me a spy.

"Peter," said Dede. "They think the sun shines out your ass."

"Fuck."

"They *do*. Is that supposed to be washing? You're such a pig."

"It's fine," he said, swabbing the last plate with the grey cloth and jamming it in the drying rack. "Let's go."

"Show me your room first."

"Why?"

"I want to see it."

They went upstairs. Sonia and Pascal were getting ready to go to the beach. She asked me if I wanted to go too. I did, but I had to study. I had to study, but I said yes. Meanwhile Pete and Dede came back down and we all met up in the hall. Dede was saying, "I just don't see any evil in furniture. What happened to all your stuff?"

"I gave it away."

"You're too noble for your own good. And the filth? Is that a statement too?"

Pete pointed to her penny loafers placed primly, heel to heel and toe to toe, by the door. "You have *Abraham Lincoln* in your shoes?"

"Can we go to a club?" she asked.

Pascal led us in a zigzag through the avenues, past Gandhi and Mandela streets, until we came to a tree whose pale blossoms formed a perfect canopy. His sketchbook was tucked under his arm, the pen lost somewhere in his hair, but he found it and drew some quick lines without looking at the page. Sonia sidled up to me. "Let's tell him. I didn't want to before. He's so sweet. But it's our responsibility."

I nodded.

Past Kropotkin Street the trees I'd seen a few weeks earlier were sporting tufts of coppery leaves, their flowers a pretty litter on the ground. Pascal went over and leaned against a trunk. "In Esterhazy we've still got snow."

"This is our snow," Sonia told him, pointing to the petals under his white boots.

"It's so beautiful here."

Sonia gave me the look then went over and took Pascal's arm. Now she was leading him, I only following, and Pascal looked pleased. "It's beautiful and it's in danger," she said.

"What do you mean?"

"You've heard about what happened to Hiroshima and Nagasaki?"

"You mean the A-bomb?"

"Yes. That was nothing compared to the weapons they've got today. The hydrogen bomb is much more powerful. And the United States has thirty-five thousand of them and a special new weapon called the cruise missile that can't be detected by radar. It's a first-strike weapon. It's meant to start a nuclear war."

Pascal said, "Really?"

"Yes."

"Good thing we're on their side!"

"No, no. We can't afford to think that way any more. The Soviet Union has twenty thousand bombs, enough to kill every one of us twenty times. Hiroshima was a beautiful city like this. It was flattened. Thousands of people died the most horrible deaths. But what happened to Hiroshima was a millionth the size of what would happen here if they dropped the bomb."

Her voice was tremulous, her eyes moist. I felt that panic grip me again. Pascal had turned white. Everything, everything in that season of life was tinged with death. "It could happen at any moment," I added.

"We don't mean to scare you," Sonia told Pascal.

Me: "Tell him about our chances."

"Fifty-fifty," Sonia said. "That's according to the Joint Chiefs of Staff."

"Who?"

"The generals. The generals themselves say a nuclear war will probably happen by 1985."

"Nineteen eighty-five? That's, like, nine months away!"

Sonia took my arm now and the three of us moved along as one. I remembered going to the beach with her after the film. It had been a November night, but this was April, the trees budding and blooming, songful with birds. The birds were singing, *Look! Look at all you stand to lose!* And back in November there had been no one around, but tonight lovers were out strolling. Families. Children. Someone was flying a kite. Run! I wanted to scream. Hide! But where? With Sonia between us, her arms around us both, we sat on a log. The mountains. Surely they were indestructible.

We worked so well, Sonia and I. I really believed that, together, we could save the world. We would do it just by talking, just by telling the truth. It was why I loved her.

Pascal opened his sketchbook and began to draw. The pen scraped across the page, never lifting until the mountains appeared, first the line of peaks like a vital sign, then their bulk, shaded in. "That's so amazing," Sonia said. "Can I see?" She took the book and started from the beginning. "Are these your parents?"

"Yes."

"In Esterhazy?"

"Yes."

She asked if he'd taken the bus to Vancouver and when. When she reached her own picture, she smiled. "Is that me?"

"Can't you tell?"

She laughed. "Look, Jane."

"I saw," I said.

Pascal flipped forward in the book. Here was something new: an entire page dedicated to her, scores of miniature Sonias. She grew flustered. "When did you do this?" Yet it was obvious she was flattered. She couldn't keep up the frown for long. Where was our terror now, I wondered. It had passed without our noticing. I wanted it back.

Sonia, sensing my discomfort, asked, "Did you draw Jane?"

"I did," he said, turning the pages. "There."

"Ah! It's you, Jane."

It was not a flattering portrait, but I didn't care. It was those adoring little scribbles, all the Sonias, that upset me. I got up and walked away. Sonia called after me and, when I didn't stop, she chased me across the sand. "Jane? What's the matter?"

"Nothing. I have to study. I'll see you later."

By the time I reached the house after the long march back, I'd managed to calm myself. I was already regretting having bolted, mostly because it made me seem childish. Dieter was in the kitchen, his books spread out on the table. He glanced at, but didn't acknowledge, me. I plugged in the kettle and waited with my back to him, annoyed because he'd never set up shop in the kitchen before.

"Where did you go?" he asked after a minute.

"To the beach."

The kettle finished its thing. I dropped a tea bag into a mug and poured the water in. When I turned, Dieter was staring at me, the lenses of his glasses misty, his face boiled. "I came down and everybody was gone!"

"We went to the beach," I said.

"Nobody ever includes me!"

I was going to point out that he had been invited, but I could see it would only make things worse. I was rattled by his anger, his hurt, as he probably was by mine, the way I'd dragged it in behind me, chained to my ankle. Between the two of us, the kitchen was thick with adolescent misery.

"So where's Sonia?" he asked.

"She's still there." I added, sulkily, "With your friend."

"Who?" Dieter asked.

"Pascal," I said.

"He's not my friend."

I remembered Dieter telling Pete that he and Pascal were from the same town, as though they had just discovered it. But Pascal had asked for Dieter by name when he showed up at the party. When I told this to Dieter, he said, "I drank a lot of beer that night."

"Well, he asked for you specifically. I thought that's why he was staying here. Because he's a friend of yours."

Dieter's nostrils dilated. Already he looked happier. "What the hell is going on?"

We sat around the table waiting while Dieter breathed on his lenses, while he polished them, solemn and half-blind. There it was, that furry eyebrow, all of us gaping at it, unable to look away until the glasses were back on his face and the shocking eyebrow hidden. "We have a problem." His voice was low, stiff with its own seriousness.

This was the next day, after Dede had left, making Pete available. "Who's we?" he asked.

"All of us. Jane and I realized something last night."

I reddened, furious to be included, and Sonia, who assumed we confided everything, cast me a wounded look. Dieter: "Pascal is a spy."

"I never said that!"

"It's pretty obvious."

Sonia: "What are you talking about?"

"Fact: he showed up here the night of the party when the house was filled with activists. He stayed till God knows when talking to people, getting their names, *drawing pictures of them.* Next thing we know he's moved in."

"You said he could stay," Sonia said.

"Because I thought you knew him! Turns out he's going around saying he's a friend of *mine.* Fact: I never saw him before the party. Who is he? I've never seen him at UBC."

Sonia shrank down. I felt queasy too. Then Pete, gusting a sigh, pushed his chair back and strode out of the room, in protest we assumed. "This is a meeting!" Dieter called after him. From where I sat I could see him stop at the French doors and knock. He returned a moment later, a bobbing Pascal in tow. "Sit," Pete said and Pascal did, wrists pinned between his knees, eyes madly darting. "Where do you know this guy from?"

"Esterhazy."

"See?" said Dieter. "He's lying. He's probably never even been there."

"I'm from there. It's the potash capital of Canada."

We waited for more. The lump rose and fell in his neck. Above it, his jawline was flecked with minute scabs where the whiteheads had been decapitated. Passing the bathroom that morning, I'd glimpsed him standing at the mirror, struggling with the razor, wearing only a towel around his waist.

Dieter: "Why aren't you answering? It's a simple question. Where do you know me from?"

"You taught me to swim."

Dieter drew back.

"Remember?"

"I remember teaching swimming obviously. But I taught about a hundred kids." He looked at us. "This is going back three years at least."

Pascal leapt up and mimed a front crawl to the sink. He backstroked back then turned to us with a laugh. We all smiled, more than charmed—relieved. So he wasn't a spy. But something else occurred to us—that there was still an impersonation going on. The way he flung himself in the chair again, limbs flying, as though he were made of cloth—it was suddenly clear that we weren't the same age, that he was younger. That he might not be a *man* at all like Pete and Dieter.

"What are you doing here?" I asked.

"Checking out UBC," he said, evidently forgetting this would sound familiar to us.

Sonia: "How old are you?"

"Eighteen." Dart, dart.

"Come on," said Pete.

"I'm turning seventeen."

"Sixteen!" Sonia cried.

We were shocked. He was close to six feet tall and maturely built. I'd seen him in the bathroom practically naked, but now that I knew his actual age, it was clear that he was going around in a borrowed body. "You should be home with your parents," Sonia said.

"Why me?" Dieter asked.

"I heard you were in Vancouver." He looked around at us. "Esterhazy's small. It's so small." A grin for Dieter. "Right? I phoned your place and said I was a friend of yours. She gave me your address. I guess it was your mom."

"And what? You thought you'd just show up and I'd let you stay?"

"That's what happened. Except you don't remember me. Or do you now?"

"No!"

"You were so great," said Pascal.

"I was?" Dieter said it, not us, but we were equally surprised. Sonia asked: "Do you have enough money to get back home?"

"Sure, but I don't want to go back."

"You have to."

He shook out his waves. "Can't."

"You can't stay here," said Dieter.

Pete: "Why not?"

"We have four bedrooms. Four people sleep in those bedrooms."

"We have a chesterfield."

"He can't just move into the living room."

"Why not?" said Pete. "Hector did."

"Hector is a refugee. He was tortured."

"Maybe Pascal's getting beaten at home. Are you?"

Pascal thought about it. "No." He sounded sorry that he wasn't.

"There are other kinds of torture," Pete said. "There's psychological torture, arguably as bad. We've got a kid here who hates his parents so much he's fled the province. I know exactly how he feels. Just because he doesn't speak Spanish doesn't mean he hasn't been oppressed."

"Tell us what's happening," Sonia urged. "Can you talk about it? Are they really that bad?"

He sat for a moment, making fists and opening them, tucking them in his armpits. When he began to cry, Sonia hurried around the table to him. "There's so much screaming," he said. "They won't listen to what I want. What I want doesn't count. Only what they want. But it's my life, too. Right? It's my life."

"Yes, it is," Sonia murmured, clutching him to her.

Pete: "Hear, hear."

"It's like I don't even have a vote or anything!"

Pete: "The nuclear family is inherently fascist."

Pascal wrapped his arms around Sonia. When he sniffed, it seemed to me that he was trying to smell her hair. But I felt genuinely sorry for him, too, having suffered parental tyranny myself. In fact, I only now realized that I'd finally escaped it, that my parents were far away in another province and I wasn't emotionally dependent on them any longer—I had friends now. It was like the pillow of their love had finally lifted off my face.

"We have to let him stay," Sonia insisted. "At least until he finds another place."

The next day Pete, Dieter, and Timo went to Seattle. Before they left, Dieter knocked on my door to say, "No matter what I see there, I'm not changing my mind."

"Why are you telling me?" I asked.

The men weren't expected back for supper so Pascal offered to cook for Dieter. When I took a break from studying, I found him in the kitchen reading one of the recipe books from on top of the fridge, *The Anarchist Cookbook*, the Ronald Reagan mask on the back of his head like a rubber snood. If I hadn't before, at that moment I forgave him for his drawings. He was just a kid in trouble.

What he eventually came up with was macaroni. Following Sonia's directions, he made the journey on foot to the food co-op to procure the harmless sort of cheese she'd eat. The pasta was overcooked, the sauce infiltrated with soft lumps; it had the look and nearly the texture of baby food. Nevertheless he seemed pleased with himself. He told us it was the first meal he'd cooked in his life.

"It's time you learned," Sonia said. "It's sexist to expect women to do all the cooking."

"My mom does all the cooking," he said, fondly, so that Sonia observed, "You don't sound all that mad at her."

"I'm not *mad*," he said, serving himself another helping.

Sonia: "What's the problem then?"

"I told you yesterday." Then he said the sweetest thing. He said, "I didn't say I didn't *love* my parents. My mom's my main squeeze."

He raised the serving spoon, cobwebs of cheese trailing off it, and asked us if we wanted more. When we declined, he pulled the pot closer and ate directly out of it while we watched, amused, and let the subject drop. Dieter and Pete behaved like this too, like pigs, though when they did we were disgusted.

At Sunday's meeting I read "A Case History" in Russian as the warm-up. This is not true. I actually read the first page and a half up to the point where Dr. Korolyov is being driven by the little coachman wearing the peacock feather—the bobbing *pyero*—into the factory yard where *everything was covered with a rather strange grey deposit that could have been dust.* There is something apocalyptic about the story. The ominous metallic sound of the night watchman beating out the hour. The grey deposit I translated as ash. *Pyepyel.* Everything was covered with ash. *Vsyo pokryto pyeplom.* And then I read the answers to the last exercise I'd done in my Russian class, which was on indefinite pronouns, adjectives, and adverbs.

"*There was a small garden with a lilac tree covered in ash, and the yellow porch smelled strongly of new paint,*" I read in halting Russian before continuing with "*I haven't decided what I'll buy you in Moscow, but I will buy you something. Give him something to drink. Why don't you read something interesting? Why does he always sit right on the edge of the chair?*" and so on, and no one knew that it didn't make sense. They listened, rapt, like good little children at story time. I put a lot of expression in my voice. "*In the evening, when I'm at home, I like to talk to someone.*" When I finished, Isis wept.

Next Timo, Pete, and Dieter reported on their trip to Seattle. Pete: "There are two possible places to chain ourselves, the front gate and the workers' entrance. Obviously the front would be our first choice except there are more guards. We wouldn't have much time. If we chain ourselves by the workers' entrance, there's just the one guard in the booth where they check ID. But it would make a different statement."

"Like the action was for their benefit?"

"I worry," said Timo, "it would seem like we're blaming the workers for the arms race."

Sonia piped up. "But if the workers *did* stop working, the weapons wouldn't get made."

"So you're suggesting we try to convince them to join us?" Isis asked her.

"Why not?"

Carla: "That's what CMCP does at the Litton plant."

"And what if we targeted the front entrance?"

"It would be for the media."

"I for one," said Pete, "am sick and tired of trying to get the attention of the media. They're collaborators."

"So what I'm hearing so far," said our facilitator, Isis, "is that we're leaning toward using the workers' entrance."

Dieter, who was cross-legged on the floor wearing a kerchief like Pete sometimes did, though not managing to look remotely like a pirate, said, "Are we?"

"You have a different interpretation?"

"You're all talking like this is a done deal. We haven't even got consensus on this action."

"Dieter, you're right. Dieter's made a good point, everybody. Okay. What I suggest then is that we decide what each action would entail, this one and the recruitment office, and then make the choice."

Pete pumping, pumping his ankle. "They do tours."

"Pardon?"

He looked at the rest of us, not Isis, whom he had treated cordially thus far but refused to make eye contact with. "They do tours inside the factory. If we timed the action to coincide with a tour, it would be for the public too, not just—"

Isis: "We could go on a tour!"

"Okay, now we're gggetting somewhere," Timo said.

Dieter: "Just a sec. The recruitment centre was Isis's first choice and Jane's, too." He looked at me hard and, with his wiry hair tucked in the kerchief, his glasses seemed gigantic. "I'm leaning that way myself. It'll just be a whole lot less complicated."

"I'm definitely for Boeing now," said Isis. "I love the idea of joining the tour. Maybe we could even chain ourselves *inside* the plant."

"We couldn't get in with chains," Carla said. "They'll search our bags."

Dieter: "Is anybody even listening to me!"

We took a second break at ten-fifteen. No meeting had ever gone on this long. Before we reconvened, Sonia beckoned me to her room to show me Pascal curled up on her bed, asleep.

Dotingly, she tucked the sleeping bag around him that she'd fetched from the living room.

Pete asked to speak again once we had gathered. He leaned forward in the beanbag, elbows on knees, holding his head in his hands. He was tired of wasting time, he said. Time was running out and he was prepared to act, whatever the consequences. He said, "I'm not afraid."

"So what are you suggesting?" Dieter asked.

"I'm suggesting that those of us who want to do the Boeing action go down and do it and those who don't, stay here and pick their ears."

"You want me out of the group," Dieter said.

"We don't," Sonia told him. "We don't at all. That's not what he means."

Pete: "This isn't about the group. It's about the whole world. I'm sick of spending all this time on group dynamics. I'm sick of hearing about everybody's feelings. People? Who cares? What I feel is irrelevant."

"It isn't, Pete," Isis started to say until something in his look struck her mute. Dieter tore off the kerchief and threw it down. He didn't agree with the plan, he said, but he wouldn't block consensus any longer.

"Are you coming with us?" Sonia asked.

"I have to think about it."

We rose for our closing embrace. "I think this was the most difficult meeting we've ever had," Isis said and those who murmured murmured in agreement. "It'll make us stronger. And thank you, Jane, for reading that story. I feel like it got right into my bloodstream."

"Yes!"

"And thank you, Pete, for getting us on track as usual."

"Fuck off," he said with an off-key laugh.

Dieter was standing on my foot, his heel pinned on my instep. When I tried to pull out from under him, he shifted so I bore the full brunt of his weight.

"We shall live in peace," Carla began.

I had two exams the following week. By force of habit I sequestered myself, though what did it matter if I took my exams or not? On the other hand, if by some miracle the world didn't end, I needed my scholarship. I hated how I waffled! Sonia was so committed. I wanted to be like her, yet I knew I never would be. I had no integrity. None. I'd lied outright about being a vegetarian and, though I avoided meat now, it was reluctantly. I ate any kind of cheese. I'd shamelessly read them that story because I didn't want to admit that Chekhov in Russian was too difficult. Even my friendship with Sonia was false. I wanted more from her but was too cowardly to tell her. Did I want to sleep with her? Yes! I wanted to lie down with her, to hear the music of her little snores, the pathetic sighs, the tossings that enraptured me through the grate. I wanted to clutch her wrist when she tried to get up in the night and hold her back for her own protection. I wanted relief from my own nightmares. With her beside me, every night would dreamlessly unfurl.

Or so I thought.

Dieter was studying just as hard as I was; I knew Sonia also had an exam that week. From all the door slamming, Pete's comings and goings, he had nothing scheduled. He'd started taking Pascal around with him. They went out to modify signage and didn't come back until after one. The slamming door woke me and their midnight snack kept me up—Kropotkin this and Kropotkin that from downstairs. Sonia's light came on. I whispered down, "Tell them to shut up."

"No," she answered. "Pete's laughing."

He did seem almost his old self. A few nights before, I came across him watching the off-air signal on the TV and asked about Dede. Instead of brushing me off, he said, "I'm worried. She's always been a country club brat. Now she's a pothead too."

"*She's* a pothead?"

"I use marijuana responsibly, Zed. Pea's stoned all the time. You wouldn't believe how sweet she used to be. I'd love her to move here. I could be more of an influence. But they'll just use her to keep tabs on me."

"They shouldn't be allowed," I said.

"What?"

"Families. They should make a law."

Pete laughed.

I was glad not to see Professor Kopanyev when I took my Russian Lit exam on Friday. They had grad students for monitors, one of whom wrote on the board that we could pick up our final papers in Kopanyev's office after the test. Not caring to read his reactionary comments, I didn't go. That's what I told myself; the truth was my feelings were still hurt.

Later, while Sonia cooked supper, I sat in the kitchen and read out the classified ads from the newspaper I'd brought home. "Kits. Large two-bedroom basement suite. $450. No pets."

"I couldn't live in a basement," she said. "I'd get depressed."

We heard laughter in the vestibule, the door percussing, then a curious metallic sound accompanying Pete and Pascal down the hall. They laughed into the kitchen carrying hardware store bags. Pete dumped out the contents of one in the middle of the floor: chains. This sparked more hilarity. I noticed their slitted eyes, that Pascal was trembling, his hair wet. "What's wrong with you?" I asked.

Pete: "He went for a swim."

"At Wreck Beach!" Pascal crowed.

"Oh my God," Sonia said. "You'll catch pneumonia."

He was shivering as though he already had it. She snatched a tea towel and, forcing him into a chair, began to dry his hair. Pete lifted one of the chains out of the pile and wound it around Pascal, their laughter soundless now, Pascal stomping his feet as Pete took a padlock from one of the other bags and secured the chain. Sonia tossed the towel on the table in disgust. She disapproved of drugs, too, though for a different reason: they led to inappropriate glee. Until all the bombs were defused, frivolity of any kind offended her.

On her way back to the stove, she tripped over the hardware bags. "Is this all for the action?"

Pascal: "Not all of it! No, siree!"

Howls now.

"Well, get it out of here!"

"How?" Pascal asked. Both his arms were chained to his sides.

Pete stuffed a piece of bread in his mouth, margarined another, and rolled it into a tube for Pascal. Every time Pascal went to take a bite, Pete plucked it back. They were hysterical now.

"Get this stuff out of my way!" Sonia shouted, and Pete finally gathered up the remaining chains and bags, leaving Pascal Houdinied to the chair with a cigar of bread hanging from his mouth.

"You are so immature," Sonia told him when Pete had gone. "What have you done about finding a place to live?" She waved the wooden spoon in his sheepish face.

I went upstairs to get the key from Pete, who laughed as he gave it to me. I didn't. It had just occurred to me that Sonia might invite Pascal to move with us.

"We're just fooling around, Zed," Pete said. "Lighten up."

Back in the kitchen, I freed Pascal. As he stood, the chains loosened, the chair dropped back on its four feet, and he slunk away with the irons uncoiling behind him. Sonia turned a bowl of biscuit dough out onto the table and began a furious kneading. "I'm going to find out what his problem is," she told me. "What happened with his parents. It had better be good."

That night I dreamed I was back in my childhood home looking out the kitchen window. Something was wrong with the trees. All the trunks were charred, yet I couldn't remember any fire. It took me another minute to notice the pairs of tattered shoulders behind the trees, the children hiding in the ashscape, young children if they actually thought they were concealed. Somewhere, someone was sobbing. Even without looking around, I knew who it was. Who else would feel so much grief for children who would never be born and who would die so horribly?

I sat up in bed. The ceiling was pretty with the light coming from the grate. "Sonia?" I called down. "Are you all right?"

Pascal's face appeared, distraught. "I can't get her to stop."

By the time I got downstairs they were in the kitchen, Sonia in her nightie, hovering over the burner, her dishevelled hair hanging too near the glowing coil. Pascal was pleading with her to move back, to turn the stove off. He was in pyjamas too, a pair of striped bottoms and a blank white T-shirt. When he saw me, relief wrote itself on his face. "What's the matter with her? Is she crazy or something?"

"What did you do to her?" I put my arm around Sonia, who burst into sobs again as I led her away. "Turn off the stove," I told Pascal. "Do you want to burn the place down?"

When we reached Sonia's room, I closed the door behind us, shutting Pascal out. She flung herself on the bed and, gathering all her stuffed animals to her, almost seemed to keen. "Did he do something to you?" I asked.

Her face was buried in the plush bodies, but her head moved back and forth. "Then what happened? Tell me."

"I can't even say it! Make him tell you!"

He was right there when I opened the door again, shoulders bowed, hair flopping in his face. He came in and stood on the braided rug. Sonia sat up, eyes glistening and wide, staring back at him. I couldn't tell what was passing between them at that moment but the snare of a feeling tightened round my neck. Finally Sonia said, "Let her touch it."

Pascal sat on the bed, drawing his right leg up so it lay alongside Sonia, pulling the pyjama cuff to his knee. "You can actually feel it," Sonia told me.

"His leg?" I didn't want to.

She beckoned me over, took my reluctant hand, and guided it toward Pascal's naked shin. When I glanced at him, I saw embarrassment radiating off him.

"Do you feel it?" Sonia asked.

The leg was hot and covered with wiry hairs. She made me stroke it. I drew back. "What *is* that?"

"Cancer," she said.

He tucked the leg under himself and turned away. I thought he might be crying too, but when I asked him if it hurt he looked at me with pure exasperation. "No! I wouldn't even have noticed except I was putting on my shin pads. For soccer. Man, I shouldn't have even mentioned it! If I'd kept my mouth shut, none of this would have happened!"

"Have you been to a doctor?"

"That's what I'm talking about."

"Jane," said Sonia. "Tell him to go home. He has to go home."

Pascal: "I'll just take off again. They can't make me. They think they can, but they can't."

"Make you what?" I asked.

He threw up his hands. "They want to cut it off."

"But you'll die," Sonia cried.

"Everybody dies. I'm not going around like a gimp the rest of my life."

"You won't. You'll get a proth—"

"Oh sure. A peg leg. I can hear it now. 'Here, Peggy. Here, Peggy.'"

"You could be like Terry Fox," she told him. "You could be an example."

He shook his head. "Have you ever seen those movies of him? I'd feel like a tool hopping around like that."

"Jane," Sonia implored, as though he actually cared what I thought. "He doesn't know what he's saying. He's too young. Tell him."

It was too horrible. I couldn't think of anything to say except what my mother always said when there was any sort of crisis. "I think we should all go to bed."

"Good idea," said Sonia feverishly. "We'll have a good night's sleep and in the morning we'll make a plan." Without a word, Pascal stalked out, back to his makeshift room, his hiding place. "Pascal!" Sonia called after him. "You're not going to run away from us, are you?"

2 0 0 4

Joe Jr. brought Simon home that afternoon. My office is at the front of the house, facing the street, so I had advance notice of their coming. (Here's something else to worry about: do they talk this loudly because they're plugged in, or is this premature hearing loss?) I got up from the computer—page 22!—and watched them from the window, the Labrador of the guitar case and the mastiff of the cello set down beside them on the sidewalk. At first they seemed to be arguing, then I recognized the outraged tones of agreement, Simon striking out at the air while Joe Jr. shook his tufts in sympathetic disgust. Someone coming along on the same side of the street caught sight of them and hurried across. Who in the world, I wondered, would be afraid of a teenager with a *cello*?

Then boots on the wooden porch. There might have been horses at the door. They burst in, instrument cases colliding, one of them letting loose a stream of really shocking invective. "I'm not fucking even going to call her," Simon said, and I guessed the whole story, that all this emoting had to do with a girl. Joe Jr. shushed him, "She's always home," which could have been a reference to me or the love interest. During the valiant struggle to get their boots off, they didn't speak at all.

It embarrasses Joe Jr. when I'm eager in front of his friends so I waited a few minutes before going out, six minutes by the clock on my computer screen, time enough for them to half-empty the fridge. Every container was out, all the lids confused, the diminishing smorg spread out between them as they sub-vocalized between mouthfuls. "Hello," I said and they sprang back like startled carnivores off their quarry.

Joe Jr.: "Thanks for the heart attack."

Simon was back to not seeing me, though I saw him because his acne glowed. Supposedly they have miracle cures now—gone the hell of tetracycline, the shame of the Ten-O-Six pad. But poor Simon is incurable. (Joe Jr., luckily, hasn't had to suffer the way his father did.) "How was school?" I asked.

Joe Jr. fed himself a chipful of salsa in lieu of a reply.

"Not too boring?" I asked.

"Mom." He glanced at Simon, who had his neon chin tucked into his shoulder to avoid me.

"Are you all right?" I asked.

Vsyo normalno?

"Yes!" he snapped.

So much for the new mother-son communication. I'd prom-ised to tell him the rest of my story but, apparently, he didn't want to hear it any more. Slinking off, smarting despite how I had been dreading confessing to him, I left them to make chew-ing sounds at each other.

Earlier in the day, transcribing Chekhov's letter, I read this one too: *Nobody wants to understand me. Everybody is stupid and unjust. I'm in a bad temper and speak nonsense. My family breathes easier when I go out.* Evidently it's viral. Now they've got it too. It must be the wonderful weather, the scented air, the flouncy trees—enough to put anyone in a foul mood. Plus, I was getting no work done, which is fine when you have no work, but when you actually do, it's frustrating.

I stumped back to the computer and just sat there.

Joe got home from the hospital a few hours later, just as my bad mood was peaking. He washed his hands in the kitchen, sliced the bread on the cutting board. Over at the stove, I manned the ladle. "Not so much," I told him. "It's just us."

"Where's Joey?"

"He went out somewhere with Simon."

"Did he skip today?"

"How would I know?"

I set a bowl of soup in front of him. Before picking up his spoon, he paused to scratch all over his head with both hands, hair standing at attention, imagined flakes swirling and descending over his bowl. "Mmm," he said, tucking in. "Good."

After a few spoonfuls, he noticed my disgust. "What?" he asked.

"You just seasoned your soup with dandruff!"

His shoulders sagged, but he carried on—buttering his bread, dipping it in his bowl. Finally, he mustered his courage. "What's wrong, Jane?"

"Nothing."

"You're presenting differently." Then he looked around the room. If I hadn't spent an hour concocting soup (after tracking down the blade of the food processor that Maria had secreted away), if I hadn't undone Maria, he would have noticed right away. She leaves this vinegary miasma behind. I thought of her departure that afternoon, trudging out to the guzzler with her belongings in a half-dozen plastic bags—change of clothes, plastic shoes and wallet, even her own rags—while her pimp idled out front, ruining the climate.

"We should fire her," Joe said.

"Finally," I said. "Thanks for offering."

He's so kind, so sweet, so cowardly. He looked horrified.

"How about we move to another city?" he said.

I sighed because here's my problem with Maria, why, even though she only comes every second Tuesday, she exercises such power over me. She reminds me of my aunt Eva, who died twelve years ago. I was eighteen when I lived with my aunt, old enough to recognize what that basement repository of flattened cans stood for. The smelly balls of wool. The way she cooked for ten then froze the eight remaining portions, just in case. In case of what? I thought I was so smart. I thought I—*I!*—could prevent a war, but it never occurred to me that my aunt and father were so odd because they'd lived through one. I dipped my spoon in my bowl of guilt, lifted a bearable dose to my lips, sipped. Across from me, Joe ate heartily because he is a man with a clear conscience. The doctor's conscience is a big glass room, shiny and full of light. I watched him bend over his bowl, dousing his bread, slurping like a Russian peasant, and it made me feel vengeful.

"So," I said. "Last night Joe Jr. told me you go behind my back all the time."

He tried avoidance. "Are we still on the newspaper? I left it out for you."

I said, "That's what he told me last night."

"Last night when?"

"When I sat on him."

"You sat on him?"

"By accident."

Now, resignation. It doesn't take much to bring on that state in Joe. I presume he's very much in charge at work, but here he's mostly resigned. He blinked wistfully at his bowl because sometimes he doesn't have time for lunch. Why was I punishing him? "Eat," I said, disgusted with myself now, and he did, with renewed diligence.

He served himself seconds, then asked if the manuscript had come.

"Yes."

"Good. You'll have something to do." He hesitated. "Is it a good book?"

"I don't know. Searching for errors spoils the effect."

"Are there a lot?"

"No." I explained how fewer errors actually made the work less enjoyable; you start nitpicking to justify your fee. He shook his head in genuine amazement and immediately, I felt lousier. How could he be impressed with that after how he'd spent his working day? Someone might have died, or been saved, yet he acts as though what he does is no more difficult than correcting *lie* and *lay*. Sometimes he'll freeze in the middle of something and call out, "Jane! Help! Am I lying this down or am I laying it?"

"I'm so critical," I moaned.

"It's your job."

"I'm so grumpy!"

"That's part of your mystique!"

"Oh, you sweet darling," I said, turning away and hating myself like in the old days.

Joe went down to The Lair after dinner. He keeps the volume low but I could hear the disquieting, irregular clank of the weights striking the concrete floor. Joe Jr. was still out with Simon and hadn't called to say where he was. Maybe they'd gone over to the girl's house, or arranged to meet her somewhere. Not, I prayed, on the infamous Granville Mall where hordes of teenagers hope to evade the ID checks in the clubs, where they loiter when they've been carded, vulnerable to pushers, to pimps, to peer pressure, to being in the wrong place at the wrong time, to et cetera, et cetera. I was too restless to work or read so I went out for a walk.

In Vancouver the streets are mainly laid out in a grid. The numbered avenues run east to west, the streets north to south

from Burrard Inlet to the Fraser River, so although our neighbourhood is much farther south than Kitsilano, the street names
are the same. I headed west and the first street I reached was
Gandhi, a.k.a. Blenheim. Along it and on the avenue ahead, the
trees were all in bloom. There were two different types, a stately
white on Gandhi and a pale, confetti pink on 38th. I'd always
thought they were cherries, but yesterday Rachel had said some
were plums. Now it struck me that I'd lived for twenty-one years
in this city famous for its parks, for its trees, for wearing green
the whole year long and all these pastel shades in the spring, yet
there was barely a tree I could name. I was trying not to worry
needlessly about my son because, after all, it was only just after
eight o'clock. I tried to enjoy the beauty of the plums (or cherries) instead, but the beauty of the plums (or cherries) reminded
me again of that spring when I loved Sonia so much that I suffered physical pain, a dull throbbing in my chest that never let
up. Occasionally stories appear in the paper about lovers separated, usually by war, who somehow reconnect decades later and
fall in love again. I always wonder how they distinguish passion from angina. Was that what Joe Jr. and Simon were going
through, that exquisite agony? I hoped they didn't love the same
girl. Me, Dieter, and Pascal—we were all in love with Sonia.

I got as far as Chomsky Street, then turned back in case Joe
Jr. called.

Joe was in the shower. I checked for messages, but there
were none so I put on my nightgown and got into bed where
I lay willing the phone to ring. A few minutes later Joe came in.

"Did Joe Jr. phone while I was out?"

"Were you out?"

"I went for a walk."

"That's nice," and he sat down on the bed and leaned over
me with his wet hair dripping on my face. "Was it raining?"
he asked.

"It just started."

We kissed for a minute, though I wasn't really concentrating. I can do it with my eyes closed, so to speak. He broke off to say, "So the kid's out? That's convenient."

"Where do you think he is?"

"I have better things to think about."

He was just trying to seize an opportunity. Tomorrow he was on call. He didn't have to get up so early. Also, it's very difficult to have uninhibited sex with an adolescent in the house. But I needed reassurance before I could get into the mood. "He has his cell. He'd call if there was trouble. Wouldn't he?"

Joe: "He'd better not. We're not answering."

He kissed me again, forcing me to run through my list in mid-act. It's different now from when he was in kindergarten; pedophile abduction, for example, has been updated to teenage prostitution. I'd never heard of crystal meth until last year. Some things never change: car accidents, random acts of violence, earthquakes, nuclear war. A cell going bad. That cell doubling, then trebling. Joe had no idea what was running through my mind during his caresses. Or maybe he did.

Then, in the middle of it, after I had peeled my nightgown off and tossed it on the floor, a wonderful thing happened. Several wonderful things, but one of them was that minutes went by, many minutes, when I stopped thinking about my son and the perils of being alive in this world, when I thought instead about my husband and what he was doing to me. And afterward, as we lay there breathing hard, Joe singing "Fucked Up Ronnie" under his breath, I realized this just might be *the thing*. Better than Chekhov even. Better than Xanax or Ativan or Tolstoy. Because pleasure is so distracting when you allow yourself to feel it.

Joe stopped singing. "I have an idea."

"I do too."

"You go first," he said.

"I think we should go to a motel. Tell Joe Jr. we're going to a movie, but go to a motel instead."

He swelled. "Am I as good as that?"

"You are," I said, lifting his hand off my breast to kiss his palm. "What's your idea?"

Second thoughts crowded onto his face; I had to prod it out of him.

"Go and see her," he said.

"Who?"

Who indeed. And how? All this time, as far as I knew, Sonia had been in Ontario. Or maybe they'd moved her again. I could have written, but I didn't. I didn't know what to say. She probably wasn't even the same person. How could she be? How long can you stay earnest behind bars? Or idealistic? If it were me, I wouldn't last a day.

"How would I find her?" I asked Joe. "Presuming I wanted to. She'll hardly be in the phone book."

"It's not hard to track people down. Contact her lawyer."

"How would I find out who her lawyer was?"

"Jane," he said. "Jane. Here in the twenty-first century? We have this thing called Google."

I rolled over. "Yes. I've heard of it."

He went to sleep. I lay awake, fluttery and anxious. All those feelings forced into dormancy by trauma, stirred up again. I didn't want to see her and, no doubt, she felt the same. Yet I couldn't help wondering what she looked like now. Immediately I pictured her long hair white, which was ridiculous because we're the same age, thirty-nine. But the very *least* thing prison probably did to you was age you prematurely. Maybe it had made Sonia the old woman she thought she'd never get the chance to be.

1 9 8 4

I couldn't sleep. All night I kept feeling that distorted ridge of bone under my palm. I sweated, tossed. Gulped water and got up to refill my glass. The next morning seemed like it would never come, but it did. It came much too soon with Sonia shaking my arm and asking, "You don't have an exam, do you?"

"No. Do you?"

"I'm not going. Let's take him to the Endowment Lands."

Pascal had not run away from us. He was still asleep on the chesterfield when I came down. During the night, one of the things I had fretted about was that the police would be looking for him. His picture had probably been in the newspaper. We didn't normally get the paper because it was full of lies, but by sheer chance I'd picked it up yesterday for the classified ads. I went out on the deck where the recycling was piled and scanned the headlines. It was a beautiful spring morning and the sun made my headache sing. But there was nothing in the paper so I went back inside.

Sonia was making pancakes. "We'll wake him in a minute," she said.

And suddenly the solution came. I had confused it with my fear. "Let's call the police."

She turned to me, shocked. "We can't have the police here, Jane. What about the action?"

"We'll take him to the university and call them there. They'll take him home."

"You heard what he said last night. He'll just run away again. We've got to make him change his mind."

"How?"

"We have to convince him. We have to show him how wonderful it is to be alive." When she said this, I sank down at the table with my head in my hands because there was no one, no one, less suited to this task than me.

Sonia went to rouse Pascal, who joined us, eating cheerfully and heartily. I stared at him. He had cancer. I had felt it myself, his tangible, bony death, not the hypothetical one I always felt for myself. Yet neither cancer nor our sombre mood affected his appetite, though that other symptom of our distress, our barely touched plates, got his attention right away. "All the More for Me" was apparently the motto he would die by.

The bus took us up Kropotkin Street. We transferred and got off where the Endowment Lands began, crossing a city street— two lanes in each direction separated by a meridian. From there we stepped directly into forest. Traffic noise ceased and it seemed we were already miles from human commerce or habitation, deep in a strata of green, leathery leaves underfoot, ferns waist-high, trunks and branches brightly furred with moss, overhead a cathedral span of boughs. "Holy shit," said Pascal, craning to take in the full height of the trees. He turned a circle on the path. Sonia, she was brilliant. This was how we'd make our case for life, without even saying anything.

For a few minutes that's what we did, walked in silence, then Pascal left the trail and set off bushwhacking in his white boots. We started to follow, but when too many branches whipped back and stung our faces, Sonia and I returned to the trail. Farther ahead, around a bend, Pascal leapt out from behind a tree and scared us. Apparently our screams were hilarious. Sonia glanced at me and, clearly worried that silliness was about to replace reverence, chose this moment to take his hand. He grinned and tried to kiss her. I was outraged, but he had cancer. He had *cancer*. I didn't even know the word in Russian.

Sonia gently pushed him off. He walked over to a mossy trunk and began caressing it instead. "Isn't it beautiful here?" she asked him. "Wouldn't you miss this?"

He said that he would. He said that was why he was determined to stay. The trees in Esterhazy were barely trees compared to these.

"I mean if you were—" She choked on the word.

Pascal: "Dead? We'll all be dead in a few months anyway, right?"

"I hope not!"

"But that's what the generals say." And he put an arm around the tree that could not refuse him the way Sonia had and swung around it, smiling at his own cleverness. "Since they're the ones with all the bombs, I guess they know what they're talking about."

Sonia glanced at me again, imploring. I just stood there. Because maybe he was right. It was our own logic flung back in our faces and it stung as much as the tree branches had.

She changed tack. "Don't you want to see your squeeze one last time?"

Right away, he softened. "I said goodbye. They didn't know it, but I did. I hugged them and said I loved them and then I snuck out in the night."

"What do they do?" Sonia asked.

"My parents? My dad works at the plant. My mom's just a mom."

"She must be heartsick," Sonia said.

"I called them from a payphone. I told them I was okay." He walked on.

"You seem so nice," Sonia said, following. "Would you really hurt her like that?"

Pascal turned. "You're always asking me questions. Can I ask you one?"

"All right."

"Why don't you have a boyfriend?"

I waited for her answer too. "I couldn't," she said.

"Why not?"

"What if something happened to him?" she said, and the way Pascal shook his head, it was clear that he already subscribed to the wonders of being alive, that it was Sonia and I who, in our fear of dying, had turned our backs on life.

Sonia gave up on the subject after that. She dropped behind and walked with me, letting Pascal lead the way. Though he had no idea where he was going and chose each fork in the trail at random, eventually we emerged onto a paved road across from a row of duplex housing for students with families. We trudged across the campus. I hadn't eaten anything, had barely slept the night before. The watery pressure of unshed tears was building up inside me.

Somehow he found the path behind the Museum of Anthropology. He must have come that way with Pete. We clambered down, using stones and roots as handholds, and arrived on a pebbled beach where driftwood logs were scattered around like sticks. Nearby stood a large concrete structure straight out of campus lore—a gun tower prettied up with graffiti, erected during World War II to repel a Japanese invasion. Pascal climbed to the top of it and made machine gun sounds while we waited, embarrassed, for this fit of childishness to pass.

"I want to go home," I told Sonia.

She grabbed my hand. "Jane. I need you."

"What can I do?"

"I don't know yet. Please stay. We'll figure something out. We always do."

When Pascal came back down from the tower, we continued walking around the end of the promontory. He spent some time here skipping stones. By then I was dizzy with hunger. Each grating step had a similar effect on my nerves. "Look," he said with mock surprise when, ahead, a number of people came into view, some lying on the beach, others reclining on logs, a few even swimming in the frigid water. He walked faster. A prudish distance away, Sonia and I halted. Wreck Beach. None of them was wearing clothes.

"Come on," he said.

She was as horrified as I was. "No!"

"I'm going in."

Pascal stripped his shirt off. We turned to face the trees, waiting until it seemed safe to look again. When we turned back, his clothes were piled on shore, but he was still working up his nerve, standing thigh-deep in the water, backside to us, pretty as a flower.

"I'm going," I said.

"Jane." She took my hand and led me to a log, never once taking her eyes off Pascal. He plunged and, a second later, bobbed up, sputtering, in a different place. I didn't notice anyone approaching. I was watching Pascal swim and thinking how it was Dieter who had taught him back in Saskatchewan.

"What about telling Pete and Dieter?" she asked.

"Pete will side with Pascal. He'll say he has a right to do what he wants."

"Even die?"

"Who knows how far Pete will go?"

"That's true. But Dieter might take him home. He doesn't want to do the action anyway."

"You really think he would?"

"He might," Sonia said. "If *I* ask him." She blushed before adding, "Or I could go."

"What about the action?"

"That's the thing," she moaned. "The action is my chance to finally do something that will count."

"There you are! You didn't come for your paper."

We both looked up. I'd never had the occasion to see a penis in the flesh. This one hung above us, rosy and helpless between shaggy thighs, a naked bird in a nest of hair. Hair covered the rest of his body too, whorling in a weather pattern round his belly. I lifted my eyes to the beard. Kopanyev? As soon as Sonia realized he was talking to me, she sprang up and ran to Pascal.

Kopanyev said, "You should come and pick it up. You didn't do as bad as that. Come this afternoon."

I was speechless. He seemed not to realize it was because he was nude.

"If you're going to have convictions, no matter how misguided, you must take little criticism, yes? You did very well on your examination. I peeked. You knew that, of course. You're very bright." He waited for me to respond and when I didn't, he sighed. "I hope our little spat won't change your mind about Russian. Or Russians. This one." He pointed to the mat on his chest. "In particular."

I dropped my gaze to his feet. He was wearing dress shoes and socks.

"You are coming back next year, ya?"

"That depends," I said. I meant the end of the world might change all our plans, but when I looked up at his face again, skipping the parts in between, I saw that he was hurt. With a brusque nod, Kopanyev walked away, bestowing on me a long, receding view of the hair concentrating in his crack.

I was wretched after that. I felt expelled from Kopanyev's favour and, by extension, Russian literature. Sonia didn't ask me what the matter was. She didn't ask about that hairy apparition, my former favourite professor, because she was too upset herself. The entire bus ride home her pale forehead pleated with worry; she tenderized her bottom lip. Pascal put his arm around her and she didn't even pull away like she usually did. When we got off at the stop, she asked me, "What's that word again? For ice cream?"

Morozhenoye.

We stopped at the corner store so she could buy some. Pascal bought a bag of chips, two chocolate bars, a pocketful of penny candy. *Konfyeta.* He was like a kid. He *was* a kid. A kid blowing his allowance and dancing around Sonia, trying to get her to eat a chip. "No," she kept saying. "No, please." Then she gave in and closed her eyes as though it was his last request, allowing Pascal, with a delicate, priestlike gesture, to place the rippled wafer on her tongue and laugh.

As soon as we got home, she asked me to keep him in her room while she went to get a spoon. Then she asked me to stay. Pascal sat cross-legged on the bed and ate the ice cream with Sonia beside him sucking on her cross. Now and then he held out the little tub for each of us to vehemently decline it. When he had eaten it all, he fell back groaning, so his capacity for taking in food was finite after all. "Listen," he said, still on his back. He pulled one leg of his jeans up and, clasping his hands behind his knee, set to pumping the leg madly. "Leg farts!" he crowed. "Leg farts!"

It was *that leg.*

It seemed so strange, the way he acted. Because I didn't know any teenage boys. They'd never been an object of fascination for me, or even interest, like they'd been for other girls.

Their capacious appetites, their Rip Van Winkle slumbers, their bravado and invincibility—all this was new to me. Sonia, though, she had a younger brother. Sonia was pretty and popular. She had experience.

That night everyone in NAG! but Dieter met at the elementary school near our house. It was a Catholic school with a high chain link fence and, above the door, a white statue of the Virgin Mary in a giant clamshell of radiant light. We had come for the fence. Sonia brought Pascal, exiling him to the playground while we worked. No one objected to him being there. He ran up the teeter-totter until it tipped, then turned and ran back in a mad race against gravity. He hung upside-down on the monkey bars. All the while he was acutely aware of what we were doing at the fence. His antics made this obvious.

We had waited till it got dark, which was happening later and later now. Pete and I unloaded the chains and locks from the packs. Isis had brought the stopwatch. For the purpose of timing the action, we divided into two groups, those who would be chained and those who would chain. In reality, we had too many chainees, particularly if Dieter wouldn't join us (and it appeared that he wouldn't since he wouldn't even come out for the practice). I paired with Timo, which required me to press against his softness spread-eagled to the fence while I struggled to weave the chain behind his back and through the links. Giggling further hindered the task and soon the whole exercise disintegrated. Then we tried with two chainers, which was faster when speed was the point; the stopwatch told us just over a minute. But only Pete and Timo were attached to the fence when we finished, leaving four of us to slosh the fake blood around.

Isis got an idea. This was her forte—telling people where to stand, how to move, what to do. We tried it *in* a chain. As soon as Sonia and I had finished attaching Pete, Sonia leaned against the fence. Carla, who had just chained Timo, simply turned to her left and helped me with Sonia. Then Carla and I went over to Isis, who was waiting, patient as a caryatid, wrists crossed above her head. Though this worked much better, we knew that valuable minutes could be saved if someone got a head start chaining Isis.

"This is bullshit," said Pete. "Pascal! Come here!"

This time we dramatized it. We pretended we were on the tour with Isis as our guide. "Go!" would be our cue to dash to the fence.

"Right this way, folks. Now we're going to enter the plant itself and see just where we manufacture our world-famous first-strike weapons. Yes, folks. Right here is where we make nuclear holocausts happen." And she mimed waving us through the gap that led to the playground. "Go!"

We were better at it now that we'd done it a couple of times. Pete and I stepped back from chaining Timo and saw the result: Isis chained to Carla, Sonia to Pascal. And I wondered what kind of bonds they really were.

There was an argument that night. It started in the kitchen while Dieter was bent over the smoking toaster saying to no one and us all, "Who put this on high?" Out on the deck, Pete was corrupting his acolyte. They came reekingly in, both of them staggering for the granola jar. Pete clawed inside it then headed for the fridge.

"What happened?" Dieter asked Pascal. "You were going to play Monopoly with me tonight."

Pascal bobbed, trying not to giggle. "I went with them."

I could see this hurt Dieter, probably more than he showed. Pascal had run away to Dieter, and for a time Dieter had taken him under his wing. But then Pascal transferred his allegiance to Pete, despite how Dieter kept trying to reinforce his and Pascal's shared Esterhazy connection, quizzing Pascal about places and people they knew in common. The more Pascal sensed Dieter's neediness, the more he distanced himself. That, or he was too weak to resist the magnetic pull of Uncle Peter.

Kneading the back of his neck madly, Dieter turned. Pete was standing before the open fridge drinking out of a carton. "That's Sonia's milk," he said.

And Pete exploded, spraying granola around the room. "There are so many fucking rules around here! It's like you're working for the Mounties! Are you?"

"What's that supposed to mean!"

"Sonia's right here." Pete pointed to where she cowered in the doorway waiting for Pascal to be released into her care. "If she doesn't want to share her milk," Pete said, "she can tell me herself. She's a big girl. She doesn't need you to speak for her."

"You twist everything to suit your purposes! We're supposed to run this house by consensus! We're supposed to respect each other's personal property!"

Pete turned to Pascal with an aha look. "See?"

Dieter: "And we're supposed to run the group by consensus too! But when that consensus goes against what you want, you ignore it! Or you start name-calling!"

"Wrong. I start calling a spade a spade. You're the one misusing consensus. It's called filibustering."

"Did I bring that kid into the group tonight?"

Pascal, slitty, blandly chewing, burst into titters when he realized Dieter meant him. Pete: "Why wouldn't *you* come?"

Sonia begging them to stop. "This is crazy. We have to work together. We have to do this action. It's our last chance. Why don't we *all* play Monopoly?"

The last time we played had been the night before the Hyatt action, when we were getting along so well. Sonia pleaded until

Dieter finally agreed and fetched the game from his room. He explained the inverted rules to Pascal and, miraculously, tensions subsided. We might even have brought the evening to a peaceful close if we had chosen a different game. A game that took less time to play. Because the longer we played, the greater the chance that tempers would flare again, which was what happened an hour later when Sonia rolled and landed on Community Chest. It was as inevitable as Monopoly is endless.

"You have won second prize in a beauty contest. Collect $10."

"You should have won first prize," Pascal said, reaching for her.

She retreated behind her hair. "Beauty contests are sexist. We shouldn't even have that card in the game."

Pete retrieved it from the bottom of the pile and tore it up.

"What do you think you're doing?" Dieter cried.

"Isn't it a house game?"

"No! It's mine!"

"Go then," said Pete, tossing him the dice.

Dieter passed Go and paid his $200, grudgingly it seemed, then immediately earned it back by landing on Income Tax. "Hold on," he said when I went to take my turn. He was still tallying his funds, trying to calculate the greater sum, two hundred dollars or 10 percent.

"Roll," Pete told me. "Just go."

"I haven't finished my turn yet," Dieter said.

"Just take the two hundred for fuck's sake."

"Now I've lost count." And he started again, meticulously counting out his ones until Pete flipped the board closed, sending all the pieces flying. "Earthquake!" he sang.

Pascal laughed but Dieter was livid. "We weren't finished!" The rest of us, bored too, started to disband, Sonia ducking underneath the table to pick the houses and tokens off the floor.

"Let's at least count our money," Dieter said.

"You lost," Pete said.

Pascal: "You're the biggest capitalist!"

As soon as the words were out of his mouth, Pascal looked sorry for having said them. But Dieter turned to Pete, as though Pete had delivered the insult and, in a way, Pete had by so assiduously indoctrinating Pascal. "You're one to talk."

Pete: "What's that supposed to mean?"

"*I sail. I play field hockey. I spend all my daddy's money.*"

"Fuck you," Pete said. "Leave my sister out of it."

"Your sister's sacred. Mine's not?"

Pete blinked. Clearly, he didn't even remember Dieter had a sister. He certainly didn't recall making a comment about her, but evidently he had. "You're such a hypocrite," Dieter went on. "About everything. You say you're anti-government, but I can't help noticing you have no problem taking what the government provides."

"What are you talking about?" Pete asked, and Dieter opened the Monopoly board like a book and pointed to the squares. "*Water Works. Electric Company.*"

Pascal said, "All that should be free anyway!"

"Excuse me? Who said that?" He squinted molishly around through the big glasses. "Oh, you! You're *still* here? Sorry. I understood you were looking for other accommodation."

"He's fine here," said Sonia, emerging from under the table with a handful of pieces. Pete took them and, tossing a house high into the air, caught it in his mouth. We gasped when he swallowed. When he did it a second time with one of the metal tokens, Sonia lunged and pried the remaining pieces away from him.

Pete: "I'm giving Pascal my room."

He went upstairs. We sat there, stunned by what had just happened. Pascal, obviously ashamed, started helping Dieter put the game away, replacing the cards and pieces and all the coloured money in their respective slots. No one spoke until Pete came back down, dragging his sleeping bag and foamie. Under his other arm was a milk crate full of clothes. He told Pascal he could have whatever was left in the room.

"No," said Pascal.

"Take it. It's yours."

"Even the boom box?" Pascal asked, incredulous.

Sonia: "Where are you going to sleep, Pete?"

"I'm moving to the garage."

"It's horrible in there, Pete. It's disgusting."

We followed him. From the outside, the garage looked uninhabitable, compost mounded on one side, shoring it up, and not a shingle visible for the moss. He wasn't going to change his mind, so we helped with the magnitudinous task of clearing out all the decades of forerenters' crap. There was an overhead light but it was burned out. I went back to the house to get a working bulb and, once it was screwed in, all was revealed: the cobwebs strung like tinsel, a hundred rusted paint cans, smashed flower pots, tires, disintegrating cardboard boxes, rodent pellets, heaps of dubious rags. There were two wooden doors at the back that swung outward, though probably hadn't in a lifetime. Pete kicked them open—squawk!—and we started moving the boxes out to the alley. The bottom fell out of the one Sonia was carrying and a reeking nest of shredded blanket landed at her feet. Both of us screamed. The remaining boxes we pushed and kicked out, then we carried out the cans. The floor, finally exposed, turned out to be planks laid across dirt. Sonia fetched the broom and swept and swept, but it wasn't ever going to make a difference.

Going by Sonia and Pete's faces, the nasty things in their hair, by the time we finished I looked as filthy as I felt. Sonia and

I went inside while Pete stopped at the outside tap and washed there. I took a long bath. Later, I looked out my bedroom window into the back yard. The light in the garage was off. I never saw it on again.

The next morning when I looked out, Pete was urinating on the compost pile. He ducked briefly into the garage for a plastic bag of bread and a mug from one of the boxes we'd left in the alley. He filled the mug from the outside tap then, finding a sunny place in the long grass, sat and ate his breakfast.

As the day progressed, it became obvious that Pete didn't intend just to sleep in the garage, but to live there and not enter the house at all. Sonia went to talk to him late in the morning, only to return almost in tears. She woke Pascal, dragged him down, and, with strict instructions to bring Pete back, sent him out. After half an hour, the two of us reconnoitred in the garage ourselves. Pascal was sketching in his book while Pete lounged on his foamie. "Pete," said Sonia in the doorway. "Please."

He kept his gaze fixed on the cobwebbed rafters. "I told you. Pete doesn't live there any more."

"You do!"

She had one last idea. Commanding me to stay where I was, half in the garage, half leaning into spring, she went back to the house. The pear tree was blooming in the yard. Pascal held up a sketch of the neighbour's gnome. Pete said, "You're nuts."

Finally, Sonia reappeared with Dieter, who looked like he'd just had his ears boxed. "Dieter has something to say to you."

"I'm sorry," Dieter said, red-faced. "I didn't mean what I said. Pascal can have the living room. I don't care." He cupped his nose. "Sometimes I feel like nobody—" Then he threw up his hands. "Never mind!"

Pete looked right at his former housemate. It was the first time I'd heard him use a gentle tone with Dieter. "Forget it,

man. You were absolutely right. Pete *was* acting like a hypocrite.
He *wasn't* living by his own principles. You showed him that."

I found a note hanging from the string on the grate. Pulled
through the fretwork and unscrolled, it was a newspaper article. *Sick Boy Still Missing.*

What was I thinking? Why didn't I do more to get him
home? He'd talked about his parents, shown us drawings of
them, but I never thought of trying to contact them. I never considered the hell they were going through. I wish I could blame
Sonia, but I blame myself, my half-heartedness. I was *neopre-
delennaya.* (In Russian there are eight words for *vague.*) Already
Pascal's cancer had started to feel unreal to me, even though I
had really felt it with my own hand, skin to skin. This was probably what had happened to Pascal, too, what would have happened to me a few days after seeing *If You Love This Planet* except
that I had Sonia there constantly stoking my dread. Everyone
was going to die this horrible death, probably very soon, and we
all knew it, but everyone carried on as usual. It was as easy for
most people to forget about the missiles as it was for me to forget there was anything the matter with Pascal. He didn't seem
sick. On the contrary, he was the liveliest person in the house.

That day on Wreck Beach Sonia abandoned her exams so
she could devote herself to the problem of getting Pascal home.
Having seen her in action many times, knowing how persuasive
she could be, I had no doubt she would succeed in convinc-
ing him to go. And so I abdicated. I abdicated all responsibility
for him.

Pete moved into the garage and Pascal became his gofer, a
boy to bring him what he needed from the house. Pete needed
books, Bakunin and Kropotkin, *The Anarchist Handbook*, his
engineering texts. He needed the two garden statues without

which the hearth looked bare and the living room unironic. The Ronald Reagan mask, too, went missing from the nail on the kitchen wall. Sonia brought him food because Pete wouldn't eat with us. But Pete was still in NAG! and he turned up for our practices every few nights (Dieter too), unnerving everyone by the way he kept referring to himself by name, in the third person.

That week we held our meeting around the fire pit Pete had constructed. The issue for him was electricity. This was why he wouldn't come into the house. He told us, "Pete will not live with state-supplied light. Pete will no longer be bought out by the forces of government."

Hunched by the fire, erratically illuminated by its flames, Pete looked weird, spooky, passing around a five-fingered bag of marshmallows. Surprisingly, the practices were going well and the decisions we made that night came easily too, perhaps from having to keep our voices low. (The neighbours were more concerned about the smoke from Pete's fire than the ultimate conflagration we hoped to save them from.) Our forced whispers and half-tones precluded argument, or the marshmallows sweetened our words, or we were just too freaked out by Pete. We settled on a date for the action—the last Sunday in April, traditionally the day of the Walk for Peace, the peace movement's Christmas, the highlight of the year. Estimates for that year's walk broke all records: one hundred thousand people. But we in NAG!, we Naggers, disdained the walk for being merely symbolic, hardly more than a parade. On April 29, 1984, eight months before the world was scheduled to end, rather than be usurped by Trots as we tramped across the Burrard Street Bridge shouldering our papier mâché cruise missiles, we would be acting to save the world, not just singing songs about it.

Then Pete's proposal to include non-Naggers in the action was accepted without a murmur. We were in need of one or two extra people. They wouldn't be joining the group per se, because an affinity group by nature must be small. It was a kind of cell, a cell for peace. "Pete's suggestion is that we invite these people in with the understanding that after the action we help them form a group themselves—something we've been talking about for a long time anyway, right?"

"I think that's a great idea, Pete," said Sonia and she named Pascal, since he had already been at the practices and knew everything that was going on. We threw other names around, including Ruth's, then Dieter said, "I'm not trying to *filibuster* or anything, but—how about we stick with Pascal? It'll be a whole lot less complicated."

Afterward we all went inside, except Pete, and I made tea. Dieter and Sonia headed upstairs, Dieter to study, Sonia to tell Pascal what we'd decided. We could hear the music from Pete's old room, where Pascal was apparently listening his way through every one of Pete's tapes. It was strange to hear Mozart in the house.

Downstairs, Isis snugged a nylon stocking over Timo's face. *Napyalivat*: to put on a tight garment with a certain amount of effort. Instantly, his placid features were erased and in his place sat this faceless giant. She plucked at the fabric over one eye, snipped the tip off with scissors. It sprang back, revealing a blinking hazel orb. She did the same with the other eye and the mouth, then removed the stocking so she could seal the edges of each hole with nail polish.

The nights were still chilly. I warmed my hands on the pot as the tea steeped, picturing Pete doing the same outside over the dying embers of the fire, nails packed with grime, face roughened with stubble, hair perfumed with smoke. I couldn't actually see him, but he would be able to see us if he stood in the door of the garage. We would look bright and comfortable under those sixty hypocritical watts, framed in the window like a diorama, discussing him.

"He stinks," Carla said. "He needs a bath."

"You need water for that."

"He's got to drink. What's he drinking?"

He'd left bowls out, but it hadn't rained in over a week. I kept my mouth shut about the tap and told them instead about the dew-catcher he'd made from stones, a pot, and a plastic bag.

"He can do anything," Isis said, blowing on the nail polish. "I tell you, he's a genius."

I wondered why Sonia was taking so long with Pascal. Should I pour her tea or would it just get cold?

Isis turned to me. "Is Pete okay? I feel terrible. Should I talk to him?"

Carla said, "No. That's why he's doing it."

"It's creepy," Isis said, "how he says *Pete* this and *Pete* that."

"He's trying to guilt you out. Right, Timo?"

"I don't know," Timo said. "I hope it isn't dissociation."

Isis shivered and laid her forehead on the table so the bronze ropes of her hair spread across her back. "The stress is killing me. Exams. Pete acting crazy. The action."

"Nuclear war," I added.

Carla got up to massage her shoulders. "Exams are done," she said.

Isis: "I think my head's going to explode. We've got to do something fun. Soon."

Timo had been sitting patiently, waiting for Isis to need him again. She was making each of us a mask, a second skin across which she was going to conjure horribly realistic burns. Now he looked at me and asked the question no one had dared bring up. "So Jane. Where's he ppppooping then?"

I had left the matter of the dying, runaway child we were harbouring in Sonia's small, capable hands so that I could concentrate on studying. It never occurred to me that this was a stupid,

selfish course, just as it never occurred to me to be jealous of a
sixteen-year-old boy until he and Sonia came in the door with
petals in their hair. When I saw them, I thought of confetti,
then the Russian word for candy, *konfyeta*, and I broke into a
sweat over my exam, my very last, scheduled sadistically on
the very last week, almost the last day, as though to prolong my
misery, the agony of learning Russian, that sado-masochistic
language. Because, unlike Sonia, I couldn't *not* study. It wasn't in
my nature. I had to keep at it until the ordeal was done. I would
still be studying when I took the bus to the university on Thursday, muttering conjugations and declensions. I would be studying even as I huddled outside the examination room, my back to
the wall, hugging my knees. Every noun in Russian had twelve
forms! All this zealotry even though I knew I wasn't going to
continue in Slavonic Studies, even though I would never get the
chance to use the Russian that I'd learned.

They came into the house together like a bride and groom,
triggering in me a spasm of hindsight. Pascal was always trying
to get near Sonia, even touch her, and she was always slithering
from his grasp or physically unhanding herself when he now
and then actually got her in his brazen teenage clutches. But at
the NAG! meeting the night before this hadn't happened. Pascal had sat on his hands and trained his idiot smile on her from
across the fire, which forced me to conclude now, with a mar-
tyrizing pang, that the touching was happening elsewhere.
Suddenly I knew how Alexei Laptev really felt in "Three Years"
*suffering the shame and humiliation of someone who had been
rejected, who wasn't loved, who was thought unattractive, repulsive
and perhaps even hateful, and whom everyone avoided* . . . and Staff-
Captain Ryabovitch in "The Kiss," that *short, stooping officer*,
the *most modest and most insignificant* officer in the brigade,
whose unremarkable appearance the ladies deem *vague*, who,
after the kiss, goes to sleep at night imagining *someone caressing*

him and making him happy, even while recognizing that these caresses are *absurd*. Now I wanted to be Kitty, because when Kitty was in love with Varenka, her love was returned.

They'd been holding hands, but let go as soon as they saw me. I hurried up the stairs. "Jane," Sonia called.

She followed me. Pascal was right behind her. I heard a chiding whisper, then Pete's door closing and the music coming on. Sonia knocked. "I'm busy," I said from my desk, but she came in anyway and lay down on my futon. I pretended to be reading. *Ya chitayu*. I'm reading. In Russian, there are twenty-six prefixes for that particular verb.

"I did it," she said.

I turned in my chair and saw her stretched out on my futon with her hair fanned out around her. All spring I had longed to see her lying there like that. "He's going back," she said. Then she rolled over and pressed her face into the pillow where I laid my head every night thinking about her.

"He's really going?"

She nodded. I heard her sob. Then I was crying too, from relief. I'd been mistaken. She didn't love him *that way*. She loved him the way she loved everyone, including me. That was the best I could do. And it was fine. Really. As long as he was leaving.

I came over and sat beside her on the futon. She pushed herself up and we embraced. After a minute, she asked, "Why are you crying, Jane?"

"I'm happy." I blotted my eyes on the sheet.

"Jane? Will you help me?"

"Of course. What?"

"Because—" She looked flushed and I couldn't tell if it was out of embarrassment or excitement. "I couldn't have a baby. I couldn't."

And I felt so stupid. I felt betrayed.

"Don't look at me like that," she said. "Please, Jane."

"Don't do it, Sonia. Don't." I thought to add, "Not unless you want to."

She swelled with indignation. "I don't *want* to. I'm not like that. Not at all. But if I do, he'll go back home and cooperate with everyone. Jane, I've tried everything."

"What about the police?"

"No." She took her head in her hands.

"But how can you? You're not in love with him." I didn't have to say anything about her being Catholic. She was already fiddling with her cross, twisting it in her guilty little fingers.

"It doesn't matter. I'm not getting married. I've made up my mind, whether you help me or not. It's the only chance I'll ever have."

"Chance for what?"

"To save someone." She held out her hands with their gnawed nails, pleading. "He's sixteen. They won't give him anything."

I stared at her.

"I can't walk into a store and ask for condoms, Jane. I'd die."

"I would too!" I cried.

"I know. Come with me. That's all I'm asking. Come with me. Be my support."

She was willing to be arrested, to go to jail even, but she couldn't walk into a drugstore and ask for birth control. I understood exactly how she felt because I'd been brought up the same way. Sex was the unutterable word. It was almost evil, worse than Communism even. Occasionally my father would rant about Communists, but he would never talk about sex, not to me and probably not to my mother either. I looked in Sonia's blotchy face, desperate and ashamed—yet triumphant too, that she had found a way to help him. Pascal would go home and I would still be here, the person who had helped *her*, the person who really loved her. We would do the Boeing action and maybe it would be the one that tipped the scales. Maybe peace would break out everywhere and we would live in it together and not die that awful death.

We walked up to Fourth Avenue in silence. I plodded the aisles of the drugstore with her, but I wouldn't help her look. When she went up to the cashier, I slipped outside and waited until, minutes later, she burst out with a paper bag under her arm. "Thank you, Jane!" she gasped.

"You don't like him, do you?"

She kissed me in the same place as before.

"Do you?" I asked.

Trutch house talked in its sleep. Every creak sounded like Sonia coming up the stairs or Pascal going down. I kept getting up, going for a drink of water, going to the bathroom. Dread. Why had I helped her buy the condoms? Why? I read for a little while, waiting for Sonia's light. It never came on, yet my room seemed so bright. When I got up and looked out the window, the moon was nearly full, ringed by blazing moondogs. Below, a paler light flickered in the garage.

A sweet tang masked the other garage odours, which may have been why Pete didn't seem particularly surprised to have a visitor in the middle of the night. "Zed," he said, wriggling an arm out of the sleeping bag and flourishing it in welcome. "Pull up a milk crate."

It was the only place to sit. I made myself small on it and asked him how he was.

"Pete's okay. He's hunky-dory. How about you?"

"I can't sleep. I was reading and saw your light."

"What were you reading?"

"'Three Years.' It's about this guy, Alexei Laptev. The woman he loves doesn't love him back. So he's always having these conversations with friends. About the possibility of life without love. About passion being a psychosis. About love not existing at all, being just a physical attraction."

I saw that Pete was shaking his head, letting it roll this way and that on the foamie, and that his stubble was starting to thicken into a beard. "What?" I asked.

"With everything that's going on in the world, Zed? You read *stories*?" He might have said *nursery rhymes*.

"It's Chekhov."

His look said, *So?*

"You read my paper. I love his stories. I love the people in them. How they strive. They have these hopes for the future, but the future seems—like it will never come. They're guilty and idealistic and jaded—all at the same time. And always there's this mood. I'm not explaining it very well. It's just that he writes the way I feel."

The candle, fixed onto a paint can, licked at the night. We both watched it. Then a line came to me and I recited it. *"My heart felt heavy within me and I kept thinking how wonderful it would be if I could only rip it out of my breast somehow."*

"That's how you feel?" he asked.

"Yes. Don't you?"

"Pete's feelings are irrelevant," he said.

"That's the problem with you," I said, exasperated. "You act like we're all creatures. It's not going to make you less of an anarchist, admitting you actually love somebody." Then, to my horror, I did cry, covering my face with my hands, wishing it all felt irrelevant to me. Pete did nothing to comfort me, but after I had dried my face on my sleeve, he offered to sleep with me.

"Pete wanted to at Christmas, but you didn't seem into it."

"No," I said.

He arched his back in the bag, a stretch or a shrug. He thrashed around. "Zed, come here," he said and when I froze on the crate, he laughed. "Fear not. Pete won't jump you."

So I came and sat beside him, wary until he turned his back to me. "Scratch?"

Between his shoulder blades, up and down his spine with its pretty, decorative knobs. "Harder," he said and I scratched it harder.

The unbearable itch that had taken over his life.

The weather turned the next day. Having grown smug with spring, we were shocked to wake to a moleskin sky, to wind. Worse, rain was predicted for Sunday when no one could remember a rainy Walk for Peace. For what it would do to the papier mâché alone, it signified disaster, though for us personally only discomfort, our fake blood thinning, the chains slippery and more difficult to handle. Nevertheless, we couldn't help seeing an omen in the forecast.

I had thought my anxiety would evaporate as soon as I finished my exam, indeed, before I finished it, as soon as I read the questions. Instead, I discovered that the exam had been a distraction and now the real worrying began. We were going to cross the border. Some of us were going to be arrested. Not me, I was support, but what if something went wrong?

Isis had promised fun and what she brought over were five identical booklets from the library, five copies of *The Cherry Orchard*, and a jug of oily-looking plonk. She gathered us on the porch where we sat along the wide wooden ledge and on the flowered chesterfield, feeling its metal skeleton through the emaciated cushions. I avoided Sonia's eye.

Since there were sixteen characters and only seven of us, excluding Pete, Isis assigned some of us multiple roles. She herself took on all the minor characters as well as the two female leads, Ania and Liuba, mother and daughter. "Pete was supposed to be Trofimov." *Piotr* Trofimov, the idealistic student.

"He *is* Trofimov," she said, meaning more than that they had the same name. She looked at the three males and decided Pascal would be Pete's understudy in addition to playing Yasha, the preening valet. "This is for you, Jane," she said, pulling a cucumber from her bag. "You're Charlotta. Because you're so funny."

"I'm funny?" I said and everyone laughed.

Isis read the first stage directions: "*The windows of the room are shut, but through them the trees can be seen in blossom.*" More laughter over Timo's Yepihodov proposing to Carla's Dooniasha, as well as Yepihodov dropping or bumping into things, which Timo didn't just read but stood to clown out. Then I had my first line as Charlotta, the German governess. "*My dog actually eats nuts.*"

They laughed again.

I had read the play once before, almost a year earlier, but remembered only the basic outline of the story—the orchard is going to auction in order to pay Liuba Ranyevskaia's debts. I remembered Gayev's speech to the bookshelf and when Pishchik swallows all of Liuba's pills, and that everyone was in love, Trofimov and Ania, too, though Trofimov pretends to be above love. But I had forgotten about the dead child at the heart of the play, Liuba's drowned son, the reason she fled Russia for Paris five years before.

By Act Two, we recognized the genius in the roles Isis had assigned us. Dieter, who was at first thrilled to play Lopakhin and be yearned for by Sonia's Varia, began complaining. "He's the biggest capitalist in the play!"

"But he's also the only one talking sanely."

"Look at me," Timo said to console him. "I'm a couple of tools."

"Still," Dieter sniffed. "Why couldn't *I* be Trofimov?"

It was true that Pascal didn't do the character justice. When he stammered through his monologues, we imagined Pete.

When he said, "*One day all the things that are beyond our grasp at present are going to fall within our reach, only to achieve this we've got to work with all our might, to help the people who are seeking after truth,*" when he said, "*Don't you see human beings gazing at you from every cherry tree in your orchard, from every leaf and every tree trunk, don't you hear voices?*" we heard Pete's.

Isis read Liuba and Ania in two different voices, sometimes as a dialogue with herself. "*I keep expecting,*" she said in a strained voice, "*something dreadful to happen . . .*"

As Charlotta I had to perform conjuring tricks. I had to say out loud the words I often thought to myself, though less poetically. "*I am so lonely, always so lonely, no one belongs to me, and . . . and who I am, what I exist for, nobody knows . . .*" I had to take the cucumber out of my pocket and bite into it while everybody whooped.

We passed around the jug of wine and it had the intended effect. Pascal, as Trofimov, rose to his feet near the end of the play and, swaying like a tree (he had been glugging the stuff), declared he was a free man. "*Humanity is advancing toward the highest truth—*"

Sonia tried to shush him. "You don't have to shout."

"*—the greatest happiness that is possible to achieve on earth—*"

Dieter kicked off a Birkenstock and came at Pascal as though to shove it in his mouth.

Pascal: "*—and I am in the van!*"

At the mention of the vanguard, Pete, seemingly on cue, darted out from the side of the house and ran across the neighbour's lawn straight for the red-hatted gnome. "No, Pete!" Sonia cried, which made us all turn and most of us laugh harder. Because when he seized it and pulled, it wouldn't release. It was cemented in this time. "Go, go, go!" Pascal chanted. Pete pulled and pulled and his hair, lank from lack of washing, began to flap around his head with the fury of each tug. Unshaven, clothes filthy, he looked completely crazy. Finally the gnome capitulated, breaking off at the ankles, and Pete stumbled backward and almost fell. "Look," Sonia groaned when he had absconded with it. Two pointed shoes, left behind in the flower bed, yellow and hollow, as though the gnome's feet had merely slipped out of them.

Isis clapped her hands and demanded we finish the play. Lopakhin buys the orchard, engages Yepihodov to run it, then fails once more to propose to Varia. She leaves to take up a position as housekeeper on a nearby estate. Gayev gets a job in a bank, Liuba and Ania go back to Paris, taking Yasha. Pishchik's financial problems are solved by the discovery of clay on his estate. And the old servant Freers, whose deafness adds so much comedy to the play, is left behind in the confusion. But was it a comedy or a tragedy? Though many of the lines were funny, the situation was sad, unbearably sad. "They were so deluded," said Carla. "Over and over again Lop—what's his name? Old Loppy tried to help them, but they wouldn't listen. They just sank deeper."

Dieter: "That's how it is with the bourgeoisie."

"It's more than a critique of the bourgeoisie," I said. "The whole world is our orchard. How are we going to save it?"

"We're going to Seattle tomorrow," Isis said.

And then we all went for a walk. Timo whispered to me going down the steps, "*My dog actually eats nuts!*" and I replied, "*Fancy that!*"

We reached one of the flowery streets where the wind had filled the gutters with drifts of petals. Cars, the tops of newspaper boxes—everything coated in pink snow. Pascal scooped up a handful and threw it in Sonia's face. She retaliated, then all of us joined in, chasing each other between parked cars, hurling fistfuls. The wind gusted and the petals swirled and lifted like so many pink, materializing spirits.

"*Did you know*—" Carla said as we ducked together behind a car to avoid the next flowery assault, "—*my dog actually eats nuts?*"

A car forced us back onto the sidewalk and we abandoned the game. Sonia came up to me then. She was embarrassed too, I realized. "The ending gave me the willies, Jane."

She meant the play, that sound *coming as if out of the sky, like the sound of a string snapping, slowly and sadly dying away.* Because we, too, were always waiting for a sound, which one it would be, we didn't know—air raid siren, a lone plane, the imagined whine of an ICBM.

"Ah!"

"What?"

"You woke me up!"

This was when I woke up.

"Where were you?"

"In the garage. What?"

"Nothing."

"I'm here now."

"Your feet are cold."

"Warm them."

They fell silent, or at least too quiet for me to hear. I moved to the edge of the futon and peered down on Sonia's dresser, where I could just make out the white teapot in the dark. Crawling partially off the mattress, I laid my head on the metal grate. Now I could hear a fainter sound. A moist one.

Then: "What?"

"You weren't very nice to your mother."

A sigh.

"In the play," she said.

Pascal laughed and the kissing resumed, louder and wetter, before breaking off. He breathed his words, "I-think-you're-so-pretty."

I pictured her in all her prettiness, lying with me instead, me kissing her cherry mouth, the little pillows of her lips, so sweet. She parted them slightly and I felt her tongue brush against mine. It was so unexpected, I drew back in surprise.

Other sounds. Rustling. I kissed her sweet foot a thousand times.

"Did you like that?"

She told me: "Yes."

He took back his inhalation. More kissing; small grunts now and sighs. I couldn't picture it. They were shadows in the dark. *Thank you*, whispered. "Thank you for picking me."

"Are you serious?" he said.

Her nightie was already around her neck. Now she tossed it on the floor and lay back, opening herself. "You remember what you promised?"

"Yeah." He was fumbling with it, that much I could hear. Fumbling with the condom I'd helped her buy.

"What?"

"I'm taking the bus tomorrow."

"Promise?"

"Yes. What?"

"You're just a kid."

"I'm almost seventeen. I know tons of guys who've already done it. Well, two."

"I mean you shouldn't be sick."

"I'll be dead here in a minute." He eased himself on top of her.

"Ouch!"

"I haven't even touched you yet."

And then the sounds came faster, confusing, overlapping. A sharp intake of breath, a gasp of surprise or pain. I writhed with them, half in agony, but it was over in a minute. Breathless apologies gushed: "I'm sorry." "*I'm* sorry. Too fast. What a tool." "No, no. Never say that." "You do like me, right?"

"I love you," Sonia told him.

The pain in my ear. The whole side of my face incised with their words.

2 0 0 4

Just after midnight I heard the back door open, then boots, possibly more than one pair. A minute later two voices confirmed this, their tone still angry, which struck me as troubling and odd. Something was going on, but if I went out there in my housecoat Joe Jr. would die on the spot. No matter what I wore, if I tried to pry it out of them they would only clamp tighter. At least they were home, I told myself.

They set upon the fridge and, afterward, stamped down to The Lair, where the volume came on low. Joe could sleep through the end of the world, and probably will, but after half an hour I couldn't take the vibrations any longer. I got out of bed and went to call down to Joe Jr. from the top of the basement stairs. Sibilants were exchanged, the volume lowered, then he appeared at the bottom of the stairs looking contrite. "Sorry. We'll keep it down."

"It's 12:30," I said. "Where were you?"

"Just hanging."

"You've got school tomorrow."

"I know."

"When's Simon leaving?"

"He's going to sleep here. Is that all right?"

"You've got school tomorrow."

Joe Jr.: "We just went over that."

"Okay," I said. "But when are you planning on going to bed?"

"Now. We'll go now. All right?" I could hear a pull in his voice, like he wanted to be sarcastic but also wanted to stay on my good side.

"Where are you going to sleep?"

"In my room."

"What about Simon?"

"On a foamie."

Under the painted bulb his hair and face looked pink. I hoped it was the light, not that he was poised to explode because, normally, he's sweet-tempered, like his dad. "Okay," I said. "Fine. But does his mother know?"

His mother, it turned out, did not.

"The cretins! That's all we care about! We don't give a fuck about his parents!"

"What cretins do you mean?" I asked Joe Jr.

"*The* Cretins! Our *band*!"

"Okay, okay," said Joe, coming in from the kitchen, where he'd made hot chocolate, a clutch of steaming mugs in each hand. His bathrobe hung open showing, above the waistband of his boxers, most of his pale, doctorly stomach and chest. Poor Joe. He finally gets to sleep in and what happens? He's up half the night in the ER of our house. I woke him as soon as I found out that the girl, the love interest, had never existed except in my mind. It was that *other* girl. The Big One. It was Mother Trouble.

"Dad's almost got a gig set up," Joe Jr. said. "A real one, not in some fucking garage. This is important. It's *so* important."

Simon, meanwhile, was practically fetal on his end of the couch, weeping silently.

Joe: "Don't swear at your mother."

"I didn't swear *at* her."

"Whatever. It isn't nice." He held out a mug to Joe Jr.

"No."

"Take one."

He did, with a huff, then Joe persuaded Simon to sit up and take his mug as well. I was so grateful for Joe's presence, for the calm he exuded, his reasonableness, when it was all I could do not to knock the boys' spikes together. Joe settled on the footstool on my side of the room and passed me my chocolate. "Okay," he said. "Let's start at the beginning."

"Simon's parents won't let him be in the band!"

"Since when?"

"Since yesterday when he told them about Mom."

I burned my tongue. Chocolate slopped onto my housecoat and I set the mug down. "What about Jane?" Joe asked, very, very carefully.

"That she was in that group when she was young."

"Let Simon answer."

Simon looked so miserable and pimply wiping his nose on his bare arm. "Joey showed me the article in the paper. I Googled her. Then I told my mom about it. I can't believe I did that. It was so stupid!"

"They're so straight!" Joe Jr. spat.

"I'm still not understanding," Joe said. "The article didn't even mention Jane."

"She got 326 hits!"

Joe looked at me, eyebrows raised, holding in the smile. "A celebrity in our midst."

"And she thinks! She said! 'Joe's mom's a terrorist and you're not going over there any more!'" This came out like bullets.

I couldn't believe it. I couldn't believe anyone could be so dumb. I strained to picture this woman, this idiot, but couldn't. She probably had no head. I thought: she lets him mutilate himself, but she won't let him play guitar with my son? Which was, of course, unhelpful. No doubt there was a long, complicated story behind Simon's grommetted earlobes.

"Jane wasn't a terrorist," Joe said. "She just fell in with the wrong people."

"I didn't!" I said. "It was all a mistake. And anyway, what were you back then?"

Joe laughed. "I was definitely the wrong person."

"Would it help if I talked to her?" I offered Simon.

"No!"

Sighing, Joe turned to me. "What now?"

"We call them," I said.

"No!" the boys screamed.

"We?" Joe said, appalled.

"Don't call them. Mom. Let him stay here tonight."

"Of course he can stay." I rose from the chair. "But I'm going to call his parents and let them know he's here."

"No," Simon moaned, curling over his mug.

Joe Jr.: "Fuck."

Joe Sr.: "What did I say about that?"

From across the room, my son looked at me in a way that made me stop in my tracks. It was the kind of look you dread your whole life and, at that moment, I almost gave in. I almost did the wrong thing again. "Simon," I asked. "What will happen to you if I phone your parents?"

"They won't let him be in—"

I shushed Joe Jr. "Simon?"

"They'll come and get me," he muttered.

"And then what?"

"I'll get grounded."

"Just grounded? Are you sure?" I turned to Joe Jr. for confirmation but he refused to meet my eye. Satisfied that this was

the truth, that a beating or reform school were unlikely consequences, I went back to the kitchen to get the phone. "Fuck!"
said Joe Jr., coming after me, begging now. "Please, Mom.
Don't call them. We have it figured out."

"What have you figured out?"

"He stays here tonight. Then he'll go to the hostel tomorrow after we get his stuff. He can't live there any more. He can't
stand them. He wants to be in the band."

"I am not letting those people wonder all night where their
child is! Do you understand me?"

I guess I screamed this because Joe Jr. blanched and returned
to the living room. Then I had to go and ask for the phone number. Both boys were staring at the rug in seething silence, which
Simon broke only to rattle off the numbers. I punched them
in and went back to the kitchen so I wouldn't have to talk to
his parents in front of him. On the way out, Joe offered me an
encouraging look and a shrug of utter helplessness to choose
between.

A woman answered, cutting short the first ring, so I knew
she'd been camped by the phone. "I'm sorry to be calling so
late," I told her. "This is Joey Norman's mother, Jane Z—"

Before I'd even finished introducing myself, a man replaced
her on the line. I told him what I'd been about to say to her: "I
just found out you didn't know Simon's here. He's welcome to
stay the night, but I wanted you to know he's safe."

"We'll come and get him," the man said.

"You can come in the morning if you prefer. It's late."

"We'll come right now. What's the address?"

When I got back to the living room, the boys were gone. Joe
said, "They're in Joey's room." I sat down and Joe handed me
my mug of lukewarm chocolate again.

"What if he bolts?" I asked.

"We'll send out a posse."

"What a mess."

"Don't worry," Joe said, squeezing my foot through the slipper. "It'll get sorted out."

"That woman? She didn't even say anything and she sounded hostile."

"Bitch," he said, trying to be funny.

Or maybe I had only been hearing that other mother's anger. Either way, I didn't care because now I was thinking about that look Joe Jr. had given me, so calculatedly disaffected. I hoped it was temporary.

Twenty minutes after I made the call, the doorbell rang. I sent Joe to the door. He answered, then, passing by the living room to get the boys, mouthed to me that it was the dad. I felt less afraid then and got up to take a look at him hanging in the open door, bulky and balding and seemingly as appalled as I was. He shook my hand when I offered it, but refused eye contact with the terrorist.

"Sorry about all this," I said.

"She's pretty frantic," he said.

"Of course. I would be too."

Simon appeared with his backpack and guitar and sank down on the stairs to put his boots on. His father picked up the instrument. "Carry them."

Simon stood.

"Say thank you."

Simon: "Thank you."

"I hope to see you again soon, Simon," I warbled, managing to pat him on the back as he ducked out.

From the window Joe and I watched father and son going down the walk, Simon sock-footed, taking mincing steps, a long boot in each hand. His father threw the guitar in the trunk, then came around to unlock the passenger door. We were relieved when he hugged the boy.

Downstairs, The Sex Pistols came on full throttle.

There are things you simply don't understand until you have a child. You might think you know about love, for example, its rigours and complications, its thousand feats, but then it turns out that you don't, that you're clueless, that love, in point of fact, might as well be a Russian word. When Joe Jr. was born safe and whole, I felt such a sense of accomplishment. I had finally made a contribution. Finally something decisive, something that mattered to the world. This tiny, purple, squalling thing? I would die for him. It would be a privilege and a joy. I'd do it twice if I could.

But those groggy postpartum days don't last. The hormonal frenzy, the ecstatic blear—it passes—and on the other side of bliss, it's still there. Death is still there, more terrifying than before.

Not mine. His.

The next day we decided to let Joe Jr. skip school. Joe Sr. got up out of habit and cooked us a big fry-up. Joe Jr. slept through this olfactory alarm so Joe and I sat down together, overtired parents of a normally trouble-free teen. Then Joe's pager went off and he had to leave for the hospital with three strips of bacon folded into a piece of toast. It was depressing to eat alone after the promise of company. Outside, spring flaunted herself against the window. She lifted her lacy skirts and bent over. Birds flew by with bits of grass in their beaks. How cliché, I thought.

I'd got as far as page 92 in the manuscript when mutterings began to issue from Joe Jr.'s room. He was on the phone to

Simon, I assumed—until I heard pounding and went to find out what was going on.

"Nothing," he said from behind his closed door.

I took a chance and opened it. He was on the bed, leaning against the wall, not on the phone at all, the laptop squeezed between his thighs and his hair flat—a bad sign. On the screen I could see bombs releasing every time his finger stabbed return. In the virtual city, people were scattering, escaping down cyber alleys, getting blown to bits.

"Dad made breakfast," I said. Joe was at the hospital that very moment tending to the sick and wounded while his son skipped school to choreograph this massacre. Joe Jr. groaned and slammed the back of his head against the wall hard enough to make me jump. "Joey!"

"I'm not hungry."

"Excuse me while I call 911."

In the time it took us to exchange these few terse words, scores of innocents died or were dismembered with every manic palpation of the space bar. Each emitted a weird, synthesized *A-a-a-a-a!!!*, truncated by the next victim's *A-a-a-a-a-a-a-a!!!*

"Have you heard from Simon?" I asked.

Joe Jr.: "There was a text."

A-a-a!!! A-a-a-a-a-a-a-a-a!!! A-a-a-a!!! A-a-a-a-a-a-a-a!!!

"And?"

A-a-a-a-a-a-a-a-a-a-a!!!

"She's taking his phone away."

If his tone had been accusatory or even cold I would have taken comfort in it. I remembered being angry at my parents when I was his age. I even remembered hating them. But hate and anger are at least feelings. They connect you to people as much as love does. This glaze-eyed-killer-zombie son gave me the creeps. I said, "The woman's a zilch, remember?"

A-a-a-a!!! A-a!!! A-a!!! A-a-a-a!!! A-a-a-a-a-a-a!!! A-a-a-a-a-a-a-a-a-a-a!!!

It was because of the computer, I thought. When I was his age, the boob tube corrupted our minds. I wasn't allowed to watch TV except in the company of my parents and then only edifying programs. There had been plenty of arguments about that. And because I never wanted to be that kind of parent, because I felt I was smarter than they, and because, admittedly, I stoop to flipping through parenting magazines at the grocery store where I tote away my organic vegetables in reusable canvas carriers or, when I'm stuck without, in recycled paper bags, I knew that I had to embrace these new technologies despite how they mystified and repelled me, so that I could speak a language common to my son.

So I asked. "Did you only Google me?"

"What?"

"Did you look up any of the other people in the group?"

"No."

I thrilled when, after a pause to off a dozen more cyber citizens, he asked, "Why?"

"I just wondered. I haven't either."

He blasted a few more. *A-a-a-a!!! A-a-a-a-a-a-a!!!*

"Why not?"

Just a tinge, a little tinge, of curiosity in his voice.

I left him alone while he ate his cold bacon and eggs. When he showed up in my office forty minutes later, he'd showered and looked more himself, more spiniferous anyway. The stud under his lip caught the light and blinked. "Hi," I said.

"Do you want to do it?"

"All right," I said, closing the editing file I'd been feigning work on. He pulled a chair over beside mine and, when he was

settled, I let him do the work. His fingers are so nimble. Compared to his, mine move like I'm decoding Braille for the first
time. He could have done this on his own, of course, but the fact
that he didn't was heartening.

He asked for a name and I gave him Dieter Koenig's.

"That was easy. Usually there's a lot of people with the same
name. He's a lawyer."

I leaned in to read the home page on his site. "He's partner
in a firm that specializes in ICBC claims." In other words, he
makes his living suing the provincial auto insurance corporation. *Think you have whiplash? You probably do!* read one of the
subject headings on his pull-down menu.

"What do you call a lawyer at the bottom of the ocean?"
I asked.

"What?"

I told him, but he didn't get it. "Never mind," I said.

"Carla Steadperson" got no hits whatsoever, though there
were a number of Carla Steadmans, one who was jailed for three
months for shoplifting in England, another who worked for the
Red Cross, and one who owned a tanning salon in, of all places,
Hawaii. It was impossible to say which of these Carla Steadmans, if any, was the one I once knew, lark-voiced lesbian, serial
scrawler of "Lies!" on newspaper boxes.

There were even more Timothy Brandts, among them an
oncologist in Colorado, a specialist in spray-on foam roof insu-
lation, and Timothy Brandt the actor, who had appeared in the
Italian cult film *Arpeggio*. There were no Timos, but numerous
Tim Brandts—a motivational speaker, a motocross racer, the
victim of a fatal 1999 car accident. Of everyone in NAG!, it was
Timo I had the clearest feelings for, an unadulterated, entirely
unconflicted fondness, which made me loath to pick his fate even
if it was only in my imagination. But if pressed, if I absolutely

had to choose, I would like to have seen him towering on a podium, one pant leg rolled to the knee, stuttering hope the way he used to pass around the Chipits.

Belinda had changed her name again. We tried Isis, Goddess, Redhead. We tried that brand of hair conditioner.

Peter English turned out to be a fairly common name. His million-plus hits Joe Jr. quickly narrowed by adding "anarchist." There were still more than a thousand references to him, many archived news articles, but also blogs which Joe Jr. read with fascination while I made and brought him a sandwich and stood by, biting my tongue, as he crumbed up my keyboard.

"He has a defence committee working for his release. They say he's innocent, that he's a political prisoner. His father was president of a mining company. He wouldn't even pay for a lawyer!" Indignation in his voice.

I sighed.

"How did you get in with them anyway?" Joe Jr. asked.

"I came out here to go to university. I wanted to live closer to campus so I moved into a shared house with three of them."

Joe Jr. took a break to go to the bathroom, but came back and threw himself into the chair again. He rubbed his eyes, then, instead of returning to the search, picked a book off the pile on the desk, as though paper had soothing properties the screen lacked. The book was *Fathers and Sons*, which I still hadn't put back on the shelf. He flipped through it. "Look at all the underlining. *Children! Is it true that love's an imaginary feeling?*"

We both laughed.

Like Pete, many of Sonia's hits belonged to other people. Many of the ones that were hers were also Pete's. And Joe was right about her lawyer. He was mentioned many times. Not only that, he was based in Vancouver. He would be as easy to contact as Dieter Koenig of Koenig, Hit, and Run.

"Anyone else?" Joe Jr. asked. He probably meant me. I hesitated, then told him, "No." I didn't remember Pascal's last name, if I ever knew it.

But I must have. I'd read the article Sonia tied to the grate. What stuck in my mind was a word not a name.

Osteosarcoma.

They come as soon as they're called, these dog-loyal tears. Joe Jr. pushed the chair back and, standing, launched into a Y—arms extending, fists unfurling, spreading. Suddenly he seemed so alive, as if some energy, some life force liberated by the stretch, was streaming off his fifteen-year-old body. He stayed like that, suspended, refracted green through my tears, for nearly half a minute until he remembered he was supposed to be mad at me. Then he dropped his arms and, rearranging his expression, turned to leave.

And what might happen to him if he walked through the door of my study now? Anything. I knew that for a fact. We had just read so many possible fates, every one of them unexpected, because all we had ever expected was to die.

Everybody dies.

And I thought—if I can hold him back for just a moment, something different will happen instead.

"Do you want to meet Sonia?" I asked.

I immediately regretted the offer, but, having made it, I had no choice but to phone. I talked to her lawyer's secretary, who said she would pass the request along. As soon as I hung up I felt elated, not just for getting the call over with. It was like waking from a pleasant dream with the feeling sticking to you, but in this case the dream was a memory. I used to know Sonia's timetable. It was tacked to the wall above her desk and I memorized it so I could correctly place her in my imagination throughout the day.

It's 11:20 so Sonia is in the Scarfe Building for Techniques in Reading Education. Whenever possible I tried to get home early and be in the kitchen making tea when she got in. Though my timetable didn't always mesh with hers, next year, when we were living together, if we were still around, if the world hadn't ended, I'd make sure it did. I'd choose my courses so that I would always be there for her. In the meantime, I stood by the kettle, urging it to boil, dried letters of spaghetti stuck to the ceiling, compost steeping in the bowl, the smell—beans, rotten table scraps, life, death—me poised and listening for the sound of the front door opening. Oh, joy.

But that was twenty years ago. We were two completely different people now. A ruined one and a saved one.

I was quite certain that she wouldn't want to see me.

In this age of e-mail, the phone doesn't ring that often any more. Every time it did I sprang for it, but it was never the lawyer's secretary with the slightly nasal voice getting back to me as promised. Sonia's lawyer must be busy these days with all those people trying to get off no-fly lists, all those terror suspects detained under security certificates, not to mention the ordinary addicts, prostitutes, and mentally ill needing counsel. For one quick glance at his website confirmed that she had engaged the St. Jude of the profession, a man no doubt kept extremely busy by injustice. The secretary didn't call back that day, or the next.

Good, I thought.

At dinner Joe Sr. broached the subject of contacting Mr. and Ms. Zilch. "I think if we had them over they would see we're not so bad. We don't eat babies. We don't do drugs."

"Or do we?" I glanced sidelong at our sullen son.

"Your mother's not a terrorist. She's perfectly harmless. And she's an excellent cook."

"I'm not cooking dinner for that horrible woman," I said.

"We could go to a restaurant then. The six of us. Talk it out. What do you think, Joey?"

He shrugged and put more food in.

Joe: "We'll call them. The worst thing that could happen is they'll say no."

"Fine," I said. "Call them."

Joe said, "Who? Me?"

It became a mental mat routine, waking hopefully but quickly putting hope out of mind—because, logically, the likelihood that the secretary would call while I was hoping she would call was virtually nil. Not that I really wanted her to call. No, I did. I wanted her to call and say that Sonia didn't want to see me any more than I wanted to see her. It was just that I had made this offer to my son, I would explain to the secretary. He's going through a phase.

I focused on other things, on work, even as my mounting wretchedness subverted the plan; it proved I *was* hoping, subconsciously and in vain. Next move: rationalizing. It wasn't as if *Sonia* wasn't calling me. The secretary wasn't. Sonia would have called me right away. Then, as four o'clock approached, I abandoned my faith in logic and entered the actively hoping phase, willing her to call, crossing fingers, muttering pleas. Because there were things I was desperate to know so that I could put it all behind me once and for all. Such as: why did she lie? Why did she say she was in any way involved?

Finally it hit, the devastation of five o'clock when legal offices everywhere closed for the day, followed ten minutes later by another bout of hope, for a lawyer like that, he'd work his clients' hours. He'd hang his shingle out all night. Then the whole cycle started again until bedtime when, dejected, humiliated, I crawled between the sheets and had a little cry without waking

Joe, who is long accustomed to these unexplained fits of sorrow and remorse.

The weekend came and went. Monday, the agony resumed. I was on page 376 of the novel when the proverbial moment of least expectation arrived, just as I was getting up from my desk to start dinner. Telemarketer Hour. The nasal secretary apologized for taking so long to call back. Sonia had given permission for me to call her.

It was a local number, which seemed too good to be true, but the woman who answered—she couldn't have been Sonia. Only a lifetime passionately committed to smoking could produce such timbre. "Who's this?" she asked.

"Tell her it's Jane calling."

"Jane?"

"Zwierzchowski," I said.

"*Who?*"

1 9 8 4

A mosaic of wet petals was pasted across the windshield. I wondered how Timo had driven over, for only now, while we were waiting out front in the van, did he put the wipers on. Swish, swish. They crushed and scraped the petals aside. He turned around to address us—Pete in the back corner, bristly, giving off a campfire fug, me hunkered in the middle seat, in misery. "Hey! We're in the vvvvan! Remember? From the play?"

Dieter, up front in the passenger seat: "What's taking them so long?"

Pete: "Honk."

But the front door opened just then and Sonia hurried down the steps, arms floating at her sides as though about to take to the air and fly. She threw her small weight back, slid the van door open, hopped inside. "Pascal's not coming," she joyfully announced.

"Fuck," said Pete. The other two asked why.

"He's sick. He's throwing up." She got in beside me, tucking her pack at her feet.

"When did that start?"

"Just now."

Hours earlier Pascal and Sonia's laughter had woken me, then their thousand little kisses had kept me awake. Maybe they made love again, I don't know—I stormed off to the bathroom so I wouldn't have to listen a second time. Beside me now, she squeezed my hand to thank me. Everything about her glowed— her hair, washed that morning and lustrous, her face, flushing now that she was with the one person who knew, who knew more than she realized. She kept her eyes demurely lowered.

Pascal was not throwing up. I'd seen him myself through my bedroom window, leaving the garage with the garden gnome in his arms. It seemed a cumbersome souvenir to be taking all the way back to Saskatchewan on the bus.

"Is everybody ready then?" Timo asked, starting the van.

I pressed the side of my face to the cold window and shut my eyes. Sonia was still holding my hand.

Dieter: "Wait. Here he comes."

Sonia let go of me and swung around. When she saw Pascal approaching the van, loaded down with his duffle bag, she tore her seat belt off. Pascal put his bag in the back and opened the side door at the same time as Sonia did. "What's wrong?" she asked.

"Sorry," he said, eyes darting at all of us.

"Are you coming or not?" Pete asked.

"I'm coming."

"No," Sonia said, pushing him back. "You're sick. Re- member?"

Pascal whooshed the door closed on its rollers and took the seat behind us, next to Pete. Immediately Sonia curled forward, as though over a stomach ache. At first I just sat there, in shock too, while Timo drove away. When we reached the Blenheim house a few minutes later, I forced myself to look back. Pascal blinked, one eye closing a fraction of a second before the other, which somehow suggested to me guilt, though nothing else on his face indicated he felt bad about what he'd done to Sonia. Carla and Isis were carrying a cardboard box and several plastic bags, which they loaded into the back too, along with their packs. Suddenly Pascal leaned forward and, taunt or benediction, placed a hand flat on the top of Sonia's head. She jerked out from under his touch.

Carla, then Isis, climbed aboard. "How y'all doing this morning?" Isis asked as an American. As a Canadian she commented that we looked tense. "This ain't good, y'all. It looks suspicious. How 'bout we take a sec to shake them jitters out?"

She, Carla, Timo, and Pascal hokey-pokeyed as best they could in the limited space of the van, Timo behind the wheel with barely enough room even to drive, let alone jiggle himself. He looked in the grip of some kind of seizure. The rest of us stayed planted in our seats for all our different reasons. Then Carla slid in beside Sonia, leaving Isis to Pascal.

"Where's my mask?" he asked. "Can I see it?"

Isis reached behind the seat, took a handful of fabric from one of the bags, and tossed it to him, saying, "*How clever you are, Pyetia!*" She kissed Pascal's cheek like she'd done yesterday when he'd played Trofimov so hopelessly. On the other side of Pascal, Pete yawned loudly and turned toward the window.

Carla noticed first and asked if Sonia was okay. Sonia wasn't. Weeping silently against my shoulder, she kept on weeping through Carla's back rub. "Shh," Carla told her. "It's going to be fine. Everything will work out." The van filled with soothing murmurs, a susurrus of platitudes that had no effect until Carla began to sing "We Shall Overcome." Then Sonia dried her tears and settled into a catatonia that lasted the rest of the trip. All the things she should have been feeling—betrayed, humiliated, used—I took on on her behalf, shooting fresh daggers back at Pascal every few minutes. He goofed around with Isis, elbowing her, pulling at her braids until she swatted him off, benignly tolerant, like he was a puppy. He was acting like one. He couldn't keep still, was practically bouncing on the seat. And while I felt a barely suppressed urge to scream things at him that weren't non-violent, eventually I started to sense that it was an act, that these antics were to distract him from what he really felt. He pulled the burn mask over his head. "Take it off," Pete said. Pascal wouldn't. He sat there between Pete and Isis, ghoulish, barely human, twiddling his thumbs. When Pete accused him of being stupid, he finally removed it.

Rain flowed across the van windows in jerky diagonal tracks. Outside, the trees looked stripped, their petals already browning in the gutters. The fan failed in its one task, and Timo and Dieter, unrolling their windows to clear the fogged windshield, let in the sweet smell of decay. Carla had stopped singing and for a long time no one spoke. We were too nervous for small talk. Isis said she wished I'd brought a story to read aloud.

We were the story now.

Over the Oak Street Bridge. Soon the sodden fields in the Agricultural Land Reserve opened on either side of the highway, the sky white like in an unfinished drawing. Up front, Dieter played with the radio dial and found an oldies station. Timo asked, "Do you think they're marching yet?" and Dieter snorted. "Who cares?" When we entered the tunnel under the river, the music morphed to an angry static and Pascal belched loudly in the dark. "Who did that?" he asked and someone sighed.

Back in the matte light of day, we reviewed the border plan. Going over the various scenarios helped dispel some of the tension. Then "The Times They Are A-Changin'" whined out of the radio and we all cheered. The drug of idealism kicked in. Ahead, a sign: Peace Arch Border Crossing.

"Peace Arch," muttered Carla. "That's so ironic."

About five minutes from the border, Pascal put the mask back on. Once again, Pete called for him to take it off.

"Take it off, Pyetia," Isis cooed.

"Off!" Pete roared, cueing everyone to start shouting.

Dieter: "I knew involving him was a bad idea. He's too immature. Look at how he's acting. No one listens to me."

Then I understood. Pascal didn't want to be recognized. They would know about him at the border, and if they asked for ID, there would be trouble. We might be arrested even before we got across. I tried to think if harbouring a runaway was an actual crime and turned to Sonia in a panic, but she was no help, sitting there in her stupor. Finally Pascal gave in and, plucking the mask off, slid low in the seat. And it came to me, what we'd done: we'd been irresponsible.

The van pulled to the side of the highway. "What are you doing?" Dieter asked Timo, whose full pink face contorted. He struggled but not a word came out. "Just say it!" Dieter snapped.

Isis spoke up from the back: "I'll do the talking." She took over the driving as well, tying her red ropes in a kerchief as she ran around the van. "Now y'all," she said, getting in the driver's seat Timo had vacated for her, "put on your happy faces, you hear? You too," she said to Sonia. And to Pascal, "Now you behave yourself, Pyetia. Everybody? Shut up. Is that understood? You're all climbing the walls here."

The park came into view, a lawned expanse with the Peace Arch in the middle of it, standing on the 49th parallel, a symbolic door between two countries, monumentally American despite the fact that one of the two sodden flags on the roof was ours. Beyond was U.S. Customs. All we had to do was move patiently through the waiting line of cars. Isis let Dieter pick a lane; he chose the only one with a black man in the booth. When our turn finally came, Isis drove slowly, unrolling the window. Beside me, a sound like a groan issued from some fathomless place inside Sonia.

"Hi!" Isis showed all her teeth to the guard in the booth. He kept his to himself. "The purpose of our visit?" she repeated. "We're a children's theatre troupe. There's this festival in Seattle.

Playtime. Have you heard of it?" She produced a typed letter, a letter typed by Isis, confirming our attendance at this imaginary festival. One glance at it and he asked for ID.

"ID everyone!" she called and we all reached into pockets and backpacks for our birth certificates and driver's licences. Isis handed them in a bunch to the guard. I watched, unbreathing, while he shuffled through them, exhaled when he handed them back. He leaned in the window to look at us.

"I need to get out," Sonia gasped.

Isis started to say that she would pull over on the American side, but Sonia cried, "Now!" and crawled right over Carla. She struggled with the door until Timo leapt up and opened it for her. Two wobbly steps across the asphalt then she vomited.

"Great," said Dieter. "Now she's puking too."

"She has what he had," Isis told the guard, pointing to Pascal, out of the van now too, standing by Sonia in his glowing boots, hands in his pockets, bobbing, neither of them speaking. They seemed to be divining a message in the puddle she had made.

"It's going around," Isis said.

"Pull over there," said the guard, indicating the customs building.

"Can we wait for her on the other side? We're somewhat in a hurry."

Then Pascal said in a pleading voice loud enough for us all to hear, "I'll go. I promise I will. I just want to do this one last thing with you. It's going to be so cool."

And Sonia bolted. We couldn't believe it. We just turned in our seats and watched her go, watched as our much-rehearsed plan completely disintegrated. Back the way we'd come, back toward the park and the arch and Canada. Pascal went after her, but she pushed him away. It must have been what she said rather than her feeble shove that sent him hurrying back to us.

"What's she doing?" everyone started screeching when he got in the van again.

"I don't know what you're trying to pull off here," the guard told Isis, "but I suggest you collect your friend and get on home." He pointed to the service road bordering the park that led to the Canadian-bound lanes.

"You're not going to let us in?" She jutted her chin in indignation, but did exactly what he said, reversed the van and turned it around. "Fuckity-fuck-fuck, fuckity-fuck-fuck, look at Sonia go," Pete started singing under his breath, the whole way back to the corner of the park where Isis pulled to the side of the road. Sonia was halfway to the arch by then, jogging more than running, the bottom of her jeans two-toned from the wet grass. Isis pressed her head against the steering wheel. The wipers went slap, slap, slap.

"What's happening?" Pascal asked, sounding like a lost child.

Isis reared up with a hammy smile. "It's fine," she chirped. "We'll go get a coffee, wait an hour, then try again."

"What about Sonia?" I asked.

"Leave her," Pete said.

"We can't do that!" It wasn't only me saying this. Timo did too, and Carla.

Pete: "Why not?"

"I say we forget about the action," Dieter said. "We'll never get across now. I say we go home."

"You would."

Dieter swung around in his seat to face Pete, but Isis aborted their exchange. "Just cool it! Calm down everybody! I'm going to pick up Sonia! We'll figure it out from there!"

She drove the road that bordered the southern edge of the park, then turned north toward the Canadian booths. When she was parallel to where Sonia was slogging along at barely a trot, Isis honked the horn. Sonia looked over at us and, taking fright, picked up the pace again.

"Is she really sick?" Pascal asked.

"You gave it to her, didn't you?"

"It's nerves," Carla said.

"She was really into it," Timo insisted. "I don't gggggget it."

I glanced back at Pascal and, for the first time, saw he was afraid.

Nearer to the booths, Isis pulled over again to wait for Sonia. "I know what we need," Timo announced. "Chchchipits!" He rooted through his bag, passed the package along. Pascal ripped it open and took some. When it reached me, I declined. I wiped a circle on the window, a peephole, to watch Sonia through. There were no other Chipits takers so, hand to hand, like a church collection plate, the bag made its way back to Timo.

Sunday morning border traffic goes the other way. Canadians go shopping in America. Americans stay home and go to church. The guard stuck his arm out the window of his booth and impatiently waved us forward. "Okay," said Isis. "This is it. Act normal. Rhubarb, rhubarb, rhubarb."

"Wait for Sonia," I pleaded as Isis drove up beside the booth. When she was face to face with the guard, she tried out her smile on him.

He asked how long we'd been in the United States.

"Actually, we haven't even been yet. We were just about to cross when we realized we left someone behind. She should be coming up any second now." Isis leaned out the window. "There she is."

Marching over to us, head down as though pushing against the drizzle, hands in fists, Sonia was a little soldier of determination. Carla opened the van door for her, but instead of coming around and getting in, Sonia stayed on the other side where she was in full view of the guard. "What's she ddddoing?" Timo asked.

She was pointing. Pointing frantically at the van. Then she dropped her arms, came round, and got inside. Carla, still standing so Sonia could sit next to me again, closed the door.

"What the fuck was that about?" Pete asked, but Isis shushed him.

"Are you sick, Sonia, or are you nervous?" Carla asked.

She was shivering violently beside me. I was shaking too, because I knew what she'd been doing. *Look inside*, she'd been saying. *He's in the van. Look.*

Carla: "Maybe you should be support."

"Everybody present and accounted for!" Isis chirped to the guard, who came out of the booth now and asked what was in the back.

"Costumes. Props. We were on our way to a children's theatre festival in Seattle. I have a letter. Do you want it?"

"Is it open?"

"The back? I think so."

"I'll need to see your ID," the guard said.

He headed for the back of the van. I watched him through my peephole, tall and hale, an entirely whole person in brightly polished shoes. A middle-aged father of three, I would later learn. Dieter turned in his seat and said to Sonia, "What if we can't even get back into Canada now? You idiot!"

The guard opened the back door and began a methodical inspection of our things.

"ID everyone. *Again*," Isis sighed. "Those are our costumes," she called back.

Pascal opened the sliding side door and—whoosh!—leapt out at a run. And then we heard it, the sound we had been waiting for all that time.

The bomb went off like a practice run for that other, bigger one. With a weird popping sound and a scream, it came, the end of the world as we knew it. Somehow I ducked and when I straightened and turned, it was Timo I saw, Timo holding the side of his head, blood coursing down his arms, though someone else was screaming, someone I couldn't see rolling on the ground outside. There was crying too and smoke, broken glass and the smell of burning chocolate. Pete was yelling, "What did you do? What did you do?" All of us scrambling over each other and out of the van as fast as we could, except Pascal, who was long gone. From how fast he ran, you would never have guessed there was anything the matter with his leg.

The second before, in that stunned pause between the future and the past, I glanced down. Pieces of someone were scattered around. An eye lay in my lap, gawking up. I thought it was Timo's and became hysterical. But it was only plaster. The gnome, turned to shrapnel.

2 0 0 4

I dreamed I was walking along a path through the woods. The trees were ordinary—nothing flowery—except that one had a door in its trunk about the size of a kitchen cupboard. Of course I stopped. I stopped and opened it. Inside was a baby, either petrified or charred, its tiny brown knees drawn to its chest. He must have been there a long time to look so ancient and discoloured. To look so cold in his nest of moss.

I just stood there thinking: what should I do? What should I do now?

A few hours later we were driving along Kingsway, that diagonal slash across the city. Without any trees around the auto body shops and strip malls, it could have been any season; spring never shed its delicate petals on these vinyl awnings. It could have been any*where* for that matter, any generic, over-franchised thoroughfare in North America, until something from another era unexpectedly appeared, the old 2400 Motel with its little modernist cabins, completely out of place, as though the eighties had never been here and wrecked everything. I tried pointing the landmark out to Joe Jr., but his eyes were closed, eyebrow rings clicking arrhythmically against the passenger window, earbuds screwed in tight.

He came to as I pulled over. "Here?"

"I'm not driving all this way with you plugged into that thing, Joey," I said. "The idea was to have someone to talk to."

"I can talk and listen at the same time."

I had the car radio off because it seemed too weird, the two of us in such physical proximity, yet mentally so far apart. Different music, different thoughts, mine anxious. What would Sonia be like? Why did she even agree to see me? I would enter his space, I decided and signalled for him to pass an earbud over. "Hendrix?" I said after a minute.

First he gaped, then he cradled his head. "Mom. Mom."

"What's wrong?"

"You don't have *any idea*?"

"No," I admitted.

"How cool you are?"

I laughed. "Jimi Hendrix was actually *way* before my time."

"You're bad," he said.

Which reminded me of Bazarov's words to Arkady: "*Don't you know that in our dialect 'not all right' means 'all right'?*"

"Would it be possible, Joey?" I asked sweetly. "Do you think? You can listen on the way back."

He looked at me strangely, but unplugged himself nonetheless, wound the wires around the little white box, and put it in his jeans pocket.

We were driving out to New Westminster, which is technically another city, though each municipality flows into the next, undemarcated, unless I missed the signs. After a few minutes of non-conversation, Joe Jr. finally initiated one. "What is an anarchist?" he asked in exactly the same tone he might have used ten years ago to ask why the sky was that particular colour.

"I don't know. There must be a hundred definitions."

"There are thirteen schools of thought."

"You know better than I do then. I guess you Googled it."

"But you weren't one?"

"An anarchist? No!"

He ticked his rings against the window again. I wondered what he was expecting from Sonia and if I had done the right thing bringing him. When he was little, if a dog approached us in a park I'd always put myself between them. This was more like me needing another body to step behind. Because, what if I fell in love with her again? We'd talked on the phone for a few awkward minutes while I took down the address. She hadn't hesitated to invite me. What if the very sight of her, my first crush, made me forget my darling Joes?

"Why didn't you go to jail?" Joe Jr. asked.

"I did. While I waited for my bail hearing."

He straightened in the seat. "You *did*? For *real*? Why didn't you say? Why don't you tell me anything?"

Touché.

"I honestly don't remember anything except I wasn't allowed to take a shower."

Then he asked me to tell him about the bomb, like I'd promised. How did they make it? Why did it go off at the wrong time? But once again, I knew less than he did.

"You can use ordinary birthday sparklers wrapped in electrical tape," he said. "Or sand down pop cans and pack the shavings in a pipe."

"Well," I said.

"It must have had an anti-tamper trigger. Probably an arming switch too, so they could move it around."

"Joey. I wish you wouldn't."

"What?"

"Talk like this."

"You said you wanted to talk!"

Nowadays bombs go off all the time, but not back then. Back then, Pete's bomb made the front pages. (Not that I read them, or I'd know more about it.) It was obviously small, or pathetically amateur, despite his genius. Or intentionally so. (This just occurred to me.)

I told Joe Jr.: "I guess the guard messing around with our stuff set it off. No one was killed, but they could have been. Which was why it was taken so seriously. The guard lost two fingers and an eye. One of us was practically scalped by shards of plaster."

"What was the plaster for?"

"The bomb was in a garden gnome."

"Man! That's brilliant!" Joe Jr. said. "And then what happened?"

We were all arrested. Sonia confessed. Because the rest of us knew nothing about the bomb and were cooperative—except Pete—we were only charged with attempting to cross the border for the purposes of committing an indictable offence. We all pled guilty and got two years' probation. Pete went to trial, but wouldn't open his mouth, not even in his own defence. There was so much circumstantial evidence he didn't have a hope.

"He was living in the garage where the bomb was made, where *The Anarchist Handbook* was found. Do you know what that is?"

"I looked it up."

"Of course you did. Also, the trial of an actual terrorist group, the Squamish Five, had just finished. Public opinion was against Pete."

"But Sonia didn't do it?" he asked.

"No way."

"And this English guy, he did?"

"I guess so. It still seems hard to believe. He wasn't like that. Or maybe he was. His girlfriend had just broken up with him. Maybe that had something to do with it. Anyway, you read all that stuff, Joey."

Then Joe Jr. asked me if I was sorry for what happened and I told him that I regretted many things, the injuries in particular, not just to the guard—to our families too. The waste of two good people's lives. But I couldn't truthfully say that I wished it hadn't happened because then *he* wouldn't have happened. Back then, when I was nineteen, I thought I would always be miserable, and I should have been. I should have ended up like a Chekhov character, always in galoshes, or like my aunt with her expired bus transfers and her flattened cans. Or I should have been incinerated along with everyone else. That was all I expected, but look what I got instead. Statistically, it was infinitesimal— my chance at happiness.

Somewhere Kingsway changed names and now, as we descended, a view opened out before us. We saw the river, the triple span of bridges, the metastasizing suburbs on the other side. I asked Joe Jr. to get out the map at the same time I spotted the street we were looking for. We drove past several blocks of near-identical apartments before finding Sonia's. There was parking right in front, the way there hardly ever is in Vancouver, because, I realized as I was taking the flowers out of the trunk, a lot of people here probably didn't own cars. The cars they did own were beaters, like the one I'd parked behind, its muffler lacy with rust, a clutch of talismans hanging from the rear-view mirror, likely the only insurance the owner had. The bouquet had cost sixty dollars. I felt like leaving it on the beater's hood.

On the little square of lawn in front of the building, dog shit was hardening next to a plastic trike. We went up the walk and looked through the glass door to the lobby where a year's worth of flyers was stacked on the floor. One wall was tiled with mirrors and, amazingly, a knee-high artificial Christmas tree stood before it, decorations intact. Once, long ago, I'd prepared a trousseau—tea towels, dish cloths, a set of utensils with pink plastic handles. The pots and pans we could get at a thrift store, but I wanted some of the things in our new life to be new. I wanted to buy Sonia a kimono to wear when she drank her tea. Now I asked myself, is this where we would have ended up?

I was sweating when I pressed the intercom button. (The name beside the number was the same as all the others: Occupied.) The one with the smoked vocal chords answered. I said my name, that I was there to— The door buzzer cut me off.

Inside, we walked the gloomy hallways until we found the apartment. I knocked, then heard her name called out. *How wonderful it would be*, I thought, *if I could rip my heart out of my breast somehow!* The sound of chains being removed. I was trembling now.

Muscular, T-shirt so tight across her biceps the tattoo looked like it was being squeezed out. Half pit bull, half dyke. She looked right at Joe Jr. and I know he felt her animosity too, because he stepped back, almost behind me. Even her hair seemed to threaten us—*natural* spikes such as Joe Jr. could only dream of. "Who's he?" she asked. Before I could answer, she called over her shoulder, "She brought a *guy!*"

"This is my son," I said and her expression softened. "Joey," I said. By then she was looking at the flowers, taking fresh umbrage, and again, I felt the urge to chuck them.

Beyond the blockade of *her* was a room straight out of the past: saggy futon couch draped in a serape, shipping trunk coffee table, posters, one of a carved First Nations mask. Sonia appeared from some place beyond, coming up silently on cat's feet, performing her usual wonder simply by placing her hands on her protector's broad shoulders so she relaxed and stepped aside. Then Sonia stood before me in the flesh, still Anna Sergeyevna, but different. That degree of thin is pretty at nineteen; at thirty-nine it looks gaunt and, with all her mournful hair shorn away, she had nothing to hide behind. I saw her bones, her delicate skull. She said, "Jane?" and put a hand over her smile. "Oh my God. You look fantastic."

Joe Jr. had not come in vain. There was at least one tattoo, a murky blue peace dove on Sonia's forearm, probably done with a Bic. She never used to wear jewellery except for the little cross, but now, as I let go of the flowers so I could hug her, two bulky silver medallions on leather thongs dug into my chest. Both her ears were fringed with rings. Then *she* reared up behind Sonia, glaring now. How ironic, I thought. But what else could Sonia be but gay, after two decades in exclusively female company? Well, there would have been guards, psychiatrists, case workers, but I couldn't bear to think about them.

The hug went on and on, as I had imagined it would, but it smelled less like spring. This was how I knew my heart was safe where it was: when I pulled back and introduced my son, who had picked the flowers off the floor, and he shook her hand so politely. When the expected angina attack did not occur. How perfectly Tolstoy had nailed the girl-crush, but I couldn't see it at that time, just as I couldn't tell who the tears were for that had sprung in Sonia's eyes.

"This is Brenda," Sonia said before Brenda actually snarled. Sonia put her arms around her and, blushing, Brenda pulled away and stalked off.

"Come in. I'll make tea," Sonia said, and we followed her down the hall. She seemed all right, I thought then. You couldn't tell.

She led us to a kitchen smelling of garbage that needed taking out, where Brenda was already lurking. Joe Jr. stood by, the embarrassment of the bouquet still in his hands. Sonia relieved him of it, gestured for us to sit at the little table, then began lifting dirty dishes out of the sink onto the counter, the flowers held in the crook of one arm, the way in a different life she might have multi-tasked with a baby on her hip.

"Do you want tea, hon?"

"Tea?" Brenda said from the open fridge. She held up a can of beer to me. "Does he want one?"

I said, "He's fifteen," and Sonia turned and looked at him again. "Give him a Coke," she said.

Brenda did, sitting down hard on her chair. Until that moment I'd thought she was older than Sonia, than us, but now I realized that, despite her experienced face, she was younger by quite a bit, young enough anyway for fits of petulance. Among the clutter on the table were rolling papers, a pouch of tobacco. Brenda got busy assembling a cigarette while Joe Jr. watched, wrists pressed primly between his knees when he wasn't drinking from the can. Sonia put the flowers in the sink. People around here, they didn't own cars and they didn't own vases.

"So you're married," she said.

"Technically."

There were only three chairs at the table I noticed then and stood. Sonia waved me back. She filled the kettle and put it on. "What does he do?"

"My husband? He's a doctor."

"What about you?"

"I freelance as a copy editor."

"Ah."

The angel of silence has flown over us, Chekhov wrote, but it was not like that. Silence dropped, like that old iron curtain. I had expected some things to be difficult to talk about, things that maybe Sonia wouldn't want me to bring up, but I hadn't foreseen how excruciating it would be to have an ordinary conversation, the routine back and forth of two reacquainting friends. How to reciprocate her questions? Her life had stopped while mine had carried on these twenty years. I couldn't ask what she worked at. What Brenda did. Who Brenda was. How they'd met. Even asking how she'd been seemed grotesquely insensitive. (I was afraid to ask.) Meanwhile, Sonia searched the cupboards for teabags. Then, as though she perceived my distress and wanted to spare me from it, she asked over her shoulder, "Do you still speak Russian?"

"God, no. I never finished that degree. Words still come though. Now and then."

"All the time," Joe Jr. said. "It can be annoying."

Sonia smiled. "How's that?"

"Like I'm talking to her and, apropos of nothing, she says something completely incomprehensible." Sonia thought that was hilarious. She laughed and laughed and Joe Jr. turned as red as the can in his hand.

"I actually didn't go back to school until about five years ago," I said.

"I finished too," Sonia said. "I finished in prison."

Joe Jr. perked up at the word while I recoiled. But I did manage to say, truthfully, "That's wonderful, Sonia. You were born a teacher. I always thought so." Brenda, listening to all this but feigning not to as she tongued the seam of her rollie, gave herself away with a grunt.

"What?" Sonia asked her.

"Nothing."

"Go and smoke your cigarette, you ingrate."

Brenda put it behind her ear and stubbornly started on another. Joe Jr. was looking around vaguely now, bored so soon, but cigarettes apparently held some interest for him and he asked, "Can I try?"

"Are you allowed?"

He was insulted, as she had intended him to be; he conveyed this to me in a glance. Then Brenda pushed the pouch of Drum over and started issuing instructions. He was probably doubly offended, but he played along and I felt proud. We watched him struggle with the filmy paper and when the kettle sounded off, it seemed difficult for Sonia to look away. Joe Jr. handed Brenda what I hoped was a novice effort. "Looks like a tampon," she said. I was afraid she'd invite him to smoke it just to make trouble, but she didn't. She stood. "I'll go give myself cancer now."

"You do that, hon," Sonia said, passing me my tea and slipping into Brenda's vacated chair. "What do you like to do, Joey?"

He turned bashful. "Play music."

"He's in a punk band with his dad," I said.

She kept looking at him, and after a minute I could tell Joe Jr. was starting to feel weirded out. He got that Maria look, that someone's-been-messing-in-my-underwear-drawer look. "What happened to Pascal?" I came right out and asked.

It took her so long to tear her eyes away from Joe Jr. that I wondered if she'd heard my question. "I'm the last person who would know," she finally said.

"Can we talk about what happened?"

"Isn't that why you came?"

"I wanted to see you, too, Sonia."

"Ask me anything you want. I'll answer if I can."

"Why, Sonia? Why did you say you had anything to do with it? You didn't. I know you didn't."

"I was scared. I thought we were all going to die anyway so I might as well be in prison." She spoke matter-of-factly, as though giving up her freedom had been as easy as giving up her chair a few minutes ago. She'd always had a self-sacrificing streak and, at that moment, it made me furious.

"Then why did you stay?" I asked her. "You should have got out on parole years ago."

She got up to pour our tea and bring the mugs over. "It's easy to stay if you want to. You just have to be a bad girl. I don't think I have any jam." She smiled at Joe Jr.

"You actually wanted to stay?"

"Not really, but other people had to."

"You mean Pete?"

Sonia glanced behind at Brenda out on the balcony, the hulk of her leaning over the railing, taking in the unscenic view of the facing apartment. She'd probably killed somebody, I realized then. "She couldn't read," Sonia said. "Can you imagine that? She couldn't read."

"No," I said. "I can't."

Sonia: "Can I talk about her in front of him?"

"Of course."

Joe Jr. got up anyway. I got the feeling he wanted to stay and listen, but he could take a hint. "Where's the bathroom?"

Sonia told him. As soon as he left the room, she said, "Jane. He's beautiful."

"Thank you."

"We're going to try to have a baby. Maybe I'm too old."

"You're not," I said.

"Brenda can't." Her lips tightened and she added, "She doesn't mean to be unfriendly."

"I know."

"What are you saying about me?" she barked even before she reached the kitchen.

"We're not talking about you. We're talking about us." Sonia took Brenda's hand, wrapping the meaty arm attached to it around her neck. Brenda just stood there, clearly unconvinced.

"We wanted to save the world," I told her.

"I wanted to be a saint," Sonia said.

"You fucking are one!" Brenda burst out and I couldn't tell if she was sincere or ironic. "Sit down," I told her, though really, I wished she'd go away. She scraped the chair over beside Sonia's, laid her protective arm along the back of it, and, from the way she looked at me across the table, bristly still, I understood how much I'd changed, all the way from a seething Brenda to the kind of woman Brendas detest. A bourgeoise. But I wasn't. *Not at all!* I wanted to say.

I broached a neutral topic. "How are your parents, Sonia?"

They were going up to Hundred Mile House the very next week. Sonia was dying to see the place again. I told her that my dad eventually forgave me, but for several years we were estranged. "After I had Joe Jr. he decided that maybe, maybe, I wasn't a Communist."

"Oh, those meetings," Sonia sighed. "Do you remember? They were endless."

"Hours. Just to decide whether to put a phone number on a leaflet."

"We put the phone number on," Sonia said. "Nobody called! But you know what I loved? I loved when you read to me through the grate. I loved those stories."

"Do you remember reading *The Cherry Orchard* on the porch?"

Sonia didn't. She didn't remember it at all.

"I think about it every spring when the cherries come out," I told her. "How Pete appeared out of nowhere and stole the gnome."

Sonia said, "I remember the gnome."

There we were, closing in on the subject again, what I wanted to tell her—the only person I thought would really understand. I wished I could have held her hand, but that was impossible now. I said, "I'm sorry I didn't write."

She shrugged. "Life gets in the way. I was busy too."

"After I had him—"

Joe Jr. hadn't come back. Sonia peeked around the corner to the living room, touched her ear. "He's listening to his music."

"I felt terrible about that poor man, the guard."

She covered her face. "I know." To Brenda: "It was awful. Awful. It went off in his hands. And poor Timo!"

"Yes. But after Joey was born? It was Pascal I couldn't stop thinking about. What his parents must have gone through. How we—I—."

"No, me."

"*We* were partly responsible. Why didn't we just call the police?"

"I wouldn't let you."

"I could have anyway. And if we'd called the police, would it have made a difference? To what happened to him, I mean. Because, as Joe Jr. gets older, I keep seeing Pascal. I can't talk about this with his father. He's wonderful. A wonderful man, but he doesn't understand."

"Tell me then," Sonia said.

"I worry I'll be punished for what I did. That the same thing will happen to Joe Jr. Pascal? Did he—?"

She stared at me with glittery eyes. "Die?"

When I started to cry, Brenda got up from the table. I thought she was disgusted, but she was only getting a dishtowel from the drawer for me to dry my eyes. She dropped it on the table and sat down with a thump. I gathered this was something both of them were used to, hearing confessions, watching breakdowns. Sonia seemed so calm. "Doesn't it haunt you?" I asked.

"Of course. But other people have died."

At first I took this the wrong way. It sounded callous. When I realized she meant friends, I felt ashamed and sobbed into the towel.

"Poor you, Jane," she said, and Brenda was big enough to let Sonia reach across the table and squeeze my arms. We made a kind of ladder, hanging onto each another. Then Joe Jr. appeared behind where Sonia and Brenda sat, all wired up, looking desperate. I quickly dried my face. "What was his last name? Do you remember?"

Her eyes slid away from mine.

"I'd like to find out what happened to him," I said.

Then she noticed Joe Jr. in the doorway behind her and jumped out of the chair so fast it almost tipped over. "You're lucky to have such a wonderful mother," she said. "She loves you so much."

Why did she change the subject? To protect Joe Jr. from what we were talking about, or to protect me from finding out? In the awkwardness of the moment, her agitation, the bird-like fluttering of her hands, I sensed it; she was always protecting someone.

All those years ago, I used to wonder what she and Pascal were doing when I wasn't there. Now I know. I have a son almost the same age. He is so charming when he wants to be and, even when he doesn't, he's charming anyway. It's that irresistible combination of boredom and worldliness and utter naïveté. It's all that masturbation.

Joe Jr. yawned. "That's the signal," I told her and he went ahead to the door while Sonia and I embraced again. She nudged Brenda, who hugged me too and almost knocked my wind out.

"See?" Sonia told her. "She's nice."

As soon as we got in the car, Joe Jr. put on the iPod. I was glad for it now. The visit had been boring for him, but shocking for me and I wanted to be alone.

One of the conditions of my parole was that I wasn't allowed to communicate with anyone from NAG! for two years. Not that I wanted to. I'd been angry, especially with Sonia. Angry that she'd picked Pascal over me. That she'd martyred herself. This was why I never wrote her even after my probation was up. But now it turned out that I'd been wrong. She hadn't been ruined at all. Far from throwing her life away, she'd probably redeemed a dozen Brendas. Without a doubt she'd done more in prison than I'd done with all my freedom. But I'd always been half-hearted. All I do is mope around and read. That's what my son said. That's what he thinks of me.

He tugged the wires so the earbuds popped out. "Who was that person you were talking about?"

"What person?"

"You talked about someone named Pascal."

I pointed to the little white box. "I thought you were listening to that."

"I can listen and listen at the same time. You were crying."

So I told him. I told him everything except how Sonia had slept with Pascal. "I don't get it," said Joe Jr. when I finished. "Who wouldn't want to live?"

"That's the right answer. Thank you. I'm relieved. But to that sixteen-year-old, losing a leg was worse than dying. At the time it was the only treatment."

"And you never found out what happened to him?"

"No. He was the only one who wasn't charged. They whisked him back home, I presume. He wasn't called as a witness at Pete's trial. He wasn't even mentioned. Because he was a minor. Or because he was sick."

"So he made the bomb?"

The bomb. The only part of the story really interesting to a fifteen-year-old. But as soon as he said it, it seemed so obvious. Pete and Pascal, they were just fooling around. God knows what they planned to do with it. Probably set it off on Wreck Beach when no one was around. But why wouldn't Pete just say that? Would he actually take the rap for a dumb prank rather than put aside his principles and speak in court? Maybe. He always was too noble for his own good.

Or he was a fool.

Joe Jr. said, "I saw these plans on the Internet? How to make a cruise missile for five thousand dollars."

I gave him my severest frown.

"It would be cool. You know, just to say you did it." Then he hunkered down again with his private soundtrack.

We spoke only once more during the drive home, when I asked, "Who are you listening to now?"

He passed the earbud over to me. Sadness poured into my head and filled it. Old Kirsanov and his cello. Joe Jr. sat smiling, waiting for me to guess, but I couldn't speak.

"Come on, Mom," he said. "It's Bach."

1 9 8 4

The lawyer came out to Oakalla prison to explain how lucky I was. That was not how I felt, still in shock and crying all the time, without any idea how many days had passed. It was a nightmare, I kept thinking. Some small detail wasn't right and if I could only figure it out, it would cue me to wake up.

Things had changed overnight, the lawyer said. The only charge against me that was going to stand was the least of them. He didn't tell me why and I didn't ask. All I wanted to know was if Timo was okay. "Oh, he's fine. But the guard's not in such great shape, which doesn't bode too well for some of your friends."

My aunt posted bail, which was what she had been saving up for all those years, I supposed. By the time all the paperwork was done it was evening. I signed for my belongings—*The Party and Other Stories*, my empty cosmetics bag (its contents exiled to a separate plastic one), wallet, a clean pair of panties—all of it packed in anticipation of an overnight stay in Seattle. I wasn't sure what relationship I had to these personal items any more. Only the book felt like mine, filled with my annotations: *p. 36 galoshes, p. 141 slippers, p. 117 felt boots.*

A police van drove me back to Vancouver and dropped me off at the Main Street courthouse where it had brought me for my bail hearing the day before. Dark by then, almost ten o'clock, the air, saturated with damp, held its odours close. Across the street a few ragged people had formed a privacy wall with shopping carts. I was supposed to go to my aunt's, but felt ashamed after how I'd treated her. Yet with the Trutch house behind police tape and the lawyer's stern warning not to fraternize, there was nowhere else to go.

I was still standing on the street working up the nerve to find a phone and call her, when a second van pulled up and Dieter got out. As soon as I recognized him, I started walking away fast, but he saw me too and caught up.

"Where do you think you're going?"

I tried to pull out of his grip. "I'm not supposed to talk to you."

"No? Well, we're getting the story straight. Because we're in deep shit here. We are fucked." He dragged me along. No one we passed looked at us twice. They thought we were drunk.

Dieter didn't like the Irish pub we came to first. He bullied me farther along the block, then down a stairwell wallpapered with photocopied posters, into a pit where everyone was dressed like ghouls. Faces were stuck through with pins, as though their features might drop off. A leper bar. He shoved me through the crowd. "What do you want?" he shouted over the noise of the band.

"Nothing!"

"Wrong!"

"Vodka then," I said.

Dieter shouted to the bartender, who was wearing a dog collar and black lipstick. When he let go of me to pay, I didn't try to escape. I didn't think I could. He stuck the glass in my hand and, on the first sip, my eyes watered and the room diffused even more, as though there were two disco balls. The band was shrieking, goading the people on the dance floor who were leaping around, smashing into each other, pogoing. "Were you in on it?"

"No!"

"I should believe you? You're such a liar!"

"I'm not," I said.

"What?"

"I'm not!"

"Right! I found out something about you! I found out you're not even Russian! You told everyone you were Russian just to get into the group!"

"I never said I was!"

"Drink your milk, Kitty!"

I took another sip, choked.

"And Pete! Pete is such a hypocrite! But you all love him! He can do no wrong! He can make bombs and that's just swell with all of you! You'll still sleep with him. Drink that! I am so fucking tense here!"

I drank down the rest.

"Or T-t-t-timo! T-t-t-t-imo's everybody's darling! Or that stupid fucking kid! I hate you all! Know why?" Saliva sprayed my face and I thought that, quite possibly, he was the ugliest person in the room. "Because you hate me!" he said.

Something that might have been a waitress brought a tray of beer to a nearby table. Dieter went to speak to her. Again, I could have left, but I actually felt sorry for him then with his headband of an eyebrow and his goggly glasses and his rage. I didn't care what happened to me anyway. My life was ruined. At any moment the bomb would fall and put me out of my misery. Good, I thought. Dieter came back, demanding money. I handed over my backpack and he dug through it, found my wallet full of dull American bills, took a few, then let the backpack drop. I picked it up and hugged it to my chest. My book was in it. That was all I cared about.

"And poor little Sonia! She's probably a lesbo too!"

"She's not!"

"Well, you're one for sure!"

I started to cry.

"You're all a bunch of man-hating dykes and I hate your guts!"

He kept on like this until the drinks came. I drank mine willingly this time. Dieter kept calling me "Kitty" in a derisive tone every time I sipped my "milk." It was so weird. He couldn't have known about *Anna Karenina*. Soon the things he was saying became inseparable from the ugly things the band was screaming. They merged into one song to thrash around to. Abruptly, half of it ended on a discordant strum and I heard someone say, "We're going to take a break." Dieter carried on. "I'm getting out of this mess! There's no fucking way I'm taking the rap for Pete and a bunch of dykes! We're going to get the story straight! Right?"

I said, "I'm going to throw up."

Somehow I made it to the bathroom, where it was twice as bright as in the bar. All the scarecrows were lined up at the sinks pinning their faces back on. When I finished vomiting, they made room for me to splash myself with water. One of them asked, "Are you okay?"

Dieter was waiting outside so he must have escorted me there. I squinted around. We were in a short dark corridor at the end of which a sign glowed. Exit. *Vykhod.* I made my way toward it, dragging one shoulder along the wall, falling against the handle—air! Taking great draughts of it, I stumbled out. In the alley, people stood around in clusters. Someone was playing with a lighter, making the flame climb higher, while someone else sliced a hand through it.

Pozhar. Fire.

A bottle went flying. There seemed a very long delay before it smashed on the cobblestoned street.

"Where do you think you're going, Kitty?"

I clutched my backpack to my chest. Book. *Kniga.* "Nowhere."
"That's right. You're staying with me until we figure out what we're going to say."
"I told you. I don't know what happened."
"You've fucked me around before. Remember? Remember the recruitment centre? You were going to back me on that. Look what happened."

Dieter's next shove prompted a few white faces with bruised eyes to turn curiously in our direction. "Did you ever talk to Sonia? You didn't, did you? Or maybe you did. Maybe you said nasty things about me."

It wasn't that I began to be afraid—I hadn't stopped being afraid—but now I realized I was going to get hurt. He pushed me again, hard enough for my head to flop back and smack the bricks. A silver ball of pain released, rattling all through my skull, binging off my synapses. I sank down and began to conjugate. "*Ya zabyvayu, ty zabyvayesh . . .*" I forget. You forget.

"Get up!"

"*On zabyvayet . . .*" I opened my eyes. Some of the ghouls were closing in behind Dieter, drawn by the scent of violence. I curled tighter, teeth chattering. Dieter slapped the back of my head again. "*My zabyvayem.*" Again. "*Vy zabyvayetye . . .*" I was conjugating for my life.

"What do you think you're doing?" someone asked me.
"*Oni zabyvayut,*" I answered.
"Fuck off, man!"
"You fuck off!"
"Leave her alone!"

I heard scuffling and grunts. Dieter: "Fuck you!" Steps running off.

Someone touched my arm. "Are you okay? Hey? Hello?"

I lifted my face. How had he spoken? His lips were pinned together. "Can I call you a cab?" He was dressed in pins too, a kind of silver armour of them. "Where do you live?" he asked. "Do you want to go home?"

His blue spikes formed a halo.

"*Nyet*," I said.

Dawn oozed through a curtain of pins. I had no idea where I was, how I'd gotten there, but I knew my headache had something to do with it. There was a guitar case propped up in a corner, but barely any furniture. The bed itself was a Murphy bed that folded into a rectangular recess in the wall. One small room I was alone in with a tiny alcove kitchen. I assumed there would be a bathroom, and there was. That was where I found him, curled up asleep in the tub.

Snippets came back as I stood in the bathroom door. A different room he'd asked me to wait in. Bottles on a table. The reek of brimming ashtrays. I could have anything I wanted except a clean glass. When the noise started up again, it was like the end of the world. Even the walls had shuddered.

The next time the pins were sparkling. Now I saw that they looked pretty with the sunlight on them, fixed together in long chains. "Oh," he said, peering down at me. "You're awake."

He looked different in daylight, less fierce by half, spikes crooked after a night spent in the tub. His nose hooked slightly, almost meeting the pin in his lip. There were pins in his ears too, but the most predominant feature was his skin, which looked purplish and sore to the touch. The pins, my headache, his acne. I winced.

"Good mor-ning! Do you understand anything I'm saying to you? No?" He sighed in his Sex Pistols T-shirt. "Coffee?"

I sat up. It was the same word in Russian. "*Kofye*."

"Bingo!" He disappeared into the alcove, returned with a mug. "Do you take milk or sugar? Forget it. Wait." A milk carton jiggled at me. I nodded, still perplexed. Something had happened last night. *Ya zabyvayu.*

"Now we're getting somewhere," he said.

But I couldn't drink the coffee. It curdled whatever was in my stomach. He sat on the bed and looked at me again. Wasn't there a bird with that same crest? Horned Grebe? Punkatoo? I was staring at his pins, but he seemed only to be thinking of what to say next. "Joe," he finally came up with, pointing to his chest.

I pointed to the same place, at Johnny Rotten on his T-shirt, extending a can of ejaculating beer. "Joe."

"Oh, crap," he said. "Listen. I've got to go. You stay. Stay." He patted the bed. "There's food by some miracle. Thank you, Mother." He went to the alcove to show me the fridge. Mimed eating. "Eat. Eat. Help yourself. Okay? I'll be back around—" Five fingers held up.

"*Da*," I said. It seemed funny now.

"Yeah. Da." His boots were by the door, black and shin high and requiring a seated position to put on. He wove the laces through the eyelets, snugged all the Xs, then stomped over to the table where a stack of boot sole–thick books waited to be loaded into an army satchel. He relieved the chair of the leather jacket. There must have been five pounds of studs hammered into it and his shoulders sank when he put it on. Thus burdened, he left the apartment, calling over his shoulder, "Stay!"

I went to the window and, drawing aside the pins, watched him clomp up the street. The view was of a commercial building with a sign over what looked like a garage door. *Shipping and Receiving.* Nothing indicated what moved in and out. I let go of the pins and looked around the room. The bookshelf was filled with science texts. The one I opened had his name written under the crossed-out previous owner's.

Joey Normal.

I cleaned his bathtub and finally took a bath. I cleaned the rest of the bathroom and the kitchen. It was the least I could do. In the fridge were a number of plastic containers with the contents written on a piece of masking tape. Chicken Soup. Meatballs. I ate a cold meatball and, though delicious, my stomach was still touchy. I considered going for a walk, but worried I'd get locked out, so for the rest of the day I slept and read. Twice the phone rang, prompting an agony of questions. Why hadn't I gone to my aunt's? I was supposed to notify the police of a change of address. Should I call them and tell them where I was? Where was I?

The phone, the questions, all unanswered.

Near five, I zipped the book up in my backpack and closed the Murphy bed.

Boring (5). *Bore* (1). *Boredom* (1). *Bored* (6). *Dull* (2). *Banal* (1). *Idleness* (1). *Monotony* (1). *Tiresome* (1). *Sad* (10).

A group of people came down the hall when the building had been so quiet all day. "So you picked up a stray?" a woman said.

I locked myself in the bathroom.

"She might not even be here still," Joe said as everyone thudded in. "Crap. She cleaned up."

"Where is she?"

"She's gone. Or—"

"Knock."

"No. She'll come out when she's ready."

"She doesn't understand anything?"

"I don't think so."

"Where's she from?"

"I don't know. I don't know anything about her. This guy was beating her up in the alley."

"She's a prostitute?"

"Maybe."

"They bring girls from other countries and make them sex slaves." She started chanting, "Joey has a sex slave, a sex slave!" Then they lapsed into silence. I heard grunting, a thunk, a sigh. Three more times. They were removing their boots. Also, though they made noise enough for four, it was just the two of them. I opened the door a crack.

The back of her head was shaved, leaving just a tuft of bang in front, dyed Barbie pink. She was bent over, massaging her feet and, when she straightened, she looked right at me, smiling under the kilt pin stuck through her septum like a bone. Her nose was a near match in pinkness to her hair. "Hi! Joe?"

Joe popped out from around the corner, all *acne vulgaris* and smiles. "You're still here! Great! Come out! Come out! It's okay!" He pointed to himself again, this time being careful not to reference the shirt. "I'm Joe. That's Molly. Molly."

"Hiya," Molly said.

When I finally sidled out, Joe repeated his introduction, adding, "Who are you?"

"Maybe she's retarded."

"Kitty," I said.

"Ah!" and just then one of his spikes gave way completely, reminding me of a dog with one ear in a flop, though in this case four blue ears stayed cocked. "Kitty's a nice name." To Molly: "Could be anything, right? Spanish. French. She understood 'coffee' this morning. I wish I could remember some French."

Molly: "*Voulez-vous coucher avec moi?*"

"I see you cleaned up. Cleaned." He mimed scrubbing. "Thank you. Thank you. Are you staying for dinner?" Forking motions. "Eat with us? Me and Molly? Yum." Tummy rubbing. "I'm just going to fix Molly up here first because she's done a really stupid thing to herself. Here. I'll take down the bed so you can sit. Here. Sit."

He patted the place.

"So where're you from, Kitty?" Molly asked me, so casually I nearly answered except she burst into phlegmy laughter before I could. Joe, who had gone to the bathroom to wash his hands, came back with a bottle and some sterile pads. "She has nice eyes," Molly told him.

"Do you want a drink first?"

"Of that?" It was rubbing alcohol. "I can take the pain," Molly said. "I love pain."

He pulled his chair up close to hers, doused one of the cotton pads. When he dabbed at her nose, she jerked her head back with a yowl. "Fuck off! Loser!"

"Hold still," he said. "I'm going to take it out."

"No!"

"I have to."

I couldn't look. Molly screeched. "Look at the pus," said Joe.

She ran to the bathroom. More howls. "I look awful! Jesus Christ!" She stomped back without the kilt pin, which Joe was cleaning with alcohol. "Now put it through my cheek like this."

Joe: "Meningococcus? That mean anything to you?"

"I want to cry. How can I go out like this?" and she retrieved her boots and began the trial of putting them back on.

"You're welcome," Joe said.

"Fuck off." She stamped one heel down.

"Aren't you eating with us?"

"I'm going home to cry. Give me back my pin."

Joe tossed it. "Pick up some Polysporin."

He sniffed in all the containers and decided on soup, heating it in a battered aluminum pot. He seemed very relaxed for a person with a giant pin through his lip, the kind of person who probably talked to himself and was grateful to have a mute overnight guest as an excuse. "I'm in med school. First year." He looked at me. "This is where I would pause to ask what you do. Honest I would."

I gave him my most dazed, uncomprehending look.

"Actually, I probably wouldn't. I'm pretty shy. I don't talk much around girls. Molly doesn't count. She's barely a girl. She's a thing."

He brought the bowls to the table and invited me to sit. His smile, the way his acne barely registered after a few minutes, reminded me of Dr. Samoylenko, who after a few days began to strike others *as exceptionally kind, amiable, handsome even.* Even with the pin. But how was he going to feed himself? He simply ate around it. "Eat," he extolled before pausing to consider his utensil. "This is a spoon, Kitty. A spoon. Say it. Spoon."

"Spoon," I said.

"Good! And this is a bowl." He clinked it. "Bowl. Say 'bowl.'"

"Bowl."

He looked pleased with himself. "Soup."

"Soup." Sweet and salty, swimming with fat noodles and pieces of shredded meat, it was the first thing I'd eaten all day. I immediately felt about that soup the way I felt about a good book, that I would probably have liked Chekhov too, if I'd ever had the chance to meet him.

"So. Med school. I almost didn't get in. I'm trying harder now. My dad's a judge. Big shoes to fill, right? Last year I decided I didn't want to. I wanted to be a musician, see?" Joe flipped back the errant spike again. "Then my old man had a heart attack. I realized I was sabotaging my whole future. Hence summer school. I can be a musician on the side. Do you remember me singing? That was me and The Fuck Ups last night." He pointed to the guitar in the corner. "I'll play something for you after."

I directed my alarm into my soup.

"Guitar. Say it."

"Guitar."

"What's guitar in your language? Me, guitar. You? What?"

"*Balalaika.*" If there was another word, I didn't know it.

"*Balalaika?* That's Russian. That's that little Russian ukulele. Are you Russian? You? Russian? USSR?"

I shook my head.

"Something like it then? Czech? What do you call this?" He lifted the spoon.

"*Lozhka.*"

Tocking his spikes. The loose one went back and forth, metronomic. "*Lozhka. Lozhka.*"

After soup, he took the guitar out. There were acronyms stencilled all over the case—D.O.A., R.I.P., a plain A with a circle round it. Another one, I thought, as he bent over the instrument, untuning it. He launched straight into a violent strumming and, immediately, a banging sounded overhead. Joe rolled his eyes and stopped playing. "That's my neighbour. He's all right. We have different taste in music is all. That was the start of 'Fucked Up Ronnie.' Remember? We covered it last night. You don't remember. You were wasted. I can't drink and play. My fingers don't work. Hey, I'm going to write you a song."

He spent a moment plucking out a rudimentary tune, then barked out:

I found Kitty in the alley
I found Kitty in the alley
Someone was being mean
Someone was being mean
Fuck that! I don't like it!
Be nice why don't you!

He fell back on the Murphy bed, a hand on his shirt, sapped by this burst of creativity. "God. These songs just pour out of

me. I don't know how. I don't even try." He propped himself
up to look at me. "You can see what my dilemma was. With med
school, I mean." Then he laughed. "You make the funniest faces,
Kitty."

He had to study. "Hit the books?" The guitar put to bed in
its case, he went for one of the tomes in his satchel, dropped it
on the table. "Book," he said. "Hit."

I slapped my hand down on the cover.

"Hey," he said. "You're getting it."

Joe was up till two humming "Fucked Up Ronnie." I wondered how he could read and hum at the same time. Obviously
he didn't know he was doing it since he was reading in the
kitchen so I could sleep. I liked him. Because I liked him, I was
going to have to leave before he found out I was a fake. I tossed
on the Murphy bed, sleepless and bored and fretting. If only I
could have read. And Chekhov was so close, right under the bed!

Eventually, he retired to the bathroom. I heard him washing, the stallion-like voiding of his bladder. The flush. I waited,
then got up and tore a page out of his notebook. *Ya Jane, nye
Kitty. Ya Kanadka. Ya govoryu po-angliski. Bolshoye spasibo. Ty
kharoshoiye.*

There was no way he would recognize a word of Cyrillic.

"Know what day it is today, Kitty? It's Cadaver Day! I have to
say I'm not really looking forward to it. When I come home
tonight? If I look a little pale? That will be the reason. Are you
staying? Here? Stay?"

I shrugged.

"Really?" He slumped a little though his spikes stayed pert.
He'd showered and regelled them, had been firing up the hair
dryer off and on for half an hour. Now he was talking at me
while he finished dressing. It constituted a project, putting on
those jeans. The outside seams had been slit, then pinned, pins

being, I realized, something of an obsession for him. When he finally got the front of his pants attached to the back, he went to get his boots.

"What's this?" He reached inside. "Ah! A clue!"

I blushed. I'd pictured him stomping around on my note all day, not noticing it until later, after I was gone. He unfolded it. "That sure looks like Russian. You're sure you're not Russian? Bulgarian? I'm going to ask around. So will you be here when I get back or not?"

I nodded yes.

"Uh-oh. I know for a fact that *this*"—he nodded—"is no in Bulgaria and *this*"—he shook his head—"is yes. So. You might be here or you might not." He paused in the doorway, looking back. "If you're not, I think I might get a cat."

I was. I was still there when he got back that evening. Because he had to cut up the dead body. What a horrible thing to have to do. He'd been there for me so how could I just walk out? I regretted the note and worried all day that he'd somehow find someone to translate it.

Alas, I underlined in my book, *the actions and thoughts of human beings are not nearly as important as their sorrows!*

He knocked—as though I had some right to the place now too!—and looked so happy when he came in. So happy to see me. Yet there was something different about him too. He wasn't making eye contact.

"Do you think that guy's still looking for you? Is he your boyfriend?"

Ugh, I thought. It was easier just to clamp my tongue between my teeth so I'd remember not to answer.

"I mean, can we go out? Out?" He pointed to the window.

Outside the building the air felt warm, like a new season, like summer, though it was only May, an evening in May with birds twittering around the warehouses and the sound of distant traffic in the air. Now I saw the apartment from the outside, old and brick, survivor, along with a few slouching wooden houses, of industrial rezoning. He'd left his studded jacket behind and today's T-shirt was full of holes, the ripped-off sleeves revealing his acned shoulders. He'd obviously forgotten about my note. Other things had happened to him that day, things more important than my confession. Clomp, clomp, clomp went his boots on the sidewalk. The few people we passed gave us a wide berth. They gave it to Joe in his blue crown of thorns.

"How was your day?" he asked. "Pause for you to answer. Question reciprocated. Thanks, Kitty. It was pretty disturbing, needless to say."

He grabbed my hand and ran me across a busy street when there was a break in traffic. On the other side we intersected with another pedestrian, all of us performing the awkward ballet of getting out of each other's way. Joe let rip a chorus, "We're The Fuck Ups! We're The Fuck Ups!" A cement truck rumbled by like a sound effect.

Under the concrete span of Cambie Bridge, boots dangling over False Creek, he patted the spot beside him. When I sat, he took my hand, squeezed it, let go. Held up his. "Hand."

"Hand," I said.

Here was where he told me about the cadaver. How he'd kept thinking about his old man. "Everybody was making jokes. From nerves, you know. It wasn't very respectful. Here's this guy. Gave his body to science and science is making cracks about his dick. Not that I wasn't." He inserted a finger in a hole in his shirt and scratched his stomach. "There's quite a difference between being dead and alive. Beyond the obvious, I mean. This guy was clearly not just sleeping. He was dead. But the weird thing is, every day a thousand billion cells in your body die, Kitty. That's a fact of life."

We walked around for a while, then went for Chinese. The waiter slammed a teapot and two stacked cups on the lazy Susan. Joe, unnesting one cup from the other, asked for beer. He filled the teacups, rotated the lazy Susan in my direction. When I went to take my cup, he steered it out of reach. Every time I tried to grab it, the cup spun away from me. Our laughter brought the waiter hurrying back with the beer. He'd put us in the corner, near the kitchen, away from the other diners. Joe seemed unoffended. The food came faster. He was finally looking at me again.

"You probably won't understand what I'm going to say, Kitty. You came along at just the right time. If you saw me last year when I dropped out of med school, you wouldn't have known me. Of course you wouldn't have known me. You didn't know me. But you know what I mean." He laughed. I laughed. Then he chopsticked a cube of crimson-sauced pork into his mouth, sombre again.

"A lot of guys would say this is an ideal situation. A girl who can't talk back."

When I bristled, he said, "You must be really intelligent. You always seem to know what I mean."

Joe unlocked the apartment door. As soon as we stepped inside, he lunged for me and pressed the pin into my lips. It almost went up my nose and I shrank back. "Sorry," he said. "I should have asked. Do you want to? Kiss?"

I wasn't sure. The mechanics seemed daunting. Yet he'd been so kind! I leaned toward him, offering the corner of my mouth, but the various positions we tried were so awkward and I worried the pin would come undone. I told myself that was silly. It was a *safety* pin.

"Fuck it." Joe bolted for the bathroom.

I'd hurt his feelings. I stood there trying to work up the nerve to knock, to finally speak, but he emerged a moment later without the pin, rendering me genuinely mute. Still in his boots, he took my face in his hands and placed his liberated mouth on mine. He tasted of garlic and tin. I wasn't embarrassed or ashamed, which was strange for me. A strange new sensation. When we finally pulled away, I touched my own mouth and saw his blood on my fingers.

Joe sat down to take his boots off. I knelt and helped unlace them, pulled and pulled and when the boot finally released, fell back into giddiness. I had to struggle harder with the other one. Joe lifted me into his lap and we kissed for a long time, finally getting the choreography right. When we came up for air, he pointed to the bed. Blue exclamation marks all around his head, but on his face, a tender question.

He had to undo all those pins first. While he was occupied with them, I got in the bed and undressed under the covers. He turned out the light, got in too, and lay beside me in the dark.

"Did you read my note?" I asked.

Joe started to laugh. "Well, I couldn't, could I? But I found someone who could. Not that easy. I had to hike all the way across campus where they have a department for that. Say something else."

"*Bolshoye spasibo.*"

"In English."

"My dog actually eats nuts."

He laughed and laughed.

"I might be a lesbian." I said it. Would saying it make me one?

Joe said, "Maybe we shouldn't then."

Strangely though, I seemed to want to.

I woke thinking of Sonia the morning of the action, so radiant as she floated down the steps. I'd thought saintliness had made her shimmer when really it was bliss. She'd actually done it. She'd shown Pascal how wonderful it was to be alive. That entire night with Joe, Reagan's infamous briefcase stayed tucked under his bed. Nancy had taken the phone off the hook. And far away, across the vast Russian steppe, in the Kremlin, Chernenko put Shostakovich on low and popped a sleeping pill.

I got up and took a shower. I was sore from keeping the world safe all night.

When I came out of the bathroom, Joe was on the phone. He hung up and said, "I'm going to take you to see my parents. You're going to need a better lawyer." Then he practised kissing me again.

I felt twice as nervous when I saw the house. I couldn't imagine that anyone who lived in Shaughnessy would want his son to have anything to do with me. Joe tried the door, then used the knocker. Loud, judgemental raps. His father probably knew all about me already.

He answered in slippers—leather, backless—and I liked him even before the landslide of relief happened on his face. Pulling Joe close, he said, "I know someone who's going to be very happy when she sees you."

"Dad, this is Jane," Joe said.

The judge held out his hand. "Joe Sr. Pleased to meet you, Jane. Come in. Come in. Rachel's all in a tizzy baking something." By the time he finished shaking my hand, my arm was numb to the shoulder.

We went through a vestibule the size of Joe's entire apartment, through a living room, then into a large rec room with windows all around it. There was a pool table, a bar at one end, and, at the other, more sittable furniture than in the living room. His father bellowed, "Rachel!"

"What?" from far away.

"They're here!"

"What!"

"Joey's here with his friend!"

"Oh!"

Joe went over to the pool table and started emptying the pockets while I sat on the chesterfield with my hands nervously clasped, his father smiling at me from his armchair, just sitting there, legs crossed and smiling, like someone waiting for the punch line. A minute later Joe's mother appeared in the doorway, aproned and in slacks. She was tiny, her hair in a tailored bob. She glanced at me, then at Joe racking the balls, and her mouth opened and her hand struck her chest with an audible thump. Joe's father began to laugh, then cough.

"Excuse me," he said to me.

"Hello," Joe's mother said to Joe. Joe came over with the cue and hugged her, then pointed it in my direction. "This is Jane, who I told you about."

"Jane!" She brisked over with her hand held out and squeezed both of mine. "Rachel Norman. So nice to meet you, Jane. So *very, very* nice."

I was finding all this strange. Their behaviour seemed over the top until it occurred to me that maybe I was the first girl Joe had brought home.

"I'm just putting the tea together," Rachel said. "Come and help me, Jane."

Joe was bent over the pool table now, eyeing up the shot, not caring that Rachel was leading me away by the hand. The room was full of light from all the windows. His hair looked crazy and I didn't want to go, but I left him there with his smiling father, the dying judge, swinging his slipper on the end of his foot.

Rachel brought me back through the living room and down the stairs we'd passed on the way in, through a dining room with china-crammed cupboards, into a surprisingly small kitchen that smelled of cinnamon. The timer was sounding and Rachel hurried to remove a loaf pan from the oven. She dropped it on a rack as though she didn't give a damn about it any more, pulled off the oven mitts, tossed them too, then turned to face me.

"Jane?" She drew in a breath while I stood there, feeling awkward and too tall.

"I don't know anything about you. I don't know what kind of trouble you're in. But let me say this, Jane—" and she took a step toward me. "I will never forget, *never*, that you were the one who got him to take that pin out."

As soon as she touched me, both hands on my shoulders, a word came to me in my own language. *Firmament*. The way it sounded, so fixed and safe, I knew everything was going to be all right. Everything would work out.

Or so she thought.

Acknowledgements

Bolshoye spasibo Shaena Lambert, Zsuzsi Gartner, Patrick Crean, and Jackie Kaiser, who all endured early versions of this novel; Tanya Tyuleneva for checking my translations and putting up with my Russian; Joan and Graham Sweeney for keeping us all warm and dry; Bruce and Patrick and the Addersons for the love. And Larry Cohen for "the tea."

All Chekhov quotes are reproduced by permission of Penguin Books Ltd. Quotes on page 15 and pages 147–150 are from Leo Tolstoy's *Anna Karenin*, translated by Rosemary Edmonds, ©Rosemary Edmonds, 1978. Quotes on pages 23, 85, 144, 145, 241, and 280 are from *Lady with Lapdog and Other Stories*, translated by David Magarshak, ©David Magarshak, 1964. Quotes on pages 29, 49, 174, 237, and 310 are from *The Fiancée and Other Stories*, translated by Ronald Wilks, ©Ronald Wilks, 1986. Quotes on pages 62, 65, 104, 146, and 301 are from *The Duel and Other Stories*, translated by Ronald Wilks, ©Ronald Wilks, 1984. Quotes on pages 122, 123, 144, 156, 201, 202, 237, and 238 are from *The Kiss and Other Stories*, translated by Ronald Wilks, ©Ronald Wilks, 1982. Quotes on pages 47, 105, and 304 are from *The Party and Other Stories*, translated by Ronald Wilks, ©Ronald Wilks, 1985. Quotes from *The Cherry*

Orchard are from *Plays*, translated by Elisaveta Fen, ©Elisaveta Fen, 1954.

Quotes from Chekhov's letters are taken from *The Selected Letters of Anton Chekhov*, edited by Lillian Hellman, translated by Sidonie K. Lederer, Farrar, Straus and Giroux, 1955. Quotes from Ivan Turgenev's *Fathers and Sons* are from the 1986 Bantam Classics edition translated by Barbara Makanowitzky. Jane's Russian text is the 1962 edition of *Russian: A Beginners' Course* by Ronald Hingley and T. J. Binyon. Helen Caldicott's quotes come from the 1982 film *If You Love This Planet*, directed by Terre Nash.

The author gratefully acknowledges the generous and unexpected support of the Canada Council for the Arts and the British Columbia Arts Council.

Efforts were made during the writing of this book to preserve our diminishing Canadian lexicon. Please, when you sit down to read, sit on a *chesterfield*.